AUNT
IVY'S
COTTAGE

BOOKS BY KRISTIN HARPER

Summer at Hope Haven

AUNT IVY'S COTTAGE

KRISTIN HARPER

bookouture

Published by Bookouture in 2020

An imprint of Storyfire Ltd.
Carmelite House
50 Victoria Embankment
London EC4Y 0DZ

www.bookouture.com

ISBN: 978-1-83888-829-9
eBook ISBN: 978-1-83888-828-2

For my sisters, nieces and aunts

Prologue

The daffodils that were meant to brighten the room were already going limp in their vase and Zoey Jansen felt as if she were wilting, too. It was a sunny afternoon in mid-April, but the thermostat was set at seventy-four. Zoey's sweater stuck to the small of her back and she wiped perspiration from her upper lip. Yet her great-aunt Sylvia, who was covered to her chest with a quilt, kept saying she was cold.

Zoey lifted the blankets only enough to gently place a freshly filled hot-water bottle into her aunt's hands. "This should help warm you up."

"Mmm," Sylvia murmured drowsily, her eyes closed. "You've always been so good to me, Ivy. More like a sister than my own sisters."

She thinks I'm my great-aunt Ivy. Zoey didn't correct her mistake. Sylvia had been so restless the past several days that she didn't want to rouse her if she was finally sleepy. As she started to withdraw her hand from beneath the blankets, Sylvia feebly grasped her fingers.

"Don't go. I need—" her voice crackled. Assuming what Sylvia needed was a cool drink, Zoey reached for the water glass on the nightstand but her aunt tugged her hand again, pulling her closer. "I need to tell you something important."

Zoey touched her shoulder to reassure her that she had her full attention. "What is it?"

"Mark doesn't deserve this," Sylvia uttered. "It's not fair. I can't let it happen."

Mark—whose given name was Marcus—was Sylvia's grandson. Ivy's great-nephew. And Zoey's cousin. His second wife had recently divorced him and Zoey figured that was what Sylvia meant was unfair. The old woman had always doted on her only grandchild, so Zoey understood it must have been upsetting for her to realize not every woman thought the sun rose and set on Marcus Winslow III. Struggling to say something that was honest yet kind, Zoey resorted to one of the platitudes she'd often heard Sylvia use.

"Sometimes, these things have a way of working out for the best for everyone." *Especially for his wife.*

"No, no. That boy can only take so much." Sylvia wiggled her head back and forth against the pillow, clearly agitated. "Enough is enough."

Zoey gently pulled her hand free to smooth down her aunt's flyaway hair, vaguely aware of how self-conscious Sylvia was about her appearance, even now, at eighty-four. "He can take it. He's a lot stronger than you think." *Some might even say he's a bully.*

"What about Zoey? She's such a dear girl. I'm concerned about her."

"She'll be fine. She'll find another job soon."

"What if she doesn't? She's lost all of her savings and she can't pay her mortgage. Where will she live?"

Zoey's breath caught. She had told her great-aunts she'd been laid off from her job as a librarian when the city closed the branch where she worked, but how had Sylvia found out that she'd lost her savings and was on the brink of losing her townhome? Zoey hadn't wanted to burden her aunts by telling them that the guy she'd been seeing for the past year, a financial planner, had risked—and *blown*—all of her savings in a series of investments that turned out to be just shy of illegal. And she was too ashamed to admit she hadn't even realized what he'd done until she tried to withdraw money from her depleted retirement funds to pay her mortgage.

Guessing that her aunt must have overheard her ranting about it on the phone to her friend, Lauren, she pleaded, "I know you're worried about me, Aunt Sylvia, but Aunt Ivy can't find out about that yet. She'll get upset and stress is bad for her heart. When the time is right, I'll talk to her about it. Meanwhile, please promise you won't tell her."

Upon hearing Zoey call her *aunt*, Sylvia opened her eyes and blinked in apparent surprise. Then she knitted her brows together, agreeing, "You're right. It'll be our secret."

"Thank you." As her aunt's eyelids fell shut again, Zoey stood to leave.

But Sylvia added in a raspy voice, "For now, it's best to let the past stay buried in the past… beneath the roses."

What does that *mean?* Although her aunt's health had been improving, Zoey wondered if she was feverish again. She leaned down and kissed her forehead. No, no fever…Yesterday, right before dozing off, she'd rambled on and on about dancing in the stars. When she woke, she had no recollection of having said anything and they concluded she'd been dreaming. Maybe she was only semi-awake now, too.

Zoey waited. When Sylvia didn't say anything else, she straightened her posture and tiptoed across the room toward the heavy old door, slightly ajar. Aware it would creak if she opened it any farther, Zoey turned sideways to ease across the threshold. Before she left, she impulsively stopped to glance back at the bed and whisper, "I love you, Auntie. Sleep well."

CHAPTER ONE

After escorting an elderly funeral guest to her car, Zoey Jansen paused on the sidewalk to appreciate the contrast of vibrant red, yellow and orange tulips against the white picket fence. Her aunt Sylvia had been an accomplished gardener and tulips were always her favorite spring flower. She had planted them around the perimeter of the yard and in abundant bunches in front of the stately sea-captain's home her sister-in-law Ivy owned and where she herself had lived for most of her adult life.

It's too bad she didn't get to see them bloom this year, Zoey thought. She quickly dabbed the corner of her eye. She couldn't start crying. Not yet. Maybe after all the mourners had left and the food had been put away and she'd made a kettle of tea and consoled her great-aunt Ivy. And after Zoey had persuaded her to go to bed early and then had sat beside her in the dark, chatting about nothing in particular until she drifted off to sleep, the way she'd done every night for the past week so her elderly relative wouldn't feel so lonely. Maybe then Zoey would creep down the hall to her own room and allow herself to have a good cry. But not now.

As she unlatched the gate to follow the walkway to the front door, a burst of raucous laughter rose from the side of the house.

What could possibly be so hilarious at a funeral reception? Worried that someone who'd had too much to drink might be about to drive home, Zoey changed course and continued down the sidewalk toward the brick driveway.

Scanning the area in front of the detached garage, which was once a carriage house, she saw four or five men, drinks in hand. Zoey had met a couple of them at the church; they were islanders who went to high school with Mark the year he stayed with Sylvia and Ivy after his father died. Apparently, when his buddies learned about the funeral, they took advantage of the opportunity to reunite with him. She'd overheard two of them planning a golf tournament for the next day while they worked their way down the buffet table, piling their plates high with shrimp and cocktail quiches and cheesecake. Now, they clustered around her square-jawed, golden-haired cousin, paying rapt attention as he dominated the conversation. That would explain the ruckus.

A sweetly pungent odor tickled her nose and she noticed Mr. Witherell, the town's notorious eccentric, leaning on his cane and smoking a pipe in the back yard. Zoey hoped her great-aunt Ivy didn't smell it; pipe tobacco reminded her of her long-departed father, and she was distraught enough already.

"Now that Sylvia's deceased, it won't be long before Ivy goes. She's not going to be able to handle the loneliness."

Mark was talking so loudly that Zoey could hear his appalling remark clear at the other end of the driveway. She set her jaw and made a beeline for him. Or as straight a beeline as she could make, given that her heels were blistered from her new shoes and the brick terrain was slightly uneven in spots.

"Who will get the house?" a redhead with his back to Zoey asked. He was the one who'd been talking about going to the golf club earlier.

"You're looking at him." As Ivy's oldest blood relative, her great-nephew Mark was next in line to inherit the estate, in accordance with the will Ivy's father had drawn up years ago that ensured the house would always stay within the family.

"You going to sell it or move here and live in it yourself?"

"Unfortunately, it has to remain in the family, otherwise I'd sell it in a heartbeat and retire tomorrow," Mark answered, rubbing his thumb and fingers together to indicate how wealthy he'd be.

Although Ivy's house wasn't nearly as grand as the other homes— some were mansions, really—overlooking the harbor, the land it was situated on was worth a mint. Last in a row of residences built on the southern end of the village's one-sided Main Street, Ivy's was the highest on the hill and it afforded the best vantage points. From the front was a panoramic view of the harbor and bay. From the back, it looked out over a shallow valley of modest cottages interspersed among sprawling summer residences, and four miles beyond that, the glittering open ocean.

But it was the widow's walk on top of the house that offered an unparalleled perspective. Accessed through a trapdoor in the attic, the balustraded, open-air platform provided a three hundred and sixty degree vista of awe-inspiring beauty; the whole of Dune Island and its surrounding waters. So Mark was right; he could have earned a bundle one day if he were permitted to sell his inheritance. Fortunately, he wasn't.

"There's no way I'm relocating from Boston to Benjamin's Manor," he continued, referring to the quaint, historic fishing village, one of the five towns on Dune Island that collectively comprised Hope Haven. "I plan to lease this place out to corporations for executive retreats. Obviously, I'll have to make major renovations first, but the investment will pay for itself in no time. Especially if Ivy goes before summer begins."

Zoey couldn't quite believe how openly callous Mark was being about their great-aunt's future death. Just as she got close enough to ask him to kindly lower his voice, a tall, dark-haired man facing in her direction greeted her with a cordial hello. The other men immediately whipped their heads around to see who had come up behind them. The tall guy nudged his way through them until he stood directly in front of her, blocking everyone else from her range of view.

"We haven't met… I'm Nick."

Momentarily sidetracked from her mission, Zoey reflexively shook his hand. *Nick who, from where?* she wondered as she peered into his hooded, deep-blue eyes. She noticed that his heavy brows, like his hair, were flecked with gray and she guessed he was about the same age as her cousin. Another pal from high school? Mark liked to be considered the best-looking person in the room, and this guy was a lot more attractive than he was. Which meant if they were friends, there must have been something about him that was useful to Mark. That was just the way he operated.

Zoey was about to let go of his hand when he leaned forward, bringing his mouth nearly level with her left ear, and softly said, "Your aunt Sylvia spoke very fondly of you. It was clear how special you were to her. I'm really sorry for your loss."

Thank you. Two words. She had been saying those two words all afternoon. All *week*. It was all she needed to say now, too. But as Nick's cool, strong hand enveloped her sweaty one and his condolence resonated deep within her heart, Zoey was tongue-tied. *Aunt Sylvia was very special to me, too*, she replied silently. She could feel herself faltering, emotionally and physically. Dipping her chin, she inadvertently pressed her forehead against his chest. Nick must have thought she wanted a hug because he lifted his other hand and patted her back. To Zoey's dismay, his unexpected gesture caused a smattering of tears to bounce down her cheeks. *Oh, please, not now*, she thought, panicking. *Not here. Not in front of* them.

She jerked her head upright and pulled her hand from his to whisk her face dry with her fingertips. Nick quickly dropped his arms to his sides and she noticed several wet circles darkening his gray tie. Embarrassed, she stepped around him and addressed her cousin as neutrally as she could manage through more tears that were still threatening to fall.

"Could you please lower your voice so Aunt Ivy doesn't hear you talking about that?"

The redhead who had been questioning Mark about the house kicked at a pebble and the other two guys studied the labels on their beer bottles. At least they had the good sense to act chagrined. Unlike Mark, who took a long, slow pull from his drink and then crudely smacked his lips.

"So Ivy doesn't hear us talking about *what*?"

The year he turned sixteen, Mark started referring to and addressing their great-aunt by her first name, as if they were peers, instead of calling her Aunt Ivy. Now that he was forty-one, it didn't seem quite as disrespectful, but it still grated on Zoey's nerves whenever he said it—an annoyance which probably had more to do with his superiority complex than with whether or not he used the title, *aunt.*

"About her…" Even though they were at a funeral reception, it seemed strangely inappropriate to use the word "death," so Zoey repeated Mark's euphemism. "About her *going.* What if one of the windows had been open?"

The rest of the men were furtively dispersing, but Mark stood his ground, wearing an amused expression. "If one of the windows had been open, I wouldn't have had to come outside in eighty-five-degree weather to cool off."

Eight months of the year, Sylvia or Ivy complained about how cold they were. They didn't turn the heat down until the end of April and didn't put window screens in until late May. So even though today was unseasonably warm, the windows remained shut. But that wasn't Zoey's point and Mark knew it.

"Someone could have opened the back door and Aunt Ivy could have heard you."

"So what? I've already spoken to her about it."

Zoey struggled to keep her volume low. "You talked to Aunt Ivy about her *dying*?"

"Dying?" Mark guffawed. "Who mentioned anything about her dying? I said she would probably be *going* soon." Mark looked at Zoey as if she were the one who had zero sensitivity. She felt foolish for misinterpreting his comments but his response begged another question.

"Going *where* soon?"

"To an assisted living facility. I think it would be advantageous for her."

Zoey was taken aback; her aunt had never mentioned anything about moving anywhere, especially not to an assisted living facility. "How would it be advantageous? She loves this house and she's managing fine on her own. When I'm not here, Carla comes twice a week to clean and Aunt Ivy still enjoys cooking for herself. And the cardiologist said her heart condition is treatable with medication."

Now it was Mark's turn to look puzzled. "Ivy has a heart condition?"

Me and my big mouth. "Yeah, she has occasional chest pain. It's called angina. But Dr. Laurent said she's in good health for someone who's eighty-seven, especially considering her medical history."

Ivy had had non-Hodgkin lymphoma when she was in her early sixties. It recurred twice, but she'd been cancer-free since she turned seventy. And until she was eighty, she routinely walked two miles a day. She also watched her weight, never smoked and rarely drank. It was only during the past five or six years that she'd slowed down a little—but she was nowhere near *stopping*.

"Her physical health might be okay. But up here...?" Mark tapped his temple.

"What are you talking about? She has all her mental faculties."

"Then why didn't she turn the gas burner off a couple weeks ago?"

She was surprised Ivy had told him about her recent oversight, considering how vexed she'd been by it. Zoey hadn't been there when it happened; she'd gone back to Rhode Island for a few days to collect documents to file her taxes. But according to her aunt, if the carpenter who was tightening the staircase banister hadn't happened to smell gas, Ivy, Sylvia, and Moby —their gray, seventeen-pound, thirteen-year-old tabby cat—all would have perished. Since the gas had only been on for a few minutes and Ivy would have smelled it eventually, Zoey was reasonably sure that was an exaggeration, but her aunt had bemoaned her error for days.

"How did you hear about that?"

"I do check in from time to time to see how they're doing, you know. You're not the only one who cares about them." Mark scowled and averted his eyes.

That was as close as Zoey had ever heard him come to expressing… well, not *love*, but at least *concern* about Ivy and Sylvia. She realized she ought to go a little easier on him. If she'd heard her aunts say it once, she'd heard them say it a hundred times, *Mark isn't good at demonstrating affection, but that doesn't mean he doesn't care.*

"I appreciate that you're concerned about her," she acknowledged. "But Aunt Ivy didn't leave the gas on because she's experiencing symptoms of dementia. She just didn't click the knob into place all the way—probably because of her arthritis."

Actually, it was probably because the knob was difficult to twist. The major appliances in her home—and a couple of the downstairs rooms—could have done with some updating but Zoey wasn't going to admit that to Mark. From what she'd just overheard, he already wanted to overhaul the entire house and she knew how traumatic that would be for their aunt. "Besides, I always check the burners when she's done using the stove."

"Exactly. So what's going to happen once you leave?"

"I-I'm planning to stay a while longer."

"How can you do that? What about your job?"

Zoey was relieved but not surprised her aunts hadn't told Mark that she'd been laid off; Sylvia and Ivy had always been tight-lipped about anything that Zoey or Mark mentioned to them in confidence. So he must have thought she'd been taking family medical leave to care for Sylvia, and Zoey was fine with letting him believe that. Losing her job wasn't her fault, but that wouldn't stop Mark from gloating. The fact that he'd only been in his current role as a pharmaceutical sales rep for a year and would probably quit or get fired within another six months, the way he usually did, was irrelevant. He'd make wisecracks if he found out she'd been unemployed for five months and she wasn't in the mood to hear them.

"It's not a problem," she hedged. "I can stay as long as Aunt Ivy needs me."

"You're just postponing the inevitable, you know. She's going to have to move eventually."

You want to bet on it? Zoey thought, but she let his remark slide. She'd challenge him again later if it came to that, but right now she didn't have it in her to keep sparring with him. When Mark tipped his head back to down the last of his beer, she took advantage of the silence to tell him she was going back inside. But as she turned toward the door, she noticed Mr. Witherell out of the corner of her eye. Apparently he'd finished smoking his pipe and he shuffled toward them, bent at the waist so that his torso and head were angled nearly parallel with the ground as he tapped his cane on the brick driveway.

The old man had been the village's lighthouse keeper until all the lighthouses on Dune Island became automated in the seventies and he was forced into an early retirement. He now lived in a rundown shack of a dwelling on a little patch of land in the lowest-lying area in Benjamin's Manor. His house was considered such an eyesore by the village's summer elite that several of them united and offered to pay to relocate him so they could raze the building. When he refused, they counter-offered to rehabilitate his home, inside and out. Again, no deal. He did, however, allow them to build and maintain a white, eight-foot wooden privacy fence with a lattice topper and lockable gate. Anyone driving by the property wouldn't have guessed his house on the other side was any different from the rest of the houses in the neighborhood; exactly the desired effect.

"Hello, Mr. Witherell. Thank you for coming," Zoey said, although she knew better than to expect a response.

As a rule, Mr. Witherell didn't talk any more. He grunted on occasion, or shook his head, but that was it. According to island lore that the school kids had been passing down for years, his jaw rusted shut during the hurricane of 1967. Although some of the adults believed he'd gone deaf, most of them generally assumed that he'd spent so much time alone keeping the lighthouse, he'd lost his social skills, and they tried to accommodate his communication style as best as they could. There were a few less tolerant people who theorized he was so cantankerous it was actually a good thing he didn't express himself verbally.

Yet Zoey's aunt said he always showed up for funerals whenever one of the old-time islanders passed away. Regardless of the season, he wore the same wool single-breasted suit, a relic from the fifties that was so faded it appeared charcoal instead of black. But beneath the cuffs of his short-cut, pleated trousers, his toe-cap shoes were polished to a shine. To Zoey, that small detail demonstrated a world of respect for the deceased. She tried to reciprocate her regard for

Mr. Witherell by speaking to him as she would have spoken to any other guest, whether or not he heard or answered her.

Mark, on the other hand, fanned his nose and scoffed as the old man passed by, "If you want to keep your title as Dune Island's oldest year-round resident, you might consider giving up that pipe."

"Mark!" Zoey hissed, "That's rude."

Mark sneered, "The old salt is deaf."

As if on cue, Mr. Witherell stopped short and spat on the grass. Staring at the ground, he asked Mark, "Who do you think you are?"

Zoey was absolutely dumbfounded to hear his voice, which sounded as if he was gurgling pebbles in the back of his throat. But his tone wasn't one of indignation, the way people usually sounded when they asked that question. It was more like a straightforward inquiry. And he appeared to be waiting for a response, which meant he certainly wasn't deaf. She glanced over at Mark to see what he'd do next.

At first, he shook his head and rolled his eyes. But when Mr. Witherell didn't leave, he snickered before announcing slowly and loudly, "I'm. Marcus. Winslow. The. Third."

Mr. Witherell pulled out a handkerchief and swiped it across his mouth. "I wouldn't be too sure of that," he said. Then he shoved the kerchief back into his pocket and continued down the driveway.

Red-faced, Mark immediately cursed him out, while Zoey stood there wondering, *What was* that *all about?* Mr. Witherell had undoubtedly been the object of far ruder remarks over the years, but as far as she knew, no one ever reported hearing him say anything in response. Why today? Was he finally fed up? Or was there something about Mark in particular that made him lash out?

It wouldn't have been the first time someone had been offended by her cousin's boorishness, but casting doubt on his identity was more of a slam against his mother than against Mark. Or it would been, if it weren't utterly ridiculous.

Oh—I get it, Zoey suddenly realized. *Mark is such a snob about being a Winslow that Mr. Witherell was deliberately attacking his point of pride to get a reaction.*

It worked: his taunt had made Mark fuming mad and he ended his tirade by saying, "Somebody should have had that guy committed half a century ago."

"I admit that was odd. But I wonder why—"

Just then, the back door opened and Helen, one of Ivy and Sylvia's acquaintances from the church they'd attended when they were in better health, tottered down the back steps hugging a large vase of white lilies. "I'm not absconding with these," she said, peering around the blooms. "Ivy insisted I take them because they make her sneeze. She wrapped goodies for me to bring home, too, but my car is parked down the street so I'll have to come back for them."

"I can help you," Zoey offered, taking the vase. While Helen was inside retrieving the goodies, Mark told Zoey he was going to say goodbye to Ivy and then he intended to take off.

"Already?" she questioned, since he had just arrived on the island that morning. She assumed he was going to spend at least one night there.

"Yeah. Check-in is at four."

"You're not staying at the house?"

"Nah. I'd suffocate in there. I booked a room at The Harborview."

Of course. Only the best resort for Mark Winslow III. Knowing him, he was charging his lodging to his company's account and claiming it was a business expense. "Are you coming back here at all tomorrow?" *Or will that interfere with your golf schedule?*

"Yeah. I'll be on the island for a few days."

"Okay. See you later."

As Zoey and Helen inched halfway down the hill in the direction of the harbor, Helen apologized for walking so slowly, explaining, "I've put on quite a few pounds over the winter."

"That's okay—I'm wearing new shoes so I'm not going anywhere fast, either."

Zoey was actually glad for the excuse to get away from the house for a few minutes and after Helen drove away, she paused to survey the seascape below, at the bottom of the hill. Benjamin's Harbor was much smaller than Port Newcomb, where the island's ferry docks were located, but it was more picturesque. She never tired of gazing at the bay's cobalt-blue water during high tide. The vivid green grass and blanched sands at low. Or at the white brick, black iron-capped lighthouse—Sea Gull Lighthouse, the one Mr. Witherell used to keep—standing tall among the bayberry bushes and juniper trees on the flat sea-level peninsula. In the summer, she could spend hours sitting on one of the many wrought-iron benches and watching boats navigate past the long, narrow jetty as they entered or exited the harbor.

There weren't many vessels docked in the slips this early in the season, but because it was such a pleasant day, the waterfront park was humming with activity. Families with small children walking dogs. Teenagers playing ultimate frisbee on the beach. Couples strolling hand-in-hand. Joggers and cyclists exercising in T-shirts and shorts. And just past the harbor, where the pavement gave way to cobblestone, people were strolling along Main Street, browsing in shops and dining al fresco at the numerous restaurants boasting water views.

At another time, Zoey might have hustled the rest of the way down the hill to be in the thick of things. But today, she chose a bench at the edge of the park so she'd have more privacy to collect her thoughts. Because of the way the bench was angled, she had a view both of the harbor and of several of the houses lining the bottom half of the hill.

Despite their differences in size and design, virtually all of them were painted white, with their doors and shutters such a dark shade of green they almost appeared black. Invariably, the yards had lush, manicured squares of lawn—or they would, once spring had fully sprung—bordered by picket fences just like her aunt's. Zoey loved the clean, simple architecture of the residences on Main Street in Benjamin's Manor. This place had always provided her a sense of order and stability whenever it seemed her own world was in chaos. Like when her parents were getting divorced. Or her college boyfriend, her first love, broke up with her. When her mother died of an aneurysm. Her father of heart failure. And especially after her sister's brief, intense battle with cancer…

Oh, Jess, I wish you were here with me now, she thought, as she'd done countless other times during the past six years. Jessica had been Zoey's best friend, as well as her big sister, and she still missed her like crazy. Unfortunately, Zoey had had enough experience with mourning to know how to endure her own sorrow over Sylvia's death, but she wasn't as confident about her ability to buoy her great-aunt through such a loss. Jessica, on the other hand, would have known exactly how to comfort Ivy.

She also would have known how to respond to Mark's suggestion that their great-aunt would benefit from moving into an assisted living facility. Although the incident with Ivy leaving the gas on had initially given Zoey pause, nothing like that had ever happened before. So, whether her aunt had forgotten to turn it off or just hadn't completely twisted the knob around, Zoey figured it was a one-off, a mistake anyone could have made. Still, she wished her sister were there to give her a reality check. And to back her up. Jess could always see through Mark's ruses but she had a lighthearted way of calling him out on his behavior without overreacting or offending him, the way Zoey did.

How am I going to handle this kind of family stuff without Jessica's advice and humor to get me through? It's going to be like… like not having an anchor in a storm, she lamented, already feeling adrift.

If she wasn't careful, Zoey was going to cry and it still wasn't time for that. She stood and took a few tentative steps toward home but her blisters were killing her feet. If she took her shoes off to walk back, she'd get runs in her newly purchased pantyhose. *Who cares? I'm never going to wear them again.* Zoey had only put them on today in deference to her aunt Sylvia's belief that a lady never wore a skirt or dress bare-legged to a formal event, like a wedding or a funeral. But the funeral was over and besides, it was stinking hot outside. Too hot for her to trudge back up the hill wearing nylons.

Zoey pivoted toward the park so she could take her hosiery off in the public restroom, some twenty yards away. But when she hobbled over to it, she found the facility was still locked for the off-season. She surveyed the area around her; not a soul in sight and she was hidden from view, too.

"Sorry, Aunt Sylvia," she apologized, removing her shoes. With her back to the wall so she could see if anyone was coming, as well as to prevent them from catching a glimpse of her derriere, she discreetly slid her hands beneath her skirt and hooked her thumbs into the waistband of the hosiery. As swiftly as she could, she brought the pantyhose to her ankles. She intended to quickly step out of them but when she lifted one leg, the nylon clung to her foot, turning inside out, so she had to roll the stockings over her toes.

"Ah, freedom!" she proclaimed when her second foot was finally bare. She flipped her hair back over her head as she stood upright again, thrusting the ropey ring of hosiery in the air like a hard-won trophy.

At that moment, a man wearing a suit came around the corner of the building. Not just any man. It was Nick. The guy whose tie she'd cried on. He stopped abruptly, a wry smile on his face. Mortified, Zoey scrunched the hosiery into a ball and hid it behind her back.

"The bathrooms are closed," she snapped as if it were somehow his fault, and tore off across the grass instead of using the walkway.

"Zoey" he called after her. When she sped up instead of slowing down, he called again. "Zoey, wait!"

Couldn't he take a hint? How could he possibly expect her to stop and chit-chat after she'd just been caught disrobing in public, especially since he knew she had a funeral reception to get back to? Then she was struck by a discomfiting thought: *He probably has women throwing themselves at him all the time. What if he misread my little teary-eyed lapse in the driveway as flirting?*

Under different circumstances Zoey might have been interested in getting to know him, but her aunt had just died, so she couldn't trust her emotions right now. Plus, she had sworn off dating—for at least six months, anyway—after breaking up with Erik. And that had only been two months ago. Not to mention, Nick was pals with Mark.

After years of giving Mark's friends the benefit of the doubt, Zoey had learned the hard way that in her cousin's case, birds of a feather really did flock together. The people he attracted tended to be duplicitous, self-centered and combative. Mark had no affinity for honest, giving, easy-going types and they usually didn't stick around him long, either—with the exception of his family, of course.

So, no. Zoey wasn't interested in Nick. She hurried across Main Street, refusing to slow down even when she heard his footsteps right behind her.

Suddenly, he had outpaced her and was walking backwards up the hill. "You forgot your shoes," he informed her, holding them out.

Still clutching her nylons in one hand, Zoey took the shoes with other. "Thank you," she said. Brusquely sidestepping him to conceal her humiliation—he must have thought she was ridiculous—she continued her trek and to her relief, he didn't follow.

Zoey felt like a sponge that had reached saturation and tears began to seep from her eyes. *No, no, no*, she told herself. *Not now. Not yet.* This time, it didn't matter; she was going to cry. In public. On Main Street, no less. She plodded onward another ten yards before giving in. Hugging one of the island's ubiquitous, colonial-style post lanterns for balance, she wept openly. The tears came hard and fast, like an April shower. Then, just as abruptly, her crying jag passed.

She was wiping her eyes when a red convertible came flying down the hill, its stereo blaring, the top down. From behind the wheel, Mark flashed his perfect white teeth and waved at her, as if today was just another day at the beach.

CHAPTER TWO

"I'm so sorry I couldn't make it to Hope Haven yesterday," Lauren apologized when she called early the next morning.

Zoey understood; her closest friend and colleague had also been laid off in December when their branch closed and she'd just begun working at a library in Cranston three weeks ago. As the newest member on staff, she had been relegated to the Saturday shift and she hadn't accrued any time off yet. "That's okay. I'd rather have you visit on a happier occasion, anyway."

"Yeah, but I wanted to be there to support you. How did things go?"

Zoey told her about the lovely memorial service and reception before confiding how ticked off she was at Mark for insinuating their aunt wasn't fit to live alone and for apparently trying to squeeze her out of her house.

"She doesn't want to move?"

"No way. That's one of the reasons she was so grateful I came to help when my aunt Sylvia got pneumonia. She was afraid the doctor was going to suggest that she go to a skilled nursing center off-island to recover. Neither of them has left Hope Haven for longer than a night or two for the past fifty or sixty years," Zoey answered. "I don't get it. Mark has never shown this level of interest in the house before. He's going to inherit it eventually, so what's the big rush to get his hands on it now?"

"Maybe he's hard up for money? Oh, that reminds me—I have a lead for you!" Lauren told her about a librarian in one of Providence's universities who was pregnant with twins and would be going on maternity leave in August. Supposedly, the woman had indicated she didn't plan to return to her post after the babies were born, so the position had a high likelihood of becoming permanent. "I get it that you need to start earning an income again, but if this job is a good fit, you could spend a few more months on Dune Island before it starts."

"You're right. It might be ideal, as long as my tenant wants to lease my townhome through the summer and I can keep on top of my mortgage payments," Zoey said. "I'd love to be able to stay with my aunt until she's a little stronger. Emotionally, I mean."

"It might be good for you, too, Zo. You've gone through a lot in the past few months," Lauren sympathized. "I know you're grieving, but Hope Haven has always seemed like, well, like a haven for you. And who knows, if you stay there for a while, you might end up meeting someone. It would be great if you could have a summer romance. Preferably with a swashbuckling type of guy who'd take your mind off your troubles."

"Swashbuckling type?" Zoey cracked up. "This is a contemporary island, you know, not the high seas in the seventeen-hundreds. Besides, I just got out of a relationship with a pirate—Erik. It's not an experience I can afford to repeat."

"You know what I mean. Someone who's very dashing. And chivalrous. An adventurer, like a fisherman or a lifeguard. Or someone in the Coast Guard."

Zoey recognized this wish list. "And it wouldn't hurt if he had a friend or a brother I could introduce you to, right?"

"Right."

While she was considering whether she should tell Lauren about her interaction with Nick, just for kicks, her phone beeped, signaling she was getting another call. Zoey looked at the screen: it was Kathleen, who she supposed was her sister-in-law, in a way. In the six years since Jessica died, her husband Scott had remarried twice. Zoey rarely spoke directly with Kathleen, his current wife, so it was alarming to see her number. Had something happened to him or to Zoey's fourteen-year-old niece, Gabi? She quickly said goodbye to Lauren so she could pick up the call.

"Zoey!" Kathleen exclaimed breathlessly. "I'm so glad I reached you."

"Is something wrong? Is Gabi okay?"

"Well, yes and no…"

Zoey's pulse thudded in her ears as Kathleen explained that Gabi had attempted to drive her father's car, supposedly on a dare from a boy. Fortunately, she didn't get very far; she backed into the brick retaining wall while attempting a three-point-turn in the driveway. Although she smashed a tail light and put a big dent in the fender, she didn't suffer any injuries herself.

Zoey's initial relief that no physical harm had befallen her niece was followed by a wave of concern for Gabi's emotional well-being. "That doesn't sound like Gabi at all."

Gabi was genuinely a kind, good-humored, smart girl who seemed to be more interested in getting good grades and playing the flute with the city's youth symphony than impressing boys or rebelling against her parents. But then, Zoey hadn't seen her in almost ten months.

In the first year following Jessica's death, Zoey spent virtually every weekend with her sister's child. But shortly after Scott remarried the first time, his employer transferred him from Rhode Island to California. Although Zoey kept in touch with Gabi by phone and text, she usually only got to visit her twice a year. And actually, she hadn't made the trip out west this past Christmas, the way she usually did. Because she'd just been laid off, money was tight. Since Gabi had planned to spend most of her school vacation performing with the symphony, Zoey decided to postpone the trip until her February break, when they'd have more time together. By then, Sylvia had gotten sick and was in and out of the hospital, so Zoey's presence was needed on Dune Island. Afterward, she'd regretted that she hadn't gone to California in December and she especially regretted it now.

"A lot has changed since you saw her last June."

Zoey didn't like the sound of that. Was her niece in trouble with drugs? Boys? School? "What do you mean?"

"It's Scott. He's been drinking. A lot. It's really taken a toll on Gabi. And on me—"

Zoey waited quietly as Kathleen wept. Geography and differences in their personalities, as well as a sense of loyalty toward Jessica, had kept Zoey from becoming close to her, but she appreciated what an excellent stepmother Kathleen had been to Gabi. Kathleen was also very supportive of Scott, who had been absolutely devastated by Jessica's death. He'd gone through a drinking phase right after she died—Zoey long suspected he was drunk when he married his second wife, Sheila—but that's all Zoey thought it was. A grief-induced phase that had ended over four years ago, along with his second marriage.

But if he was drinking again, that explained why he'd seemed so indifferent when Zoey called to tell him about Sylvia's passing. It wasn't as if she had expected him to come to the funeral or to send Gabi back east for it. But she had at least expected him to reminisce with her about her aunt for a moment, considering all the summers Sylvia and Ivy had hosted him and Jessica. Instead, he'd expressed perfunctory condolences and quickly ended the call.

"I'm sorry to hear about this," she said after Kathleen regained her composure. "How long has it been going on?"

Kathleen sniffed. "Almost two years."

Why hadn't Zoey noticed Scott's drinking when she'd visited their house? "I had no idea."

"Scott used to be able to hide it, but it's gotten a lot worse. It's ruining his career, his health and his relationship with his daughter. And I can't tell you what a strain it's putting on our marriage. We're fighting all the time."

Zoey winced, remembering the months—the *years*—leading up to her own parents' divorce. No wonder Gabi took her father's car; she was probably trying to get as far away from the two of them as fast as she could. And at this moment, Zoey wished she could help her escape. She didn't know what to say except, "That's awful, Kathleen."

"Yeah. That's why I finally gave him an ultimatum. Either he goes through a recovery program and gets sober, or I'm leaving him and I'll do whatever it takes in order to bring Gabi with me."

Zoey was afraid to ask. "Which did he choose?"

"Recovery—he's going to a residential center."

"That's great!"

"It's hardly great," Kathleen said sarcastically. "But it *is* necessary."

Don't get snitty with me. I'm kind of on the edge here, myself. "I meant it's better than the alternative. And it's a very hopeful step. But it's still going to be difficult. For all of you." *Especially for my niece—and she's the one I'm most worried about.*

Kathleen seemed to read her mind. "Yeah, it is. I don't know how Gabi is going to behave once Scott isn't here." She explained that Scott was either drunk or hungover so often that he'd become something of an absentee parent. Which meant she'd had to play bad cop when Gabi banged up the car. She'd taken away Gabi's phone and in retaliation, Gabi hadn't spoken to her for over three weeks. Kathleen anticipated Gabi would blame her for sending her father away and she was concerned the teenager would act out and get into even more trouble.

"She refused to tell us the name of the boy who dared her to drive the car, but obviously I'm concerned about his influence on her. And I can see how the tension between all three of us has negatively affected her, too. I think it would be helpful for her to be in a healthier, more positive environment. That's why I'm calling—to ask if Gabi could stay with you for a while."

Zoey bit her lip to keep from blurting out, *How fast can she pack?* She recognized a decision of this gravity needed to be considered from all angles. "Don't most programs want the family members to be involved in the recovery process? Like go to counseling and stuff?"

"Eventually, but Scott's not going to be allowed to have visitors for the first thirty days, at least. And he only gets to make phone calls once a week."

Thirty days, at least? "What about school?"

"She can transfer. There's not that much of the school year left, anyway."

"I'd like to take her, but I'm… I'm still unemployed. And I've been spending most of my time at Hope Haven, on Dune Island. I don't know if Scott mentioned it, but my great-aunt Sylvia just passed away."

"Oh, I'm so sorry. I totally forgot. When is the funeral?"

"We, uh, already had it." Zoey didn't want to make Kathleen feel worse by telling her it was the day before. "Anyway, I've been subletting my townhome on a month-to-month basis. But if I land a job, I'll need to go back to Rhode Island and start work. Which means Gabi might just get settled into a school here in Benjamin's Manor and then I'd have to uproot her again. That could be really disruptive."

"Trust me. It would be a lot less disruptive than what's going on here."

Zoey's head was swimming. "Have you talked to Scott about this?"

"More like he talked to me. It was his idea. Obviously, he trusts you deeply. We both do."

"What does Gabi think about coming here?"

"Who knows? Like I said, she won't talk to me." Kathleen sighed. "I'm not sure she should have much of a say in this decision, considering her behavior lately. But before we even considered asking you to take her, Gabi told Scott she wished she could go stay with her cousin in Virginia, so she clearly wants to get away. Not that we'd ever let her live with Sophie."

Zoey understood why they wouldn't: Scott's niece was a year older than Gabi but she acted as if she were twenty-one and she had absolutely no parental supervision. Then it occurred to Zoey that if Gabi was willing to go to Virginia, it meant she was willing to give up playing her flute in the spring concert. And if she was willing to give that up, things at home must have been really, really bad.

"I'd be happy to have her. I'll have to talk it over with my aunt, first, but I can't imagine her objecting," Zoey said. "When will she arrive?"

"Um… is Tuesday too soon?" Kathleen explained she was concerned that if she didn't put the plans into motion immediately, Scott would change his mind.

Zoey agreed Tuesday was fine and they arranged to discuss Gabi's itinerary and the details involved in enrolling her in the local high school later that evening. Kathleen thanked Zoey profusely, saying, "I can't tell you how much this means to me. And to Scott. We know you're the best person to take care of her."

After disconnecting, Zoey stared blankly at the phone, wondering, *Am I really the best person to look after Gabi? Or am I the* only *person?*

She'd always had a close relationship with her niece, but that was before the teenager started acting up the way Kathleen had just described. And how was she going to talk to Gabi about boys or be a good role model for responsible behavior and healthy relationships when she herself had allowed her last boyfriend to all but bankrupt her?

It was mortifying to acknowledge the part she'd played in her own financial ruin by signing off on all the transactions Erik had suggested without fully researching them. Later, she tried to convince herself it was because she'd been too distracted by her job search. Or that she hadn't had enough time to examine the fine print because she'd been ferrying back and forth between her place and Dune Island to care for her aunt Sylvia. But the truth was, she'd been stupid to trust Erik with her money. And stupider to trust him with her heart. Or was that the other way around? Regardless, Zoey wouldn't be making the same mistakes with any man again any time soon.

Hopefully, Gabi feels the same way about the boy at school, she thought and went downstairs to talk to her aunt about their youngest family member coming to Dune Island to find her footing again.

*

As she waited for the line of vehicles in front of her rental car to disembark the ferry on Tuesday morning, Zoey glanced at her niece dozing in the passenger seat. Then she looked at herself in the rearview mirror. She fully felt every one of her thirty-eight years. This was partly because the spray of lines near the outer corners of her eyes—which reminded her more of a cat's whiskers than of a crow's feet—always appeared deeper when she hadn't gotten enough sleep.

It was also because seeing her niece brought Zoey back to when she and her sister were teenagers, another lifetime ago. With her fair skin and hair and pale blue eyes, Gabi had always generally resembled her mother, but this past year the girl had blossomed into her spitting image. The same high cheek bones, straight nose and slightly pointed chin. She'd inherited Jessica's long legs, too.

When she was growing up, Zoey desperately wished she looked more like her mom and sister. Instead, she was short, had a heart-shaped face, hazel eyes, and an aquiline nose. Although her hair was thick and wavy, it was a decidedly ordinary shade of brown. As a kid, Zoey envied her sister's golden locks. When they became adults and Jessica lost her hair because of the chemo treatments, Zoey couldn't look at her without tearing up.

"Why are you crying? I'm the one who's bald," her sister had asked.

Zoey had confessed she used to fantasize about waving a magic wand and making Jessica's hair all fall out at once. "Now that it has, I wish I could wave a wand and make it all grow back."

Ever practical, Jessica had replied, "It will, eventually. You don't need magic for that."

"Yeah, but I can't believe I wished such a thing on you. I'm sorry, Jess."

Zoey recalled Jessica's charitable response. "That was only petty jealousy, Zo. It's not as if you made *this* happen. And if it helps you feel any better, sometimes when I used to watch you curling your eyelashes, I wished they'd break off. It drove me nuts that mine weren't even long enough to use a curler—every time I tried, I pinched my eyelids."

Zoey did have really long, thick eyelashes, but until that discussion, she'd never known Jessica envied them as much as she'd envied Jessica's hair. For the most part, the Jansen girls were so close that any sibling rivalry between them was negligible. If anything, Zoey admired her sister. She was proud of how charismatic and smart Jessica was, especially in the sciences and math. And she marveled at her optimism and intrepidness. Her singing voice. Her wit... *Does Gabi remember any of these things about her mom?* Zoey wondered.

She peeked at her niece again. Her eyes were still closed. After a red-eye, cross-country flight, it was possible she was truly sleepy, but Zoey got the sense Gabi was avoiding conversation. At the airport, the teenager had allowed her aunt to hug her hello, but she had barely returned Zoey's embrace—a first. And although she'd replied to Zoey's questions on the way to the ferry terminal, Gabi's answers were practically monosyllabic and she didn't initiate any conversation on her own. *Is she afraid if we start talking, I'll grill her about smashing up her dad's car?* Zoey hoped not; the two of them had always had such an easy rapport and she didn't want her niece to shut her out.

Gabi's eyes opened and she caught Zoey looking at her. "What?"

"I was just thinking how much you look like your mom did at your age."

Gabi scowled. "Not really. I have my dad's overbite."

Zoey was secretly glad her niece had to wear braces; they kept her from appearing more mature than she was. Kathleen mentioned that Gabi had shot up so much this past year she was now taller than most of the boys and virtually all of the girls her age at school. So Zoey was counting on her orthodontic hardware to prevent the juniors or seniors at school from mistaking her for being in their grade.

"I hope you brought some cooler clothes to wear. Aunt Ivy keeps the house awfully warm."

"I'll be fine." She crossed her arms in front of her.

After they drove down the ferry ramp and merged onto Port Newcomb's Main Street, Zoey pointed to a restaurant. "Do you

remember the first time you went to Captain Clark's? You were
about five years old and your dad asked you to help him choose
a lobster from the tank. They had bands on their claws, so you
thought he was going to let you keep it as a pet. When you found
out he was planning to eat it for supper, you threw such a tantrum
we had to leave before we were served."

Gabi shook her head and closed her eyes again. "That was a long
time ago. I hardly remember anything about being here."

Really? Zoey was disappointed. Her sister had loved Dune Island
as much as Zoey did, and Jessica, Scott and Gabi had spent two
weeks there every July from the time Gabi was a baby until she
was eight years old. Zoey always joined them. Summer vacations
together in Benjamin's Manor had been a family tradition since they
were girls themselves and the sisters looked forward to it all year.

In fact, when it became clear Jessica's cancer was terminal, even
though it was only May she insisted on going to Dune Island, so
they could enjoy one last vacation there as a family. It had been
Jessica's hope that her daughter would consider Benjamin's Manor
her second home, too. *Even if Gabi doesn't remember much about
being here as a little girl, maybe if I show her what her mom loved about
the island, it will become meaningful to her, too*, Zoey ruminated.

It was gloriously sunny and there were plenty of interesting
things to see on the brief trip back from the ferry dock. Hope Haven
was made up of five towns, also called hamlets or villages by the local
old-timers. In addition to Benjamin's Manor and Port Newcomb,
there was Rockfield, Highland Hills, and Lucinda's Hamlet—Lucy's
Ham, for short. Each community had a distinct vibe and offered
unique vistas of both land and sea. Zoey would have pointed out

Jessica's favorite views to Gabi, but her niece didn't open her eyes again until they were parked in the driveway.

"Look who's here," Ivy said when they came through the back door. "My great and grand niece."

When Gabi was little and her mom was trying to explain how they were related to Ivy and Sylvia, she said, "My mother was their niece. I'm their great-niece. And you're their great-grand-niece."

Gabi had asked in wide-eyed astonishment, "They think I'm great *and* grand, Mom?"

Jessica had managed to suppress her laughter, saying, "Yes, honey. You're definitely the greatest and grandest niece they have."

Gabi might not have remembered going to Captain Clark's restaurant, but she hadn't forgotten about this. Either that or her father had repeated the anecdote when she was older because now she giggled self-consciously and replied, "The greatest and grandest."

When Ivy held out her arms for a hug, Gabi hesitated. Their aunt was still very emotional over losing Sylvia and Zoey hoped Gabi wasn't going to give her the same lukewarm reception she'd given Zoey at the airport. But then, Gabi set down her flute case and carry-on bag and enveloped Ivy with both arms, proving that she was still the same warm-hearted girl she'd always been, just like her mother before her.

"Dad didn't tell me about Auntie Sylvia until Sunday," she said. "I feel so bad. I wish she was still here."

"So do I," Ivy agreed.

There was something so poignant about the sight of Gabi's long, flaxen locks brushing against Ivy's silver halo of hair as they embraced that Zoey got choked up and she had to look away.

Then Mark came around the corner from the kitchen. "I think it's time to flip the pancakes," he announced.

"You're right!" Ivy let go of Gabi and spun toward the kitchen, instructing over her shoulder, "Show Gabi to her room and then hurry back down. Brunch is almost ready."

While their aunt disappeared around the corner, Gabi picked up her flute and carry-on bag and Zoey grabbed her other suitcase, since Mark clearly wasn't going to give them a hand.

"Hi, Mark," Gabi said as she squeezed by him.

"Hey, kiddo. You've gotten tall." Mark patted her shoulder. Coming from him, that was actually a rather demonstrative gesture, however awkward. "Tall and thin. It obvious you come from the Winslow family line. Not like Doughy, here."

When Zoey was learning to talk, she couldn't pronounce her first name, so she called herself 'Doughy'. Her family thought it was adorable and the nickname stuck for years afterward as a term of endearment. But she knew that's not how Mark meant it now. He meant it as a crack about her weight. Not that it was any of his business either way, but she *wasn't* doughy; she was muscular and athletic, a former soccer player. But ever since they were young, her cousin seemed to relish drawing attention to the fact that she wasn't as thin as the rest of the women in their extended family.

Zoey ignored the juvenile dig. "Aunt Ivy usually isn't so active at this time in the morning. You didn't come here and wake her up to make breakfast for you, did you?"

Mark smirked. "You're the one who told me she still loves to cook."

As he ducked into the kitchen, Zoey said to Gabi, "Let's take the back stairs. Be careful—they're steep."

Ivy's rectangular, Federal-style home was built at the turn of the nineteenth century. Some of its original features included the narrow servants' staircase in the back of the house, and the wider, split-level "grand staircase" in the front. A kitchen and formal dining room, as well as the "keeping" and "best" rooms, both with fireplaces, made up the lower level; and four bedrooms—also with original fireplaces—were found upstairs. As simple as the floor plan was, the house was spacious and elegant and Zoey hoped her niece would feel comfortable there.

At the top of the stairs, Gabi abruptly stopped. "I'm not going to use Aunt Sylvia's room, am I?"

Did Scott tell her that Sylvia had died at home in bed? Although unexpected, her passing was peaceful. Even so, Zoey understood why the young girl would have been reluctant to sleep there. "No. You'll be at the other end of the hall, across from me. You get the room with the fireplace—not that you'll need to use it."

"I might. I'm actually kind of chilly."

"You are? I guess that's one way you don't take after your mom. She and I always ran hot. We used to beg our parents to let us sleep up on the widow's walk because we thought it would be nice and breezy up there. Of course, they never did."

"Yeah, well I'm from southern California, so this weather is colder than what I'm used to."

Zoey was surprised she identified herself as being *from* California. She *lived* in California, but she wasn't *from* there. Not originally, anyway. Even in terms of duration, Gabi had resided on the east coast longer than on the west. Zoey knew it was irrational, but it made her sad to hear her niece say she was from a state that Jessica had never visited. It was almost as if she were distancing herself from the first part of her life. Or from her mom.

I'm hypersensitive because I'm tired, Zoey told herself as she splashed water on her face in the bathroom. *I should be glad Gabi sounds so proud she lives in California—it's a beautiful place and it shows how well she has adjusted to being there.*

She went downstairs into the kitchen, where Mark had begun eating. A few minutes later, Gabi came in and when she did, Moby padded over to rub against her legs.

"Aww, hi Moby." She picked up the portly animal, turning him around and stretching her arms straight out to examine him before cuddling the monster cat to her chest. "You've lost weight, you poor thing," she cooed, pressing her face into his fur.

Her sincere yet ludicrous remark must have tickled their aunt's funny bone because for the first time since Sylvia died, Ivy laughed. Which made Zoey laugh, too.

Maybe having Gabi here will be good for all three of us, she dared to hope.

After Mark, Gabi and Zoey had eaten more blueberry buttermilk pancakes than seemed possible—their aunt had made a double batch and insisted they couldn't let them go to waste—Zoey offered to do the dishes. Gabi went upstairs to sleep. Then, probably because Mark had woken her up so early, Ivy said she needed to lie down again, too.

Which left Mark in the kitchen drinking a third cup of coffee. Zoey figured he was killing time until he went to the golf club again, and as she cleared the table she tried to think of something to say to him. Ever since Mr. Witherell's remark after the funeral, her cousin had seemed edgier than usual, so she had no intention of bringing that subject up. Nor did she want to quarrel with him again about his opinion that Ivy should move. So, she nonchalantly asked, "When are you going back to Boston?"

Mark immediately sounded defensive. "Why? Are you eager to get rid of me?"

"Just wondering what your schedule is like." *But why are you being so cagey about how long you're staying on the island? Usually, you can't wait to leave.*

"Well, when I'm done with my coffee, I'm going up to the attic. Ivy said Sylvia stored a couple of containers up there and I want to look through them."

Zoey was taken aback. Sylvia had diffidently shown her and Jessica the contents of the trunks once or twice when they were girls but Mark had never demonstrated any interest in her keepsakes. *Kitsch*, he called them. Most of the knickknacks she'd put into storage in the attic weren't worth more than fifty dollars apiece, but they held a wealth of sentimental value to her. It seemed odd that he'd taken a sudden interest in his grandmother's favorite doilies, bric-a-brac and the dress she'd worn when she got married.

Or was he hoping to find something else, something more valuable. Like… what? Mark knew that Sylvia had given her wedding ring to his father so he could use it when he proposed to Mark's mother. After Mark's mother died, his father sold the ring and used the money to buy a new one for his second wife. Zoey tried to imagine what else Mark may have been looking for, but she drew a complete blank. And it wasn't as if she could have asked him about it outright; while Mark had no problem drilling others, if someone asked him a question he didn't want to answer, he accused them of interrogating him.

So she squelched her curiosity, and at the risk of offending him by pointing out what he should have thought of by himself, she asked, "Could you please wait until after Aunt Ivy and Gabi get up from their naps? Otherwise they'll hear you tromping around overhead and they won't be able to sleep."

"I didn't plan on *tromping*, but whatever. I'll come back this afternoon." Clearly insulted, he left his cup on the table and headed out the door.

Couldn't he have at least brought this to the sink? Zoey thought as she lifted the cup and wiped the wet ring beneath it. *I'm not his personal servant.*

As with other things Mark sometimes said or did that irked Zoey, this trivial gesture wasn't particularly offensive in itself. But it bothered her because it reflected his deep-seated sense of entitlement. Or maybe it reflected what Zoey's father had referred to as "poor training." Which was his way of saying that Mark's parents hadn't taught him how to be responsible for himself and considerate toward others. And as much as it pained Zoey to admit it, because she loved her great-aunts dearly, they had spoiled him rotten, too.

While she poured the rest of Mark's coffee down the drain and washed his cup, Zoey recalled that when her family used to come to Sylvia and Ivy's house for their annual two-week vacation, Mark was usually already there. His mother had died when he was seven and although his father remarried six months later, neither he nor

Mark's stepmother seemed to know what to do with him when school wasn't in session. So, they'd ship him off to visit Sylvia and Ivy. In retrospect, Zoey realized it must have been upsetting for the young boy to know his parents essentially didn't want him around. But at the time, she resented how self-centered and lazy he was.

Zoey and Jessica's parents had always expected them to pick up after themselves, as well as participate in chores that benefitted everyone else. But Mark refused to clear the table or take out the trash. He wouldn't help load beach chairs into the car's trunk. He never even dashed through the house closing the windows when it rained or took a turn filling the basin everyone used to rinse the sand off their feet before entering the house. What was really maddening to Zoey was that her aunts hadn't seemed to mind, especially Sylvia.

"It's not fair," she'd once complained to her mother as a child. "Can't you tell him to take out the garbage tonight?"

"No."

"Why not?"

"Because what Mark does or doesn't do is between him and his grandmother and great-aunt. And how your cousin behaves shouldn't have any bearing on how *you* behave. You should help your aunties because you love and appreciate them and because it's the responsible thing to do," her mother had lectured her. "But if you really feel it's such a hardship to set the table or dry the dishes while we're here, just let me know and next year we don't have to come back."

Zoey smiled, remembering how effectively her mother's threat had shut down her adolescent grievance. Years later, her mom admitted that Ivy and Sylvia had mollycoddled Mark's father, too. But by then, Zoey had learned a lot more about Ivy and Sylvia's history through the stories they'd shared, as well as secrets her mother confided, and she'd come to understand why they may have indulged "the boys."

So, Zoey's cousin had grown into a man who still expected his grandmother Sylvia—and more notably, Ivy, since she was the wealthy one—to cater to him. Not just in little ways, like getting up earlier than usual to make him breakfast because he had a craving for buttermilk pancakes. Oh, no. They babied him on a much bigger scale; like buying his first car and then paying for his speeding tickets. Giving him the down payment for a house he moved out of after less than a year. Compensating his attorney the first time he divorced. They even settled his gambling debts—and those were just the things Zoey knew about. It was safe to say there was no financial crisis or legal jam Mark got into that Sylvia and Ivy didn't get him out of. According to Zoey's mother, they had done the same kind of things for his father, too.

Although Jessica and Zoey had many private discussions about Mark exploiting their aunts, Zoey had followed her mother's example and held her tongue about it in front of everyone else. It wasn't her money or her relationship, so it wasn't her business. As she matured, she came to the realization that if she had asked them to, her aunts would have helped her just as much as they'd helped Mark. But that was the difference between the two cousins; Zoey never would have expected Ivy or Sylvia to rescue her, especially not from a mess she'd made herself. *Like allowing Erik to deplete my life savings*, she thought ruefully.

But dwelling on her regret was a poor use of her time. With the funeral behind them, Zoey needed to resume her job search. After putting away the last dish, she decided to follow up on a few leads she'd researched earlier in the month. She tiptoed upstairs to get her laptop, stopping to peek in on Ivy and make sure she was actually napping and not weeping.

Downstairs again, she went into the living room, or the "keeping" room, as it was originally known. When the house was built in the early 1800s, the room was intended to "keep" family members warm. It was right next to the kitchen, where the woodburning stove provided a major source of heat, and contained a fireplace of its own, as well as a small beehive oven for baking bread.

Of course, keeping warm wasn't a challenge any more; over the years the house had been modernized to include a heating system, as well as electricity and a landline for the only kind of phone Ivy ever used. The servants' cramped quarters, both upstairs and down, had also been converted into bathrooms with functional plumbing long ago. The kitchen had been remodelled in the late seventies, but otherwise, except for essential updates and the occasional fresh coat of paint, Ivy declined to make many superficial changes to the rest of the house's interior, including to its original wide-plank floors and simple but elegant molding and chair rails. Nor did she replace her numerous antique tables, chairs, lamps and mirrors because, as she said, they were tangible reminders of her family's history.

She was especially fond of the "best parlor" or "best room," which was still solely used for its originally intended purpose of entertaining guests on special occasions. It also housed numerous Winslow family heirlooms in two floor-to-ceiling built-in china cabinets. The best parlor's décor had virtually remained unchanged, for better and for worse, for at least the past seventy years. Ivy treasured the room so much that not even Moby was allowed to tread across its threshold without explicit permission from her, and most of the time, the door was kept shut.

Zoey preferred the living room anyway, where she could settle into an antique mahogany lady's writing desk in front of one of the windows facing the harbor. She opened her laptop to type an email inquiry, but the room was so warm and her stomach was so full of pancakes that she lowered the lid again. Crossing her arms, she rested them on her laptop and put her head down. *Just for a minute…*

Zoey woke to the muffled pitter-patter of Moby slinking across the floor behind her. But when she turned, she discovered it was her niece who had entered the room. The teenager yawned and gracefully folded her legs behind the coffee table as she took a seat on the sofa. Getting up to join her there, Zoey resisted the urge to tell her again how much she looked like Jessica.

"Did you have a good rest?"

"Yeah. Except when I woke up I couldn't figure out where I was." Gabi pushed her bangs out of her eyes and pointed to the dome-shaped, brick opening in the wall to the right of the Rumford-style fireplace. "I used to be scared to walk past the beehive oven. I thought bees really lived in there."

Zoey chuckled, happy that her niece was starting to remember more about being here.

"Hey." Mark had come in without her hearing him. He plunked himself into an armchair across from them, causing the antimacassar to slide off the back of the headrest. "What were you two laughing about?"

When Zoey told him, Mark said to Gabi, "That's not so silly—Zoey used to be afraid of the dentil molding."

Zoey had forgotten all about that and she was surprised her cousin remembered. "I wasn't *afraid* of it. I was *disgusted* by it."

"What's dentil molding?" Gabi asked.

"It's the kind of wood trim in the best parlor." Zoey gestured to the edge of the ceiling opposite them. "But it's not as plain as this crown molding is. Dentil molding was considered very ornate and at the time, it was expensive. So the original homeowner could only afford to put it in one room, the best one."

"It's really called dental molding?" Gabi clarified. "Dental, like dentist?"

"Sort of. It has the same root word as dental, *dens*. But it's spelled *d-e-n-t-i-l*. It was named that because it's composed of little blocks that look like teeth."

Mark hooted. "Except Zoey thought they actually *were* teeth."

"I wonder who gave me that idea?" Zoey tried to glare accusingly at him but she couldn't keep a straight face.

"One day Zoey overheard Ivy say that a section of the dentil molding in the best room was rotting out and it was going to have to be replaced," Mark explained. "Ivy was really upset because it had been there almost since the sea captain, Captain Chadwell, first built the house."

Zoey cut in. "He was actually a *whaling* captain. But we weren't supposed to make that distinction, for obvious reasons, even though back in those days whaling was a highly regarded occupation. Anyway, I didn't know what dentil molding was but I couldn't ask my parents because they would have figured out I'd been eavesdropping."

"So she asked me instead—"

"*Big* mistake." Zoey shook her head, but she was enjoying this.

"I came up with a story about how Captain Chadwell was out at sea for so long, he got scurvy and all of his teeth fell out. Which was tragic, because the one thing his wife had always loved…"

Because Mark was laughing too hard to continue, Zoey picked up where he left off. "The one thing the captain's wife always loved best about him was his pearly white smile. So when his teeth fell out, instead of tossing them overboard, he put them in a leather pouch and brought them home to give to her. At first, she was heartbroken but then she realized if she put the teeth on display she could be reminded of her husband's smile even when he was at sea "right hunting," meaning hunting right whales. Her china cabinet was already full of other valuables, so she secured his teeth to the molding instead." By this point, Zoey was clutching her sides and she could hardly get the words out. "Mark told me that's why Aunt Ivy referred to it as *dentil molding.* So, you can understand why I was so grossed out by it."

Gabi wrinkled her nose. "Eww! That's a terrible story."

"What are you talking about? It was *romantic*," Mark exclaimed with mock indignation.

Tears were rolling down Zoey's cheeks. "That explains a lot about your love life!"

"Seriously, I can't believe you told something so gruesome to a little girl," Gabi repeated.

Red-faced from cracking up, Mark snorted. "A little girl? She was thirteen!"

"I was not!" Zoey protested. "Don't listen to him, Gabi. I was only seven or eight... eleven, max."

All three of them burst out laughing again. When they settled down, Mark boasted, "You have to admit, I had you convinced."

"Yeah, at first. But when I told Jessica about it, she said you made the whole thing up." Jess never allowed anyone—especially Mark—to steer her little sister wrong. Remembering, Zoey thought, *If she'd been here when I was seeing Erik, she would have tipped me off about him right away, too...*

"Later that night you hid my skateboard behind the beach roses in the back yard for payback, remember?"

"Yeah. You looked for it for two days—Aunt Sylvia was the one who found it when she went out to clip flowers for her bud vase."

"You two loved ganging up on me," Mark accused, but he was grinning.

Zoey had forgotten about the pranks she and Jessica played on Mark and she was pleased he seemed to have such fond memories of the trio's childhood antics, too. It occurred to her that over the course of the last ten years, she'd heard him laugh on occasion but she couldn't recall ever hearing him howl in amusement the way he'd done just now about the Legend of Captain Chadwell, as they later titled it.

Gabi pointed to the oversized, black and white portrait photograph of a young man with a brilliant smile hanging above the fireplace. "At least your grandfather never got scurvy, Mark."

"That's not his grandfather—that's Aunt Ivy's husband, Dennis," Zoey told her niece. "Mark's grandfather's portrait is hanging in the other parlor, with the rest of the paintings of Aunt Ivy's closest relatives."

"Oh, sorry." Gabi narrowed her eyes at the portrait, her cheeks going pink.

"It's hard to keep track of how we're all related," Zoey said, waving away her niece's embarrassment.

She went on to explain a little about Ivy's family. Ivy had been the eldest child of Thomas and Adele Winslow. Next came Charles, who was Zoey's grandfather and Gabi's great-grandfather. And then Ivy's younger brother, Marcus—he later married Sylvia, who had become as close as a true sister to Ivy. Their son and grandson were both named Marcus, too, but everyone called their son *Marcus Jr.*—or sometimes just *Junior*—and their grandson *Mark*, so there wouldn't be any confusion. Ivy's immediate family members had sat for the portraits when she was sixteen and the paintings had hung in the same places ever since. Thomas Winslow had barred all other portraits, including those of spouses and offspring, from the best room.

After his death, Ivy continued to honor her father's wishes, and she positioned the photo of her husband, Dennis Cartwright, prominently above the mantel in the living room, instead. The armchair opposite it was tacitly understood to be "Ivy's seat" and no one else ever sat in it. She presumably had situated it there so she could gaze across the room at her long-deceased, handsome husband's likeness. On occasion, Zoey had caught Ivy talking to him, too.

"When Aunt Ivy is up to it, we'll ask her to tell you more about her father and brothers and her beloved Captain Denny—that's what she calls her husband. She loves to talk about them and it's so interesting to learn about our family hist—"

Wiping his forehead with his palm, Mark interrupted, grumbling, "It's really hot in here."

For once, Zoey agreed with him. "Yeah, it is. If you give me a hand, we could install the window screens earlier than usual this year."

"I think Ivy hired a guy to come and do that in a couple of weeks," Mark said, missing her point. Or ignoring it on purpose.

"But if we do it ourselves, she doesn't have to pay someone else."

"The kid's a high school student. The same one who takes care of the lawn. He probably needs to earn the money."

That's a convenient excuse, Zoey thought, as the moment of camaraderie they just experienced seemed to dissipate into thin air. "Have you ever considered that maybe Aunt Ivy needs to *save* money? She's on a fixed income, you know."

"She's hardly strapped for cash. She's got a trust fund," Mark replied.

"You don't know how much of that she has left or what she might need to reserve for the future if she gets sick or needs long-term care."

"If it means that much to you, fine, put the screens in yourself. I'll tell the kid's dad not to bother sending him over here."

Zoey was about to say she *couldn't* put them in herself—she was too short, that's why she needed Mark's help—when what he'd said sunk in. "How do you know so much about who she hired?" *Don't tell me—Aunt Ivy asked you for help with the screens and you pawned the job off on someone else.*

"His father's a buddy of mine from high school. He takes care of all Ivy's repairs—and he did her flooring in the spare room last spring. We're meeting on Friday to discuss the kitchen renovations."

"Wa-wait a second," Zoey stuttered. "*What* renovations?"

"I just told you. *Kitchen* renovations," Mark said drolly. "You know, granite countertops, new cabinets. Maybe we'll even knock out that wall, open the space up."

"Whose idea is that?" *As if I have to ask.*

"I was the one who brought it up after the incident with the gas, but Ivy seems to agree it's a good idea—who wouldn't? That room is hideous."

On one hand, Mark had a point. With its dark cupboards, yellow laminate countertops and brown appliances, the kitchen's 1970s design was appallingly outdated. And it was completely incompatible with the style of the other rooms. So Zoey didn't blame Mark for wishing their aunt would make some alternations.

In fact, years ago she'd spent her summer vacation trying to convince Ivy to remodel the kitchen, too. Or at the very least, to allow Zoey to paint the cupboards. But she backed off after Ivy confided the reason she couldn't bear to change the room. Apparently, the water damage that necessitated the renovation in the 1970s had occurred shortly after Sylvia's son, Marcus Jr., got married and moved off the island permanently. Sylvia was absolutely despondent from missing him, but after Ivy got her involved in planning the remodel, she began to perk up. Sylvia had taken special delight in choosing the yellow color scheme, which she said made her feel as if it was sunny inside the house no matter what the weather outside was like. Decades later, Ivy still refused to re-do the room, knowing how much designing it had meant to her sister-in-law.

Now that Sylvia had died, Zoey anticipated that her aunt would be even more resistant to making unnecessary alterations to the kitchen. So, while Zoey personally hated the décor as much or more than Mark did, she wasn't going to let him force Ivy to change something that held so much sentimental value for her.

"She might need a new stove, but countertops and cabinets? Knocking out a wall? No way. She loves this house the way things are."

"She may be ready for a change."

"Everyone knows it's unwise for people to make major changes or decisions when they're grieving. I don't want Aunt Ivy to do something now that she regrets later, when she's thinking more clearly. What's the rush, anyway?"

It was a stupid question. Zoey knew what the rush was; Mark wanted to get a jump start on profiting from his inheritance. Why wait until Ivy died to begin renovations, when he could literally pull the rug out from under her now? This way he could lease the house out the moment she passed away. And although the house would go to Mark, any money their aunt had leftover from her trust fund would be divided equally between him, Zoey and Gabi. So it was in his best interest to have Ivy pay for the renovations now, instead of footing the bill later himself.

"No rush. No need to get all worked up about it, either. Like I said, we're just going to discuss it with the carpenter. He's not bringing a wrecking ball with him." Mark casually yawned, stretching his arms.

Zoey hated it when he dropped a bombshell like that and then implied she was blowing things out of proportion. Especially in front of people like Gabi, who weren't familiar with how crafty he could be when he wanted his way. But Zoey refused to allow him to make her look bad. So when he changed the subject to ask if she'd made lunch yet, instead of telling him off, she just shrugged. "There's tuna in the pantry. Help yourself."

"You're not making something special for Gabi's first day here?" Ivy and Sylvia had always made "special" meals to welcome their guests to Dune Island, as well as when it came time to say goodbye—and for any occasion they could think of in-between. Even though Mark knew Zoey wasn't much of a cook, he apparently assumed because she was an aunt, she'd carry on this tradition. But the way he was playing the guilt card on her for his own benefit was so obvious it was almost laughable.

"Yes, I do intend to make a nice meal for *Gabi*. But I thought I'd wait until suppertime, since we had such a big brunch."

Gabi leaped up. "I can make tuna fish sandwiches for all of us."

"Thank you, Gabi. That's really nice of you." For being an absolute ingrate, Mark could sound genuinely appreciative when it suited him, the big phony.

"It *is* nice, but you don't have to make lunch for us on your *first day here*, Gabi," Zoey said, throwing her cousin's words back at him.

"I don't mind. I'm hungry, too." Gabi was inching toward the door.

"You kids are hungry already?" Ivy asked as she teetered into the room. She was always a little unsteady when she first got out of bed or rose from a chair. She glanced at the clock on the mantel. "No wonder. It's half past one. You shouldn't have let me sleep so long. I'll go fix you something."

Now Zoey jumped up. She didn't want her aunt to get dizzy. And she didn't want to let Gabi set a precedent of waiting on Mark; she was supposed to be teaching her niece good boundaries. She didn't especially want to make Mark a sandwich, either, since he was perfectly capable of making one himself, but she had to pick her battles. And she planned to save her energy for the war she was about to wage.

Because it was one thing for Zoey to keep her mouth shut when her aunt was turning a blind eye to Mark's laziness or forking her money over to him so he could waste it on himself. It was quite another thing for him to take advantage of Ivy's emotional vulnerability and twist her arm into altering—or giving up—what was still *her* house. *There's no way I'm going to sit idly by while Mark hustles Aunt Ivy the way Erik hustled me.*

"No, Aunt Ivy, that's okay. *I'll* fix lunch," she insisted. "Have a seat. You, too, Gabi. It will only take me a minute."

She patted the cushion and Gabi returned to the sofa. Ivy took her usual seat in the armchair opposite Denny's photograph portrait. And as Zoey left the room, Mark gave her such a smugly victorious look that she would have liked to add a few of *his* teeth to the dentil molding.

CHAPTER THREE

Ever since Mark mentioned meeting with the carpenter to discuss kitchen renovations, Zoey had been waiting for an opportune moment to bring up the topic with her aunt. She wanted to spare her the hassle of listening to a high-pressure sales pitch from Mark and whatever swindler he knew from high school if all she wanted was a new stove. In which case, Zoey could research stoves online, order the model her aunt wanted and a technician from the appliance store undoubtedly would install the new one and take the old one away.

But she had difficulty finding the right time to mention it, since Ivy was prone to intense bouts of weeping, especially in the mornings when she first rose and realized she'd have to face another day without Sylvia. Having lost her own sister, Zoey understood how overwhelming that must have been. Especially because in the past sixty-some years, the only time Ivy and Sylvia had ever spent more than a few hours apart was when one or the other of them had to be hospitalized.

As for the evenings, on both Tuesday and Wednesday after climbing the stairs to go to bed, Ivy experienced chest pain. Although she'd suffered from it on occasion before, it was rare for her to have two consecutive episodes. The nitro pills her cardiologist prescribed helped within minutes both times, but once her discomfort let up, Zoey didn't want to agitate her by discussing what was potentially a distressful subject.

That left the afternoons, which were also inconvenient because that's when Mark dropped in. Surprisingly, on Wednesday after gobbling down the Philly cheesesteak sandwich Ivy made him for lunch, he intimated to Zoey that it was his turn to keep their aunt company. "Why don't you go run your errands or do something by yourself for a while?" he suggested.

Zoey was immediately skeptical. Was he going to work their aunt over about selling the house while she was at the grocery store? *Will I find a FOR SALE sign on the front lawn when I come back?* she wondered.

But Gabi was jet lagged and had gone upstairs to nap, so Mark's presence gave Zoey the opportunity to walk to the market in town without rushing home to check on Ivy. It wasn't that her aunt *couldn't* be left on her own, but when she was she had a tendency to be overcome with sadness. Sometimes she cried so hard she got a headache and Zoey was concerned she might wind up with angina, too.

So, she left and when she returned an hour later, Ivy and Mark were in the living room, playing cribbage. After they finished, he took off for the golf club and Zoey unabashedly asked her aunt what they'd discussed while she'd been shopping. Ivy said they'd been too busy playing cards to talk about anything in particular.

Maybe I'm too suspicious of him, Zoey thought. *It could be that he truly enjoys playing cribbage with Aunt Ivy. Or maybe he's just frittering away an hour or two until his friends are free to meet him at the club?*

But her suspicion that Mark was up to something intensified when he hung around again after lunch on Thursday. "You and Gabi should take a walk down to the harbor," he recommended. "Enjoy this gorgeous weather before she starts school tomorrow."

Gabi jumped at the idea, so Zoey gave in, hoping some quality one-on-one time would do the teenager good. On hearing the news—via Zoey, since Gabi was refusing to answer the phone to her stepmother—that her dad had officially checked in to the recovery center, Gabi had seemed indifferent, but Zoey sensed her attitude was a façade. She hoped while the two of them took a walk, she would open up about what had been happening at home. Or how she felt about going to a new school the next day.

"Your skin is so fair, Jessica. I have sunblock in the bathroom cupboard if you need it," Ivy offered before they set out.

"That's not Jessica," Mark immediately corrected her. "That's Jessica's daughter, Gabi."

Ivy rattled her head. "Oh, did I call you Jessica? What am I thinking?"

Mark raised an eyebrow at Zoey, as if to say, "I told you she was losing it." Which was absurd—Gabi looked so much like her mother that Zoey had to stop *herself* from calling her Jessica on a number of occasions. It was a slip of the tongue, not confusion.

"I already put sunblock on. In California, I wear it every day. But thanks for the reminder, Auntie." Gabi answered sweetly.

Why would such a gentle-spirited girl attempt to take her father's car? Zoey wondered as they descended the hill. More importantly, how could she make sure Gabi didn't get into the same kind of trouble here?

"Are you nervous about tomorrow?" she asked, struggling to match her niece's long-legged stride.

"Not really."

"That's good. I've heard wonderful things about Hope Haven High. But, if anything goes wrong, you can talk to me about it. You can talk to me about anything. Anything at all."

"You mean like my dad going into a recovery center or why I'm not answering Kathleen's phone calls." It was a statement, not a question.

"Yeah, like that," Zoey responded frankly. "I'm happy to just listen or to provide help if I can, whichever you need, whenever you need it. And you can count on me to keep whatever you say between the two of us."

"Thanks, but I don't want to talk about that stuff right now," her niece told her and Zoey nodded, indicating there was no pressure. Then the girl deadpanned, "But you don't have to worry about me stealing Aunt Ivy's car from the garage or anything like that while I'm here."

Sometimes, she's too perceptive for her own good, Zoey acknowledged to herself. "I know I don't, honey." She linked her arm through her niece's. "And do you know how I know that?"

"Because you trust me?"

"I *do* trust you. But that's not how I know."

"Is it because Aunt Ivy doesn't have a car?"

"Oh, she has a car all right. You might not remember it, but she's had the same car since before you were born. Since before *I* was born. It's a champagne-colored Cadillac Coupe DeVille with leather seats, a real beauty. She has literally only driven it to church or to the market, so it's in mint condition. She has someone start it for her throughout the winter, to make sure it's still running. But you'd have to be crazy to attempt to back it out the driveway—it's as big as a boat."

"Is that why you picked me up in a rental?"

"Yeah. Even if I managed to maneuver the Caddy to the ferry, they probably would have charged me a double fare to board. It's so wide, it would overlap two lanes!"

"What happened to your car?"

Zoey hesitated. If she wanted her niece to be honest with her, she supposed she'd have to lead by example. "If I tell you, do you promise not to tell Aunt Ivy? And not Mark, either?"

"I won't even tell Moby," her niece quipped, reminding Zoey so much of Jessica's humor that the flash of nostalgia made her breath hitch.

Zoey slowed her pace. Meandering through the park toward the beach, she explained that she'd lost her job in December. Although she'd been eligible for unemployment benefits, she'd had to stop collecting once Sylvia got sick because the rules required a claimant to be available and actively seeking work. Since she was gone so often anyway, Zoey sublet her apartment, along with the use of her car, to the friend of a friend, in order to pay her mortgage.

She didn't go into detail about Erik, simply summing up what happened as, "I sort of let my boyfriend talk me into a series of bad investments, so I lost a lot of my savings." She fought the impulse to add, *The moral of this story is not to allow someone to convince you to do something you'll regret later.*

Gabi gave her a playful nudge. "Wow. And I thought what *I* did was dumb."

"What you did *was* dumb." Even though she was an aunt, Zoey could assume a mom-voice when she had to. "But as I said, I trust you not to do something like that again."

Her niece came to an abrupt stop, dropped Zoey's arm, closed her eyes and inhaled deeply. At first, Zoey thought she may have been offended by her admonishment. Then she realized she was savoring the briny scent wafting toward them. Zoey understood; frequently the sight or sound or smell of the ocean stopped her in her tracks, too. As she glanced at Gabi's profile, she wondered if the tear streaking her cheek was from the wind or from emotion. What was it she was feeling? Did she remember coming here with her mom?

Her eyelids snapped open. "Which way do you want to go?"

Zoey suggested they walk in the sand to the end of the jetty, which was easier than tramping atop of the uneven, rocky surface. Since the tide was out, they could make it all the way to the tip without getting their shoes wet. Gabi asked why there were NO SWIMMING signs posted nearby.

"Because when the tide is in, there's a lot of boat traffic. This is more of a walking beach. When it gets warmer, we can go swimming at Rose Beach. It's not too far from here, just on the other side of Sea Gull Light." Zoey pointed to the sandy arm jutting into the water. Against the bright blue backdrop of the sky, the white lighthouse appeared even more radiant than usual.

"Is the house next to it really where Mr. Witherell used to live?"

"Yes, but now it's a museum. Why, do you remember him?"

"No. When I saw him go past Aunt Ivy's window yesterday afternoon, Mark kind of filled me in."

"Oh? What did he tell you?"

"That Mr. Witherell used to be the lighthouse keeper. But now he lives in a decrepit little house in the valley. He said he's mean. That twice a day he roams from one end of Benjamin's Manor to the other, no matter what the weather's like and that he growls at people. He told me I should stay away from him—to cross the street if I see him coming. I didn't know if he was trying to trick me, like when he told you the Legend of Captain Chadwell."

Zoey figured her cousin must have still been annoyed about the verbal dig Mr. Witherell made at his expense. If Mark felt spiteful toward the old man, that was his business, but to malign his character to an impressionable teenager was taking his resentment too far. While she thought it was a good idea for Gabi to be cautious around strangers in general, Zoey didn't want her to feel uncomfortable if she crossed paths with Mr. Witherell.

"It's true that he lives in a little house and walks every day. I'm not sure how good his hearing is. He can speak, but he usually doesn't say much. I've never heard him growl at anyone, but sometimes he sort of clears his throat.

"As for Mr. Witherell being mean, I can only guess why Mark would say that. Unfortunately, you might hear kids at school or people in town saying the same thing. Aunt Ivy once told me that's because when he was a lighthouse keeper, Mr. Witherell used to report boaters for speeding in the harbor and he broke up a few bashes—that's what they called parties—which were prohibited on the beach after dark. Supposedly, he considered Benjamin's Harbor his domain to protect, so he was a real stickler for the rules. A few people held grudges against him for that and they passed their attitudes down to their children and grandchildren."

Zoey repeated the advice her mother gave her when she was about Gabi's age, warning her that on such a small island she was going to hear a lot of gossip from the locals. New rumors, as well as old ones going back several decades. Some had an element of truth and some were completely unfounded, so she should take them all with a grain of salt.

"Regardless, I think Mark's suggestion to cross the street if you see Mr. Witherell coming your way is rude. Mr. Witherell has served this island well in his capacity as keeper of Sea Gull Light and he deserves respect. You saw him, so you know he's a fragile, elderly gentleman who couldn't hurt a fly even if he wanted to. There's definitely no need to be afraid of him, if that's what you're worried about."

"I wasn't. Not really." Gabi's half-hearted denial told Zoey otherwise. "Besides, Aunt Ivy told me he used to carry a torch for Aunt Sylvia—that's how she put it—but that she wasn't interested in him."

Her aunt had once told Zoey the same thing, boasting, "Young men were drawn to Sylvia like bees to honey, but she was only drawn to Marcus." It was hard to tell if she was prouder of Sylvia for being so attractive or of her brother, for capturing Sylvia's heart.

Curious, Zoey asked, "Did talking about Aunt Sylvia make Aunt Ivy sad?"

"No, she was okay. I think she actually wanted tell me more stories about Aunt Sylvia but Mark was hungry for something sweet so she went into the kitchen to make those raspberry crumble bars we had last night for dessert."

As they continued their hike, Zoey silently mulled over Mark's instructing Gabi to shun Mr. Witherell. Giving him the benefit of the doubt, she supposed he may have been concerned Mr. Witherell would say something insulting to Gabi, too—but that was unlikely since Gabi would never provoke him with an obnoxious comment the way Mark did. Zoey couldn't put a finger on it exactly, but something wasn't adding up and she decided she was going to wheedle the truth out of her cousin when she got home, even if he accused her of asking nosy questions. However, when they returned, Mark was nowhere in sight.

"He's in the attic again," Ivy informed her. "That's the third time this week. First it was Sylvia's bedroom, now this. He's going through everything with a fine-toothed comb. The poor boy, I think he's hoping his grandmother left him a personal note or something special to remember her by."

Is that *why he's been hanging around in the afternoon?* Zoey wondered. She'd thought it was because he wanted time alone with Ivy to cajole her into vacating her home. But perhaps it was merely because he was still combing through Sylvia's mementos. Or maybe it was a little of each. Otherwise, why would he have chased Zoey out of the house on both days? He'd already told her he wanted to check out the trunks Sylvia kept in the attic. In fact, Zoey had seen him go up there after they'd eaten lunch on Tuesday, so it wasn't any big secret.

That's when it struck her: it shouldn't have taken Mark *three days* to sort through his grandmother's possessions. For one thing, the attic was too organized. Ivy had never been one to purchase more than she needed; she used everything until it was no longer functional and then disposed of it and got a replacement. All her valuables and heirlooms were on display in the best room. So aside from seasonal items, such as Christmas ornaments, lawn decorations and window screens, the attic was nearly empty, and Sylvia's two trunks were readily accessible.

For another thing, Sylvia's belongings amounted to little more than a couple of dresser scarves and half a dozen figurines. Except for her clothes and a few personal items, everything else in the house belonged to Ivy, so it's not as if it should have taken Mark more than half an hour to peruse the contents of Sylvia's bedroom, either.

He had *to have been searching for something else! Something specific that he hasn't found yet. Something that's so important to him that he's willing to stick around Dune Island until he does,* she deduced. *And I doubt very much it's a personal note from his grandmother!*

Her curiosity piqued, Zoey decided to pop upstairs so she could catch Mark unawares, but before she could, he came back down. "Did you discover anything interesting?"

"Nah." He turned his empty palms up as if to prove it.

"If you tell me what you're looking for, maybe I can help you find it." *You're not the only one who has ulterior motives for being helpful,* she thought.

"That's okay. I'm done up there."

Zoey knew it was futile to ask whether he was done because he'd found whatever it was he wanted to find (and was hiding it in his pocket), or because he'd searched the attic thoroughly enough to conclude that whatever he was looking for wasn't there. But she decided that after he left the island she was going to do a little snooping upstairs on her own.

Mark clapped dust off his slacks and said, "I've got to run, Ivy. I'll be back by eight tomorrow morning for our eight-thirty meeting, but don't feel obligated to make breakfast."

Ivy furrowed her brow. "Our meeting?"

"Yeah, you know—with the carpenter."

"The carpenter?" Ivy echoed him again.

"We spoke about this at length. Don't you remember?"

Mark's patronizing tone made Zoey want to scream, *So what if she forgot! Don't you have the slightest inkling of how difficult it is to concentrate when you're grief-stricken?* As far as Zoey was concerned, in the weeks following her sister's death, if she could remember her email address and phone number, it meant she was having a good day. So she thought nothing of Ivy forgetting about Mark's self-serving meeting.

"Sometimes, it can be helpful to jot important details down on a calendar," she suggested, looking pointedly at Mark, meaning that's what he should have done on their aunt's behalf.

"I'd probably forget where I hung the calendar, too." Ivy clucked, shaking her head. "What will we be discussing at this meeting?"

"The kitchen renovations. Getting a new stove, that kind of thing," Mark answered.

"Ah, now I remember," Ivy claimed, but there was no spark of recognition in her eyes. It made Zoey wonder if Mark had actually discussed the renovations with her at all. He'd been acting so sketchy lately that she wouldn't put it past him to use Ivy's supposed forgetfulness against her and trick everyone into believing she'd okayed the meeting.

"You don't have to meet with anyone yet, if you're not ready. There's no hurry," Zoey told her aunt.

"Actually, there is. I'm leaving tomorrow afternoon on the twelve thirty-five ferry. That's why I reserved a block of time in my schedule in the morning."

The elation Zoey felt upon hearing that Mark was leaving was counterbalanced by her resentment of his pressure tactic. *Whatever happened to you saying, 'no rush' when we talked about this on Tuesday?* she fumed to herself. Clearly, he'd just been pacifying her to shut her up. Well, two could play that game.

"You've obviously got a lot on your plate right now—that's all the more reason to postpone the meeting. You could always come back to discuss the renovations later in the summer." *Or in the fall. Or never.*

"Yeah, but I'm concerned it might be hazardous for Ivy to continue using the stove. Besides, who knows what the carpenter's workload will be like later in the season."

"The Armstrong boy?" Ivy asked. "The one who does all my repairs?"

"Yup."

"Oh, you're right. He does excellent work at a very fair price. We can't miss out on booking him," Ivy agreed. "I worry he doesn't eat right, you know. He's divorced and he doesn't have a girlfriend. I'll make a quiche for breakfast."

"It's not necessary for you to feed him, Aunt Ivy," Zoey was half amused, half exasperated by her aunt's attitude and belief that men didn't know how to cook for themselves. "Besides, we don't have enough eggs."

"I can walk to the market and get some," Gabi volunteered.

"Thanks, but we prefer local eggs. I'll stop at the farm stand on the way home from taking you to school in the morning. There will still be plenty of time for me to make a quiche before our meeting."

"You don't have to take me—" Gabi began.

At the same moment, Ivy protested, "I can't let you make breakfast when I'm the one who suggested it."

Simultaneously, Mark spoke over both of them, saying, "There's no need for you to attend the meeting, Zoey."

"Wait—just listen to me!" she barked, startling everyone, including Moby who hopped off Ivy's lap and trotted out of the room. Feeling like a shrew, she lowered her voice. "Yes, I *do* need to go to school with you, Gabi. There's some paperwork they want me to sign and I have a few questions I'd like answered… And Aunt Ivy, please let me make the quiche. It takes you a while to wake up in the morning. If you get up early or have to rush around, you'll be too distracted to tell Mark and the carpenter what you want—and don't want—done to your kitchen."

Then, her voice disingenuously syrupy, she added, "I'm happy to sit in on the meeting, Mark. I'll take notes so we can all remember what was discussed and agreed upon."

Zoey relished the look of dismay that melted his features. He recovered quickly though. "Suit yourself. But as long as you're going to the trouble of making breakfast, I'd prefer an omelet instead of quiche."

"Sure. Whatever you want." Under her breath she muttered, "A special meal in celebration of *your last day here*."

Later that evening, Zoey relaxed in the living room with her aunt and Gabi, both of them sipping chamomile tea, the way Ivy and Sylvia routinely used to do together at bedtime. Moby was settled peacefully on Gabi's lap and Zoey, who was too hot for tea, was drinking ice water.

"Are you planning to audition for the school symphony?" she asked her niece.

Gabi shrugged. "They might not have a symphony at this school."

"They must have a band, at least." Zoey remarked to Ivy, "Gabi is an excellent flutist. She made second chair in the youth symphony this year, even though she's only in ninth grade."

"I know. Her father gave me… I think it's called a *link*? To her Christmas concert. The boy who plows the driveway played it for Sylvia and me on his phone. It brought tears to our eyes, we were so proud."

That was news to Zoey. "I wonder why Scott didn't send me the link."

Gabi blew her bangs out of her eyes with a puff from the corner of her mouth. "Probably didn't think you were interested."

Her aloof manner told Zoey what must have happened; Scott had forgotten to send it to her because he'd been drinking. Trying not to show her disappointment, she said, "Oh, well. You could give us a private performance now, couldn't you?"

"I'm too tired. And I haven't had any practice."

"You can practice here any time," Ivy said. "Don't feel like you have to be quiet on my account, even if I'm napping. I don't hear anything unless we're in the same room."

"Yeah, but my flute might bother Moby. Cats have very sensitive ears."

Zoey was perplexed by Gabi's response. Why had she brought her flute if she didn't intend to play it? Maybe she'd change her mind. It was possible she was more nervous about starting school the next day than she'd let on and she couldn't focus on playing her instrument right now.

Switching the subject, Zoey hinted, "Aunt Ivy, I don't think Gabi knows the story about how you met Captain Denny."

Because Zoey's great-uncle had died so long before she was born, she never thought of him as Uncle Dennis. To her, he was always *Denny* or *Captain Denny.* Or sometimes *Aunt Ivy's husband.* She glanced at her aunt, hoping his name wouldn't trigger tears. But the elderly woman smiled as she set her teacup and saucer on the coffee table.

"Oh, that's right. The last time you visited, Gabi, you would have been too young for me to tell you about my clandestine courtship." There was a sparkle in her eye as she beamed at the portrait above the mantel, obviously pleased for the opportunity to tell the story again. Zoey had heard it so often she could have recited it verbatim. But this time, Ivy began by repeating the genealogy Zoey had previously mentioned, since Gabi didn't have a good grasp of her family's background.

"Growing up, I lived in Brookline, a suburb just outside Boston. My father was a criminal court judge and my mother was a homemaker. They had three children; me, Charles—your great-grandfather—and Marcus."

Ivy recounted how when she was a girl, her family rented a house on Dune Island for the entire summer. Although her father's work kept him in Boston, he'd visit on the weekends or whenever court wasn't in session. They all loved Benjamin's Manor so much that her parents bought the Captain Chadwell house the year Ivy was twelve, with the intention of relocating there permanently when her father retired.

"Unfortunately, my mother died when she was forty-one of an aneurysm. Two years after that, my father, a pipe smoker, was diagnosed with esophageal cancer. He lost his voice from a surgery and had to resign from judicial office. I was in my second year of college, so I dropped out in order to care for him."

"You had to drop out of college when your father got sick?" Gabi asked. "What about your brothers? Didn't they help you?"

"Well, Charles had his sights set on law school. And Marcus wasn't in the best health himself. He'd go through bouts of fatigue and respiratory illness. Problems with his muscles, too, especially in his ankles. My mother thought it was because he'd contracted polio as a child, even though he recovered. My father said he was just born with a weak constitution. It left him exhausted and it was assumed I'd take care of him, too. Men weren't expected to assist with things like that—nursing an ill person back to health was considered women's work. Regardless, I wanted to do it because I loved my father and my brother dearly."

Noticing Ivy's eyes brim with tears, Zoey said, "Maybe we should wait until another time to continue this story."

"No, no. I haven't gotten to the best part yet," Ivy insisted. She took another sip of tea before telling Gabi that since her father needed to stay close to his doctors and the hospital in Boston, they couldn't relocate to Dune Island year round, as he had planned. But they continued to go there in the summers, when his health permitted. Sometimes his condition improved; more often, it worsened. Toward the end, he decided he wanted to live out his last days on the island, against his physicians' advice.

When her aunt got to this part of her family's history, Zoey stole a glance at Gabi. Would it evoke memories of her own mother's quest to return to Benjamin's Manor one last time before she passed away?

"So, my father finally sold our house in Brookline. The three of us—Marcus, my father and me—moved to Benjamin's Manor for good and Charles stayed behind in Boston to continue his studies. We arrived the first of June, right after Memorial Day weekend. I had arranged for someone to open the house and prepare it for the season, since the rest of the year it sat unused. In the past, we had a housekeeper come in twice a week during the summer. But because my father's illness was so severe and my brother was going through a stretch of sickness, too, I was overwhelmed. So I hired a maid to do the cleaning every day and give me a hand with the cooking, which allowed me more time to care for my father and brother... You know who I hired, don't you?"

When Gabi shook her head, Ivy revealed with a flourish, "It was your great-grand-aunt Sylvia!"

"Really?"

"Really. But I can't get ahead of myself or I'll spoil the rest of the story."

Zoey was glad for Gabi's sake that Ivy skipped over the details of her father's death, simply stating, "By mid-June, my father had passed, as we knew he would. Even so, I was utterly dejected. Sylvia had to move in with us because I was useless. I didn't want to get out of bed because I missed my father terribly and also because I believed my best years were behind me. At almost twenty-five, I was considered an old maid and I resigned myself to that. No one thought Marcus would ever marry, either, because of his health. Or they said the only reason anyone would marry us was for our money."

"That's terrible," Gabi objected. "Who would say something like that?"

"My brother Charles, for one. And before him, my father had said it, too. He wasn't trying to be cruel—he was worried about our future. That's why he set up the will to ensure the estate would always be passed down to a blood relative. He didn't want someone taking advantage of Marcus or me or our descendants. He was especially worried an 'outsider' would be awarded the house in the event of a divorce.

"Anyway, after his death, Sylvia saw how miserable I was and she insisted I go for a walk every day. 'Just down to the harbor and back. If you do nothing else today, do that,' she'd plead with me. 'I'll take care of everything else at the house.' So that's what I did. Sometimes it took me until three o'clock in the afternoon to get dressed, but then I'd drag myself down to the harbor. And little by little, day by day, I started to feel better."

It's too bad you can't walk down to the harbor now, Zoey thought. She wondered if there was something else her aunt could do every day that might alleviate her grief. Or at least provide a pleasant, momentary distraction.

"I felt guilty leaving Sylvia alone to care for Marcus, but he got it into his head he was going to teach her how to play chess. He'd set up the board on that round table, right there by the front window. Little did I know, he was falling in love with her!"

Ivy always seemed as happy to share the anecdote of how Sylvia and Marcus fell in love as she was to recount how she and Dennis met. Which was fortunate, since Sylvia had always been too shy to tell the story herself. She couldn't even be in the room when Ivy told it; always finding some reason to leave. Zoey wasn't sure whether that was because she felt insecure about coming from a poor family and being a housekeeper, or because she was embarrassed by how highly Ivy spoke of her.

"I shouldn't have been surprised," Ivy said. "Sylvia was so beautiful she could have been on the cover of a fashion magazine. She was wasp-waisted, had eyes like a doe and a peaches-and-cream complexion. She was lovely on the inside, too. So soft-spoken and patient. Sometimes I thought my brother was exaggerating his pain to win her sympathy and keep her attention. Sylvia later admitted she'd been smitten with him, too. She said even though he was more intelligent than anyone she'd ever known, he wasn't the least bit conceited. She told me she wasn't accustomed to a man being so kind to her and listening to her opinions."

Ivy never stated it explicitly, but over the years she intimated that Sylvia's father had been abusive. Her stepsisters, who were intensely jealous of her appearance, were cruel to her, too, constantly telling her she was homely and useless. By contrast, Sylvia took after her mother. She'd been gentle to the point of timidity; in all the time she'd known her, Zoey had never heard her raise her voice. The closest she'd come was when the squirrel would eat food from the bird feeder and she'd tap on the windowpane and say, "Scat."

Ivy continued to extol her sister-in-law's abilities, gushing, "My, how she could cook! I had no interest in food after my father died, so Sylvia had to take over in the kitchen completely or else Marcus would have starved. That girl could make a four-course meal out of two sticks and a stone! Between boosting me out of my depression and keeping Marcus fed, Sylvia was a godsend. I don't know what we would have done without her.

"Anyway, one hot afternoon in mid July, I began my usual excursion but instead of stopping at the harbor, I continued walking until I got to Bleecker's ice-cream parlor on Main Street—this was long before they moved their shop to the boardwalk in Lucinda's Hamlet. I had a craving for a scoop of strawberry ice cream, so I purchased a cone and then ambled back to the harbor and along the jetty. After barely eating anything for a month, I was savoring my treat—it was as if I was tasting food for the first time—and I was completely oblivious to the fishing vessel slowly passing by as it entered the harbor. It could have been floating backward and I wouldn't have noticed, if someone on board hadn't whistled. It was a catcall, loud and sharp, there was no missing it. Now, I know today you girls would consider that demeaning, but to us, it was a compliment. Especially to me, because I usually didn't get that kind of attention. I had long legs and a big bosom but a short torso, just as I do now and my face wasn't anyone's idea of pretty."

"I doubt that was true!" Zoey challenged, as she did every time her aunt got to this part of her story.

As usual, Ivy waved her hand. "Whether it was true or not, it was how I *felt*. But the man on the boat apparently saw me differently. And what a man he was! His arms were so muscular that if he hadn't rolled up sleeves, his biceps would have split the seams. He was backlit by the sunshine, which made his tanned skin and blond hair even more dazzling. But it was his smile that nearly blinded me. Oh, what a smile he had! At first, I thought there must have been some mistake. There were a few other people on the jetty and I wondered if perhaps he'd whistled at one of them. So the next day, I came back when I knew the tide was in. Except instead of meandering down the jetty, I sat on a bench near the docks."

She stopped and put her hand to the side of her mouth, indicating she was about to reveal a secret. "To be honest, I didn't *sit* as much as I *posed*. Like this." She crossed her legs and half-twisted in her chair, her spine elongated and her chest out. She placed one hand flat beside her and cupped the other above her brow, as if to shield her eyes as she surveyed the waves. Zoey could imagine her how striking her silhouette must have been, no matter how she'd joked about her appearance.

"You see, I knew how to accentuate my best features," she said with a wink, her old familiar humor momentarily outshining her present grief. "It worked, too. This time, he hopped off the boat and sauntered over to where I was, with his hands behind his back. 'Hi, Doll. Were you looking for this?' he asked and presented me with a fish wrapped in a newspaper. It was a sea bass and it was so fresh it was still wiggling." Then, Ivy added the line she always said, "I couldn't have been more delighted if he had given me a bouquet of roses—although roses would have smelled better."

After eliciting a giggle from Gabi, Ivy quickly skimmed over the details of her "whirlwind courtship with Dennis Cartwright," saying that at first she didn't tell Marcus or Sylvia about him. She'd time her daily walks to coincide with when he'd be docking. Or else she'd excuse herself in the evenings to meet him on the beach for moonlit strolls. Since Ivy wanted to be discreet about their relationship, they never went to a sock hop at the dance hall or even to eat at a restaurant, although Dennis occasionally bought Ivy an ice-cream cone or she packed a picnic for them to enjoy on the beach.

"Sylvia and Marcus were oblivious, just as I was unaware they were falling for each other. They must have thought it was beneficial for me to get as much fresh air as I could. Or perhaps they were so eager to have time alone that they didn't question my whereabouts. I'd see Dennis every day except on Sunday, which was Sylvia's day off. She'd go visit her friends, the other seasonal maids and nannies she'd lived with briefly in a boarding house before we asked her to stay with us full-time."

Gabi nudged Moby off her lap and stretched. Zoey hoped she wasn't getting restless because she knew Ivy wasn't finished with her story yet.

"Sundays were agonizing. I couldn't stand being away from Denny, so after about a month or so I broke down and asked Sylvia if she could stay home and keep Marcus company so I could go be with my "steady," as we called our boyfriends then. She was surprised but delighted I'd met someone and suggested I invite him to the house for supper. That put me in a tizzy because I was afraid Marcus would object to our relationship since Denny was working class. But I should have known my littlest brother disagreed with my father and Charles on that issue."

Gabi snickered. "My great-grandfather was kind of an elitist, wasn't he?"

"I suppose, but Charles learned to think that way from my father," Ivy acknowledged. "I loved him to pieces, but he could be very… influential. Not that it's any excuse but as the eldest son, Charles was expected to follow in my father's footsteps, including adopting his opinions. Marcus and I didn't always share their views but we weren't necessarily outspoken. If my father hadn't died, I don't know if I would have had the courage to marry Captain Denny or if Marcus would have married Sylvia…" Ivy's voice faded. She bent forward and absently touched Moby's back as the cat wove between her ankles before stealing out of the room.

"Where was I? Oh, yes. As nervous as I was about bringing Denny home, I found out later that Marcus was even more anxious. We were both worried Denny would take one gander at Sylvia and we'd be out of the picture! Instead, he didn't give her a second look. She didn't warm to him, either, although she was always polite. Shortly after that, Marcus professed his love and proposed to her and they got married a couple of weeks later. Talk about a whirlwind! I think Marcus was afraid of losing her and she didn't want to have to return home to Connecticut in the fall, like her family expected her to do. Denny and I weren't in as much of a hurry—we wed on October the fifteenth," Ivy wryly jested.

"You met him in July and got married in October?" Gabi asked.

Zoey wagged a finger at her niece. "Don't get any ideas!"

"I wasn't. I just wondered how Aunt Ivy planned a wedding that quickly."

"Oh, I didn't need a big to-do. We got married at the courthouse, just like Sylvia and Marcus did. Denny didn't even have a ring to give me—I used my mother's. He didn't feel right about that but I didn't care. I had everything I'd dreamed of when he proposed to me on bended knee, right there." She gestured to the area in front of the fireplace. "Afterward, we celebrated with champagne in the best room, didn't we, Captain?"

Gazing at his portrait, Ivy absently raised her teacup as if toasting him, a faraway look in her eyes. Then she took a sip and blinked several times. "I'm sorry I rambled so long. You girls must be bored to tears."

"No, we aren't! I'm really glad you told me your love story, Aunt Ivy. It's really amazing even thought parts of it are sad. It reminds me of some of the historical romances I've read, only it's a lot better because it was about you. And about our family." Gabi's response couldn't have been more earnest or endearing and Zoey could tell by the expression on Ivy's face how pleased her aunt was to hear it, even if she shook her head and apologized again for blathering for so long.

Gabi walked over and kissed her aunt's cheek before collecting the tea cups and saying goodnight. Shortly after her niece left, Zoey accompanied Ivy up the stairs, cupping her elbow for support. On the first landing, her aunt paused to take a rest.

"I must have used up all my breath telling that long-winded story," she said. "I can't seem to help myself. I only have to catch a glimpse of the chess table or Denny's hat on the mantel and all my favorite youthful memories come rushing back… You know, my brother Charles's wife—your grandmother—used to try to get me to take home movies but I never had any use for them. She'd say, 'When you're old and gray, you'll be sorry you don't have anything to remind you of the people you loved or what you did in your younger years.' But I *do* have something to remind me. This house reminds me, if that makes sense."

"Yes, it does," Zoey assured her. *And that's why I'm going to do whatever I can to keep Mark from forcing you out or making any changes to your home that you don't want to make,* she silently promised her aunt.

CHAPTER FOUR

Since Ivy's house was just under two miles away from the school, Gabi wasn't eligible to take a school bus and of course, Zoey didn't want to drive her in Ivy's car. The teen could have taken public transportation—there was a bus stop right down the hill—but Zoey was glad when Gabi said she'd rather walk.

It was a gray and mizzling morning and a foghorn sounded as they strode down Main Street in the opposite direction from the harbor. They passed the golf course before cutting east, down a slope and through the valley. Zoey pointed out landmarks along the way: the library, a historic gristmill, the site of the island's first church and even the road leading to the part of town where Mr. Witherell lived.

"Do you want me to meet you after school in case you forget how to get back home?"

Gabi pretended to suck her thumb, ridiculing, "No, Mama. Me a big girl."

That was *exactly* what Jessica would have done and Zoey elbowed her. "Fine. Did you at least bring an umbrella?"

"No."

"Here, take mine."

"It isn't raining."

"It isn't now, but if it starts this afternoon, Aunt Ivy will worry about you and then she'll make me drive down to pick you up in the Caddy. And I can't guarantee I'll be able to stay in my lane—or even on the road. Is that really the first impression you want to make on your new classmates?"

Gabi groaned as she accepted the umbrella and shoved it into her bookbag.

Once they arrived at the school, Zoey discussed the questions she had with the vice principal before signing the required paperwork. Then, a cheerful girl a head shorter than Gabi and a skinny boy wearing glasses arrived to take her on a tour. Zoey dawdled in the office threshold, watching them flank her niece as she ambled down the corridor, her long, blond hair hanging down her back, her bookbag hoisted onto one shoulder.

It reminded her of how she'd accompanied Jessica when she walked Gabi to school on her first day of kindergarten. Usually unflappable, her sister had cried all the way home. Since Scott was traveling on business, Zoey ended up taking a personal day off from work so Jess wouldn't have to be alone.

"Gabi will be fine. She's going to *thrive*," she'd comforted her.

"I know she will and more than anything, that's what I want for her," Jess had sobbed. "But it's still hard to let her go."

She said the same thing about leaving her daughter at the end of her life, too—except she used the word 'excruciating,' Zoey recalled, the lump in her throat growing bigger. She shot out of the school and dropped onto the cement bench encircling the flag pole. After a few moments, when she'd caught her breath again, she blotted the dampness from her face and got up. *You know I'll do whatever I can to help Gabi thrive*, she mentally reassured her sister, just as she'd done the day before Jessica died. She only hoped her best was enough.

On the way home, Zoey was so melancholy she wandered at least half a mile beyond the farm stand before she remembered she was supposed to stop for eggs. It was drizzling harder now and the clouds on the horizon had darkened from gray to charcoal, so she quickly backtracked and made her purchase.

She had just scuttled half a block down the road when the sky let loose. Because she'd been too warm to wear a coat and she'd given her umbrella to Gabi, she had no protection from the nickel-sized raindrops. She tried jogging, but she was worried the jostling would break the eggs. *Not that I care if there are shells in Mark's omelet*, she thought sardonically as she slowed her pace to a brisk walk. *But I don't want to hear him complain.*

Within a minute, Zoey was soaking wet. By then, she figured it must have been eight o'clock, maybe later. Her backtracking had made her late. Although she didn't want Ivy to attempt to come get her, she hoped if Mark had arrived at the house, her aunt would at least send him. She didn't want to call and ask, for fear that Mark would twist her request and send Aunt Ivy out to drive in the rain, leaving him alone to conspire with the carpenter about the renovations.

The egg carton she carried was a recycled donation that must have been used repeatedly because once the flimsy cardboard top got soggy, it began to tear. Zoey slipped the package beneath her

T-shirt and hugged it against her chest to protect it, although by that time, her clothes were so wet she doubted it did any good. The rain was falling at a slant against her face and even though Zoey tucked her head against it, droplets dripped from her lashes into her eyes. Squinting, she didn't see the pedestrian approaching from the opposite direction until the last second.

It was Mr. Witherell and he was bent so far forward he didn't see her, either, so she quickly leaped aside to avoid colliding with him and breaking her eggs. He wasn't carrying an umbrella, but he was wearing a hat and a dark rain jacket that looked as old as his funeral suit.

"Good morning, Mr. Witherell. Crummy weather, isn't it?" she asked but he scuffed on without replying.

I'm sorry about Mark! she had the impulse to call after him, but didn't. *Please don't hold his behavior against me. I'm a nice person, really!*

A few minutes later, the friendly beep of a horn sounded behind her. She stepped farther away from the pavement. It beeped again, so without turning to look she swept her arm in a semi-circle, signaling the driver should go around her. Another honk. She could tell by the volume the driver was much closer now. He yelled something that sounded like, *you're on the wrong side.*

Hardly able to see through the deluge, she kept her head down. "I'm not in your way—go around me!"

"You want a ride?" The driver's remark was clearer this time. He had stopped and lowered his passenger-side window.

Zoey came to a standstill, too. Squinching her face against the rain, she peered at him. There was something familiar about his thick eyebrows and angular features but it took a second for her to remember how she knew him: it was Nick. The good-looking guy from the funeral reception. From the park restrooms. She'd already embarrassed herself in front of him twice. Considering her current state of mind and the condition of her apparel, Zoey realized it was almost inevitable she'd do it again a third time if she got into his truck.

"That's kind, but no, thanks." She resumed hiking but instead of driving off, he coasted forward, matching her stride.

"I promise I'm a not a creep," he called out. "Your aunt Ivy can vouch for me."

Zoey had to give him credit; he was persistent, and she was soaked. She stopped walking as the car came to a halt, and tugged the door open.

"Wait!" Nick grabbed a cloth from his dashboard and wiped off the upholstery where the rain had come in. Zoey couldn't help noticing he wasn't wearing a wedding ring.

"That's very gallant," she said, tongue-in-cheek. "But it's going to get twice as wet the moment I sit on it." She climbed in and discreetly pulled the carton out from under her T-shirt so she could buckle her seatbelt.

Nick grinned when he saw the eggs. "Incubation?"

"No. Breakfast," she retorted, rolling her eyes. But inwardly she was laughing. Wittiness was one of her favorite qualities in a man and a shiver flicked up her spine and across her shoulders.

"Want me to turn the heat on?" he asked, reaching for the dial.

"No, thanks. My aunts—" Zoey caught herself. She still thought of her aunts in the plural. Aunt Ivy and Aunt Sylvia; their names went together in a pair, like salt and pepper. "My aunt keeps it really warm in the house. It feels good to be cold for a change."

"Is that why you went for a walk in the rain, to cool off?"

"It wasn't raining when I started out." They had almost reached Ivy's house and Zoey noticed Nick put his signal on. "You don't have to turn into the driveway. You can just pull over here at the curb."

"No I can't. Street parking isn't allowed on weekdays between nine and five. I'll get a ticket."

Parking? That meant he intended to stay. "You want to come in?" It wasn't an invitation, it more of an expression of surprise. Not that it would have killed her to have a cup of coffee with him, but she needed to change her clothes and make breakfast before the meeting.

"Yeah, of course." Nick gave her a quizzical look. "I have an appointment this morning with your cousin and aunt. Didn't they tell you?"

"*You're* the Armstrong boy?" She was so thrown off that she accidentally used her aunt's wording; Ivy referred to anyone under fifty as a boy or a girl. Zoey had long since given up trying to convince her that some adults might be offended by those terms.

"Actually, my son's the Armstrong boy. I'm the Armstrong *man*." Nick made a muscle, but Zoey no longer found him amusing.

"You're the carpenter Mark is planning to hire to renovate my aunt's kitchen?" She wanted to be sure she understood correctly.

"I hope so, yeah."

Is that why he was at Aunt Sylvia's funeral—to drum up business with Mark? Zoey got out of the truck and shut the door harder than she needed to. Nick got out, too, and followed her up the driveway, past where Mark had parked his convertible. Given the soaking she had just endured in pursuit of eggs for *his* breakfast, the sight of his car made her want to kick his tires.

Neither Mark nor Ivy was in the kitchen, so she told Nick he could have a seat while she went to look for them. She poked her head into the living room but it was empty, too. Zoey dashed upstairs. The doors to the bathroom and her aunt's room were both closed, so she went to dry off and change into clean clothes.

When she came out of her room, she knocked on her aunt's door. "Aunt Ivy? Are you awake?"

"Yes. Come in." Her aunt was fully dressed but her silver hair formed a helmet of tight curls atop of her head, her locks holding the shape of the rollers she'd worn to bed. Ivy used to have hair as thick as Zoey's, but after she lost it to chemo, it grew back baby-fine. Every evening she put it up in rollers so it would appear fuller the following day. "Look at me," she fussed. "I can't find my brush anywhere."

Zoey scanned the vanity table. It contained a jar of moisturizing cream, two tubes of lipstick, a bottle of lily of the valley perfume and half a dozen pink and green plastic rollers. But the hairbrush was missing. Zoey lifted the table skirt; no brush there, either.

"Did you bring it into the bathroom with you?"

"I haven't used the bathroom yet. Mark just came in and woke me up. He's been in there ever since."

Zoey checked beneath the bed and under the bureau. She lifted the quilt and overturned the pillows. "Is it possible you used it last night and it fell behind the headboard?"

"No, the last time I used it was when I was putting my hair up. I was so tired I fell asleep right after that."

It was true; Ivy had been too weary to sit in her usual place at the vanity, so she'd propped herself up in bed against the pillows. Zoey had brought the rollers and brush to her and when Ivy was finished, Zoey returned the brush to the vanity table. She distinctly remembered because she had to put it back before she turned off the lamp beside Ivy's bed, otherwise she wouldn't have been able to see what she was doing. By the time she'd set the item in its place and crossed the room to the nightstand, Ivy was already sleeping.

"I'm sure it will turn up somewhere. I'll get mine for you."

She was halfway down the hall when Mark opened the bathroom door and stepped out. "Hey, Zo. Is breakfast ready yet? I'm starving."

You. Have. So. Much. Gall. Zoey thought, but she ignored his question and asked her own. "Have you seen a brush in there? It's got a blue handle."

He reached back into the bathroom and produced the brush. "Is this it? 'Cause I don't think it's sturdy enough to get through those snarls."

"It's *Aunt Ivy's.*" She grabbed it from him and hurried down the hall.

"Where did you find it?" Ivy asked. When Zoey told her, she said, "I don't know where my mind is lately. I honestly don't recall going into the bathroom. I'm starting to think something is wrong with me."

"You're just not a morning person," Zoey assured her, even though for the first time her aunt's forgetfulness bothered her, too. Not necessarily because she initially didn't remember using the restroom that morning, but because she still couldn't remember once she'd been told that's where she'd left her brush. *Yet she had no problem recalling everything that happened last night right before she fell asleep*, Zoey thought. She was probably worrying over nothing, but she silently resolved to pay closer attention to her aunt's short-term memory in the future. For now she said, "Take your time doing your hair and when you come down, I'll have a cup of coffee waiting for you."

In the kitchen, she found Nick taking measurements of the cupboards, while Mark leaned against a counter, watching.

"Don't get ahead of yourself, guys. Aunt Ivy hasn't decided if she even wants to replace the stove, much less do any other renovations," Zoey warned.

"Oh, sorry," Nick pushed the button on his measuring tape and it snapped into place. "Mark said—"

"This isn't Mark's house." *Not yet, anyway.*

"It's not yours, either," Mark shot back.

"No joke. That's why—"

Nick quickly cut in, "I'm happy to do—or not do—whatever your aunt wants. No pressure. We'll leave it up to her."

Satisfied, Zoey suggested the men go wait in the formal dining room, where she planned to serve breakfast. The first three omelets she made were warming on a platter in the oven and she was ready to fold the last one when her aunt came in. "That smells good. Where are the boys?"

Zoey motioned toward the dining room. "I thought we'd eat in there."

"That's much too formal. Let's eat here, at the family table." Ivy peered into the skillet. "Uh-oh, I think the edges of that are browning."

Zoey smiled; if her aunt was giving her cooking tips, it meant she was feeling a little more like her old self again. She lifted one side of the egg with the spatula and gently folded it over.

"I'll take care of this so you can go fix your hair," Ivy offered. Somehow, that hint didn't seem as insulting when it came from her aunt as when her cousin said it.

Zoey ran upstairs and brushed her hair into a high pony tail, revealing wet marks on her shoulders. She changed her T-shirt again, vaguely aware that she would have left the same one on if Nick wasn't eating with them. Then she hustled downstairs to tell the men breakfast was ready.

"Good morning, Mrs. Cartwright," Nick said when he entered the kitchen.

"Good morning, Nicholas. It's good to see you again. But what did I tell you about calling me Mrs. Cartwright? It makes me feel old. And I'm not old—yet. Am I?"

"Being called Nicholas makes me feel like I'm in trouble. And I'm not in trouble—yet. Am I?"

Both of them laughed; obviously this greeting this was a running joke between them.

"Have you met my great-niece yet?"

"Yes. I've had the pleasure—twice." Nick gave Zoey a sidelong glance and then smiled broadly at Ivy.

Is he trying to charm his way into a major remodel gig? Zoey wondered. She couldn't let herself forget that Erik had seemed charming at first, too. *And* that Nick was Mark's friend.

Once everyone was seated and served, Ivy asked Nick how his son, Aidan, was doing in school.

"He's doing great, thanks, although he's looking forward to summer, of course. By the way, if you want him to get started on the flowerbeds, he can drop off a load of mulch some time next week. I noticed he's got a few trees to edge out back, too." Nick explained to Zoey, "Aidan's mother and I are divorced. He'd been living with her in Connecticut, but he decided to finish out his last two years of school here on the island. He takes care of Mrs. Cartwright's—of your aunt's landscaping and other small projects. We had a mild winter, so he hasn't had to do it since January, but your aunt lets him start the Cadillac during the colder months to keep it running. Makes me jealous—*I've* never been behind the wheel of a Caddy."

"Aidan's such a nice, polite, handsome boy," Ivy gushed. "He takes after his father."

Nick chuckled. "Ugh. Please don't wish that on the kid."

"My great-grand-niece, Gabi, came here to complete the school year, too. She just started classes today."

"Oh, yeah?" Nick took a swallow of coffee. "If she needs anyone to show her around Hope Haven or introduce her to kids at school, I'm sure Aidan would do it. He knows what it's like to be the new kid on the island."

"Thanks," Zoey replied noncommittally. No matter how much Ivy raved about Aidan, he was two grades ahead of Gabi, which automatically made Zoey wary.

When they finished eating, Mark asked Nick to get his laptop from the truck. Apparently, the two men had already discussed what kinds of cupboards and countertops might look good in Ivy's kitchen and Nick had created a gallery of photos to show her.

"Hang on, not so fast," Zoey warned. "The first thing that needs to be discussed is whether or not the stove even needs to be replaced. Aunt Ivy doesn't need to see photos in order to make that decision—she needs her stove evaluated."

"Right," Nick readily agreed. "I evaluated it the last time I was here and I have some concerns I'd like to draw your attention to. If I get my laptop, I can show you what the experts online recommend, so you don't have to take my word for it."

"Don't be silly, Nicholas. I trust your opinion," Ivy said.

So he pointed out a few issues he thought could be potentially hazardous if left unchecked. He also asked Ivy questions about the burners and whether her food was cooking evenly and discussed the cost differences between repairing and replacing the range. By the time he was done talking, both Zoey and her aunt were convinced it was imperative for Ivy to get a new stove, and they gathered round Nick's laptop as he showed them a few models. Zoey was impressed with his recommendation of a vintage-look freestanding range that would go perfectly with the house: he had good taste. And when Nick confirmed he'd fit the new stove for half the price of the manufacturer, her trust began to deepen.

"Didn't I tell you he's the best contractor on the island? Appliances, carpentry, plumbing—he does it all." Ivy proudly patted Nick's forearm.

"It's more like I do a little of everything."

"Now show her the photo of the fridge that will complement that stove and then we can move on to the cupboards," Nick ordered Mark.

Ivy appeared baffled. "My refrigerator works just fine. Why would I want to replace it?"

"Because you're getting a new stove!" Mark's exasperation was evident. He lowered his voice and clarified, "Aunt Ivy, if you replace the stove without making other changes to the kitchen, it's going to stand out like a sore thumb."

Zoey thought her head was about to explode. Since when did he address her as *aunt*? And "like a sore thumb" was one of Ivy's idioms—obviously Mark was mirroring her language in order to win her over. "If you're concerned about the colors of your appliances clashing, I could paint the fridge to match the stove, Aunt Ivy."

"It's not just that the colors won't match, the styles won't—" Mark began to argue, but Ivy interrupted him to consult with Nick.

"You're the professional, Nicholas. Do you think I should get a new fridge?"

"If it's working well, then the only reason to replace it would be aesthetics. So unless having different styles of appliances bothers you, I'd say don't waste your money."

Mark huffed and crossed his arms, clearly dissatisfied with his friend's answer, but Nick was undeterred.

"Eventually, if you want a new fridge, I know some places off island where you can get a good deal on a trade-in. But there's no rush. Changes can be very difficult. Give yourself time to adjust."

As Ivy visibly relaxed her shoulders and exhaled, Zoey sensed Nick wasn't just talking about kitchen appliances and she could have hugged him for being so understanding about what her aunt was going through. She tried to catch his eye so she could mouth, "thank you," but he was studying Ivy's face, patiently waiting for her to think it over. *He seems more concerned about her well-being than Mark does*, Zoey thought. Had she judged him prematurely?

"I think I'll only purchase the stove for now," Ivy said. "And I'd like you to install it, Nick."

"Sure thing." He lowered the lid to his computer.

"Wait, we still haven't discussed the cupboards and countertops," Mark said.

Nick looked as incredulous as Zoey felt. Somehow she managed to modulate her voice when she replied, "She just said she only wants to purchase the stove for now. Right, Aunt Ivy?"

"She meant she didn't want a fridge. That's not the same as not wanting new countertops or cupboards," Mark answered for their aunt before she had the chance to answer for herself. "Ivy and I have already agreed this place needs to be brightened up."

Ivy nodded. "It is rather dim in here. The other day I nearly tripped over Moby. The room is so shadowy he blends right in."

Mark was all over that. "Yeah—it's *unsafe* to keep the décor the way it is."

"There are ways of brightening up the room without tearing up all the cupboards and countertops. We could put a different bulb in the overhead light," Zoey suggested. *Obviously.*

"Will that be enough to make a difference?" Ivy asked Nick.

"It's a good start, sure. We can look around and see what else might be contributing to the dimness. For example, that big rhododendron shrub right outside the side window. If we trim that back, we could let a lot of light in."

"Oh, but Sylvia always likes to look at the rhododendrons while she's washing dishes," Ivy objected.

Just as Zoey was wondering whether anyone else noticed she'd referred to her sister-in-law in the present tense, Mark said, "Uh, Sylvia isn't here any more, Ivy."

You think she doesn't know that? Zoey seethed. *She's aware of it almost every single waking moment.* If Zoey's legs were longer, she would have given him a swift shin kick beneath the table.

Fortunately, Nick quickly jumped in, replying, "Yeah, that's right. I remember Sylvia telling me how much she enjoyed watching the bees opening up the blossoms, but she was glad they were on the other side of the window screen."

His recollection made Ivy smile. Zoey was so moved by the genuine connection he seemed to have formed with both her aunts that she decided she shouldn't hold it against him that he was also friends with Mark; clearly, he was the exception to the rule.

"So, we should leave the rhododendrons just as they are and I'll buy new bulbs for the light, right Aunt Ivy?" Zoey asked.

When her aunt said yes, Zoey expected Mark to put up a fight again, but he was silently rubbing his temples. Their meeting might not have gone according to his plans, but she didn't think he should look so dour; at the very least, he'd eventually be inheriting a modern, upscale stove.

Zoey cleared the table and washed the dishes while Nick, Mark and Ivy placed the order online and worked out the details for the delivery and installation. Finally, Nick got up to leave, asking, "How is that balustrade holding up, Mrs.—I mean, Ivy?"

"I haven't been sliding down it since you fixed it, so it's still nice and sturdy," Ivy joked. Nick offered his arm and she used it to pull herself up from her chair. Turning to Mark, she said, "I didn't tell you this because I knew you'd worry I'm becoming too forgetful, but your friend here saved me from certain death when I left the gas on, without the flame lit. He was working on the balustrade that day and he smelled it. I'm grateful he keeps an eye out for me."

Zoey's ears perked up. *But Mark already knows about the gas. He said Aunt Ivy told him about it when he was checking in on her*, she thought. *It's strange that she'd forget admitting something like that.* Zoey was beginning to wonder if she was wrong about her aunt's memory. Maybe Ivy wasn't just distracted because she was mourning. Maybe her forgetfulness was more serious than Zoey wanted to believe... Noticing movement in her peripheral vision, she looked over just as Mark shook his head and pressed a finger to his lips, signaling Nick to keep quiet. Nick nodded.

It took a moment for the realization to click. *So* that's *how Mark knew—Nick was here that day and* he *must have told him.* While Zoey was relieved to be wrong about her aunt having another memory lapse, she was disappointed to be right about Nick being in cahoots with her cousin. *When Mark said he checked in from time to time to see how Aunt Sylvia and Aunt Ivy were doing, I assumed he meant he called them. But apparently, he's been checking in with* Nick.

Zoey could appreciate that Nick was trying to be helpful by reporting the stove incident to Mark; it was the responsible thing to do. But she resented it that her cousin had involved him in keeping tabs on Sylvia and Ivy in the first place. Nick wasn't family. He didn't even work at the house very often—Carla, who came twice a week to clean, had been there far more consistently over the years than any other contractor. And Zoey was the one who'd been living with Sylvia and Ivy for the past three months. But Mark never called *her* to ask how they were doing. He virtually never called her at all.

So why had her cousin made an arrangement to check in with his high school buddy? And what was in it for Nick? Had he been looking after Sylvia and Ivy as favor to Mark, so that Mark would hire him for the big, future renovation projects he had planned?

Furthermore, if everything was on the up-and-up, why were the two men acting so conspiratorial? *Probably because they know that Aunt Ivy would be offended if she found out Nick's been spying on her as if she were a batty old woman!* Okay, that was too harsh. Zoey had seen too much evidence of Nick's respect for Ivy to believe that's what he thought about her. But something about the whole situation made Zoey recognize she'd been hasty in thinking she could let her guard down around Nick.

She flicked water from her fingers and wiped her hands on the hanging tie towel. Facing the others, she said, "You're right, Aunt Ivy, it's very helpful to have an extra pair of eyes looking out for you." *Which is why I'll be keeping an even closer watch on Mark and Nick from now on.*

CHAPTER FIVE

Zoey had planned to poke around in the attic on Friday afternoon to see if she could gain any insight into what Mark may have been trying to find. But once he left the island, she felt so relaxed that she wound up taking a nap instead. Then Gabi came home and both aunts peppered her with questions about her first day at school, which she said she liked in general, although the classes were a lot smaller than what she was used to in California.

It rained on Saturday and Sunday and even though she usually loved listening to it pattering against the rooftop, Zoey didn't go into the attic then, either. The longer Mark was out of sight, the farther out of mind she wanted to put him and his 'monkey business,' as Ivy would say. After the stove was installed, she'd be able to forget about Nick, too.

Meanwhile, she had more important things to focus on, like continuing her job search. And shopping for and preparing appealing no-cook meals, since she was worried about using the stove in its current condition. She also played cribbage with her aunt and niece more times than she could count. The card game had been something Sylvia and Ivy enjoyed daily; they even bet on it, awarding the winner a penny per point. Teaching Gabi how to play provided a brief distraction for Ivy when she became overwrought with loneliness for Sylvia, which happened several times a day. It made Zoey worry about how she'd fare once she herself went back to Providence and Gabi returned to California, but maybe if she got her aunt involved at the senior center or with the ladies' fellowship at church, that would help. *And I can come here on the weekends*, Zoey thought. In any case, that was a bridge she'd have to cross in the future.

By Monday, she was itching to get out of the house, so while Ivy was napping she walked halfway to the high school to meet Gabi. On the way home, she suggested instead of using the sidewalk for the final half mile, they cut over the dunes to Rose Beach and follow the shoreline that ran parallel to Main Street. As usual, Zoey was hot and she convinced Gabi they should remove their shoes and roll up their pants' legs so they could splash through the tidal pools.

"When you were a baby, you used to put everything in your mouth—even more than most toddlers do. Your mom and I would take you to this beach and she'd have to watch you like a hawk. If we turned our backs for even a second, you'd be licking a fistful of sand or eating seaweed. One time your mom caught you sucking on a pebble and you wouldn't spit it out. She freaked and did a finger sweep of your mouth. Guess what you really had in there?"

"I don't know."

"A live periwinkle snail!"

"Gross."

Zoey had expected more of a reaction. Gabi had been quiet this morning, too, and she wondered if she'd had an argument with Kathleen yesterday, because for once Gabi had actually answered the phone when she called. Or maybe something happened at school. "Are you okay?"

"Yeah. Just tired."

"Oh. Were you too warm last night to sleep? I know *I* was." The heat was on again but Zoey hadn't wanted to open her windows because without the screens on them, insects could get in.

"No. I heard something creaking in the middle of the night. It woke me up."

"That was probably Moby going in or out of Aunt Sylvia's room. One of these days, I really should oil that door."

"Oh, so that's what it was!" Gabi snapped her fingers, suddenly animated.

Zoey heard the relief in her voice and wondered if she felt nervous because she was used to having her father in her house instead of living with all women. "Benjamin's Manor is very safe, you know. Dune Island has one of the lowest crime rates in the country, except in the summer, when there's an increase in trespassing. But that's because the vacationers want to take shortcuts to the beach, not because they're stealing stuff from houses or hurting people or anything like that."

Gabi stopped to a balance a slipper shell on her big toe. She kicked her leg at the knee and the shell flew upward but she wasn't quick enough to catch it. Scott used to be pretty good at that trick. Had he taught it to his daughter on a beach in California or did she remember it from when she was here as a kid?

"You know how you said I could talk to you about anything?" the girl asked tentatively.

Suddenly, Zoey's stomach felt as if *she'd* been sucking on a periwinkle snail. She hoped nothing serious was upsetting Gabi but if it was, she hoped she'd know how to handle it. "Yes. I meant it, too."

"Okay... so today at lunch I told some kids where I'm staying. And a boy from my trig class said a woman who lived in Aunt Ivy's house used to go up on the widow's walk during a full moon and make a screeching sound that people could hear all over the island."

Zoey had heard variations of this rumor when she was young, too, but she thought it had died out a long time ago. She should have known better. And she probably should have prepared Gabi better, too. But the truth was even more unsettling than the myth and she hadn't wanted to tell her about it if it wasn't necessary.

"Hmm. Sounds like that kid would have believed Mark's story about the dentil molding, too," she said, stalling until she could figure out how much of their aunts' history she should disclose. Would it be too troubling for Gabi to hear it, especially considering everything else that was going on in her life right now?

"Yeah, that's what I thought, at first. But then a different boy said he'd heard that story, too. Except the woman didn't go to the widow's walk during a full moon, she went up there every time it rained to look for her husband, who was lost at sea. And she wasn't screaming, she was crying. He said her name was Sylvia and she had a newborn baby and he said some other stuff, too." Gabi stopped and faced Zoey. "Is this one of those unfounded rumors I shouldn't believe or is it true?"

"Well..."

"Aunt Zoey, you just said I could talk to you about anything." Gabi crossed her arms over her chest. "I'm not a little kid any more. I'm old enough to know. If my mom was here, *she'd* tell me."

That's the first time I've heard you mention your mother, Zoey noticed. Although she didn't especially appreciate the guilt-trip comparison, she realized her niece was right; Jessica would have been open about it. Besides, she and her sister were both close to Gabi's age when they found out and it had helped them understand their family dynamics better. "Okay. C'mon. Let's sit a minute."

They walked farther up on shore and sat in the sand at the very foot of a dune, so they wouldn't disturb the new beach grass that had been planted higher up to protect it from erosion. Peering across the flats toward a ship on the horizon, Zoey began, "What I'm going to tell you is, well, it's sort of a family secret. Or at least it's something we want to be discreet about, out of respect for our aunts' privacy. So you have to promise not to share it with anyone else. Even if they say things you know are false, don't try to prove them wrong by telling them what really happened. And please don't talk to Aunt Ivy about it unless she brings it up first, because it might make her sad." Zoey faced her niece and narrowed her eyes. "You promise?"

When Gabi nodded her agreement, Zoey continued hesitantly, "It's kind of complicated and I'm not sure where to start... You might not know why Aunt Ivy always refers to her husband as Captain Denny, do you?"

"Isn't it because he was a sea captain?"

"Actually, when she met him, he was a boatswain—that's like a boss for the other deckhands. He was working his way up to become a first mate because he was very ambitious and it was his dream to become a licensed captain, buy his own boat and hire a crew instead of fishing for someone else."

Zoey explained that Dennis had been saving up since he was eighteen but he didn't have nearly enough money to make a purchase that big. So the spring after they got married, Ivy decided to use some of the money she'd inherited to help him buy a forty-two-foot trawler. And she'd convinced her brother, Marcus, to co-invest in exchange for a percent of the profits from Denny's fishing business. He also agreed to do the bookkeeping since he was really good at figures but couldn't hold a full-time job because of his illness.

"In early April, the boat was christened *Boston Ivy*, which was a play on Aunt Ivy's name and birthplace, as well as another name for the ivy known as woodbine. He assembled a crew and appointed Marcus his honorary first mate for the maiden voyage. It was in title only, since Denny wasn't officially a captain and his brother-in-law had no maritime skills, but Marcus felt very complimented by it and he was looking forward to the expedition. Aunt Sylvia, however, was pregnant and didn't want him to go because he'd been experiencing one of his weak spells. She was worried he'd get seasick and pass out. But Aunt Ivy convinced her Captain Denny wouldn't let anything happen to him, so off they went. According to the crew, they brought in a good haul and they were all excited about their success."

Zoey paused. She hated telling this next part. "That afternoon as they were returning, the fog was so thick they decided to dock at Port Newcomb instead of Benjamin's Harbor. Even though they were advancing slowly, the visibility was very poor and the boat edged alongside the jetty, too close, like this." Zoey demonstrated with her hands.

"It grated against the rocks and tipped at about a forty degree angle, grinding to a halt. Marcus and another man were thrown overboard. One crew member said Denny jumped in to rescue them so fast the other guys hardly had a chance to comprehend what was going on. He swam to Marcus, first, probably because he knew how frail he was." Zoey inhaled deeply and then blew out through her lips, equivocating about whether she should keep going.

"Did Marcus drown?" Gabi questioned bluntly.

"No, but he must have landed on a rock just beneath the surface because the medical examiner's report indicated his back was broken and he probably died from the impact. Denny didn't know that though, so he was trying to keep Marcus's head above water while he swam backwards, pulling him toward the jetty. As he got closer, a wave slammed him against the rocks and he gashed his head, but he didn't let go of Marcus. The crew members managed to scramble off the boat, toss a rope to the other guy in the water and somehow they hoisted Denny and Marcus out, too. When the ambulance arrived, Denny was barely conscious, but his arm was still wrapped around his brother-in-law." Even though it happened long before she was born and to people she had never known, Zoey's eyes brimmed at the thought. "He, um, he died of a brain injury about an hour after he got to the hospital."

"Wow. That's awful. No wonder it makes Aunt Ivy sad to talk about it." Gabi hugged her knees, her hair obscuring her profile. Zoey waited silently for the teenager to absorb what she'd been told. Eventually Gabi remarked, "Everyone in our family dies young."

Zoey felt as if she'd inhaled a shard of glass. Was Gabi thinking about her mother's death? Was she worried about her own? "We might not have the healthiest—or the most fruitful—family tree, but not *every*one dies young," she reassured her. "Look at Aunt Ivy, she's eighty-seven and still going strong."

"Yeah, I guess." Gabi stretched her legs out in front of her and wiggled her toes. "If she never talks about how Captain Denny died, how did you find out?"

"Every now and then she'll make a general reference to it. But I heard most of the details from my mom, who heard them from her parents. And the accident was reported in all the newspapers, even the ones in Boston." Zoey had looked it up in an online archive a couple years ago.

"Oh. So does that mean the kids could have been right about Aunt Sylvia going on the widow's walk? Was she up there because she was grieving?"

"Mm, yes and no. See, when Aunt Sylvia and Aunt Ivy got to the hospital and were informed that their husbands had died, Aunt Sylvia was so traumatized she immediately went into labor. Even though it was more than a month before she was due, she gave birth to a baby boy."

"That was the second Marcus, right? Marcus, Jr.?"

"Exactly. He was Mark's father—Marcus Winslow the Second. He was born perfectly healthy, which was amazing, all things considered. But Aunt Sylvia was so distraught about losing her husband, she wouldn't touch the baby for three or four months. Today she'd probably be diagnosed with postpartum depression or maybe post-traumatic stress disorder, but at the time everyone called it a nervous breakdown. Since she didn't have any income or family support, Aunt Ivy moved her and Marcus Jr. out of the rented cottage and into her house, so she could take care of the baby and look after her sister-in-law, too."

"And that helped Aunt Sylvia feel better?"

"Yes, but it took a while. The turning point came one night at the end of the summer when she went up to the widow's walk. Aunt Ivy didn't hear her overhead, which meant Aunt Sylvia must have been very quiet. In other words, she wasn't howling at the moon. She wasn't crying in the rain or watching for her husband. She wasn't doing any of the things your classmates told you she was doing. And it was just that one time, not something that happened repeatedly," Zoey emphasized.

"Lots of people went up to their widow's walks at night in the summer to stargaze and have a drink, or whatever, just like they do now. It wasn't a big deal. But the islanders knew what had happened to Aunt Sylvia's husband and how emotionally fragile she was. A concerned neighbor must have seen her up there, feared the worst and called the police, because a couple of officers showed up, banging on the door. Aunt Ivy's afraid of heights, so they had to go bring Sylvia down. By that time, Marcus Jr. had woken up and he was wailing his head off. The neighbors might have heard him or seen the police vehicle in front of the house and that's how some of the stories you heard got started. They may have been more accurate at the beginning, but I'm sure the details changed the more they were retold over a couple of generations. That's what I meant when I said some of the gossip you'll hear has an element of truth…"

As gingerly as she could, Zoey confided that the police surmised Sylvia went to the widow's walk with the intention of jumping off the roof. Which wasn't true—she later told Ivy that's where Marcus had proposed exactly one year ago to the day and she just wanted to feel close to him again. But when the police questioned what she was doing up there, she wouldn't tell them, for fear she'd sound unstable. Ironically, her silence made them even more determined to take her to the hospital for an evaluation, which she adamantly resisted.

"Back then, mental health care was… well, let's just say it's understandable why she refused to go with them. Aunt Ivy later told our grandmother, Charles's wife, that was the only time she'd ever heard Aunt Sylvia raise her voice. She insisted, 'I can't leave. My son needs me. Now, please get out of this house.' Zoey chuckled to herself; only her docile great-aunt would say "please" when she was telling someone off. "Aunt Ivy handed her the baby and then she escorted the police to the door while Aunt Sylvia took Marcus Jr. to his room and rocked him back to sleep."

"So she bonded with him after all?"

"Are you kidding me? She *adored* him. Just like Aunt Ivy did. Some people—like our grandfather—said they overdid it. They said the two of them spoiled him rotten and they were probably right. But doting on the baby helped them through their grief. Aunt Ivy once told me that taking care of her brother's son made her feel as if she was taking care of *him*, in a way. She said it gave her a reason to get up in the morning… I also think they pampered Marcus Jr. because they felt so guilty."

"Guilty? Gabi sat up straighter. "About what?"

"Well, even though it was an accident, Denny was technically at fault. Aunt Ivy felt horrible about that, especially because she had convinced Aunt Sylvia that Marcus would be fine on the boat.

Instead, he ended up leaving his wife a widow and his son father-less. As for Aunt Sylvia, I don't think she ever forgave herself for neglecting the baby right after he was born. It's almost as if they both believed—mistakenly—that they'd ruined his life. So they kept trying to make it up to him."

"That must be why Aunt Ivy spoils Mark, too. Because he's Marcus Jr.'s son."

Zoey hadn't realized that Gabi had picked up on the dynamic between their aunt and cousin. Ordinarily, she'd be careful not to criticize Mark in front of Gabi but since the girl was so perceptive anyway, Zoey felt she could level with her. "Yes, I suppose that's part of it. I mean, Mark isn't shy about getting what he wants, regardless. But how Aunt Sylvia and Aunt Ivy have always treated him is definitely an extension of how they treated his father. And once Marcus Jr. died, they lavished Mark with even more attention and... and with other things, too."

Zoey intended to leave it at that, but Gabi asked, "Like with making him the beneficiary of the house?"

"How do you know about his inheritance?" It wasn't a secret but Zoey couldn't imagine anyone discussing it with Gabi. Even if Scott knew and remembered, he would have thought she was too young to be privy to that kind of information. And Ivy rarely talked about the will.

"I heard Mark telling someone on the phone—I wasn't being nosy. He made the call right in front of me and he was talking really loud."

Now, who is he trying to impress? Zoey wondered. "It's true he'll inherit the house some day, but Aunt Ivy had nothing to do with that. It was her father's decision." She explained that Thomas's ironclad will designated the eldest Winslow blood relative as sole beneficiary of the house, for generations to come. Whatever was left over from Ivy's trust fund, however, would be divided among *all* of her living blood relatives, meaning Mark, Zoey and Gabi.

Gabi was thoughtful as she slowly drizzled sand onto her knee-caps, one at a time. "You mean if Mark wasn't in the family and Aunt Ivy passed away, you'd inherit the house?"

"Yeah, I'd be next in line. And then you." Zoey swatted a bee away from her niece. She comforted her, "Don't worry. Neither Mark nor I intend to die any time soon. Nor does Aunt Ivy, for that matter."

"No, I don't mean if Mark *dies*. I meant if he was never really in the family."

Zoey cocked her head, puzzling over her niece's peculiar question. "What do you mean by never really in the family?"

"Like, if Aunt Sylvia had a lover and Marcus Jr. was the lover's baby, not Marcus's. Because that would mean Mark isn't related to Aunt Ivy by blood, either."

"Is that what the students at your school are saying?" Zoey asked. "I can't imagine Aunt Sylvia even *using* the word lover, much less, having one. "

"But you haven't heard the theory yet. It totally fits with what you just told me."

Zoey sighed. "All right. Go ahead and tell me. I'll try to keep an open mind."

"One of the kids said everyone in Aunt Sylvia's generation knew she never loved Marcus—that she just married him for his money," she chattered breathlessly. "She got pregnant by someone else and she planned to wait a while and then get divorced so her husband would have to pay her alimony. When she saved enough, she was going to run off with her lover, who was very poor, like her."

Zoey winced. *Gabi is so gullible. No wonder Kathleen's worried about her being easily influenced*, she thought. *If she's not careful, she'll wind up like me—letting some smooth-talking guy drain her savings.*

The teenager prattled on, "Except Marcus spent every penny he had buying a boat and when he was lost at sea—well, technically his boat crashed—he left her destitute, which is essentially what happened, right? This boy said Aunt Sylvia felt so guilty, she couldn't even look at her baby, and that's exactly the same as what you just told me. She couldn't stand the sight of her lover any more, either, so she completely ignored him. And since he didn't want to disgrace her and he couldn't afford to support a family anyway, he never told anyone the baby was his." Gabi concluded melodramatically, "But he was so heartbroken, he'd walk past the house every day, hoping to catch a glimpse of her and his son. Eventually, he grew so bitter, he could hardly eat or speak or sleep."

"Hmm." Part of Zoey found all the gossip amusing, but another part of her was hurt on her aunt Sylvia's behalf. She would have hated to know she was the subject of any gossip, and Gabi's casual attitude and dramatization of real people's pain—even if it was all made up or just teenage chatter—caused Zoey's to wince. "Did your classmate offer any theories about who Marcus Jr.'s real father was?"

"Yes," Gabi answered triumphantly. "He said it was Mr. Witherell."

The tiny hairs on Zoey's forearm stood on end as she instantly recalled the exchange between the old man and Mark on the day of Aunt Sylvia's funeral.

"Who do you think you are?"

"I'm Marcus Winslow the Third."

"I wouldn't be too sure of that."

"That's ridiculous," Zoey scoffed, more to herself than to her niece. Mr. Witherell was undoubtedly aware of the rumor that he'd fathered Marcus Jr. and he would have known Mark had heard the same gossip. He was just capitalizing on it to provoke the younger man's ire because Mark had insulted *him*. Mr. Witherell wasn't *seriously* indicating he was his father. What purpose would that have served? "It's completely illogical."

"No, it isn't. Even Aunt Ivy said he carried a torch for Aunt Sylvia, remember? And Mr. Witherell *still* walks by her house every day."

"Mr. Witherell walks by a *lot* of peoples' houses every day. It doesn't mean anything," Zoey reasoned. "Besides, why would he still try to catch a glimpse of Aunt Sylvia? He knows she's not here any longer—he came to her funeral."

"See? That's even more evidence of his devotion." Gabi's eyes were shining. "Plus, he fits the profile—he hardly ever speaks. That's because when he lost the love of his life, he also lost his voice."

The notion was so ludicrous Zoey would have laughed but she was too disturbed by her niece's naivete. "You've got it backwards, Gab. He doesn't fit the profile—the profile fits him. Don't you see? That's why gossip like this can be so convincing."

"But the boy at school swore that if his grandfather was alive, he could prove it because he was friends with Mr. Witherell. And he saw a photo of Aunt Sylvia that Mr. Witherell still keeps in his house beside his bed," Gabi insisted. "We could ask him if it's true and—"

"Ask Mr. Witherell? No way. We are *not* doing that."

"But you said he wouldn't hurt a fly."

"That's not the point."

"Then what is?" Gabi challenged. Kathleen had warned Zoey how flippant she could be, but until this instant, Zoey hadn't seen any real evidence of it.

"The point is we don't know him and that's an intrusive, offensive question." *And he'll think you're even more audacious than your cousin Mark is.*

"Fine." Gabi harrumphed. "I'll ask Aunt Ivy about it, then."

Zoey leaped to her feet. Clapping sand off the seat of her pants, she said, "You promised you wouldn't mention this subject to Aunt Ivy and I expect you to keep your word."

Gabi didn't budge. Shielding her eyes with her hand, she peered at Zoey and argued, "But this is a *different* subject. It's—"

"Don't split hairs. I know you can't remember Aunt Sylvia well, but she wasn't anything like what your classmates described and it's unfair to say things like that about someone who isn't alive to defend herself." Zoey picked up her shoes and started walking. Then she twirled around and admonished, "You can't be vulnerable to every suggestion someone makes, Gabi. You have to start learning to think things through for yourself. Like have you considered how Aunt Ivy would feel if you suggested her sister-in-law was only using her brother for his money? Or that Aunt Sylvia had been deceiving her all these years about Marcus Jr.? Even though it's utterly preposterous,

I can't fathom why you'd want to hurt your aunt by planting ideas like that in her head!"

Gabi's face went red and a frown gnarled her mouth. She faltered at first, but then her words came out in a rush. "Be-because if… if Mark isn't really a blood relative and Aunt Ivy dies, you'll inherit the house and then you won't have to worry about subletting your townhome and earning back all the savings you lost." Tears bounded down her cheeks and she brought her legs to her chest and tucked her head behind her knees.

I am such *an idiot.* Zoey plopped back down in the sand and wrapped her arm around Gabi as she wept. "Sh-shh-shh."

It was the same sound Zoey used to make when her niece had colic as a baby. When Jessica, desperate for sleep, would drive to the library and take a nap in the car as Zoey spent her lunch hour pacing the parking lot and jiggling the stroller in an attempt to soothe Gabi.

As it did then, it took a while today for her niece to grow quiet. When she did, Zoey said, "I appreciate it that you're concerned about me, Gabi. But my financial situation is too much of a burden for you to think about—not because it's so bad, but because it's my problem, not yours. Besides, I promise you, I'm fine. I've got lots of resources and if I felt desperate, I'd take any job I could get. But right now, my priority is staying with Aunt Ivy and making sure she's all right. I consider myself very fortunate to be in a position that allows me to do that."

Gabi's voice was muffled, her face still buried in her knees. "Then why are you so upset that Mark's going to inherit the house?"

Is that what he's been saying? Or is that how I've been behaving? Fingering a strand of her niece's silken hair, Zoey replied, "I love Aunt Ivy's home and I've often daydreamed about what it would be like to live on Dune Island permanently. And for some reason— maybe because Aunt Ivy and Aunt Sylvia lived alone in the house for so many years—I think of it as a *woman's* house. Or as a place for family, not a place for strangers to lease. But since there's no getting around the will, I decided a long time ago I'd better come to terms with it.

"Besides, how could I begrudge Mark his inheritance when Aunt Ivy has been so generous to me? She's shared her home with me every summer—and whenever else I've wanted to visit. She's welcomed my friends and my boyfriends to Dune Island, too. Not to mention, my entire family, including you. Being able to come here has been one the best gifts I've ever received." Zoey's eyes smarted. "So I promise you, I'm not upset Mark will *eventually* inherit the house. However, I'd hate to see him push Aunt Ivy out before she's ready to leave."

Gabi sniffed. "You don't want him to remodel her kitchen, either, do you?"

"Not unless that's what Aunt Ivy wants."

"I hope she doesn't." Gabi lifted her head. "I like it."

"Seriously? I actually agree with Mark on this one—I think it's awful."

"It may be ugly but it's retro, so that makes it kind of cool."

"Hmm, I wasn't born all that long after those cupboards were installed. I wonder if that's what people say about me, too. 'She's retro, so that makes her kind of cool.'"

"At least you're not as old as the wallpaper in the best room. Now *that's* hideous. It looks like a scary museum in there." Gabi stood and pulled her aunt to her feet. Before she let go of her hand, she said, "I promise not to tell anyone anything we talked about, Aunt Zoey."

"I know. I trust you."

When they got home, Zoey was pleased to discover her aunt still in bed, faintly snoring. The past three nights when Zoey had gotten up to fill a glass with water, she'd noticed Ivy's light was on. Each time she'd gone into her room and stayed with her for at least an hour while Ivy wept, reminiscing about Sylvia. Since the older woman hadn't been getting enough sleep, even though it was almost five o'clock, Zoey decided she'd let her nap a little longer.

"Are we having salad again for supper?" Gabi asked when she came back downstairs.

"Why, is there something else you'd rather eat?"

"Anything that's warm."

"We can't use the stove, remember?"

"I know how to make healthy microwave mac and cheese. All I need is cauliflower, cheese and cream."

"And a microwave." Zoey chuckled. "In case you didn't notice, Aunt Ivy doesn't have one."

Gabi's eyes darted around the room. "I guess that makes sense. They probably weren't invented yet the last time Aunt Ivy renovated, were they?"

Zoey was about to reply when someone knocked on the back door. She hurried to get it so the rapping wouldn't wake her aunt.

"Hi, Zoey," Nick said. A kid who could have passed for his taller, thinner twin stood beside him. "I need to double check a couple of specs for the stove and my son has some mulch to unload in the back yard. He can also put the screens in like we talked about. Aidan, this is Ms.—sorry, I don't know your last name."

"Hi, Aidan. My last name is Jansen but please call me Zoey." Her niece's remark about the invention of the microwave had already made her feel outdated. If Nick's son called her Ms. Jansen, she'd feel downright ancient. *Now I understand why Aunt Ivy doesn't want Nick calling her Mrs. Winslow.*

She gestured for them to follow her into the kitchen. "Go ahead and take a look at the range. But my aunt is napping and the screens are in the attic. I'd prefer that you didn't go up there. You might wake her and she really needs her rest."

"No problem. I can come back another time," Aidan amicably agreed. He stopped short when he spotted Gabi standing on her tiptoes, reaching into a cupboard. "Hi. I've seen you at school but we haven't met. I'm Aidan."

Gabi lowered her arm and Zoey noticed she smiled without showing her braces—was she trying to disguise her age? Aidan was probably one of the few really tall boys on the island and he was undeniably cute. "I think I've seen you, too. I'm Gabi."

"You play the flute, right? I showed a clip of your performance to your aunts once. It sounded really good."

"Thanks."

Is she blushing or did she get sunburned at the beach? Zoey wondered.

Nick cleared his throat. "Hi, Gabi. I'm Nick, Aidan's father. I'm installing your Aunt Ivy's new stove for her."

"Oh, good. Now we don't have to have salad and sandwiches for supper again."

"Uh, sorry to get your hopes up. I didn't mean I'm installing it *now*. I meant once it's delivered." Nick turned to face Zoey. "You do know you can use this range until the new one gets here, don't you?"

"But you told us it wasn't safe."

"I said it had several things that needed repair or replacement. Things that could be hazardous sometime down the road if they went unchecked," Nick reiterated. "Believe me, I wouldn't have left the stove hooked up if I thought it posed a danger to you or your aunt. And I definitely wouldn't have allowed you to make breakfast on it, either, no matter how much I wanted an omelet made from freshly gathered eggs."

A smile wrinkled his skin but Zoey was flabbergasted. Had she really been worried over nothing? What's more, had she encouraged her aunt to buy a major appliance for no good reason? He must have known what she was thinking because he added, "As I mentioned, my biggest immediate concern regarded safety as it relates to the stove's performance. Like if your aunt's meals were cooking unevenly or weren't cooking all the way through, she could get sick."

"So you're sure it's okay to use the stove?"

"Yes, I'm sure. I should have been clearer about that." He looked so remorseful that Zoey took the blame herself, although her response was as much of a warning as it was an apology.

"No, I misunderstood. I can be hypervigilant when it comes to my family. Sorry."

"Don't apologize—that's a lovely quality in a person." When Nick's eyes met hers, Zoey was disarmed by the sincerity she saw in them. "Listen, Aidan and I were going to grab pizza for supper when we're done here. Why don't we bring it back—my treat, for inconveniencing you with my miscommunication."

Thoughtfulness seemed to be second-nature to Nick—unlike his pal Mark, who rarely made an effort for anyone else unless it served him, too. While she appreciated the gesture, she still said, "Thanks, but that isn't necessary."

At the same moment, Gabi exclaimed, "Pizza? Yesss!"

"What's this about pizza?" Ivy tottered in from the hall. When she saw they had visitors, she announced, "Oh, look, who's here. The Armstrong boys, two of my favorite people."

"Hello, Mrs. Winslow," they chorused, sounding even more identical than they looked.

"I was telling Zoey that after Aidan and I unload your mulch, we'd like to pick up a couple of pizzas and bring them back for all of us to eat here. Is that all right with you?" Nick asked.

"That would be wonderful. The girls and I will make a salad, too."

Nick's grin was outshone by his son's. *Why do I feel like the two of them just received permission to take my niece and me on a double date?* Zoey asked herself.

But an hour later when they were all seated around the table and she tasted the pizza, she was glad her aunt had said yes; it was so delicious she devoured as many slices as the teenagers did.

"Now, who's ready for a game of cribbage?" Ivy asked after they had eaten. "We can play with partners."

"No, we can't. We've got an odd number of people. I'll sit the game out," Zoey quickly volunteered.

About five years ago, Ivy confided the reason she had always challenged Zoey, Jessica and their boyfriends to play cribbage against her and Sylvia when they were younger: she was secretly assessing the boys' characters and compatibility with her nieces. She claimed a card game was a much better indicator of whether the couple had a future together than whatever the boyfriends said and did when "they were working hard to make a good impression on your two old aunties."

"So if they cheated or they were poor sports, that disqualified them?" Zoey had asked.

"For starters, yes. But I wasn't just watching them—I was watching you two girls, as well. I'd look for patience. Teamwork. Willingness to forgive each other's mistakes. I was also looking for a spark of enthusiasm. You need that in a partnership, you know."

At the time, Zoey had found her aunt's practice comical, but tonight it seemed uncomfortably close to matchmaking. She wasn't sure whether Ivy intended to evaluate her and Nick or Aidan and Gabi's compatibility, but she wanted no part of it.

"I don't know how to play," Aidan said. "So I should be the one to sit the game out."

Gabi immediately told him it wasn't that hard and Ivy said, "You and I can share a hand, Aidan. The oldster will be on the same team as the youngsters. You and Zoey will be the middle-ster team, Nick. We always bet a penny per point so I hope you brought your wallet."

As happy as Zoey was to hear her aunt in such good spirits, she was still reluctant. "Aidan will get the gist of it after a couple practice rounds. Then you and Gabi can be a team, Aunt Ivy—women against men. I've got other things to do."

Ivy looked her squarely in the eye and Zoey understood her undertone when she said, "It's only a game. It's not a lifelong commitment."

"Zo-ey. Zo-ey. Zo-ey." Nick drummed the table with each syllable, and Aidan and Gabi joined his chant.

"Stop ganging up on me," Zoey whined, covering her ears. Which only made them chant louder, until she finally conceded, "All right, all right. I'll play. But only if you make it worth my while… a *dime* per point."

"Now you're talking." Ivy beamed. "This is going to be fun. Trust me, you won't regret it."

CHAPTER SIX

If only we hadn't played so many games of cribbage, Aidan might have had time to put the screens in my windows and I wouldn't be so hot I can't sleep. But even as she kicked the sheet off her legs, Zoey knew the heat wasn't the real reason for her insomnia; it was because her mind was whirling with uncertainty and mixed emotions. So she lay awake, staring at the ceiling and trying to get some perspective on everything that had happened that day.

She smiled when she thought about how she and Nick had won at cribbage three times in a row. Then they switched teams and played men against women—or "boys against girls" as Ivy called them. The foursome was so competitive that every time one couple won a game, someone from the other pair insisted on a rematch or a new partner. It was by far the most raucous evening Zoey had ever spent playing cards at her aunt's house and she completely forgot Ivy was likely sizing everyone up for their romantic rapport. But even if she had remembered, she wouldn't have cared because she was having such a good time.

Just after nine o'clock, her aunt had announced she needed to call it a night. "Now that the range isn't off-limits, I'm going to make a cup of tea and drink it in the living room before I amble upstairs to bed." She undoubtedly was planning to gaze at the portrait of Denny, too, as was her evening ritual.

"I'll go up with you in a few minutes," Zoey offered, knowing that her aunt often needed her arm for support and balance.

"No, no. Don't interrupt your game on my account. You kids are getting on like peas and carrots." She shot Zoey a self-satisfied look.

"Yeah, we are, but it's a school night. We should go," Nick said.

He suggested before they left that Aidan should bring the screens down from the attic and store them in the garage so they'd be handy the next time he came over. Gabi volunteered to help so Nick stayed in the kitchen with Zoey.

After counting the change she'd won, she announced, "Two dollars and thirty cents. Not too shabby. A couple more hands and I would've have been able to afford to buy an ice cream cone at Bleecker's tomorrow."

"No, you wouldn't."

Zoey snickered. "You sound awfully sure of yourself for a man who won... how much? Twenty cents?"

"Forty," he admitted. "But I meant you wouldn't be able to buy a cone because Bleecker's doesn't open for the season until Saturday."

Zoey groaned. "That's torture. I've been craving their cranberry ice cream all winter."

Dune Island was home to a commercial, organic cranberry bog. Local restauranteurs and eatery owners added cranberries to everything from lemonade and cocktails to ice cream and hot dogs, as well as in the usual things like stuffing, muffins and juice.

"Choco-cran or van-cran?" Nick used the popular abbreviations for the flavors.

"Choco-cran, of course."

He hung his head, shaking it sadly. "Just when I was starting to like you…"

"You were only *just* starting to like me?" Zoey feigned haughtiness. "Kind of slow, aren't you?"

"Why, when did *you* start to like *me*?" Nick's tone was light but his eyes were intense and Zoey felt startlingly self-conscious beneath his gaze.

"Mm… I'll let you know when that happens," she teased, breaking the spell.

"Ouch." He slapped a hand over his heart as if he'd been shot. "That hurts because it's true."

She laughed and said, "Nah, I'm just kidding."

"Seriously though, we'll have to go to Bleecker's on opening day. You know they have a tradition of giving the first hundred customers an extra scoop for free, don't you?"

"That's cool." Zoey's answer had been deliberately noncommittal. And now as she lay in bed, she pondered if he'd been suggesting all five of them should go? Or just him and her? As friends or on a date? She couldn't decide how she felt about the prospect of going out with Nick.

On one hand, if her relationship with Erik had taught Zoey anything, it was that she could have saved herself—and her retirement fund—a world of hurt if only she had paid attention to the warning signs when they first cropped up. Although Nick was growing on her now, the fact that she'd started out with qualms about him, due to his friendship with Mark, was not a good sign. And emotionally, she still wasn't ready to start dating.

On the other hand, as Ivy suggested, it wasn't as if Zoey needed to make a lifelong commitment. And her best friend Lauren certainly would have been thrilled for her if she had a casual summer fling. After such a difficult couple of weeks—such a difficult *winter*—hanging out with Nick tonight had been a pleasant diversion from the things that had been occupying her time and thoughts. Zoey wouldn't mind repeating the experience.

The more she got to know him, the more she doubted that Nick's interest in her aunt—and in her aunt's house—was solely motivated by financial gain. Now that Mark was off the island and Zoey didn't feel quite so uptight, she could better appreciate the ways Nick demonstrated real fondness for Ivy. Like by coming to Sylvia's funeral. Or by not pushing her to remodel the kitchen. Even by helping her out of her chair or laughing at her jokes. Maybe the two things were both true: he *was* fond of Ivy *and* he wanted to profit financially from whatever renovation projects Mark convinced her she needed to do.

In any case, since he hadn't explicitly asked her out, not even for an ice cream cone, Zoey figured she was getting ahead of herself, and she didn't have to decide tonight whether to say yes or no. Obviously, Aidan hadn't asked Gabi out, either, but that didn't stop Zoey from worrying that a romance would develop between them.

She could tell by her niece's giddy behavior that the evening had provided as much levity for Gabi as it had provided for her. She desperately wanted the young girl to be happy here. To feel stronger and more serene than when she'd arrived on Dune Island, just as Zoey always had. Which was exactly why she was concerned about the two teenagers becoming more than friends.

Granted, Zoey's impression of Aidan was that he was well-mannered, diligent and smart. She couldn't imagine many other guys his age who'd be so content to spend an evening playing cards with his dad and the elderly lady they worked for, even if it also meant he got to be around a pretty, winsome girl like Gabi. So there was nothing about him in particular that gave Zoey pause.

Her hesitation was that Gabi was sensitive, easily influenced and had a tendency to be a people-pleaser. Plus, her birthday was in August, which meant she was one of the younger students in the ninth grade. Although in some ways she was mature for a girl who wasn't quite fifteen, she was still nearly three years younger than Aidan, who mentioned he'd turn eighteen in October. At those ages, a few years made a big difference. And Gabi had already demonstrated, through her antics with her father's car, that she didn't exercise good judgment when she was involved with a boy. Zoey wanted to prevent her from making any more mistakes like the kind she'd made at home, as well as from getting her feelings hurt.

I've already hurt her feelings enough myself, she lamented, recalling their conversation on the beach. Although she'd been trying to model openness, Zoey regretted ever telling Gabi about her financial situation. She hadn't expected her disclosure to affect her niece the way it did. Inwardly, she resolved to be more careful about what she shared. She wondered how often Gabi worried about her father's and Kathleen's problems, too. *I'm glad she has some distance from them right now. I hope the longer she's here, the freer she feels.*

Still sleepless, Zoey reluctantly contemplated Gabi's theory about Sylvia and Mr. Witherell. She would have preferred to dismiss it out of hand, but that was the problem with gossip: once the seed was planted, it took root, no matter how inane it was.

One thing Zoey *did* know for certain was that it would have been completely out of character for her aunt to execute a scheme like the one Gabi suggested. Sylvia was too kind and frankly, too mild-mannered. Zoey couldn't imagine her plotting to deceive anyone—especially not Ivy, who loved her like a sister. Furthermore, Ivy often described how tender Sylvia had been to Marcus, patiently nursing him through bout after bout of illness. From her own experience, Zoey understood how much love and compassion that must have taken. No, Sylvia hadn't married Marcus for his money—Zoey was sure of that.

However, she kept thinking about the curious exchange Mr. Witherell had with Mark at the funeral. She was still 99.9 percent confident that Mr. Witherell had been trying to rile her cousin in retaliation for his arrogance. But if Zoey allowed herself to entertain Gabi's theory—as implausible as it was—that Mr. Witherell was Marcus Jr.'s father, then his comment to his "grandson" made a *bit* more sense.

If he was able to hear Mark's rude jab about quitting tobacco, then he might have been able to hear him bragging to his friends that one day he'd inherit the house, she speculated. According to Gabi's classmates, Mr. Witherell resented being shut out of Sylvia's and the baby's lives. If that was true, it might explain why he'd want to take Mark down a notch. To let him know that carrying the Winslow name didn't necessarily make him a Winslow. Maybe after keeping his son's paternity a secret all his life, Mr. Witherell felt more at liberty to disclose it after Sylvia died.

"That's absurd," Zoey said aloud.

And yet… what about the fact that her aunt delivered Marcus Jr. more than a month early? She'd never heard any stories about him being underweight. One explanation for that *could* have been that she was pregnant before she got married. According to Ivy, whenever she and her sister-in-law went shopping or out to the bank, all the men vied for her attention. What if Mr. Witherell had been one of them? Sylvia and Marcus had had a very short courtship. It was entirely possible that on the day they wed, she wouldn't have known for certain that she was already pregnant by someone she'd dated earlier—or pregnant by Marcus, for that matter. *Maybe Marcus Jr.'s paternity was always a question in her mind,* Zoey hypothesized. *In Mr. Witherell's mind, too.* After all, he didn't tell Mark he absolutely *wasn't* Marcus Winslow III. He only said he wouldn't be too sure of that.

Which brought Zoey to her cousin's reaction—rather, to his *over*-reaction—to Mr. Witherell's remark. Not only had he harangued the old man long after he'd hobbled out of view, but he'd instructed Gabi to cross the street if she saw him, too. It was understandable that Mark didn't appreciate what he'd said, but why not shrug it off? And why go to the lengths of telling his young cousin to avoid him? Was he afraid of what she might find out once they started talking? *It makes me even more sure that when Mark attended school here, he heard the same rumors Gabi heard—but it seems as if he's not entirely sure they're baseless.*

Zoey bolted upright in bed. *Could Mr. Witherell's remark have anything to do with what Mark was looking for in the attic? Was he searching for proof of his father's paternity?*

Down the hall, a door creaked. Zoey froze, her skin prickling. But it was only Moby, making his rounds. Her reaction to the eerie noise reminded her that she was letting her imagination run wild about Mr. Witherell being Marcus Jr.'s father. It was understandable why Gabi would believe the rumor; she was a gullible teenager who wanted Zoey to inherit their aunt's home. And it was equally understandable why Marcus would fear that kind of gossip; he was a money-grubber who imagined his inheritance was at stake. But Zoey knew the possibility that Mr. Witherell was Marcus Jr.'s father was infinitesimal at best. And as she'd told her niece, there was no way she was going to bring up the topic with him or with Ivy, anyway. *So I might as well put the idea out of my mind*, she thought, before falling back against the pillow and going to sleep at last.

*

"Guess what?" Zoey excitedly asked Gabi the following Friday. She had just finished running a three-mile loop around Benjamin's Manor, ending at Rose Beach where she met her niece after school. It had become her daily afternoon ritual, since that's when Ivy was napping.

"My dad called?"

Ack. Why don't I think before I speak? "No, sorry. Nothing as exciting as that."

"Oh."

"I'm sure he'll call as soon as he can. Kathleen told me the center discourages the patients from—" She interrupted herself mid-sentence, unsure whether 'patients' was the right word. "I don't know what they call the people who are in a recovery program, do you?"

"Drunks." Gabi's tone was decidedly sarcastic. Since she'd arrived on Dune Island, she'd said very little about her father, causing Zoey to suspect she was angry at him. The edge in her niece's voice now confirmed her suspicions. Zoey didn't blame her, but she wasn't going to refer to Scott that way herself.

"Kathleen said your dad isn't allowed to make phone calls for couple of weeks."

"Why? Did she take away *his* phone, too?"

"No. It's one of the rules at the cen—" Zoey started to say until she realized Gabi was being sarcastic again. That wasn't like her. Had she had another argument with Kathleen? Was there a problem at school? "Is something bothering you?"

Gabi shook her head. "What were you going to tell me?"

Zoey's excitement had flagged, but she said, "This morning I got a call about a librarian position I applied for. I have an interview in Providence a week from Monday."

"Providence?"

"Yeah, but if I get the job, it doesn't start until late August. So you don't have to worry about moving and enrolling in a new school again."

Finally, a smile on Gabi's face. "Good, because I think I'm going to join the band."

"Hey, that's great!" Zoey had been hoping she'd start playing her flute again but she didn't want to nag her so she hadn't said anything.

"Yeah, but we'll have practice after school and I'm not sure how long it lasts, so… I'm probably not going to be able to meet you here any more."

"That's fine. You never want to go in swimming anyway," Zoey teased. Most people considered the water and weather still too cold for swimming, but she didn't. Every day she'd suggest they zip home, change their clothes, and then return to the beach to take a dip. And every day, Gabi refused.

"You sure you're okay with that? I mean, with me not coming home right after school?"

Would Kathleen and Scott have objected? Gabi was so motivated to excel academically that Zoey didn't see any reason not to let her manage her own schedule. "Of course I'm fine with it. I know you'll keep up with your school work. Just call us if you're going to be late for supper or you need a ride." Zoey stopped walking and held up her index finger. "Hey, I have an idea! If this is going to be your last free afternoon for a while, why don't we zip home and change and then come back here for a dip?"

"That's original," Gabi said drolly. "I'll give you two guesses what my answer is."

"But it's so refreshing. Feel." Zoey bent beside the nearby tidal pool and tossed a scoop of water at her niece, lightly spraying the side of her head, arm and leg.

"Aunt Zoey—quit it!" Gabi kicked water back at Zoey, splattering her with wet sand, too. When Zoey retaliated, Gabi shrieked, "No, don't! I've got my laptop in my book bag. It'll get ruined."

Brushing the sand off her T-shirt, Zoey said, "I might as well go in now. It's easier just to rinse off."

"You're wearing a suit under your clothes?"

"Yes, my *birthday* suit."

"Aunt Zoey, you wouldn't!"

Actually, she would have. And she *had,* on various occasions. But not at a public beach and not when the tide was so far out that she'd have to run naked for a hundred yards before she could fully immerse herself. "No, I won't. But I've got a sports bra on. With my underwear, it'll look like I'm wearing a two-piece suit."

What if a park ranger sees you? You're going to get a ticket."

Zoey was already stripping her leggings off but she decided to leave her T-shirt on since she had to get the sand off it anyway. "Why? This covers more than what most people wear to the beach."

Gabi kept marching, calling over her shoulder, "I'm going home."

Whose daughter are you, anyway? Zoey thought but she was glad she had the presence of mind to censor herself. Whenever Jessica wanted to go swimming or bodysurfing, she'd never let a little thing like the lack of a swimsuit stop her.

Zoey waded in as deep as her waist. She stretched her arms out to the side and rested her palms on the water as if it were glass. Her eyes fixed on the horizon, she savored the stillness of the moment as her body adjusted to the chilly water. Then, on the count of three, she took a deep breath and dove in. Her sister once said that coming up from the first plunge of the season was like being born. Zoey understood what she'd meant; she felt newer, if not younger, when she surfaced.

"Wah-hoo!" she shouted at the sky as she stood, tipped her head and slicked back her hair.

She took a few more steps, dove again, and kept swimming, submerged, until she ran out of breath. Then she rolled onto her back and floated, her eyes closed as she let her mind wander to her sister's last trip to Dune Island six years ago, when Gabi was eight.

The doctor had cautioned Jess about going in the water—something about marine illness or infection and her having a compromised immune system. But she had wanted to take one last look at the bay from her favorite vantage point, a secluded little spot between two low dunes overgrown with roses and honeysuckle, about half a mile south of Rose Beach.

Jess had been so weak she'd barely walked a fraction of the distance before she needed to rest. Scott had wanted to turn around but Jessica said she wasn't leaving until she saw what she'd come to see. So Zoey had unfolded the beach chair she'd brought for her sister and as the adults waited until Jessica felt strong enough to keep going, Gabi searched the high-tide line nearby for beach glass and other treasures. When Jessica was ready, Scott picked up the cooler with one hand and supported his wife with his opposite arm, while Gabi ran up ahead and Zoey trailed behind, carrying the chair, towels and a beach blanket. The foursome would continue their expedition until Jess got tired again and then they'd stop and repeat the process.

When they'd finally reached their destination, Jessica put the seat of her chair into a reclining position and within a few minutes she had closed her eyes, although she wasn't sleeping. Scott had been incredulous that after insisting she needed to see the view, she barely looked at it. But Zoey had understood; her sister was breathing it all in. Memorizing it, just like she did every summer when it was almost time to leave Dune Island.

Even though it was May at the time, it had been unseasonably humid and eventually Jessica announced she was going to wade into the water to cool off.

"Dr. Freedman said you shouldn't," her husband had lectured. "It's dangerous. Your skin is cracked. You could come into contact with algae or bacteria and get an infection."

"Yeah, but I'm dying to go in." Jessica had giggled at her own glibly dark humor, but Scott stormed off, calling for Gabi to accompany him down the beach. Jessica had turned to her sister. "Could you give me a hand?"

"You sure about this?"

"I'm positive. It's hot out and I'm getting uncomfortable."

So Zoey had helped her up from the chair and held her steady while she took off her jeans. By then, Jess was so skinny she didn't even need to unzip them; one tug and they slid down her legs. And when Zoey had wrapped her arm around her sister's waist to support her as they walked, she could feel her sharp hip bone beneath the fabric of her over-sized shirt.

The tide had been only halfway in, so they'd treaded across the flats and passed through several shin-deep tidal pools before they entered the actual surf. Even then, it took a while for them to wade deep enough for the water to reach their midriffs. The bay had been calm that day, but its tiny swells made Jessica teeter as they lapped against her stomach. And yet, after a few moments, she'd said, "You can let go now. I want to go under."

"No, Jess. It's too cold. It'll be too much of a shock your system and—"

"Zoey, let me go. I'll be fine."

"*I* won't be." Zoey had begun sobbing because by then everything seemed like a metaphor for her sister's death.

Fearless to the very end, Jessica had threatened, "Don't you dare ruin this for me. Stop bawling and let go. *Now.*"

So Zoey had released her and Jessica pitched herself forward, disappearing beneath the water for what seemed like an eternity. Zoey held her breath until her sister's head popped up some thirty feet farther out. Gasping and blinking, Jessica looked stunned when she turned to face her.

Zoey rushed forward, running through the water instead of swimming. "Are you okay?"

"I'm *alive*!" her sister had shouted—or she tried to, her voice was more of a squawk—and raised one hand over her head, exultant.

When Zoey dove toward her, she kept her eyes open so if Jessica told her to stop bawling again, she could say her tears were from the salt water. When she swam within sight of her sister's bright, skinny legs, she had emerged and declared, "I'm alive, too!"

"You are *such* a copycat." Jessica flicked a few droplets at her, clearly trying to keep the mood light. "Just like when we were kids."

"That's because I've always admired you. I—"

"Knock it off, Zo. It's not time for my eulogy yet." Jessica's no-nonsense tone indicated she meant business.

Zoey wiped her eyes with the back of her hand, which made them sting even worse. "Did you know—"

"I mean it. Not another word."

"Stop being so bossy. And so vain. I wasn't going to say any more nice things about you," Zoey retorted. "I was only going to ask if you knew you lost your headscarf when you went under."

Jessica reflexively patted her skull. "Something felt different but I thought I was just lightheaded from holding my breath."

"It came off over there. I'll go find it."

"No, don't. I hate that thing."

"But your scalp might get sunburned."

"Good. I've always wanted to be a redhead. Come on, let's float."

Jessica had gingerly lain back on the water as if onto a bed, but she was all bones, no body fat, and she immediately began to sink. This, too, struck her as funny, but Zoey had to force a laugh as she took her arm and they began their long trek back. Every few yards, Jessica would pause and Zoey couldn't tell whether she was winded or if she didn't want to get out yet.

When they'd made it to where the water was knee-deep, Jessica pointed to her husband and daughter down the beach. "He's really going to be lost."

Even though Scott had a notoriously poor sense of direction, Zoey doubted it was possible he'd lose his way back. "All he has to do is follow the shoreline. Or follow Gabi."

"No. He's not going to *get* lost. He's going to *be* lost. When I die."

"Now *you* knock it off," Zoey rasped.

"Wait, you have to hear me out on this. Scott is… he's the love of my life. Everything I could have hoped to have in a husband. But I know his faults. His weaknesses. He's going to be an absolute disaster when I'm gone. I'm not asking you to take care of him or to set him straight or anything like that. I'm only telling you what to expect, so you'll cut him a little slack when he screws up or does something stupid… like marrying someone I'd detest." Jessica had laughed but Zoey couldn't even fake a smile. Her sister's voice was wheezy as she continued, "I'm only kidding. I want him to be happy and I think he's better off married than on his own. The most important thing is that he always puts our daughter's well-being first. That's what matters to me more than anything else. Understand?"

Zoey had understood. Jessica meant she could accept Scott remarrying as long as his new wife was a good stepmom for Gabi. She'd nodded, not trusting herself to speak.

"Scott's the love of my life, but Gabi, Gabi's my heart. And I know I don't even need to ask you to remind her how much I love her. Or to tell her what I was like. I already know you'll do that. Just like I know she'll always be able to turn to you if…"

Jessica couldn't finish her sentence because her teeth were knocking together and Zoey had noticed her lips were bluish. She let go of her waist and hugged her shivering upper torso sideways with both arms, trying to warm her.

"Of course she will, Jess," she had whispered into her sister's ear. "But don't talk about that right now. Concentrate on walking. Only a little farther and we'll be out of the water. Then you can sit down and I'll run and get you a towel."

She tried to sound confident but inside she was panicking. If her sister had hypothermia, Zoey would never forgive herself. Scott wouldn't forgive her, either.

They barely made it to dry ground when Zoey noticed Scott and Gabi were also heading back from the opposite direction. She beckoned him, yelling, "Jess is freezing!"

Scott broke into a sprint toward where they'd left their things spread on the beach. Shouting at Gabi to stay put, he grabbed the blanket instead of a towel and raced across the sand faster than she'd ever seen him move. When he reached them, he peeled off his T-shirt and replaced Jessica's with his before cocooning her in the blanket and gathering her to his chest. Zoey expected him to be livid but instead he hummed and softly caressed his wife's back, as if they were slow-dancing to their favorite song.

After a few minutes, when Jessica stopped quaking, he kissed the top of her white, baby-bald head and casually asked, "How was your swim, hon?"

"It was *awesome*," she croaked, peering up at him.

"Good. I'm glad."

Then he had picked her up and carried her back to the car. When Zoey and Gabi arrived some fifteen minutes later, the heat was blasting and the windows were rolled up. Scott had been dripping with sweat but he and Jessica were laughing about who knows what.

"Hey, Zoey…" His voice was a growl when she got into the car.

Uh-oh. Here it comes, she thought. *He can't get mad at Jess because she's sick but he's going to light into me for helping her go swimming.* She just hoped his rant wouldn't upset Gabi. "Yeah?"

"If I knew you were going to take so long, I would have carried the cooler myself. Pass me a sandwich, would you? I'm starving."

He never did chew her out. And because of that—more than because of anything Jessica said about cutting him some slack—Zoey had always known she couldn't hold it against him when he made errors in judgment, either.

Thinking about Scott now, floating in the same bay where her sister had her very last dip in the ocean she'd loved so much, she decided, *When I get back to the house, I should write him a note to tell him how well Gabi is doing.* At least, she *hoped* Gabi was doing as well as she seemed to be.

But first, Zoey dove and swam and floated until her toes and fingers were numb and goosebumps rose all over her skin. Quivering as she got out of the water and retrieved her leggings, she couldn't imagine ever complaining about being too warm again.

*

The next morning Zoey woke to what she immediately recognized as the aroma of freshly baked cinnamon raisin sticky buns. *Aunt Ivy is already awake and making breakfast?* That could only mean one thing: Mark was coming for a visit. Maybe he was already here. Zoey wondered why her aunt hadn't given her a heads-up.

I can't believe he's coming back so soon, she thought. Not that she should have been surprised; Mark had called Ivy three times during the past week, a record. The calls lasted close to half an hour on each, yet whenever Zoey happened to pass the living room, she didn't hear her aunt saying anything other than the occasional "Mm-hm." Clearly Mark had been doing all the talking.

One time after hanging up, Ivy told her he'd called to ask if the new stove had been delivered yet, since it hadn't arrived according to schedule. Another time, he supposedly just wanted to see how she was doing. Zoey found that hard to swallow. She suspected Mark's real reason for calling—and for visiting—was more self-serving. Like maybe he was still trying to persuade their aunt that she should purchase a new fridge. Or he could have been laying the groundwork to ask her for something else he wanted. *I just hope he hasn't been talking to her about moving into an assisted living facility again*, Zoey thought.

She pulled on a pair of running capris and a T-shirt and stepped into the hall. Gabi's door was open, but she wasn't in her room so Zoey went downstairs to the kitchen, greeting her aunt as she poured herself three-fourths of a cup of coffee. Ivy and Sylvia had used the same kind of electric percolator ever since they began drinking coffee. Zoey's dad used to complain to her mom that for being such a meek woman, Sylvia made the strongest coffee he'd ever had the misfortune to taste. Ivy had gotten used to making it that way, too, so Zoey added a generous splash of cream to her mug. It occurred to her that the only thing she really missed about her townhome was her single-serve coffee maker.

"Those buns smell delicious. I can't believe you and Gabi are both up and at 'em earlier than I am. Did she go somewhere?"

"Yes. She went for a long walk and on the way home she's picking up more eggs for my frittata. She's been gone for quite some time so I expect her back any minute now."

"Can I help with anything? Would you like me to set the table?"

"No, I'll do that. But I'd appreciate it if you'd bring the croquet set down from the attic. After brunch, you kids might want to have a game to pass the time."

I'll help get breakfast ready for Mark, but I am not *entertaining him until his friends are available to go to the club*, Zoey thought. "Sure, I'll bring it down, although I doubt I'll play. When Gabi gets back, I'm going for a run and then I plan to do some research about the library in preparation for my interview. What time is Mark getting here, anyway?"

"Mark's coming?" Ivy had been bending over to peer into the refrigerator. She stood up, a baffled look on her face. "I must have forgotten."

Feeling sheepish that she'd made the wrong assumption, Zoey rushed to clarify. "No, you didn't, Aunt Ivy. I just smelled the sticky buns and thought you were making them because Mark was coming for a visit."

Relief melted the frown from Ivy's face. "No, I'm making breakfast in commemoration of it being the last time I'll use this oven before they haul it away."

"The new one is being delivered today?"

"Yes. Some time between ten and twelve. That's why Nick and Aidan are coming for brunch. They're going to install it right away." Ivy bent over again and removed a container of feta cheese from the shelf. She closed the fridge door. "I thought I mentioned it to you."

She definitely hadn't. "I would have remembered that."

"Ack. I'm sorry. It must have slipped my mind." Ivy wasn't looking at Zoey, but her voice didn't carry any note of the consternation that crossed her face when she thought she'd forgotten Mark was coming. "You'd better hurry and go bring the croquet set down so you'll have time to change your clothes before breakfast."

Now I know where Mark gets his sneakiness from! Zoey grumbled to herself, recognizing that her aunt was pushing her and Nick together. She took a sip of coffee before setting down her mug and, although she had zero desire to play croquet, headed upstairs to the attic.

Zoey had always been jumpy in the presence of insects and spiders—it was why she refused to keep the windows open unless the screens were in. But Carla vacuumed, dusted and aired out the large, rectangular attic space whenever she did a deep cleaning of Ivy's entire house, so Zoey didn't mind going up there. She usually only passed through to get to the widow's walk, accessed up a ladder through a trap door in the middle of the roof, in-between the two chimneys. It wasn't as hot today as it was during the summer, when the rising heat made it uncomfortable, but it was definitely warm, so Zoey intended to be quick.

She climbed the attic stairs, switched on the light and glanced across the empty room in the direction of the storage shelves and Sylvia's trunks. She immediately recognized the blue linen fabric draped askew over the top of one of the trunks: the dress Marcus had bought Sylvia to wear on her wedding day. *Mark must have left it there. He's such a slob.*

Unlike Ivy, Sylvia had rarely spoken about her courtship or relationship with her husband. But one rainy afternoon when Jessica and Zoey were teenagers, she'd invited them to see her wedding dress. After she removed the wasp-waisted, full-skirted frock from its garment bag, they urged her to hold it up in front of her so they could picture how she had looked in it, since the only wedding photos they'd seen were black and white. Zoey had never forgotten how Sylvia's entire demeanor changed. With one hand clasping the fabric to her stomach, the other hand pressing it against her shoulder, she elongated her neck and held her chin high as she took a little twirl. It was so unlike her that the girls had squealed with laughter.

"You look beautiful," Zoey had told her.

"Yeah, you do. When I get married, I'm going to wear a blue dress, too," Jessica decided. "Not some ridiculous foofy white gown."

Compliments, especially about her appearance, always seemed to embarrass Sylvia, who dropped her chin and quickly put the dress away again. Even at that young age, Zoey recognized that her aunt cherished the dress because it was a symbol of how much Marcus had cherished *her*. It incensed Zoey that Mark had flung it aside in his quest to find whatever he'd been looking for. *He has no regard for his grandmother's past*, she seethed.

Suddenly, she recalled the nonsensical comment her aunt had made the day she died. *It will be our secret... for now it's best to let the past stay buried in the past... beneath the roses.* It had been such a peculiar thing to say, so she had assumed her aunt hadn't been aware of her remark. She still believed that was the case, but she questioned whether Sylvia happened to babble the same sentiment in front of Mark. *That could have been why he was so interested in searching her trunks, since they contain the only remnants from her past*, she thought. It certainly would have made a lot more sense if he'd been motivated to go through Sylvia's things because of something *she'd* said than because of anything Mr. Witherell had said the day of the funeral, as Zoey had been mulling a couple of nights ago as she struggled to sleep. Either way, she didn't want to waste any more time pondering it—she needed to get downstairs to change or else Nick was going to think all she owned was running clothes. *Not* that she cared. Not really.

She picked up Sylvia's dress and opened the trunk. The small boxes inside were piled every which way, but at least the trunk wasn't very large, so it was easier to straighten than Sylvia's room—Zoey had spent an hour rehanging and refolding her aunt's clothes after Mark had searched it the other week—and it didn't take her more than a few minutes to restack the boxes. She carefully placed the dress into its garment bag, laid it on top of the boxes and shut the lid of the trunk.

As she pulled the croquet tote from the wire rack, its contents shifted to the opposite end. Someone—Mark?—must not have zipped it all the way shut because a ball popped out and rolled to the edge of the room.

Fantastic. Zoey crouched down and inched across the plywood beneath the most sloped section of the roof. She retrieved the ball from where it had come to rest atop of the insulation that was overflowing the wall cavity and turned around. She'd almost made it back to the solid floor boards again when she felt something crawling across her neck.

"Eww!" she screamed, brushing it off. A large dark spider dropped to the floor and scurried away, unharmed. Zoey wasn't as fortunate. Her erratic movement caused the plywood to shift sideways and her leg to slip between two joists. Although she managed to boost herself upward and narrowly avoid crashing through the ceiling of the room below, her left calf grazed the thick and ragged wood.

As she lay sprawled on her stomach—amazingly, still clutching the croquet ball—it occurred to her the spider might still be close by. She rolled onto her back on the solid flooring and sat up. But when she tried to stand, a searing pain shot through her lower leg and she reflexively plopped down on her backside again. Given how much her leg hurt, she expected to see a lot of blood where she'd scraped her calf against the joist, but there was only one small blob. When she bent to examine it closer, she understood why: it was a puncture wound, not a scrape, and above the wound she felt a hard line.

Aware that a sizable sliver of wood was embedded in her flesh, she felt queasy as she tried to figure out what to do next. She couldn't walk on her leg unassisted, but Gabi wasn't home to support her. If she shouted for help, her aunt would be alarmed and she might rush up the stairs and suffer from chest pain. Then how would Zoey help *her?*

Using her hands and the heel of her good leg, she inched toward the staircase on her rear end, but the effort and movement intensified her pain, so she gave up. *I'll just have to wait until Gabi gets back and comes upstairs to look for me… If she comes to look for me,* Zoey thought, feeling sorry for herself.

She stretched her left, injured leg flat and hugged her right knee to her chest as she kept watch for any more spiders. The day must have been shaping up to be unseasonably warm again because a rivulet of sweat trickled down Zoey's face along her hairline. Within another ten minutes, her T-shirt was sticking to her back. She was thinking about how much she wished she had an iced coffee when she heard footsteps on the staircase. "Gabi? Is that you?" she called.

"No, it's me," Nick answered, cresting the staircase. He was wearing a deep indigo short-sleeved Henley that made his eyes appear even bluer and his biceps appear even bigger, if that was possible. Just seeing him looking so pulled together when she was coming unraveled made Zoey wish she had tried harder to make it downstairs on her own. Why did he always have to catch her at her worst possible moments?

He crossed the room and squatted beside her. "Are you okay?"

She knew what he was really wondering was why she was sitting immobile in the middle of the attic floor holding a green croquet ball. But the concern she saw in his eyes—those beautiful eyes—was so heartfelt and it had been so long since anyone had asked her that question that she teared up.

She wanted to answer, *No, I'm not okay. I'm worried about whether I'm doing a good job looking out for my aunt and taking care of my niece. And I'm worried about my finances and about whatever scheme my cousin may be plotting. And lately I miss my sister so much I can hardly breathe.* Instead, she stuttered, "I-I got a splinter."

Understandably, Nick tipped his head as if he couldn't believe something so trivial had nearly reduced her to tears. "A splinter?"

"Yeah, the plywood slipped out from under me and I scraped my calf against an old tattered joist." She turned her leg to the side. "See?"

Nick took one look at the nail-sized hole and his expression went grim. "That's not a splinter in there—it's a two-by-four."

"I know. It really hurts. I couldn't stand up."

"You shouldn't try to. I'll carry you downstairs."

"No." Zoey didn't want him to get that close; she had coffee breath and her back was all sweaty. "Thanks for the offer, but if you give me your arm, I should be able to make it."

Nick pointed to her calf. "Listen, I can barely see the tip of that thing as it is. You don't want to drive it in there any farther. And you really don't want to put pressure on it and snap it in half. So if you insist on walking downstairs on your own two feet, at least let me go get a pair of needle-nose pliers from my toolbox so I can pull the splinter out first."

Nauseated at the thought, Zoey covered her mouth. "I don't think I can handle that," she mumbled between her fingers.

"So you'll let me carry you downstairs?" Nick pleaded, his eyebrows almost touching together.

"Oh, all right," she groaned, but she sounded more reluctant than she felt.

He wrapped one arm around her torso, slid the other beneath her knees and adroitly straightened into a standing position in one smooth motion. And as Zoey rested her cheek against his chest, the thought flashed through her mind that maybe it wasn't such a bad thing that he'd arrived at one of her worst possible moments after all.

CHAPTER SEVEN

"This is all my fault. I never should have sent you up there," Ivy lamented after Nick brought Zoey into the kitchen and she told them the story of what happened.

"No, it's not your fault," Nick objected before Zoey could say anything. "It's my son's fault."

Aidan balked at that. "*My* fault?"

"Yeah, *yours*. I distinctly remember telling you to secure that plywood into place last autumn when you were putting the screens away."

The teenager squinted at his father, as if he'd spoken in a language he didn't comprehend. Then he smacked his forehead. "Oh, yeah! I remember that now. I mean, I remember that you asked me to do it—I don't remember why I didn't. I'm really sorry, Zoey" he said, laughing nervously.

"You think this is a joke, Aidan?" Nick glared at him. "You think it's funny that she got hurt?"

"No, Dad, of course not. I feel terrible about it."

"*You* feel terrible? How do you think Zoey feels? She's just lucky—*you're* just lucky she didn't fall halfway through the ceiling! How would she have felt then?"

Aidan's ears were scarlet and he appeared to be shrinking, Ivy was flustered almost to tears, and Gabi hid beneath her hair as she knelt in front of Zoey, applying antiseptic to her wound. Zoey appreciated why Nick was frustrated with his son for not following through and she didn't want to interfere with his parenting, but she could also see that it was demoralizing for Aidan to be lectured in front of everyone.

"Like a chandelier," she joked, hoping to break the tension. When everyone stared at her, looking stumped, she awkwardly explained, "Nick asked how I would have felt if I fell halfway through the ceiling…"

Gabi got it first. "Good one, Aunt Zoey."

Then Ivy swept her hand through the air. "Oh, you!"

Zoey could tell Aidan was trying not to laugh, but when Nick rolled his eyes and cracked a smile, the boy gave in and chuckled. Zoey winked at him, confessing, "If anyone is to blame for me falling in the attic, it's the ginormous spider living up there."

"Why? Did it trip you?" Gabi asked, loosely fastening an adhesive bandage to her aunt's calf.

"No, smart aleck. It crawled on me and I got creeped out and slipped." Zoey imitated the spider's movement on her skin by tickling her niece's neck, which made Gabi giggle and roll back on her heels.

"There. That should keep the germs away until you get to the ER."

Nick commanded Aidan, "While we're gone, I want you to nail down that plywood *and* put the screens in the windows. Got it?"

Aidan nodded but Zoey protested, "You can't take me to the ER. I might be there for hours. I don't want you wasting half your day waiting around for me. The new range is coming and you guys have to install it."

"They don't have to install it today. We can wait until the next time they're both free," Ivy opened a small purple thermal bag and set something inside it.

"No we can't, Aunt Ivy. The delivery people are taking your old oven away and we won't have anything to cook on," Zoey reminded her. "I'll submit a ride request. Gabi, could you bring me my phone? It's in my room on the—"

Nick cut her off. "No. *I'm* taking you to the ER." Before she knew what was happening, he'd scooped her up again.

I could get used to this, she thought as her aunt looped the handle of the thermal bag over her wrist. "What's in here?"

"Sticky buns and milk. There are napkins in the side pocket," she said. Zoey half expected her aunt to add, *Have fun you two*, as if they were going on a picnic instead of to the hospital, but instead Ivy kissed her cheek and told Nick, "Take good care of her, okay?"

"I will, Mrs. Cartwright," he promised, using her surname as if to show how seriously he meant it.

Before they pulled out of the driveway, Nick said, "I'm sorry for what happened in there. I shouldn't have bawled Aidan out like that—not until we got home, anyway. Sometimes I try so hard to keep him in line that I end up being out of line myself."

"It's okay. Nobody gets it right every time—I know *I* don't," Zoey said. "It might not mean much coming from me, since I'm a novice as far as being responsible for a teenager goes, but Aidan seems like a really good kid—he works hard and he's smart and friendly and well-mannered. A lot of that has to be to your credit."

Nick glanced her way, beaming. "Thanks. That actually means more to me than you know."

As they drove, Zoey asked him what it was like living on the island year-round, saying, "Until this year, I've never stayed here for longer than a week or two in the winter. I've always wondered if the islanders go stir crazy by the time spring comes because they're so isolated."

"A few people get cabin fever, sure, but most of the full-time residents are used to it. Those who can't hack it usually move after the first year," he answered. "I actually prefer the off-season to the summers, when the island gets so crowded. But even then, it's not nearly as crowded as the NYC suburb where I used to live."

Zoey couldn't keep the surprise from her voice. "I thought you were a die-hard islander."

"No. I left here after high school to go to college in upstate New York. Majored in computer science. Graduated. Got married—too young. We moved to the city and lived in a cell of an apartment. I was working for a tech analyst firm, in a cell of an office."

"I sense a theme here."

"You're right about that. But after Aidan was born, we moved into a better place, a house in the suburbs. Which meant I needed to get a better job—actually, the job wasn't better, it was worse in terms of how mismanaged the company was and how many hours they expected us to clock. But the salary was better. I got a lot of my fulfillment from being a husband and especially from being Aidan's dad. And I was happy we could afford to live in a nice, safe area, so it was hardly a sacrifice to work at a job I didn't exactly love.

Unfortunately, Aidan's mother…" Nick cleared his throat. "Anyway, we divorced when he was twelve and two years ago I decided to return to Dune Island to get a fresh start. Or maybe I should say I started over again, since I moved back to my home town and into my parents' house."

"You live with your parents?"

"Ha!" Nick snorted. "No. I inherited their house when my dad died, since my mother passed away about two years before that."

"And Aidan relocated with you? Wow. From NYC to Dune Island is a huge adjustment for a teenager. Gabi's only visiting, but I'm glad that the town she lives in in California is pretty small, otherwise I'd worry about her experiencing culture shock, in addition to all the other changes that come with moving to a new place and starting a new school."

"Yeah, I know what you mean. But Aidan's thriving here. He went through a lot in New York… not because of school, but because of my ex-wife's new husband's drinking. Aidan's found some kids here who have been really helpful to him though. And I enjoy the work I do as a contractor so much more than when I was working in a box for someone else… Anyway, that's my life in a nutshell." He brushed his hand through his hair. "What's yours?"

Zoey told him about her family, how much she loved coming to Dune Island every summer, about getting her masters degree, living in Providence and being a librarian.

After she finished, he asked, "Right now, you don't have—I mean your aunt said you aren't…"

He seemed embarrassed to finish his sentence. Zoey realized her aunt must have mentioned to him she was unemployed, so she confirmed, "No, I don't have a job. The branch I was working in closed in late November. But I have an interview in a week and I'm very hopeful about it."

He pulled his chin back. "You lost your job? I'm sorry to hear that."

"Yeah. Wasn't that what you were about to ask me?"

His face reddened. "Actually, I was going to ask if you were seeing anyone."

"Oh. No, I'm not." Zoey answered absently; all she could think about was how careless she'd been to let it slip that she was unemployed. What if Nick told Mark? She really didn't want him to know. "Please don't mention it to Mark, though."

"You don't want your cousin to know you're not seeing anyone?"

"No. That I'm unemployed."

Nick chuckled. "Okay."

"Seriously, it's important to me."

"I understand and I won't say anything about it."

"Then why were you laughing?"

"Because I hardly ever talk to him anyway and when I do, it's not about anything personal, like our families."

"You guys aren't old friends from high school?"

"I suppose some people might refer to us as old, but I wouldn't call us *friends.* In fact, when we were in our final semester, senior year…" He shook his head. "Nah, never mind."

Zoey *had* to hear this. "Go on, say it."

"We both liked the same girl. Amber Grant. And we both asked her to the prom."

Nick had the same taste in girlfriends as Mark did? That wasn't a good sign. "Which one of you did she choose?"

"Neither. She went with Brent Harris."

"Smart girl."

Nick laughed—Zoey liked that about him; he could take a joke. "Yeah. And we were stupid boys."

"Why, what did you do?"

He coughed into his fist. "I'm not admitting to anything on the record. But I will say before either of us found out Amber had already agreed to go to the prom with Brent, we may or may not have had a shoving match that got a little rough. And there may or may not have been some after-school detention involved.

"And by 'may or may not,' you mean 'definitely,' don't you?"

"*Definitely*. As I said, we were stupid boys. We were idiots." He shook his head. "But please don't tell your aunt."

"Why? Are you afraid the next time Mark comes here, she'll ground him?" Zoey teased.

"No, I'm afraid she'll fire *me*."

Zoey giggled. "Nah, at worst she'll forbid her nieces to hang out with '*those incorrigible Armstrong boys.*'"

"Hey, just so you know, your cousin threw the first punch."

"I thought it was a *shoving* match."

"It was. But as I said, things got out of hand."

Zoey understood how that could have happened since Mark was involved. The fact that Nick wasn't actually friends with her cousin came as a relief but there was still something she needed to address.

"I want to ask you a favor, and I'm being serious, okay?" After he nodded, Zoey said, "I know your intentions are good and I can appreciate that until recently, you didn't know me. But the next time something concerns you about Aunt Ivy or about her house, could you please let me know, instead of Mark? Or if you've already made an agreement to tell him first, could you let me know in addition to him?"

"What are you talking about? I don't have any concerns about your aunt and if I notice anything that needs to be fixed in her house, she's the one I talk to about it. I don't involve *anyone* else in repair or renovation decisions unless a homeowner has specifically requested me to. That's not the way I do business."

They had pulled up to a stoplight in front of the hospital and Nick looked over at her, his eyes lit with indignation, his mouth a harsh line. Either he was telling the truth or he was an even better actor than Erik had been. Zoey had to be absolutely sure which one it was.

"Mark doesn't check in with you about my aunt?"

"What? Of course not! Like I said, I hardly ever speak to him. And I certainly wouldn't ever *spy* on a client on behalf of her family members."

"You didn't tell him about Aunt Ivy leaving the gas on?"

Zoey could practically see the lightbulb going on above his head when he remembered. "Yeah. I did. But only because he happened to call right in the middle of the incident." Nick explained that even though the fumes were negligible, in an abundance of caution he brought Ivy to Sylvia's room, opened all the windows and closed her door. Sylvia was too weak to get out of bed or leave the house and he didn't want either woman to feel nauseated from the smell. Which meant Ivy wasn't available downstairs to answer the landline when Mark called.

"It kept ringing and I thought there might be an emergency, so I picked up and told Mark that she'd have to call him back later.

Understandably, he wanted to know what was going on. I gave him the bare facts, that's it. The only other times I've spoken to him lately have either been when I came to Sylvia's funeral or when we discussed the kitchen remodel and the stove—and I had Ivy's approval to do that that."

Zoey swallowed. "I'm sorry. I misunderstood something he told me." Nick blinked a couple of times but didn't say anything in response, so she feebly joked, "Didn't I warn you I was hypervigilant when it comes to my family?"

Someone behind them honked to indicate the light had turned green, so Nick pulled forward into the hospital parking lot, slowing as they approached the ER department entrance. He put the transmission into park. "I'll go get you a wheelchair."

"Why? Are your arms too tired to carry me the rest of the way?" she chaffed him, but he got out of the truck without laughing. Without even smiling. Her heart dropped two ribs lower in her chest, heavy with regret for insulting him. She intended to apologize again as soon as he returned, but a medical assistant came with him, pushing a wheelchair.

Nick helped transfer her from his truck into the chair so the assistant could wheel her inside. "Good luck," he said curtly before leaving to find a parking space.

The nurse brought Zoey into an exam room and took her medical history but it was another thirty minutes before the physician came in. He had a mop of dark ringlets, tanned forearms and bright blue eyes, although they weren't as pretty as Nick's—not that Zoey was comparing. No surprise, he wore a wedding band.

"Hello, Ms. Jansen. I'm Dr. Socorro. Sorry for the wait. I'm actually an ER pediatrician but we're short-staffed today," he explained.

"When they paged me to cover a shift, I was surfing, so if you smell something fishy, it's me."

"I'm glad there's someone else on this island who doesn't think it's too early in the season to go swimming."

"It's never too early. Never too late, either." The skin around his eyes crinkled when he grinned. Zoey had become glummer and glummer about Nick the longer she'd been waiting but the doctor had such a magnetic personality she couldn't help but chuckle. "So, tell me how you got your owie—sorry, force of habit. Tell me about your injury."

After she explained, Dr. Socorro removed the three-inch splinter with an instrument that actually looked a lot like a carpenter's pair of pliers—but unlike Nick could have done, he numbed the area, first. Before he left he gave her the contact info of a doctor who could do a wound check and said he'd give her printed information about how to keep the area clean.

"It should heal up nicely," he assured her. "I think the worst part of this accident is that it's going to prevent you from going swimming for a few days."

No, the worst part of my accident is that I've messed up the… the friendship I was just starting to form with Nick, Zoey thought.

It took a while for the nurse to bring her the necessary paperwork and when she ambled into the waiting lounge some fifteen minutes later, she saw Nick before he saw her. Sitting in the chair nearest the exit, he was resting his forearms on his thighs and gazing down as he swung the purple thermal bag back and forth like a metronome in the open space between his knees. *He must be so bored*, Zoey thought. *How many other guys would wait this long in an ER for someone they hardly know?*

He didn't notice her until she lowered herself onto the chair beside him and said, "Hi, Nick."

He sat up straight and swiveled his head to look at her. "All done?"

"Yeah. Sorry it took so long. Thanks for waiting."

"What else was I going to do? Make you take the bus home?"

"After what I said to you about my aunt, I wouldn't have blamed you if you did… I really jumped to an unfair assumption, but it wasn't because of you. It was because of me. Because I took something my cousin said the wrong way and I have this fear that…" Zoey didn't know how to explain her error without telling Nick that she was concerned Mark was trying to take over their aunt's house—and she didn't think it was appropriate to go into all of that with him. So she just said, "I'm really sorry I insulted you and I hope you'll forgive me."

For an agonizing moment, Nick rubbed his forehead before responding. "It's okay. I get it. Family dynamics can affect a person's perspective in strange ways." He handed her the thermal bag. "But I did eat both of the cinnamon rolls your aunt packed for us while I was waiting—I figured you owed me that much. I drank the milk, too."

Zoey threw back her head and laughed. "Were they as good as they smelled?"

"Better." Then he stood up and offered her his arm. She didn't refuse it, even though her calf was still too numb to feel any pain and she could have sprinted to his truck if she'd wanted to.

*

Zoey had to admit it, Mark was right. With its black, shiny finish, brass trim, and classy design, Ivy's modern-but-vintage-looking stove really did emphasize how outmoded and unsightly the rest of the kitchen was. Sylvia may have once described the white tile backsplash and yellow laminate countertops as sunny, but over the years the colors had dulled several shades. Zoey had installed higher-wattage bulbs in the overhead light, but they only accentuated the contrast between the old and new.

It's not my house, it's not my business, she reminded herself. *As long as Aunt Ivy is happy with it, that's all that matters.*

The problem was, Ivy *didn't* seem happy with it. In fact, for that first week after Nick and Aidan installed the range, she wouldn't allow anyone to use the oven. They were permitted to use the burners on the stovetop, but not to bake or broil anything inside it. Ivy claimed it was because she'd never had such a sparkling clean oven before and she didn't want it to get dirty right away, but Zoey had a hunch she regretted purchasing it. And that the real reason she didn't want to get it dirty was because she was considering returning the appliance.

After preparing stovetop or cold meals all week—since the gas tank for the outdoor grill was empty—Zoey was growing tired of it. Ivy had suffered several crying spells that week, so she didn't want to say anything that might make her feel pressured, for fear she'd send her spiraling into sorrow again. But on Sunday evening while Gabi and Ivy were drinking tea in the living room and she was sipping ice water, Zoey hinted that it was time for Ivy to break in the new oven.

"Do you know what would be really good for supper tomorrow night? Lasagna. I've got my interview in Providence in the morning.

On the way back I'll pick up some of that Italian sausage you like so much from the deli downtown. I should be home by twelve-thirty or one, so you and I could make the lasagna together in the afternoon."

Because this would be the first time after Sylvia's death that Ivy was going to be alone for several hours, Zoey scheduled her interview as early as possible, so her aunt would only have to spend the morning by herself.

"I'm going to be late because I have band practice and then I'm going to Amy's house," Gabi said. "Her mom always invites me to stay for supper, so you two should eat without me."

Amy was the fourth-chair flutist in the school band, a sophomore, and Gabi had practiced with her three times last week. Zoey was glad her niece had made a connection with someone other than Aidan, but it surprised her that Gabi never played her instrument at home. She repeated the excuse that she didn't want to hurt Moby's ears. Zoey supposed that was possible, since the girl seemed to have adopted Sylvia's pet, or vice versa, and she went out of her way to tiptoe past Moby whenever he was taking a cat nap.

"A whole lasagna for just two people? That's too much food. I can make chicken soup on the stovetop," Ivy proposed.

"It's kind of hot out for soup," Zoey objected. "Gabi, why don't you invite Amy here to practice for a change? Then she could eat supper with us."

"I already told her I was going to her house."

Zoey tried a slightly different tack to get the cooking ban lifted. "Later in the week you should have Aunt Ivy show you how to bake a strawberry-rhubarb pie. Yesterday I bought strawberries at the market and I saw rhubarb at the farm stand when I went for a walk on Friday. I could pick some up," she suggested. "Aunt Ivy taught my mom and yours how to make the most delicious, flaky crust you've ever tasted. She tried to teach me, too, but I never got the knack of it. It always turns out tough."

"That's because you handle the dough too much," Ivy chided.

"I bet Gabi will catch on right away, like Jess did."

Ivy clasped her hands together. "Gabi, did I ever tell you about the time your mother found rhubarb growing in the woods in Rockfield? She was about your age and she loved to bake, so when she happened upon all that free fruit, she must have picked a hundred stalks. She had so many she couldn't fit them all in the bicycle basket, so she wrapped the rest in her beach towel and carried it over her shoulder, like Santa's sack. 'Aunt Ivy, Aunt Sylvia, look what I found!' she shouted when she cycled up the driveway. You would have thought she'd discovered gold, she was so excited. She brought it into the kitchen and even before she unwrapped it, I knew from the smell, it wasn't rhubarb. It was—"

"Skunk cabbage!" Zoey chorused with Ivy. The two of them had to wipe their eyes from laughing but Gabi hardly cracked a smile. Zoey figured that was because she didn't know the difference between the two plants, but when she explained how nobody would want to make skunk cabbage pie, Gabi just rolled her eyes.

"My Denny loved strawberry-rhubarb pie, too," her aunt remarked, her eyes sparkling. Zoey knew exactly what she was going to tell Gabi next. "Every time after he'd eaten his last bite, he'd scrape the plate clean with the side of his fork, push back his chair and pull me onto his lap. 'Ivy,' he'd say, 'The best pie is like my best girl. They're both sweet enough to savor and tart enough to make me pucker up.' Then he'd kiss me."

Again, Gabi's smile seemed like an effort. Kind of like *she'd* tasted something sour. Zoey couldn't tell if she was embarrassed by her aunt's saucy anecdote, if something else was bothering her, or if it was just run-of-the-mill teenage moodiness.

Before she could ask her what was on her mind, Gabi excused herself to go finish her homework. She kissed Ivy's cheek as she usually did. "Good luck with your interview tomorrow, Aunt Zoey," she said before leaving the room.

Zoey understood that her niece had other things she'd rather do than hang out with her aunts, and she had no intention of pressuring her into it. But she had kind of hoped Gabi would want to learn to bake a pie. Not only because that might motivate Ivy to use her new oven. But also because Zoey was trying to drum up an activity her aunt might enjoy besides playing cribbage or sitting in the living room, staring at the photo of Denny.

Ivy had frequently commented that she didn't know what she'd do without Sylvia and Zoey was beginning to see that was no exaggeration. Now that her sister-in-law was gone, Ivy seemed at a loss for ideas about how to occupy her time. Unless Zoey did the same things with her that Sylvia had always done, Ivy aimlessly flitted from room to room, often breaking down in tears. She was fairly confident that after the worst of her aunt's grief passed, Ivy would be able to manage —albeit, slowly—most of the physical tasks that were required in order to take care of the house and herself. And she could increase Carla's visits or employ an additional person to do the more arduous chores and errands. But, even though it was important to Ivy that she maintained her independent lifestyle, Zoey wasn't quite as certain about her aunt's ability to cope emotionally with Sylvia's absence. So, before she left, she hoped to help her develop a social network, as well as to become engaged in a hobby or a daily practice she enjoyed.

Suddenly, inspiration struck. "Aunt Ivy, I've got an idea. Why don't I go online to check out what kinds of programs the senior center offers?"

"You're far too young for that, dear. But I read in the *Gazette* that the library offers watercolor and oil-painting classes. A local artist teaches them for free. Emily-something-or-the-other is her name… I still have the article in the kitchen. I'll go get it." Her aunt leaned forward to put her teacup and saucer on the coffee table.

"Thanks, but that's not what I meant. I was suggesting we could check to see if there's an event or class that might interest *you*."

"Me? I'm too old for the senior center."

Zoey had heard some of her friends say their parents or grandparents who were in their sixties, seventies and even eighties felt they were too *young* to go to a senior center, but she'd never heard that anyone had claimed to be too *old*.

"I'm sure there's not an age cut-off."

"Maybe not, but I've read the center's calendar listing in the newspaper, too. Yoga classes. Computer tutorials. Trips to go wine tasting and to the theater in New York City. I wouldn't be able to keep up with any of that. And a penny per point is as much as I'm willing to gamble so I have no interest in playing Bingo on Tuesdays with them, either."

It was a fair argument. Zoey had read somewhere that the year-round senior population was fewer than two hundred people, and the vast majority of them were in their mid to late sixties and still working. And since it was so secluded on the island, no one had ever built assisted living or senior housing. But Zoey kept trying to persuade her aunt, saying, "There must be at least three or four people your age living here. If not in Benjamin's Manor, then in one of the other Hope Haven towns."

"The only person on Dune Island who's my age is Phineas Witherell. I can't really picture the two of us being friends again, even though it's been, what, some sixty years since our... our falling out."

After years of listening to her aunt's stories, Zoey thought she'd heard everything Ivy had wanted to tell her about her life on Dune Island. But now, in a single sentence, she'd dropped two bombshells regarding local lore. The first was that Mr. Witherell's given name was Phineas. No one, including Ivy, had ever mentioned that in front of Zoey before now. When she was a girl, she didn't think he even *had* a first name. Phineas. Phineas Witherell. *It suits him*, she thought.

The second shock was that he and Ivy had once been friends. As soon as Zoey heard that, the rumors Gabi told her about Sylvia and Mr. Witherell fleetingly came to her mind. But she knew better than to give them credence; just because Ivy and Mr. Witherell had been friends didn't mean Sylvia and Mr. Witherell had been lovers.

"I didn't realize you and Mr. Witherell were close. I thought you hardly knew him."

"'Close' is too strong of a word. But for a time when we were young, we were more than acquaintances." She explained that the summer after her mother died, she was so inconsolable that she'd walk to the end of the peninsula where the lighthouse was and sit by herself, watching the boats coming in and going out for hours. She'd bring a lunch that the housekeeper had made, but in Ivy's words, she was "off her food." So she'd give it to Mr. Witherell when he'd come out to survey the grounds before going to bed.

"His schedule was upside down, since he worked all night. So he thought nothing of eating pickles and coleslaw and fried chicken at ten o'clock in the morning," she marveled. "Sometimes he'd show me the notes he'd made in his log book. His position required him to keep track of the tides and the weather and such. He was very smart but he could really go on and on—not at all like he is now, hardly a word out of him. I think he was even lonelier than I was, back then.

"Anyway, by the next summer my mood had improved and I only walked to the end of the peninsula once or twice and when I did, he wasn't there. I'd cross paths with him on occasion in town, but we never struck up a real conversation again… until our rift." Ivy's bottom lip quivered. "I've often regretted how I treated him that day."

Zoey's aunt was consistently gracious to everyone, so she couldn't imagine her saying or doing anything so offensive it would have caused an estrangement that lasted for years. For *decades.* Nor could she quite believe that a simple attempt to help her aunt get interested in a hobby, or something to get her out of the house, had led them down this path of reminiscences, and that Mr. Witherell had come up again for what seemed the dozenth time since she'd been on the island. But clearly something was troubling Ivy, so Zoey proceeded cautiously. "Do you want to tell me about it?"

Ivy hesitated, her eyes brimming. "You know I don't like to speak ill of anyone."

Zoey *did* know that; it was the reason Ivy never directly said Sylvia's father was abusive. It was why she called her own father *influential* instead of *opinionated* or *domineering*. And said that Mark *"isn't good at demonstrating affection,"* rather than admitting most of the time he was too self-centered to care about anyone else's feelings. Her aunt's tendency to sugarcoat the truth used to drive Zoey nuts.

"Why doesn't Aunt Ivy see how conniving Mark is?" she'd asked her mother once.

"Just because she doesn't *say* it doesn't mean she doesn't *see* it," her mother had replied. "She grew up in a different era, with a mother who told her if she couldn't say something nice, not to say anything at all. And a father who didn't want her speaking her mind, period. Besides, what's the harm in demonstrating a little grace instead of calling attention to someone's flaws?"

Zoey acknowledged to her aunt, "You're always very generous in your attitude toward others. But if talking about it makes you uncomfortable, you don't have to tell me about your fight with Mr. Witherell."

"It wasn't a fight. No, nothing like that. But I did use stern words—too stern," Ivy brooded. "Looking back, I wish I hadn't, but I didn't know how else to stop him from pestering Sylvia."

Once again, Ivy's revelation made Zoey feel as if she had to lift her jaw off the floor. Mr. Witherell had once been bothering Sylvia? *That just proves how wrong Gabi's theory about them was—he didn't even* like *her,* she reassured herself. "What do you mean, he was pestering her?"

"He wrote her a couple of letters. Two or maybe three. Then he'd drop them through the mail slot here at the house. She wouldn't show them to me or tell me what they said, but the letters flustered her so badly that she'd cry and run upstairs to her room. It didn't take a genius to figure out what was going on—he didn't want her to get involved with Marcus."

Zoey's heartbeat skittered. Was Gabi right after all? Had Sylvia and Mr. Witherell been a couple? She struggled to sound casual when she asked, "Why not?"

"I couldn't be certain because Sylvia was so modest and wouldn't talk about it, but I assumed it was because *he* wanted to date her. Maybe he'd even gone out with her once or twice. As you know, Sylvia was quite a looker. A lot of men's hopes were dashed when she married Marcus. Although it's funny that Phineas found out that she was falling for my brother, since they never went out in public together. She must have confided her feelings for him to one of the maids from the boarding house and the girl let it slip. Gossip spreads like wildfire around here."

Even if Mr. Witherell didn't want Sylvia and Marcus to date because he wanted to date her, that doesn't necessarily mean she was pregnant with Mr. Witherell's baby, Zoey reasoned as Ivy continued her story.

"Sylvia never answered Phineas's notes so one day instead of dropping an envelope through the slot, he rang the bell. Sylvia and I both went to answer it at the same time. When she saw who was standing there, she turned as white as a sheet. She might have fainted if I hadn't helped her to the kitchen and given her a cold drink. Marcus was upstairs napping so I had to take control of the situation myself. I returned to where Phineas was waiting on the step and—oh, Zoey, I shouldn't have been so harsh…" When Ivy dissolved into tears, Zoey went over and perched on the arm of the chair, patting her aunt's shoulder.

"It was so many years ago. And I'm sure whatever you said, your intentions were good—you were protecting Sylvia." *Probably because you knew how cruel her family had been to her.*

"Yes, I was, but I shouldn't have hurt Phineas in the process." Ivy pulled a tissue from where she kept it folded in the cuff of her sleeve and dabbed her cheeks, confessing, "I told him he was a bully for harassing a docile young woman like Sylvia, instead of accepting it that she wasn't interested in him. He tried to say Sylvia wasn't as innocent as I thought and that he was only looking out for our family. You know what he was implying, don't you?"

Yes. That she was pregnant with his child, Zoey thought, her heart palpitating. "What?"

"That she was only interested in Marcus for his money." Ivy shook her head in disgust. "So I said, "Phineas, if you were any kind of gentleman, you'd bow out gracefully. But since you *aren't* a gentleman, as long as Sylvia is living in my home, I don't want you darkening my doorstep. I don't even want you coming through the front gate.' Then I warned him if he couldn't be civil to her in public, he shouldn't bother speaking to me, either."

"That's not so bad at all, Aunt Ivy. You had to be firm with him." *Although you may not have known the whole story.*

"Perhaps, but you should have seen how forlorn he looked."

"Did he apologize?"

"That's the worst part. I didn't give him a chance—I slammed the door in his face. And he scampered off like a kicked puppy." Ivy cried harder.

Setting aside the remote possibility that Mr. Witherell may have been right about Sylvia's intentions, Zoey replied, "You and Aunt Sylvia were like sisters. If anyone had insulted Jessica's character, I would have said something a lot worse. It was necessary for you to establish your boundaries. To tell him what kind of behavior was unacceptable. Who knows, maybe by being firm you set a good example for Aunt Sylvia. Maybe that's how she found the strength to ask the police to leave when they wanted to take her to the hospital the time she went up to the widow's walk."

Ivy blotted her eyes and then blew her nose. "I didn't realize I'd told you the story about the police coming to the house. Sometimes I think Mark is right—I'm becoming too forgetful."

Oops. Ivy *hadn't* told her; Zoey had heard about it from her mother. Fortunately, her aunt didn't give her the chance to clarify.

"You know, I always suspected Mr. Witherell was the one who called the police that night."

"What makes you think that?"

Her aunt turned her palms up. "Who else would have spotted her up there at that hour? He had the perfect vantage point from the lighthouse."

Thinking aloud, Zoey asked, "Do you think he did it out of revenge—to get her in trouble with the police or to humiliate her in front of her neighbors?"

"Revenge? Not at all. I think he was genuinely concerned for her safety. Just like when he reported boats for speeding or bonfire parties on the beach, it was because he didn't want someone getting hurt. Most people never understood that about him." Ivy grew silent for a moment before murmuring, "Gulls in his lantern room."

Zoey didn't understand the non sequitur and her heart thrummed with alarm. Was her aunt speaking gibberish? "What did you say?"

"Do you know the expression, 'you have bats in your belfry'?" Ivy asked and when Zoey nodded, she said, "That's what they used to say about Mr. Witherell. Except they'd say he had 'gulls in his lantern room' from living alone in the lighthouse for so long. It wasn't clever. It was cruel. I didn't appreciate him making Sylvia so upset, but I think certain people haven't shown him enough respect."

Yeah, including Mark. "Well, *you* weren't disrespectful to him, Aunt Ivy. I've seen you and Aunt Sylvia pass him in the streets and you've always been cordial. He has, too. And he came to Aunt Sylvia's funeral. That must mean he isn't holding anything against you." *And it might mean more than that*, Zoey realized.

"He came to Marcus and Denny's funerals, too. He said he was very sorry. I didn't know if he meant because they'd died or if he was apologizing for what he said that day he came to the house. Either way, I think that's when we tacitly agreed to let bygones be bygones. We never chatted with each other the way we did the summer after my mother died, but at least things were less strained between us."

"Then maybe he'd be open to a closer friendship again now." Zoey knew it was a reach but she added, "He loves to walk and you used to, too. I know sometimes your angina flares up, but maybe if Dr. Laurent says it's okay and you built your endurance, little by little…?"

Ivy waved a finger at her. "Now look who's matchmaking! Next thing I know you'll be pairing us up for cribbage."

That wasn't what Zoey had in mind but she laughed, pleased her aunt's mood seemed lighter. Then Ivy said she was getting tired and Zoey walked her up the stairs. On the first landing, her heart hurt so acutely Zoey told her to sit on the step while she ran and got her a nitroglycerin pill. Ivy placed it beneath her tongue, holding her hand to her chest and rocking her upper torso. If Zoey hadn't seen this happen before, she would have called 9-1-1 but Ivy's cardiologist said she could take up to three nitro pills in a row, at five-minute intervals. She had never needed more than one, but tonight she had to take two before the pain subsided and she felt comfortable enough to climb the rest of the steps. *Her angina is always worse if she exerts herself after being upset*, Zoey acknowledged. *I wonder if that will pass in time or if I should suggest that she might benefit from a stair lift, especially once I leave...*

She helped Ivy with her nightly regimen and then sat beside her as she drifted in and out of sleep. Zoey considered canceling her interview the next day. But she'd scheduled it so early in the morning that she wouldn't have been able to give the staff advance notice that she wasn't coming. Also, she'd already picked up the rental car and she was close to maxing out her last credit card so she didn't want to add another charge if she could avoid it. Besides, her aunt seemed fine now, as she always did after the medication kicked in.

When Ivy's breathing grew heavy and rhythmic, Zoey sneaked out of the room. Noticing there was no light shining from beneath Gabi's door even though it was barely nine-thirty, she decided she might as well go to bed, too, since she had to catch the early morning ferry.

But instead of sleeping, Zoey ruminated over what Ivy had disclosed about Sylvia and Mr. Witherell. While she tried to rein in her imagination, there were just enough similarities between her aunt's and her niece's stories to make it seem almost plausible that Mr. Witherell, not Marcus Sr., had fathered Marcus Jr. Whether that was true or not, one thing was for certain: Ivy had no clue about it.

Zoey had already concluded that Mark must have heard the same rumors Gabi heard when he attended school on Dune Island. But what she wondered now was if Ivy had told *him* the same story she'd just told Zoey about Mr. Witherell leaving letters for Sylvia at the house?

"Hey!" she said aloud and snapped her fingers before hushing herself. *What if* that's *what he was looking for in the attic—Mr. Witherell's letters to Aunt Sylvia?* Zoey had straightened the boxes in her aunt's trunk the day she'd injured herself, but maybe she should take a more thorough look at their contents?

She quickly dismissed the impulse. If the letters affected Sylvia as deeply as Ivy said they did, she wouldn't have saved them. And if she *had* kept them, Mark surely had discovered and destroyed them already. But even if there was a million-in-one chance that Zoey *did* find them and they indicated Sylvia *was* pregnant with Mr. Witherell's son, what then? Her aunt had already told her how upset she'd gotten when Mr. Witherell suggested Sylvia wasn't as meek as she acted. As Zoey had told Gabi, she had to consider how hurt her aunt would feel to find out he'd been right. Especially because she'd already shared the better part of her life—and her wealth—with her sister-in-law, as well as with Marcus Jr. and with Mark.

If the new stove has taught me anything, it's to leave well enough alone. And that's what Zoey was going to have to do about the issue of Marcus Jr.'s paternity, too—even if the curiosity was killing her.

CHAPTER EIGHT

Usually Zoey experienced a rush of excitement as she drove into the city, but today she'd felt as if the traffic and high-rises were closing in on her. Nick's phrase, "a cell of an office" came to mind more than once during her tour of the library, although she did like the staff and could imagine herself being happy working with them. And while she regretted not being able to meet up with her friend Lauren after work, Zoey was equally glad that for her aunt's sake, she had to leave the city immediately after her interview. Or almost immediately; she stopped to get the sausages she'd promised her aunt first.

When she pulled into the driveway and saw Nick's truck, she practically skipped to the back door, expecting to find him and Ivy drinking coffee in the kitchen. She hoped he had convinced her to try out the oven. They weren't there but there was noise—almost like voices, but not exactly—coming from the living room. Was Ivy weeping? *I knew I shouldn't have left her alone today,* Zoey thought, hurrying to greet them.

"Hi, Nick. Hi, Aunt Ivy."

As soon her aunt saw her, she gasped. "Oh, Zoey, you're safe! I've been so worried." Her nose and eyes were red-rimmed and there was a box of tissues on her lap. She pulled one out and wiped her cheeks, and then added it to the pile on the coffee table.

"Yes, I'm safe and sound." Zoey cocked her head, confused. "Why? Did you hear about an accident on the radio or TV?"

Nick quickly explained, "Your aunt said you've been gone for hours and she didn't know where you went. We tried your cell, but we couldn't reach you and we couldn't get a hold of Gabi to ask her, either. I even checked with the hospital to see if you returned for a follow-up appointment."

"I-I went to my interview in Providence. Remember, Aunt Ivy?" It was a stupid question, something Mark would have asked. If Ivy had remembered she wouldn't have been crying and frantically trying to locate her. "I'm sorry you were worried. I turned off my phone so it wouldn't ring while I was meeting with the director. I must have forgotten to turn it on again. I feel terrible."

"No, no. I should have remembered," Ivy said, pulling another tissue from the box. "But when I couldn't get you, I thought you went swimming alone again and that you might have dived in and bumped your head on a rock."

There weren't any sizeable rocks in the bay on Rose Beach and Zoey was still avoiding the water because of the sore on her leg, but she didn't point that out. She knew her aunt had an irrational but understandable fear of her loved ones drowning ever since the boating accident. She gave her a hug, repeating, "I'm sorry I worried you, Aunt Ivy. Next time, I'll leave you a note or put a reminder on the calendar."

Her aunt inhaled and straightened her shoulders, gathering her composure. "Now that you're here, I'll make lunch. How does lemon pepper chicken sound? It will be my first time using the oven, but in the old one it didn't take more than thirty minutes."

"I'd love to have chicken for lunch, but Nick probably has to get back to work now, don't you?"

"Yeah. As tempting as it is to stay, I need to pick up an order at the lumber yard."

When Zoey noticed how crestfallen Ivy appeared, she seized the opportunity to suggest her aunt could make a lasagna and Nick and Aidan could come for supper instead.

"That sounds great, but I'm working late every day this week."

Now it was Zoey's turn to feel disappointed, until Ivy asked, "What about on Sunday?"

We'll have to freeze the sausage I picked up in Providence until then, but that's okay, Zoey thought when Nick accepted the invitation. She told her aunt she had to move the rental car because she was blocking Nick from leaving, but that she'd be right back in for lunch.

Once outside, Zoey said, "I can't thank you enough for staying with my aunt until I got here. She's never forgotten something major like this before, ever. But last night she was really upset about something and I think she's overly tired." Zoey didn't know whether she was trying to convince herself or Nick.

"I'm glad I could be here for her. Except..." Nick shoved his hands in his pockets and kicked a pebble onto the grass before meeting her eyes. "I called Mark. Not because we couldn't find you but because your aunt was having chest pain and I thought we should call 9-1-1. She insisted her physician would have advised her to take a nitro pill, first. I was really torn—I felt it was important for someone in the family to know what was going on in case..."

"It's not a problem," Zoey heard herself saying even though it was a *big* problem. Mark was going to have a field day with this one. "I would have done the same thing if I were with someone else's family member and I didn't have any knowledge of their medical history. I might have even called 9-1-1 regardless of what they told me. You can't be too careful, especially when it comes to cardiovascular symptoms."

"I'm glad you're not upset. After that last conversation we had, I didn't want you to think I was intruding."

"No. I appreciate it that you were so conscientious about my aunt's health." Zoey took a deep breath. "So, was Mark… helpful?"

"Uh, well, when I first called he wasn't there, so I left a message. By the time he called me back, Ivy's pain was gone. And she'd already called the cardiologist, primarily so I'd feel more comfortable. The doc said she did the right thing but if the pain got worse or didn't go away after taking a couple of nitro pills, she should call an ambulance. I think he moved her annual appointment up a few weeks, too—you'll have to check with her on that," Nick rambled nervously. "Anyway, Mark confirmed she has a heart condition but he didn't know what it was so he wouldn't have been able to provide much insight anyway. He, uh, he was pretty upset even though the issue with Ivy's heart had resolved itself."

"Upset with *me*, you mean. Because I wasn't here." When Nick gave a small nod, Zoey sighed. "What did he say?"

Nick winced. "I'd tell you but I was raised not to talk like that."

"Ha!" What else could Zoey do but laugh? "You know, in most families, a person would be worried if his cousin suddenly went missing. And they'd be grateful that someone like you was there to help his aunt. But not Marcus Winslow, the Third. I'm really sorry you had to listen to him go off like that."

"It's okay. I interrupted his little, uh, *invective*, by telling him you'd give him a call when you returned and then I hung up." Nick grinned. "How did the interview go?"

"Pretty well, I think. They said they'd be inviting a couple applicants back for a second round of interviews in a week or two, so I hope I'm one of them. How about you, how have you been?"

"Good. Busy. This week I've got two projects going. A deck I'm building at a cottage in Highland Hills. And a bathroom renovation—that one's in Lucinda's Hamlet. So I'm looking at some pretty tight deadlines."

Zoey realized she should stop yakking so he could leave but his eyes were so mesmerizing she couldn't seem to move or look away. "I suppose that's what you get for being the bluest contractor on the island."

"The bluest?"

"I meant the blest. The *best*," Zoey bumbled. Embarrassed that it must have been obvious she'd been thinking of his eyes, she abruptly started walking toward the house, calling, "See you on Sunday. We'll probably eat around six or six-thirty but feel free to come over any time after five."

"Thanks. Hey, Zoey?"

She stopped. "Yeah?"

"Aren't you going to move your car so I can get out?"

"Ack. Where is my head today?" she asked, much like her aunt would do. *I'd better be careful or else Mark is going to try to move me into an assisted living facility,* she thought as she backed out of the driveway.

*

While Zoey and her aunt ate lunch, Ivy kept apologizing for her memory lapse.

"It's completely understandable—you had a rough evening yesterday and you're overly tired. You'll feel better and think more clearly after you've caught up on your rest." Or so Zoey hoped. She didn't want to make too big of a deal over her aunt not remembering where she'd gone, but neither did she want to chalk up her forgetfulness to distress or distraction if there was something more serious at play. *It might be worth it for her to ask her doctor to evaluate her memory the next time she has her annual physical,* she thought.

Ivy agreed a nap was a good idea so Zoey assisted her to her room, telling her, "I'm not used to getting up so early. I feel sleepy, too."

Her aunt patted the bed. "Here, lie down next to me."

Zoey figured she'd stretch out for a few minutes until her aunt fell asleep and then she'd go email the library staff, thanking them for the interview.

Instead of dozing, Ivy continued to fuss. "I'm such a burden. First to Sylvia—she was always helping me, you know. With Marcus and my father. Then she nursed me back to health when I had cancer. And until she got pneumonia, she'd been doing the lion's share of the work around here. I relied on her too much, just like I'm relying too heavily on you now."

Zoey propped herself up on her elbows so she could meet her aunt's eyes as she replied, "Aunt Ivy, you helped Aunt Sylvia just as much as she helped you. You took her into your home when she had nowhere else to go. You loved her like a sister and you helped her raise her son. And to some extent, her grandson. You've nurtured me, too, by being a constant, loving presence in my life. By sharing your heart and your humor and your home. Most of my best, most fun memories are of being here with you and Aunt Sylvia and my mom and sister. And I don't know what I would have done if I hadn't been able to come to the island over the years to be refreshed and get my head together. So whatever little bit of help I can give you now pales in comparison to all you've given me."

Quite unexpectedly, a sob escaped her lips. She covered her mouth but her aunt had already heard it. She squeezed Zoey's other hand. "That's one of the loveliest things anyone has ever said to me, but don't cry, dear, or I'll start up again, too."

A few more tears fell after Zoey laid her head back against the pillow and watched the leafy shadows dance across the curtain. "Ignore me. I'm just releasing pent-up stress now that my interview is over." Intermittently wiping her face on the sleeve of her blouse, she told her aunt about the position and how much she liked the library director and the other staff members. "I think I have a good shot at getting a second interview, but I can't count on it. There are more applicants than I expected."

"Oh, you poor kids. The workplace is so competitive, I'm surprised you don't all have ulcers. Mark is stressed about securing a new position, too. To think, in the past six months his marriage fell apart and then he lost his job and now it looks as if his ex-wife will get the house."

Zoey stopped crying to ask, "Mark is unemployed, too?" *And what's this about him losing his house? That would explain his sudden urgency to push Aunt Ivy out of hers.*

"Uh-oh. I thought you knew. Please don't tell him I told you."

"I won't," Zoey promised.

"I keep telling him he's going to make himself sick. That he shouldn't worry so much because even if his ex-wife takes the house, he can always live with me. But he says Hope Haven is no place for a traveling sales rep, since most of his clients would be off-island. It would be too inconvenient to have to travel back and forth by ferry every day."

I'm glad for that, Zoey thought. She was even gladder her aunt had invited Mark to live with her because it meant she wasn't considering forfeiting the house to him any time soon.

"I wish I had a way to help him." Her aunt sighed.

"Mark is very resourceful. Very tenacious. He's not going to give up his house without a fight. And he'll find a job again soon—he always does. But if not, you've already told him he could come here to live. So it's not as if he's going to be homeless."

"I should say not!" Ivy rubbed her eyes. "But you know, I think that's what my sister-in-law was afraid could happen. She was too ill to discuss it with me, but when she found out Mark's ex-wife might get the house, she was terribly distraught. Sometimes I'd hear her mumbling about it in her sleep. Saying it just wasn't right."

Zoey recalled that on the last day of Sylvia's life, her great-aunt had made a similar remark to her, too. "It's not fair... That boy can only take so much." Zoey couldn't agree that Mark was being unduly victimized, but she appreciated why his grandmother's love or guilt or fear might have colored her perspective. And to be fair, Sylvia had sounded equally concerned about Zoey losing her job and savings. What was it she'd said? Something like, "What about Zoey? She's such a dear girl... Where will she live?"

As she recalled that some of her great-aunt's final thoughts were about *her* well-being, Zoey felt like crying again. She reassured Ivy that Mark would land on his feet and then she quickly changed the subject. "I've been meaning to ask you if you noticed whether there was anything going on between Gabi and Aidan?"

"They're friends, if that's what you mean but there's nothing romantic between them."

She turned her head to face her aunt, who didn't seem half as sleepy as Zoey felt. "Gabi told you that?"

"She didn't have to. I gleaned it from how they played cribbage as partners."

Zoey tittered. "Love isn't in the cards for them, is that what you're saying?"

Her aunt missed the pun, replying earnestly, "No, it isn't. They're both bright but she was so focused on helping him learn the game that she wasn't playing her best. There's a time to help, but she overdid it. And he didn't mind because he wasn't trying to impress her. Otherwise he would have made more of an effort. They enjoy each other's company, but they're like siblings. Nothing more."

As confident as Ivy sounded, Zoey wasn't sure she agreed with her aunt's appraisal. "You got all that from a card game?"

"Yes. Now let me tell you what I observed about you and Nick."

"No. Please don't."

Her aunt ignored her. "As far as whether the two of you will wind up together, it's hard to say. There's definitely a spark. But I noticed you didn't seem to trust him to make the right move. Every time it was his turn to play a card, you held your breath."

That's because the last time I didn't watch what someone was doing, he cleaned out my retirement account. "What can I say? I wanted to win—I'm competitive."

"My dear girl, you even did it when you weren't on the same team."

Zoey chuckled, in spite of herself. "What did you notice about Nick?"

"He shuffles too long."

"That's it? His shuffling? What's that got to do with anything?" *Especially with whether or not he and I would make a good couple.*

"Think about it." Ivy tapped her head knowingly. "The longer you take to shuffle, the longer it takes to get in the game. Meanwhile, the other players get restless. They lose interest."

She's forcing that metaphor, Zoey thought. Yet she had to admit, she *had* been disappointed that until today, she hadn't heard from Nick all week. Despite her blunder, they'd hit it off so well on Saturday, that even though she'd supposedly sworn off dating until the fall she had kind of hoped he'd ask her out. Or at least make some excuse to touch base with her. Was this him procrastinating, as Ivy indicated? Or wasn't he as interested in her as Zoey was becoming in him?

She wanted her aunt to do an assessment of one more pair of partners. But who? Not her mother and father. Although on occasion they'd indulge Ivy and Sylvia in a game, they both hated cribbage and would slap down any card just to get the hand over as quickly as possible. Zoey was already painfully aware of the similarity between how they'd partnered in cards and how they'd partnered in marriage.

"What did you see about my sister and Scott's relationship when they played cards?" she whispered because Ivy's eyes were closed and she didn't know if she was sleeping.

"Scott and Jess? Now *they* were a good pair. You wouldn't have thought so because he could be so conservative and she was so daring. But there was a give and take between them and it all evened out." Ivy's voice was so soft Zoey hardly heard her mumble, "As soon as I saw them playing cribbage—they weren't married yet—I told Sylvia, 'Mark my words. Their union will last a lifetime.'"

The ironic accuracy of her aunt's statement socked Zoey right in the chest and she barely managed to choke back another sob. *If a benign remark about Jess can reduce me to tears six years after she died, how can I expect Aunt Ivy to be okay by autumn?* she worried, as sleep overtook her.

Zoey had fallen into such a deep slumber that Ivy had to wake her for supper instead of the other way around. By then she remembered she still hadn't called Mark—she hadn't turned on her phone, for that matter. But she put it off until after she'd eaten and done the dishes. And then Gabi returned home and she chatted with her about Nick and Aidan coming for supper on Sunday evening.

"Can I invite Amy and Connor, too?"

Zoey was secretly delighted that she'd finally get to meet some of Gabi's friends, but she played it cool. "Sure, as long as it's okay with Aunt Ivy."

When she couldn't postpone it any longer, she took her phone to her room and powered it up, discovering that Mark had left her a long text and three messages. She didn't bother to read or listen to them, since she figured she'd get an earful when she called him anyway. Even on a good day, she could only tolerate so many of Mark's diatribes.

"It's about time," he snarled by way of greeting. "Where were you?"

"Eating supper in the kitchen." Zoey hadn't intended to sound so derisive but Mark's demanding tone immediately sent her off.

"You know what I meant. Where were you when Ivy was practically having a heart attack?"

"She wasn't practically having a heart attack. She has chronic chest pain. It's called angina, for future reference. Her cardiologist has been monitoring it and he prescribed nitro pills. As soon as she took one, she was fine. I'm sorry if you were alarmed but it wasn't a big deal."

Why am I apologizing? You weren't *alarmed. By the time you called Nick back, Ivy was fine and the pseudo emergency was over,* Zoey wanted to say, but didn't. *Furthermore, I could have sworn I told you about her angina before.*

"Not a big deal? Then why did the handyman call me in a panic?" Before Zoey could respond, he repeated. "You still haven't answered my question—where were you?"

Maybe it was his reference to Nick as "the handyman" or just his controlling, condescending attitude in general, but Zoey shot back, "I'm not under house arrest and you're not my jailer. But for your information, I had an important interview in Providence." She hadn't meant to let that last part slip but sometimes when Mark affronted her, she spoke faster than she thought.

"A job interview? Are you unemployed?" He sounded incredibly disdainful for someone who didn't have a job himself. "All this time I thought you'd taken a leave from your position because you cared so much about Ivy and Sylvia—"

"That's *exactly* why I came here," Zoey interrupted. "My library branch just so happened to close at around the same time Aunt Sylvia came down with pneumonia. It was either I came here to help or she would have had to recover in a rehab center off-island because Aunt Ivy couldn't have given her the kind of care she needed."

"What a coincidence. Are you sure the real reason you're there isn't so you can save on living costs in Providence?" Mark jeered. "Do you even have your apartment any more?"

Zoey had to bite her tongue to keep from asking if he was talking to *her* or to the mirror. *Lucky for you I promised Aunt Ivy I wouldn't say I knew anything about your situation*, she thought.

"It's a townhome and yes, I still own it. Thanks for inquiring about my welfare. And hey, thanks for checking up on Aunt Ivy later this afternoon—oh, wait. You didn't, did you?"

"Don't act as if I don't care. I'm not the one who abandoned her for hours without telling her where I was going or how she could reach me."

"Are you kidding me? I don't even go to the back yard without telling Aunt Ivy, first!"

"So you told her and she forgot?"

I fell right into that trap, Zoey thought. She'd rather take the blame unjustly than to give her cousin ammunition to imply their aunt wasn't fit to live alone. "I mentioned it to her but I should have written it down." Zoey faked a self-deprecating laugh, hoping to lighten the tension. "I can't even remember my own schedule sometimes, so it's not fair to expect Aunt Ivy to keep track of it."

"What's not fair is that for some reason you don't want her to get the help she obviously needs."

What part of what I just said about why I came here don't you understand? Zoey silently fumed. "I *am* helping her."

"What's she going to do when you leave? Or don't you ever plan to?"

"Of course I plan to leave." Zoey stopped herself before she blurted out that if she got the job, it wouldn't start until late August. The fewer details Mark had about her schedule, the better. She decided to try to empathize with her cousin. "Listen, Mark. I understand you're concerned about Aunt Ivy and I am, too. She's just suffered an enormous loss and she's not quite herself. I believe it's temporary. It's going to be challenging, but eventually she'll adjust—her background shows how resilient she is. If she doesn't, we can talk to her about… about making some changes. Meanwhile, I'm here to help. And before I go, I intend to line up resources for her, whether that means additional housekeeping, medical intervention, a social network. Whatever she needs, I'll make sure she has it before I leave."

"I don't get it. What's in it for you?"

Only you would have to ask that question. "I *love* her."

"Then why would you put her through this?"

"I'm not *putting* her through anything! She's grieving. It's a process. I'm trying to support her."

Mark was relentless. "By upsetting her like you did today?"

"That was a miscommunication."

"It was a miscommunication that left her in tears and affected her heart. If you hadn't been here—if you were still living at your own place in Providence, she wouldn't have been worried about where you were."

Zoey hardly knew how to respond to that kind of logic, it was so twisted. "If I weren't here, she'd have no emotional or physical support."

"That's *exactly* my point. And that's why I think she should move to an assisted living facility."

"Aunt Ivy doesn't want to live in a *facility*. She wants to live in a home. *Her* home."

"What she wants and what she needs are two different things."

"You're not the judge of that."

"Neither are you."

Aware the conversation was devolving into the kind of "you started it first—no, you did" argument they'd had when they were kids, Zoey said, "I don't think we're going to get anywhere talking about this tonight, so why don't we shelve it until another time and say goodbye for now?"

Mark disconnected without another word, which was actually the best response Zoey could have hoped to get.

*

On Friday evening, Lauren called shortly before supper time to see if Zoey had been invited back for a second interview. To her disappointment, she hadn't, but she was still hopeful. They chatted for a few minutes about the guy Lauren was going out with for the first time that weekend. Then her friend asked how Zoey was adjusting to living with a teenager.

"Is it as challenging as everyone claims it is?"

"No. I love having my niece here—not that I see her that often. After school she's either playing her flute in the band or practicing with her friend. In the evenings, she spends most of her time upstairs doing homework. I don't remember being that disciplined when I was her age."

"Maybe it's not that she's so disciplined. Maybe she's avoiding you."

"Hey! I'm not *that* uncool."

"The fact that you'd say *uncool* shows just how uncool you are," Lauren kidded her. "But I didn't mean that. I meant maybe you never see her because she doesn't want to be seen... Have you considered she might be hiding something?"

No, I only think that way about my cousin. "Like what?"

"I don't know, it could be anything. When my niece started withdrawing from my brother and his wife, they thought it was typical teenage behavior, but it turned out she was pregnant. And my coworker just found out her kid's addicted to dexies—"

"*Dexies?* I don't know what they are but I can assure you my niece isn't addicted to them," Zoey interrupted. "And there is *no way* she's pregnant." She'd just begun feeling more confident that Gabi seemed to be doing well and Lauren's remarks were discouraging. "Just because she made one mistake in California doesn't mean she's continuing down the wrong path."

"That's true," Lauren acknowledged. "But even if she were struggling, I wouldn't judge her—or you. I'm not judging my brother's family, either. I'm just saying it's different from when we were young.

Kids are dealing with all kinds of stuff we never had to face. You wouldn't be the first parent who found out her child was keeping something serious from her."

"Yeah, well, Gabi's not keeping anything serious from me and I'm not a parent."

"Actually, Zo, right now you kind of are."

"But no pressure, right?"

After their phone call ended, Zoey helped her aunt prepare supper. As usual, Gabi was eating at Amy's house—an occurrence that now gave Zoey pause. She'd been trying not to be overly restrictive about her niece's schedule because she knew Gabi had been burdened by Scott and Kathleen's problems this past year. Zoey remembered what that felt like from when she was a teenager and her own parents were at each other's throats all the time. So she'd wanted her niece to enjoy the freedom of being away from that. The freedom of being young. But after talking to Lauren, Zoey wondered if she should be limiting how much time Gabi spent at her friend's house. She decided to have a heart-to-heart with Gabi when they had a little time alone, just to make sure everything was okay with her.

"Still no word from the library?" her aunt asked as they sat down in the formal dining room to begin their meal. Ivy preferred they eat in there these days, even when it was just the two of them.

"Not yet, but that's okay. It's better not to hear anything than to have them confirm they've rejected me as a candidate." Zoey hoped she sounded convincing. Mark had been calling their aunt every day since Monday's miscommunication and each time she got off the phone Ivy remarked about how worried she was about him. Zoey didn't want her aunt fretting about her, too.

"I see," she replied, absently poking at her potato.

Halfway through her meal, Zoey noticed her aunt had hardly touched hers. "Is the fish too dry?" she asked. The new oven was much more efficient than the old oven and Zoey had overcooked the first few meals she'd made in it.

"No, it's fine." Ivy set down her fork. "But there's something I need to talk to you about. I've hesitated to bring it up, but it's been eating at me for days and I can't keep it to myself any longer. Mark tried to tell me way back when, but I didn't want to accept it. I wanted everything to stay as it was."

Oh, no! Zoey pressed her napkin to her mouth to stifle a gasp. *Mark did it—he wore Aunt Ivy down.* She dropped her hand flat against the table, steeling herself for her aunt to tell her she was moving into an assisted living facility. "You didn't want to accept what?"

"I loved my sister-in-law, but now that she's gone..." Ivy bit her bottom lip and shook her head, her eyes filling with tears.

Zoey waited a moment before prompting, "Now that she's gone, you want to..."

"To make another change," Ivy confirmed. "And I hope you won't be too disappointed in me."

No, but I am furious at Mark. Zoey took a sip of ice water to dilute the bitter taste in her mouth before she could say, "Aunt Ivy, it's *your* life and *your* house—so as long as it's *your* choice, I'll support whatever you do."

"Oh, I am so relieved to hear that." Blinking away her tears, she patted Zoey's hand. "Because now that the new range is installed, it makes the rest of the kitchen look so... It's *unsightly* by comparison.

I don't even like to dine in there any longer. I feel terrible saying that because I know how much thought Sylvia put into designing the room. But I think if we'd had to replace the stove while she was here and she saw how mismatched the new one was with everything else, she'd want to make additional updates, too. Don't you think so?"

"Yes, I do," Zoey agreed matter-of-factly even though she could hardly contain her glee that she'd been wrong that her aunt had given in to Mark about moving. And they could get Ivy involved with the minutiae of planning the remodel just as Ivy had involved Sylvia after her son, Marcus Jr., moved to Boston. "What would you like to change? The cupboards? The countertops? The fridge?"

"All of it. Everything but the kitchen sink, as the saying goes." Ivy chortled. "Although, I'd change that, too, if I could."

"You *can*, Aunt Ivy. I'll show you some examples of sinks online. This will be fun!"

"We'll have to get the Armstrong boy to do the work. I wouldn't want anyone else to do it."

"The Armstrong boy?" Zoey teased, "You mean Aidan?"

"Right. Aidan," her aunt answered sincerely. "He's such a fine craftsman."

Zoey was gripped by momentary apprehension. Had Ivy been calling Nick *the Armstrong boy* because she couldn't keep him and his son straight in her mind? *It's no big deal,* she convinced herself. *They look like twins. I used to get Erik's sisters' names mixed up, too. I'm overthinking it because of Mark's comments.*

Then it occurred to her that Mark would have a conniption if he knew Ivy was going forward with the remodel without his input. But with any luck, by the time he visited Hope Haven next, the remodel would be completed and it would be too late for him to try to interfere.

*

On Sunday, Nick presented Ivy with a tall bottle in a wine tote. It turned out to be gourmet extra-virgin olive oil from Sicily. Although the teenagers were still outside, he confided softly, "I would have brought wine but… I didn't know if that would be appropriate." Zoey wasn't sure what he meant by that but she figured it had something to do with Aidan's stepfather being an alcoholic.

"It's a lovely gift, Nicholas. Thank you," Ivy said and Zoey was relieved to notice she had no difficulty with his name.

Then he handed Zoey a plain white paper bag. She peeked inside: it contained a quart of choco-cran ice cream. Before she could thank him, Aidan came in with the other kids. "Hello, Mrs. Cartwright. Hi Zoey. Special delivery." He held up another white bag. It held a second quart but this time it was strawberry ice cream.

Zoey couldn't stop smiling; not only did Nick remember her favorite flavor, but somehow he knew and remembered her aunt's, as well. *How could I have ever thought he and Mark were two of a kind?* she asked herself. *Mark doesn't even remember the name of Aunt Ivy's heart condition.*

Gabi came downstairs just then and introduced Amy and Connor, who had gotten a ride with Nick and Aidan. It took a second for Zoey to recognize Connor as the boy who gave her niece a tour on the first day of school. He seemed self-conscious, as if he couldn't decide where to stand and he kept pushing his glasses up on his nose. By contrast, Amy made herself right at home, plunking into a chair, cuddling Moby to her chest and blathering merrily to whoever made eye contact with her, including the cat. Connor chuckled at everything she said, so Zoey couldn't tell whether he was interested in or going out with her, or if he was just nervous.

After serving cold drinks, Ivy chased everyone except for Zoey out of the kitchen so they could put the finishing touches on supper. Aidan had brought the croquet set down from the attic while he was waiting for his father to return on the day Zoey injured herself, so Gabi and Amy challenged Aidan and Connor to a game and Nick watched them play until Zoey summoned them back inside.

In-between lively conversation and good-natured banter, the seven of them polished off both pans of lasagna; to Ivy's delight even Gabi had a second helping. Whether it was because she was enjoying all the youthful energy in the house, because Nick had been so thoughtful or because her aunt seemed more vivacious than she'd been all week, Zoey didn't want the festive occasion to end and their guests to leave.

So she was glad that when they finished eating, Amy asked if the teenagers could go up on the widow's walk. Ivy told them they were welcome to, but Gabi hesitated. "Let's go to the beach instead."

"Why don't you want to go to the widow's walk? Are you worried because I told you I saw a couple of gigantic spiders in the attic the other day?" Aidan heckled her.

"Spiders?" Connor ran his palm over the back of his head as if he was smoothing down a cowlick. "I'm not going up there."

"What's the matter? You afraid they might build a nest in your hair?" Aidan razzed him.

"*I'm* not afraid," Amy boasted. "I'll go with you, Aidan."

"I'm not afraid, either," Gabi scoffed. "You sure you don't want to come, Connor?"

"No. I mean yeah. I don't want to go. Spiders freak me out," he admitted, which, in an ironic way, struck Zoey as a brave thing to do.

While the other three went up to the roof, Connor remained in the dining room with the adults. Beneath the table, he jiggled his leg so fiercely that Zoey felt queasy from the vibrations. In an attempt to quell his anxiety and simultaneously get more information about her niece's social life, she asked, "How do you and Gabi know each other, Connor?"

As soon as she asked it, Zoey recognized it was a stupid question since obviously they knew each other from going to the same high school on a small island, but she was new to this kind of parental detective work.

"Yeah, so." Connor adjusted his glasses on his nose. "She's in group with me."

Zoey didn't know whether that meant a group chat or if that was what high school home room was called now or what. "Oh, right, group. That's…" she left her voice drift off, hoping he'd fill in the blank so she wouldn't seem so out of touch.

"Tuesdays and Thursdays after school. Sometimes on Saturday morning, too, but that's rare. No one wants to get up that early."

Oh, this must have something to do with band practice, Zoey realized. Gabi had mentioned the band teacher occasionally divided them into groups accordingly to their abilities. "What instrument do you play?"

Connor abruptly pushed his chair back. "'Scuse me. I'm going to see if I can spot them on the roof."

"Be careful," Nick warned. "Knowing Aidan, he brought water balloons with him."

"Okay. Yeah."

After the door slammed behind Connor, Zoey told Nick about Ivy's plan to remodel the rest of the kitchen and asked if he could take on the project. After deciding that Nick could start as soon as possible, in-between his other jobs—which pleased Zoey, as it would give Mark less time to find out and interfere—she left Nick and her aunt chatting about colors and design as she took care of the dishes.

When the teenagers returned from the widow's walk and announced they were going to Rose Beach, the adults settled down with ice cream and the cribbage board. But after just one game, Ivy declared, "It's almost time for the sun to set. If you hurry, you kids can watch it from the widow's walk."

Subtle, Zoey thought, but for once she didn't mind her aunt's efforts to push her and Nick together. He seemed game, too, saying, "Yeah, I'd really like that."

He followed her up the stairs and once they reached the landing in the attic, Zoey started toward the foldable ladder in the ceiling between the two chimneys. But Nick veered toward Sylvia's trunks on the side of the room. He pushed on the plywood in several places, presumably to test Aidan's handiwork in securing it to the joists.

Then he crouched down, running his hand over the solid floor. "Do you know what it is?"

"Dust? Some kind of pollen?"

Nick chuckled. "No. Come here, look. I'm almost positive this is the house's original flooring—it's probably close to two hundred years old."

He explained that in the early 1800s, builders often used very long, wide-plank boards—up to 14 or 16 feet long and 18 to 24 inches wide—because they covered more space and needed fewer joints and fasteners. Since attic flooring wasn't treaded on as frequently as the flooring in the rest of the house, some of the original saw marks hadn't been worn away. Nick pointed to what looked like dark, thin stripes running across the width of the boards. "See?"

"Yeah, well if you were two hundred years old, you'd have a few flaws, too."

"These aren't considered flaws—they're considered a rare find. Some people go out in search of old attics and barns so they can reclaim wood like this and use it in remodels or for other purposes."

"Oh. You're not going to suggest that Aunt Ivy puts this in the kitchen, are you? She's open to some superficial changes, but it would unsettle her if you started ripping up the floors."

"No, I wasn't thinking of that at all. The floor in the kitchen looks like it's pretty old, too, which is why I steered her away from covering it with tile. It's been stripped and painted over a few times, but it's still very valuable and with a little gentle sanding, I think it'll look amazing. But this—this is really something."

Just don't tell Mark about it or he'll try to auction it online or something—if he hasn't already, Zoey thought. "We'd better get going or we'll miss the show," she said, gesturing to the hatchway.

She climbed the ladder first, emerging onto the platform, which was bordered by a low, white balustrade made of square-top wooden spindles. Moments later, Nick joined her. Facing the back yard, he rotated slowly, clearly awestruck by the sweeping view of the island and seascape: the lowland behind Ivy's place, with its mix of quaint cottages and expansive summer homes, as charming as dollhouses. The neat, verdant lawns eventually gave way to hills scattered with pitch pines and junipers. A long stripe of blond dunes stretched beneath a wider stripe of the ocean, which in this light appeared royal blue. And all of it capped by a pastel sky—so much sky!

The scenery was similar to the left and right, with landmarks from the neighboring towns which made up Hope Haven—including Port Newcomb's ferry dock and the boardwalk in Lucinda's Hamlet—as well as marshlands, streams and kettle ponds. In the direction of the front yard was the bay, its water a glimmering mirror; its harbor, lighthouse and jetty, a postcard.

"I've worked on a lot of houses and I've seen a lot of incredible views, but this perspective beats them all," Nick commented.

"Yeah. It's hard to choose which way to look because there's so much beauty in every direction and I don't want to miss any of it."

But since they'd come to see the sun set, they faced west. Ivy was right: they arrived just in time. The sky over the bay was streaked with enough clouds to emphasize the dramatic hues—orange and yellow, pink and purple—without obscuring the golden sun as it dipped closer and closer to the horizon.

They were both quiet, squinting toward the horizon as the disc appeared to slip behind the bay. When it did, they automatically applauded; a popular Dune Island tradition. But Zoey continued to watch the setting. She'd always liked the after-effects of the sunset as much as the sunset itself, especially at low tide, when long rows of shallow pools reflected the pink sky and contrasted with intermittent strips of damp, dark sand. And because she didn't know when she'd have the opportunity to chat with Nick alone again, this evening she particularly wanted to linger in the dusky glow.

"I'm glad you're going to work on Aunt Ivy's kitchen. She's really excited about it and it will be nice to see you around," she hinted.

"Yeah, I'm glad, too. I wish I could do the entire project right away, but like I said, I've got to work straight out for the next couple of weeks and it will have to fit in around that. It was a slow winter, and right now the island is inundated with seasonal carpenters. They come here to work for guys who've been in business here a lot longer than I have. So I can't afford to turn down any projects. Especially since I, uh, I've got a, a kind of major debt I need to repay ASAP."

Ordinarily, Zoey would have considered it prying to ask about his finances, even if he was the one to bring it up. But he seemed so nervous that it made her uneasy, too. "Like, what, a gambling debt?" she questioned, only half-joking.

"No. Nothing like that." He hesitated before explaining that Aidan's situation at home with his stepfather had contributed to the teenager failing some of his classes at school and getting into some major arguments with his friends. Nick felt like his son needed counseling and more support than he knew how to give him, so he'd encouraged Aidan to go to a type of treatment center for children of alcoholics. "The program wasn't covered by insurance so I had to pay out-of-pocket. I'd do it again in a heartbeat because it was a huge help to him, but it was also super expensive."

Touched that he'd confided in her, Zoey shared a little about Gabi's situation, too. And she asked Nick to tell her more about his family, his home and growing up on Dune Island. He said he had two sisters and his parents were married for forty-three years before his mother passed away. His father died two years after that.

"My house is small. It's in Rockfield and we don't have a water view but it's one of only three houses on the street, so it's nice and secluded." Standing behind her, he took Zoey by the shoulders and angled her so she was facing southeast. "It's right over there beyond those trees. It's got a basketball hoop—the net is torn. See it?"

He was joking; Rockfield was too far away for her to distinguish any properties in particular except a church and the library. Zoey couldn't concentrate anyway; all she could think about was how much she wanted to lean back against his chest and have him embrace her until the *moon* set. But he dropped his hand and pivoted toward the bay again, so she did, too.

The beacon from Sea Gull Lighthouse was more noticeable now that the sun was down and when it flashed in their direction, Nick remarked, "When I was young, I used to think one of the best jobs on Dune Island was to be the lighthouse keeper."

"Because of the view?"

"Because of my sisters—they drove me nuts." He grinned, his bright teeth still distinguishable in the waning light. "Like I said, we lived in a small house, so being a keeper seemed like an ideal arrangement. I figured I'd get to live alone *and* have the best bird's-eye view of the harbor and beaches in Benjamin's Manor. But now that I've been up here, I realize I was wrong—your aunt's house has the best view."

Thinking of Mr. Witherell, Zoey replied, "I imagine living in the lighthouse would get awfully lonely after a while."

"Yeah. Once I got older, I wondered how Mr. Witherell managed to do it for all those years, especially without a wife or children for company. But maybe he became a keeper because he preferred living alone."

"Maybe." *Or maybe he had no choice in the matter.*

"Seems like a shame, though."

Zoey swung around to look at him, wondering what else he'd heard about Mr. Witherell. Was he going to bring up the rumor about her aunt Sylvia? "What was a shame?"

"He had access to one of the most romantic views on the island, but he didn't have anyone to share it with."

Zoey relaxed, directing her gaze toward the bay again. "You want to hear something really romantic? My great-uncle Marcus proposed to my great-aunt Sylvia up here."

"That's cool."

"Yeah. All sorts of romantic things have happened on this widow's walk." Laughing, she told him about how Jessica once sneaked up there with a boy, a lifeguard she'd been flirting with all vacation, to make out with him during his lunch break. She'd thought it was the perfect location since Zoey and her parents were at the beach and her aunts were napping. But their father had decided he'd gotten enough sun for the day, so he walked home. As he was tramping up the hill, he happened to glance toward the widow's walk.

"Jess was pretty young—she'd never kissed anyone before—and the boy was at least three years older, so my father... well, let's just say voices really travel from up here." Zoey smiled, thinking about how her sister later told her that kissing the boy was worth every minute of being grounded.

"Did you ever sneak up here to kiss any boys when you were a teenager?"

"Me? No way."

"Ah. You learned from your big sister's mistake, right?"

"No, I just never had the chance. Jess was always more popular than I was when we were growing up. She looked just like Gabi. The boys loved her."

Nick nudged her arm. "You're not so bad yourself, you know."

"Gee, thanks."

"No, listen." Once again he gently took her by the shoulders, twisting her around to face him. Zoey could feel the warmth of his palms and fingertips through the fabric of her blouse. "If I had known you then, I definitely would have wanted to kiss you. Maybe not on a rooftop in broad daylight with your dad nearby, but yeah. I would have considered myself lucky."

My father's not here now and there's hardly any daylight left... she thought, heady with longing. Tilting her chin upward, she peered at him from beneath her lashes. "Me, too," she murmured.

For a moment, neither of them moved. Then Nick shifted his weight and Zoey let her lids fall closed as he began to caress her shoulder—but no, he was withdrawing his hand. He was moving away.

"The kids will be back soon, if they're not back already," he said. "We should go in now."

"Yes, we should," she agreed, since the since the moment, like the sky, had completely lost its luster.

CHAPTER NINE

During the next several days, Zoey puzzled over what happened on the widow's walk between Nick and her. Rather, what *didn't* happen between them. Although it was possible that it was merely wishful thinking on her part, she was almost positive he'd been about to kiss her. Then why didn't he? *Maybe he wanted to, but he changed his mind because he was afraid Gabi and Aidan might see us. Or because we both had spicy sausage breath*, she guessed. Her aunt had said he didn't have a girlfriend, but maybe he'd started seeing someone else since then—could that have been it?

Only a couple of months ago, Zoey had pledged she wouldn't get involved with another guy until the fall, at least. And until a few weeks ago, she didn't want anything to do with Nick. Yet here she was now, acting like a teenager, obsessing about whether he *liked* her or not. She'd even told Lauren about him. They had analyzed the minutiae of Nick's behavior for over an hour and still hadn't come to any conclusions. As frustrating as his behavior was, Zoey realized hers was even more pathetic and she finally resolved to put the incident—the *non*-incident—on the widow's walk out of her mind.

Instead, she concentrated so intently on helping her aunt research kitchen designs and décor online that by Thursday she felt as if her eyes were crossing. The time and energy were worth it; Ivy's crying jags decreased in number and intensity and she'd finally decided what she wanted for cupboards, countertops and a backsplash. Nick agreed to stop in later that evening to discuss her choices and make sure the design was workable.

"I hope I'm doing the right thing," she wavered all of a sudden.

It was almost four thirty and Zoey was sliding a chicken into the oven for supper, so her attention was on setting the timer, not on Ivy. "I really like what you selected, but if you're not sure about it, you should ask Nick for his opinion."

"I mean I still feel disloyal to Sylvia. It's as if I'm trying to remove every trace of her from memory, isn't it?" Ivy removed a tissue from her sleeve, a sure sign that she was on the brink of crying.

"Aunt Ivy, you couldn't erase Aunt Sylvia from your mind if you tried. You were too much a part of each other's lives. Of each other's hearts. The countertops are superficial reminders—your memories go much deeper than that." When Ivy blinked rapidly, fighting tears, Zoey quickly suggested, "Why don't you choose one thing in this room that Aunt Sylvia picked out and keep it exactly as it is?"

Ivy's eyes darted around the kitchen. Then her shoulders slumped and she wailed, "I can't. Everything in here looks too awful."

Zoey couldn't disagree. Thinking quickly, she said, "Aunt Sylvia was the one who planted the rhododendron by that window. I realize it's not technically inside the kitchen, but she loved to look at it when she did the dishes."

"Yes, that's true. And I did tell Nick I didn't want to cut it down, so I suppose not every visual reminder of Sylvia will be gone, right?"

"Right," Zoey agreed, just as there was a knock at the door. She expected it to be Aidan, who had been coming over to put down mulch and take care of the other spring yard work. But instead, it was Amy.

"Hi," the girl chirped, stepping inside before Zoey invited her. "Gabi forgot her trig book at my house yesterday, only I didn't know she'd left it there until she told me in class, otherwise I would have brought it to school today because she's got a quiz tomorrow and she needs it to study," she burbled before stopping to take a breath. "I'll run upstairs and give it to her real quick—my mom is parked outside."

"Gabi's not there," Zoey informed her and Amy came to a halt. "She's at band practice."

"No, she's not," Amy contradicted, shaking her red curls. "We don't have after-school practice on Tuesdays and Thursdays because we practice during sixth period instead. Seventh period on Friday. We only practice after school on Mondays and Wednesdays. That's because some of the kids in band also play sports and the band director and coaches didn't want to force them to choose just one activity."

She spoke so fast Zoey couldn't quite keep up with the schedule but she understood enough to know Gabi hadn't been where she said she'd been after school. She took the book and assured Amy she'd give it to her niece. As the teenager hopped down the back steps, Zoey leaned against the wall in stunned disbelief. *There has to be a good explanation for this*, she thought, unwilling to accept that her niece had deliberately deceived her. *That's just not like her. We have a better relationship than that.* Or was she fooling herself?

Was it possible Zoey had a big blind spot about her niece, just like Ivy—and Sylvia, when she was alive—had a blind spot about Mark?

Zoey's brooding was interrupted when her phone vibrated in her back pocket; it was the library director. She went into the living room to take the call and her disappointment in her niece was tempered by the news that she was being invited back for a second interview the following Thursday.

"They've only invited three of us back, so that increases my odds of getting the position," she told her aunt after she got off the phone.

"That's terrific!" Ivy clapped. Almost immediately, her face fell. "But if you get the job, you'll have to return to Rhode Island, won't you?"

Zoey didn't want her aunt to start dreading her departure already. "Not until the end of the summer. That's three full months away."

"But you'll still be coming to Benjamin's Manor on weekends and vice versa, right?"

Zoey was surprised her aunt was willing to visit her in Providence, since she rarely left the island. "Yes, I'll definitely come visit you. And I'd love it if you wanted to stay with me in Providence, too."

"Me? No, no. I was speaking about you and Nicholas. Now that you two are an item, you don't want to lose momentum, especially because he's so skittish—"

"We're *not* an item, Aunt Ivy."

"You're not?" She sounded almost as disappointed as Zoey had been that nothing romantic had come of their time alone on Sunday. "But you both seemed so eager to go out on the widow's walk the other evening. I was sure you wanted privacy to smooch."

"No, I think Nick was just excited because it was the first time he got to see the view from up there."

"Aha, but you didn't deny that *you* were eager to be alone with *him*," Ivy exclaimed.

Once again, Zoey belatedly realized that her aunt had tricked her into disclosing the information she wanted to know. Since it was useless to deny it, she said, "You're right. I *was* kind of hoping he'd kiss me and for a moment, it seemed as if he was going to. But he didn't. So now it's sort of like what you said about waiting for him to deal the cards in cribbage… I'm getting restless. I don't really feel like playing any more."

Ivy shook her head. "I don't know what's wrong with that boy. Someone needs to light a fire under him."

Aware that this conversation would be fresh in her aunt's mind when Nick came to the house later that evening, Zoey pleaded, "Aunt Ivy, you can't tell him—"

"Don't worry, I won't say anything to embarrass you," she promised. "Not today, anyway."

After supper, Ivy went upstairs to shower before Nick arrived. Zoey was doing the dishes when Gabi came in and she wasted no time asking her niece where she'd been that afternoon.

"Where I always am," the teenager nonchalantly replied, peering into the cupboard as she stood on tiptoe.

"I happen to know you weren't at band practice, Gabi."

"I didn't say I was."

"You *implied* it." Zoey took a deep breath and then let it out. She had skirted the truth often enough herself to understand Gabi was hiding something, but hadn't wanted to tell a boldfaced lie about it. That was a good sign, but Zoey still needed to know the whole truth. "If you weren't at band practice, where were you?"

Gabi mumbled something Zoey couldn't hear so she asked her to repeat it. "What does it matter to you whether I'm practicing my flute or not? You didn't even come to my Christmas concert this year."

The accusation plunged into Zoey's heart. Was that why her niece never played her flute in the house? Because she thought Zoey didn't want to hear it? Or because she was getting back at her for missing her performance? "I'm sorry, Gabi. I'm so proud of your talent and I wish—"

"Whatever. It doesn't matter." She snapped the cupboard door shut and started to leave the room.

Zoey decided she'd talk to her about missing her Christmas concert again later, when Gabi was more receptive. For now, they had to stay on topic. "Hold on. We're not done talking yet. I told you before that I trusted you and I do. But in return, I expect *you* to trust me by telling me the truth. So I'll ask you again. What have you been doing after school on Tuesdays and Thursdays?"

Gabi dipped her chin and picked at her fingernail, her hair veiling her face. "Hanging with my friends."

Zoey wasn't buying it. If her niece wasn't hiding anything, why would she have led Zoey to believe she was at band practice all this time? "Where?"

"Does it really matter?"

"Yes, it matters."

"Why? Aren't I entitled to privacy? It's not as if you tell *your* aunt everything about your life. You've even asked me to keep your secrets from her!"

Gabi's point was beside the point, a distraction tactic. Zoey ignored it. As evenly as she could, she answered, "I'm an adult and you're fourteen, so I'm legally responsible for you and I need to be sure you're safe. I also need to know I can find you quickly if there's an emergency here."

"You sound just like Kathleen."

Good. That means I must be doing something right. "So, are you going to tell me where you've been hanging out with your friends?"

She huffed. "At the beach."

This entire island is a beach! "Which one?"

"I don't remember what it's called. I just moved here."

"How about your friends' names? Can you remember *them*?" Zoey shot back. When Gabi shrugged, she realized she was on the verge of losing patience, so she was silent a moment, trying not to let her frustration get the best of her. Her voice low, she tried again. "Listen, I understand that you want your privacy. Your freedom. And I've been very careful not to infringe on that. But when you won't tell me what you've been doing, it makes me wonder all sorts of things. Like maybe you're out with a boy, maybe Aidan, or—"

Gabi snickered in a way that reminded her *exactly* of Mark. "You don't know *any*thing."

That was more than she could tolerate. Zoey glared at her, saying, "I'm not asking you to share every detail of your social life with me, Gabi. But I do need to know who you're with and where you're going. If you refuse to tell me that much, I have to assume it's because you're doing something you shouldn't be doing. So from now on, except on Mondays and Wednesdays when you have band practice, I expect you to come directly home from school."

Gabi backed away and yelled, "Why? So I can sit around with my two old spinster aunts while they stare at a picture of a dead person and tell the same stories over and over again?"

She stomped out of the room but before she reached the stairs, Zoey raced into the hall and shouted the first comeback she could think of. "For your information, I'm not old—I'm thirty-eight. And Aunt Ivy's not a spinster. She's a *widow*!"

Her hands shaking, she returned to the sink and filled a glass with water but she couldn't drink it. She heard a rustle in the living room. *Please let that be Moby*, she thought. But when she approached the threshold she saw Ivy in her usual chair, a newspaper folded on her lap. She hadn't gone upstairs to shower after all; she must have heard everything.

"I'm so sorry, Auntie." Zoey squatted in front of her, touching her knees. "She's behaving like a little monster. Just like her mother used to." Although Jessica rarely wielded it, she'd had a formidable mean streak. "Gabi didn't mean those things. She was lashing out at me. And I shouldn't have reacted the way I did, either."

"She's right, though. I do tell the same stories over and over." Ivy seemed so far away. So withdrawn. As if she'd closed herself up, like one of Sylvia's tulips in the evening.

"I love hearing your stories," Zoey insisted. "Especially that one about the time Captain Denny tried to surprise you on your twenty-fifth birthday and you stumbled upon his gift. Where had he hidden it again?"

But Ivy shook her head. "Not tonight, dear."

Seeing the pain on her aunt's face, Zoey felt like sending Gabi on the next flight back to California. Then she wished *she* could fly away…

Instead, she offered to make tea for her aunt and while the water was heating, she finished putting away the dishes. *Everything's going to be okay. Everything's going to be okay,* she repeated. But she only half-believed herself—which seemed fair, considering she could only half-believe what anyone else told her lately, either.

*

Zoey figured she'd start anew with her niece in the morning, but Gabi didn't come downstairs for breakfast and she left the house without saying goodbye. Nick had come by the previous evening—looking as handsome as ever, in a shirt which showed off his biceps even more than usual—to discuss the new kitchen design, and had confirmed that Zoey could begin painting the cupboards and drawers. So Zoey turned her attention to emptying the cabinets and carrying their contents to the dining room so she could clean, prime and prep. Since Ivy hadn't commented about being cold for a while and she no longer wore a long-sleeved sweater, Zoey decided she could open the windows and start painting on Monday.

She slid a box of dry goods under the living room table and noticed crumbs beneath one of the chairs. *That was where Connor sat*, she thought, smiling. As nervous as he'd been, there was something about him that was as loveable as an overgrown puppy dog.

Suddenly, she recalled what he'd said about Gabi being in his group on Tuesdays and Thursdays. Zoey had assumed he meant she was in his group in band, but now she realized he meant she was in the group of kids who hung out together after school. That made Zoey feel a little more at ease. Maybe it was because he'd refused to let Aidan pressure him into going up to the attic, but Connor didn't seem like the type of kid to be easily influenced by peer pressure or to pressure someone else. *Of course, I didn't think Erik was the type to lose my life's savings in a shady deal, either,* she reminded herself.

She still had three cupboards left to clean when Gabi returned from school, otherwise Zoey would have suggested they take a walk so she could broach the subject of where she'd been going after school again. But Gabi went straight upstairs and by the time Zoey was ready to put away her supplies, Ivy was up from her nap. Yawning, she said she was going to relax in the living room until she was a little more awake.

Then Gabi came down and Zoey overhead her asking their aunt, "Do you want to play cribbage?"

"That's okay, dear. I know you have other things you'd rather do."

"No, I don't. Please, Aunt Ivy?"

Zoey didn't hear what her aunt said next, but a few minutes later their giggling floated down the hall. Zoey was so relieved that any discord between her aunt and niece had been resolved that she didn't even mind that Gabi still gave *her* the cold shoulder during supper. *Now I understand how Kathleen feels when Gabi only talks to Scott,* she thought.

That didn't mean Zoey intended to let her keep it up, however. So the next morning when Gabi came into the dining room to look for a box of cereal, Zoey told her, "Before you leave for school today, there are a couple of things I'd like to talk about."

Gabi's eyes were steely as she crossed her arms. "I'm not telling you anything else about what I've been doing on Tuesdays and Thursdays, so you might as well not ask me again."

That wasn't how Zoey had hoped their conversation would go, but she nodded slowly. "Okay. If you'd rather continue coming right home from school on those days, that's up to you. But what *I* want to tell *you* is that I'm very sorry I didn't visit you this past Christmas. I'd just gotten laid off and I was really stressed. More importantly, I thought you were going to be busy with symphony and I figured it would be better if I came during your February break so we could spend more time together. But by then, Aunt Sylvia had pneumonia so I had to help her and Aunt Ivy... Anyway, I just want you to know that visiting you has always been a highlight of my year and I don't intend to miss spending another Christmas with you again."

Gabi's features expression remained impassive, but Zoey noticed the tiniest flicker of emotion in her eyes before she said, "Can I go now?"

Zoey inhaled deeply. *She's only fourteen*, she reminded herself and then she exhaled. "Yes. You can go."

Gabi turned to leave without taking the cereal box. "See you later," she said, which wasn't a lot, but it was better than nothing.

*

"Zoey!" Ivy called urgently when Zoey entered the house on Monday morning.

On Saturday, she'd gone to the hardware store and brought home several paint sample cards in various shades of white. So this morning she went back to buy two gallons of the color Ivy selected.

She set them down and rushed into the living room where her aunt was sitting with one hand on her chest. Her face was flushed and she appeared dazed.

"My heart's aflutter," she said.

"Did you take a nitro pill already or should I go get you one?"

"No. I mean my heart is aflutter because I finally did it. I mended a fence I should have mended a long time ago."

Zoey couldn't imagine her aunt swinging a hammer and she wondered if she was… if she was *losing it*. "What fence?"

"The broken one between me and Mr. Witherell."

Zoey dropped onto the couch, relieved. *That makes more sense*, she thought. *Sort of.* "When did you see him?"

"On his daily excursion past the house this morning. See, last night I couldn't sleep because I was thinking about how Gabi said I spend too much time in the past."

"She didn't say *that*. Besides—"

"It's okay. It's true that I spend a lot of time thinking and talking about people from the past; people in my life who have died. I have my reasons for doing that, but today I decided I was going to talk to someone from the past who can talk back to me—Mr. Witherell. So I waited on the front steps and when I saw him, I called him over. 'Phin,' I said, 'This is a long time in coming, but I want you to know I'm sorry for speaking so harshly to you when we were young. If you haven't already, will you forgive me now?' Guess what he said?"

"That he'd be glad to?"

"No. He said, 'Uhn.'" Ivy imitated his grunting noise, delighted. "Which was as good as saying *yes*. And I told him, 'The next time

I bake a rhubarb pie, I hope you'll stop in and have a piece with me.' And he nodded and then he doddered away."

Zoey wasn't sure she would have interpreted Mr. Witherell's response the same way her aunt had interpreted it, but she supposed if Ivy knew him well enough to call him Phin, she also knew what his grunting meant. "That's wonderful," she said.

But was it? Mr. Witherell's enigmatic comment to Mark after the funeral proved he was capable of conversing. Although Zoey blamed her cousin for provoking him and she believed the remark was only meant to be facetious, she couldn't be one hundred percent positive Mr. Witherell wouldn't repeat it to Ivy. Not out of revenge or because it was true, but possibly in the course of owning up to angering her great-nephew. And the slightest whisper of all those rumors, no matter how fabricated they were, would hurt her aunt's feelings. So while she was glad Ivy had rectified her falling out with Mr. Witherell, out of a sense of protectiveness, Zoey wished she'd keep her distance from him.

"Yes, it is wonderful. It goes to show it's never too late to ask for forgiveness. Righting that wrong with Phineas makes me feel so… so *alive*," she gushed. "Now, if you pull out the drawers and set them on some newspaper on the table, I can sit down and paint the front of them while you work on the cupboards."

Zoey hadn't seen her this energetic since… since she didn't know when. They spent the day painting and chatting, stopping only to eat lunch. Ivy didn't even take a nap. When they were finished, Zoey could see that the cupboards would need a second coat, but her aunt was jubilant about the overall effect.

"Nick was right—a simple change can make a world of difference," she said. "Now that I've put things right with Mr. Witherell and we're painting the kitchen, there's no telling what other changes I'll make!"

Just as long as they're changes for the better, Zoey worried to herself. But she smiled at and agreed, "The sky's the limit, Aunt Ivy."

*

"Aunt Ivy and I will be at the cardiologist's office this afternoon but I still expect you to come home immediately after school," Zoey informed her niece on Tuesday morning. She thought she'd be met with indifference, but Gabi furrowed her brow.

"Why does Aunt Ivy have to go to a cardiologist?"

"For her annual check-up," Zoey said. Then she caught herself. Knowing how sensitive Gabi could be, she didn't want to worry her, yet she didn't want to be deceptive, either. "Well, it's not exactly a regular check-up. She's been having more heart pain than usual so the doctor wanted her to come in for some tests. But I think he's erring on the side of caution."

"Oh." When she blinked her big blue eyes she looked so childlike that Zoey instinctively opened her arms to comfort her with a hug. But Gabi abruptly turned on her heel, nearly clobbering Zoey with her book bag as she slung it over her shoulder.

This time, she said to herself, *I don't care if she is only fourteen— her attitude still hurts.*

It seemed to take forever for Ivy to get through her EKG, echocardiogram and bloodwork. Finally, Zoey reunited with her as they waited while the cardiologist read her results and then a nurse escorted them into his office. Zoey had only met Dr. Laurent once before but she'd immediately liked him. Although he was relatively young, he was considered one of the best cardiac surgeons in New England. But he didn't seem to have an ego about it and Zoey appreciated that he was kind, thoughtful and treated her aunt—and undoubtedly everyone else he saw, judging from the wait time—as if she were his only patient.

After he greeted them, Ivy pointed to a seascape painting hanging on the wall. "I recognize that painting. It was in a newspaper article about a class at the library in Benjamin's Manor."

"Yes. It's an original by Emily Vandermark, the artist who's teaching that class. What do you think of it?"

"It's beautiful.   Is the artist your patient?" Ivy asked and Zoey cringed, knowing privacy laws would have prevented the doctor from admitting it if she was.

"She's my sister."

Ivy's mouth dropped open. "What if I had said I *didn't* like it?"

"I would have appreciated your honesty—although I probably wouldn't have repeated the comment to my sister. She's the type who'd shoot the messenger," Dr. Laurent joked. Then he grew serious. "I know you want honesty from me, too, Mrs. Cartwright."

"That depends on what you're going to tell me." Ivy made him chuckle, but a knot tightened in Zoey's stomach.

"I'm going to tell you the same thing I've been telling you, and that's that I think you need a pacemaker."

Zoey pounced on that. "What do you mean, 'what you've been telling her'?"

Dr. Laurent glanced at Ivy, who nodded, so he answered, "I've been advising your aunt she needs a pacemaker for the past three, three-and-a-half years." He continued, explaining why he thought she had an increased risk of suffering sudden cardiac death and how a pacemaker could keep her heart beating regularly.

"Why have you put this off, Aunt Ivy? I'm sure your insurance covers the cost."

"Yes, but there are risks associated with the surgery. And there can be unpleasant side effects from the device."

Dr. Laurent elaborated, saying the procedure was a minor surgery—her aunt would only have to stay in the hospital overnight. The doctor did caution that because of Ivy's age and health history, her recovery time would be a little longer. But all things considered, the procedure and side effects seemed like a walk in the park compared to what her aunt had experienced when she underwent cancer treatment. And nothing he described worried Zoey nearly as much as the increased likelihood that Ivy could suffer a fatal heart event without the pacemaker.

Her mind reeling, she exclaimed, "I thought you were fine. I thought Dr. Laurent was managing your heart pain with medication."

"The chest pain—the angina—is a *symptom*," Dr. Laurent clarified. "The nitroglycerin helps, but it doesn't treat the arrhythmia, which is the underlying condition."

He's only been treating the symptom, not the cause? "I don't understand how you could let her walk out of your office year after year, knowing she's in danger. That seems unethical—"

"Zoey!" Ivy admonished but she'd been too distressed to censor herself.

"It's okay. I wish all my patients had family members who care about them as much as your niece cares about you. And I welcome her expressing her questions and concerns." He turned to Zoey and gently said, "I don't think we can say for certain that your aunt's in danger of suffering a significant cardiac event. She's been declining this procedure for years and so far, she's been all right. I only know what the risks and probabilities are. Based on that, my best advice has been for her to have the device implanted—the sooner, the better. But ultimately, the decision is hers to make, not mine."

Zoey could read between the lines; he was also implying the choice was Ivy's, not Zoey's. She countered defensively, "Would you leave the decision up to the patient if it was *your* great-aunt sitting here instead of mine?"

"Yes, I would." He glanced at his hands, folded on his lap. There was such compassion in his voice that Zoey knew he understood her when he added, "But it would anguish me if she didn't make the choice I thought was best."

"Oh, stop pressuring me, you two," Ivy burst out, shaking a finger at both of them. If Zoey hadn't been so exasperated and frightened, she might have found it funny. Her aunt fell back in her seat and threw her hands in the air. "If I can remodel my kitchen, I suppose my heart deserves an update after all these years. You win. I'll get the pacemaker."

Dr. Laurent was going to be out of town the following week, but he said they could schedule the surgery for the week after that since he was the only one Ivy wanted to perform the procedure. Meanwhile, he encouraged her to do what she'd been doing; taking the nitro pills for chest pain, eating healthful foods, getting lots of rest and avoiding stressful situations.

"If you're at a loss for a pleasant way to relax, you might consider signing up for one of the painting classes my sister is teaching. Just don't repeat that crack I made about her being the type to shoot the messenger." He and Ivy both laughed but Zoey was having a difficult time not crying.

While her aunt was checking out, Zoey went to hold the elevator since she needed a moment to pull herself together. As she was waiting, her phone pulsated in her purse. "Hi, Gabi," she said when she answered it. "What's up?"

"I just wondered where you are."

That's a switch. "We're still at the hospital."

"The *hospital?* I thought Aunt Ivy only had a doctor's appointment."

"She did. Her doctor's office is located in the hospital."

"Oh. I didn't think it would take so long."

That's why she called—she's worried. Zoey's tone softened, "Aunt Ivy just got done with her appointment. We'll be home soon."

"Is she okay?"

"She's…" Zoey realized her aunt was now within earshot. "I'll tell you about it later."

"I can make supper tonight if you want me to."

"That would be nice, except there's wet paint on most of the cupboards so we decided to order takeout from Captain Clark's." As Ivy stepped into the elevator, Zoey pointed to the phone and mouthed, *Gabi.* Then she pressed the button for the lobby and the door closed. "We can either have an early meal or reheat it later. Is there anything in particular you'd like us to bring back for you?

"A pet lobster?"

It took a moment for her to get the reference to the time when her niece was a little girl and wanted to bring a lobster home from the restaurant as a pet. Gabi was making a joke. Making amends, of sorts. Zoey appreciated the effort. "Moby would get jealous. He thinks he owns you."

"All right, then bring me chowder, please."

As they waited on a bench outside for their ride to come, Zoey stared toward the port, only vaguely aware of the small passenger ferry coming in to dock and the gulls squawking overhead. *We shouldn't have takeout for supper*, she brooded. *Aunt Ivy always orders onion rings and those aren't good for her heart. She shouldn't have been painting for so long the other day, either. It was probably too much activity all at once…*

"Stop worrying about me." It was uncanny how Ivy could read her mind. "I'm going to be fine."

"I know you are." Zoey's smile belied her fears.

Ivy patted her hand. "You've been such a help to me. Just like Sylvia always was. I can't tell you how much I've appreciated it."

Zoey didn't like the way her aunt was talking in the past tense. It felt as if she was saying goodbye. "We've discussed this, Aunt Ivy. You don't have to tell me how much you appreciate my help. I already know."

"Yes, but what I do need to say is that even though I'm grateful for all you've done, I don't want my surgery or recovery to interfere with your plans. If you get that library job, don't put off starting it on my account."

So was that why her aunt hadn't had the pacemaker implanted sooner—because she hadn't wanted to be a "burden" to Sylvia or to Zoey? "It doesn't begin until late August and you'll be better long before then."

"Yes, but if there's a change. Or if another opportunity comes up sooner. Because I could always recover in one of those rest homes Mark has told me about."

Ugh. I'd forgotten all about Mark. Anticipating that one of them would have to let him know about Ivy's upcoming surgery, Zoey ruefully mused, *He'll probably try to lease out the house as soon as she's under anesthesia.* But since it wasn't the right moment to contradict the suggestion that her aunt could recover in a rest home, Zoey stood up and said, "I think that's our car coming."

Ivy took hold of Zoey's arm for balance. As they made their way down the sidewalk, she gave her skin a little pinch. "Dear girl, listen to your aunt. Most of my life is behind me. Most of yours is ahead of you. And I want you to live it fully, no matter what, understand?"

Zoey nodded. Yes, she understood what her aunt was saying, but that didn't mean she could accept it. Not yet. Not now.

CHAPTER TEN

On Wednesday morning, Gabi said she felt too sick to go to school. "My stomach hurts. My head does, too."

Even though she'd explained to her niece that the implantation was a common procedure, Zoey suspected Gabi's malaise was the result of being told that Ivy needed a pacemaker. But a stomachache was a stomachache, so Zoey let her stay home.

Since Gabi said she'd keep an ear out in case Ivy woke up and needed something, Zoey set out on her daily run. Her interview was the next day and although she knew she should be delighted, she'd been far too busy and worried to really let it sink in. But a run might clear her head.

It was earlier than usual when she began the three-mile loop and she wondered if she'd pass Mr. Witherell on his morning jaunt around town. Then a morbid thought flashed through her mind: *wouldn't it be terrible if—now that she's finally made up with him—Aunt Ivy dies before she gets to have him over for pie?*

Zoey had barely made it halfway down the hill when her lungs felt so tight she came to a sudden stop, wrapped her arms around her chest and doubled over. No, no, no. She couldn't allow herself to cry in public on Main Street for a second time this spring. Her feet leaden, she hobbled to the park and dropped onto a bench facing the water. How tidy it looked, with its flat, blue-green surface, a sharp line for the horizon, and the bright, white ferry cutting a straight path toward the island. As usual, the pristine scenery helped Zoey organize her thoughts.

Knowing what I know now, I can't leave Aunt Ivy alone tomorrow. I'll have to reschedule my interview. Or maybe I could pay Carla to come and stay with her? Then her thoughts drifted to Mark. She was going to have to tell him about their aunt's upcoming surgery. *I wonder if he'll come to see her. He only visited his grandmother once when she was sick and her illness lasted for* months…

"Aunt Zoey? Are you okay?" her niece asked breathlessly.

Zoey hadn't seen or heard her coming. "What are you doing here, Gabi?"

"I was looking out my window and I saw you stop running and hold your chest all of a sudden. I thought maybe something was wrong."

Was she worried I *was having a heart attack? She's too young to worry so much.* "I'm fine. Just lazy. You shouldn't have rushed down here when you're sick." She tapped the bench. "Catch your breath."

Gabi took a seat and immediately blurted out, "I don't want Aunt Ivy to die."

"Neither do I. But I think she'll be fine once she gets the pacemaker implanted."

They both were quiet as they watched a gull fly by with a spider crab dangling from its beak. Not the most appetizing breakfast.

"I shouldn't have yelled those things about her telling the same stories over and over again," Gabi acknowledged. "I know she heard me and it hurt her feelings. I told her I was sorry and she said it was okay, but I still wish I could take it back. I'm sorry I called you a spinster, too."

"I forgive you and so does Aunt Ivy, so you don't need to feel guilty. It's behind us now." As delicately as she could, she took the opportunity to level with her niece, saying, "You weren't entirely wrong. Aunt Ivy does talk about the past a lot, maybe too much. I do, too. But sometimes people need to share their memories about times and people they love because it helps make them happy, or gives them strength or keeps them from feeling so lonely."

"Yeah, but sometimes it makes them sadder. It makes them *miserable*." As teardrops streamed down Gabi's cheeks and dripped from her chin, it struck Zoey that the girl wasn't referring to Ivy. She must have meant herself.

"Is that why you don't talk about your memories of your mom?"

Gabi pressed her palms against her eyelids, her sobbing punctuated with hiccups. She surprised Zoey by answering, "No. It's because Dad talks about her *all* the time. And then he gets depressed and he drinks. It's been, like, six years. Why can't he get over his dead wife?" It made Zoey wince to hear her refer to Jessica so callously but she understood the girl's bitterness was directed toward her father, not her mother. She was quiet, allowing Gabi to get it all out. "Kathleen's the one who's living. Doesn't he care about her? Doesn't he care about *me*?"

Her question was so plaintive it sounded more like a howl than like speech. *Gabi is my heart*, Jessica had once said and Zoey had assumed she'd meant her daughter was her joy. That was part of it, of course, but she understood the girl was also her mother's sorrow.

Whenever Gabi's heart had ached to the point of breaking in half, so had Jessica's. And, as it turned out, so did Zoey's now.

"Shh-shh-shh." She stroked Gabi's hair down her back. "He cares about you more than anything. About Kathleen, too. I know for a fact the two of you are the reason he agreed to get help. He doesn't want his behavior—his grief—to keep hurting you. Trust me, sweetheart. If he didn't love you and Kathleen as much as he does, he'd never even try to stop drinking."

She put her arm around her niece and pulled her toward her. As Gabi cried a while longer, Zoey said, "I'm sorry if it's been upsetting for you to hear me talk about your mom. But I do that for a couple of reasons. One is that I miss her, yes. But not always in a sad way, if that makes sense. I loved your mom so much—she was my best friend, as well as my sister. And if I never talked about her, it would be as if she never existed.

"Another reason is that she trusted me to remind you what she was like. Not to feel lonely for her but because she wanted you to get to know her better, the way you would have if she were still alive. And sometimes, you remind me so much of her, it's as if you give her back to me again. Which doesn't mean I don't appreciate how unique you are, because I do. But when I see a similarity between you and her, it's almost as if I can't help saying it out loud because I want to give her back to you, too."

Now Zoey's eyes were overflowing and when she sniffed, Gabi sat up straight and announced, "I *do* remember some things about her, Aunt Zoey. Especially when I'm here. I just didn't want to talk about them."

"Will you share one thing you remember about her before we head back to the house?"

"You know how the thunder here is super loud because it reverberates over the ocean? Well, when I was little and we'd get a storm and I couldn't sleep, my mom would sing to me. Even after it stopped thundering I'd still pretend to be afraid so she'd sing another song. I always wished I had a voice like hers but I didn't, so that's why I took flute lessons instead."

And that's *why you were devastated when I didn't come to your concert this year.* Zoey felt as if she might start crying all over again. "She'd be so proud of you."

"We're having a concert right over there by the pavilion." Gabi pointed across the lawn. "It's going to be the next-to-last week of school."

"Do Aunt Ivy and I have to wait that long to hear you play? Couldn't you practice at home?"

"I suppose," Gabi said. "But it's up to Moby."

They walked up the hill and when they entered the house, Ivy was waiting for them at the door. She was already dressed and had taken out her rollers and combed her hair. "Quick, girls, I need to get to the library. The painting class begins in half an hour."

Zoey was surprised. Although a few days ago she would have been happy to see her aunt getting involved in something out of the house, Ivy hadn't mentioned anything specific about wanting to go to a class, and she hesitated. "I don't know if that's a such good idea, Aunt Ivy."

"Why not? You're the one who's been pushing me to take a class. I'll enjoy this one more than any of the classes at the senior center.

And Dr. Laurent seems to think I will, too. Otherwise, he wouldn't have recommended it.

"Okay, but—"

"But nothing. The only thing that has changed between yesterday morning and this morning is your awareness of my arrhythmia. The arrhythmia itself hasn't changed. I'm no worse off. So I don't want anyone treating me any differently. Now, let's go!"

"I was just going to say I'm not sure we can get a driver to pick us up that quickly."

"Who needs a driver?" Ivy dangled a set of keys in front of Zoey's nose. "I have a perfectly good car in the garage. Which is where I'm headed."

"Me, too," Gabi said. Zoey was going to tell her if she was too sick for school she was too sick to go to the library. Then she realized Gabi was volunteering to go so Ivy wouldn't charge down the steps without support while Zoey dashed upstairs to grab her wallet.

After getting into the boat of a car, Zoey tried multiple times to reverse into the narrow driveway, fearing she'd knock over the picket fence on the side if she was too hasty. By the fifth time she'd backed out and pulled into the garage again, Ivy said, "Move over. Let me give it a try."

Aware that she'd dampen her aunt's newfound sense of adventure if she objected, Zoey nervously relinquished the driver's seat. She intended to stand outside so she could signal Ivy if she got too close to the fence, but her aunt told her to get back in the car or risk being flattened. She'd barely buckled her seatbelt before Ivy pressed on the gas pedal and expertly maneuvered the car down the brick driveway on her first try. When she stopped at the sidewalk so she could switch places with Zoey again, Gabi hooted, "Who-hoo! That was *awesome*, Aunt Ivy. Will you give me driving lessons?"

"Oh, I'm afraid I couldn't do that."

"Why not?"

"The last time my license expired, I didn't bother to renew it. Legally, I'm not allowed to drive except on private property."

"You could teach me how to back down the driveway, then. That's one of the hardest skills to master."

"And you're speaking from personal experience, right Gabi?" Zoey teased.

"No, I'm speaking from the experience of sitting in the back seat while *you* were trying to drive in reverse," she retorted drily. But when Zoey glanced in the rearview mirror, she caught her niece smiling to herself and she smiled, too, happy that things were starting to get back to normal between them.

They made it to the tiny library in the nick of time. While their aunt was in her art class, Gabi browsed the local history section and Zoey chatted with the librarian, who informed her the library would be closing permanently on July 15. That's when she was relocating to Colorado because her husband was starting a new job. The town hadn't found a replacement to fill her role.

"It's a shame that this place is going to close, but there are only a handful of librarians in Hope Haven and they're already staffing the other libraries," she said. "Unfortunately, the salary isn't high enough to counterbalance the cost of living here, so we haven't attracted any qualified off-island candidates."

When Zoey inquired about the exact figure, she understood why the pay rate was an obstacle. And yet, the thought ran through her mind that if she continued to stay with her aunt and lease out her townhome, she'd be able to afford to live on a lot less. Theoretically, *she* could take the librarian position. The prospect certainly had its appeal, because even though she'd been trying to keep Ivy from feeling apprehensive about her eventual return to Providence, lately Zoey was finding that *she* felt anxious about her departure, too. Not only because it would mean saying goodbye to her aunt, but also because it would mean saying goodbye to Hope Haven. The longer Zoey stayed, the more accustomed she was becoming to island life. The more she *preferred* island life.

But what if she passed up the position in Providence to take this job and her aunt had a health-care need that forced her to move six months from now? Or, heaven forbid, if she died? Mark would take over the house and Zoey would be in almost the same position financially that she was in now. Plus, she'd have nowhere to live. *Unfortunately, staying in Hope Haven permanently isn't an option for me*, she concluded. And for the rest of the hour, she researched additional employment opportunities online, just in case the one she was interviewing for the following day didn't pan out.

On the way home, Ivy raved about the artist, Emily, who also taught elementary-school kids in the island's school system. "She was so creative and encouraging. You'll never guess who her husband is—he's that pediatrician who took your splinter out, Zoey. They met when she came to the island to paint a mural for the children's wing at the hospital," her aunt babbled. "She was only supposed to stay for the summer but then she met the doc and they fell in love and got married. Isn't that romantic? Her story gives me hope for you and Nick."

"You and Nick?" Gabi taunted, "Wait till I tell Aidan he's going to get a new mommy!"

"Don't you dare! I mean it, Gabi."

"Okay, okay. I won't… if you stop so we can get an ice-cream cone."

"It's too early. Bleecker's isn't open yet," Zoey fudged. She actually didn't know what time the shop started serving, but she was concerned about Ivy's diet, since Dr. Laurent had emphasized that she ought to stick to healthy foods.

"Can we stop to get more strawberries and flour instead? Aunt Ivy's going to teach me to make a pie now that the paint's dry on the cupboards."

"I thought you had a stomachache," Zoey grumbled as she pulled into the supermarket parking lot. "I'll let you off by the door and then I'll circle around so I don't have to dock this ship."

"I'm going in, too," Ivy announced. "I can't remember the last time I went into a grocery store."

Zoey was impressed that she was expanding her interests and taking on new challenges and she understood that Ivy didn't want anyone fussing over her health. However, as she watched her niece and aunt inching toward the supermarket, she couldn't help but worry that Ivy was overexerting herself physically.

It took fifteen minutes for them to return to the car and when they did, Ivy insisted that Bleecker's had to be open by that time. Once again, Zoey drove as close to the shop's entrance as she could and then kept circling the block while Ivy and Gabi placed their order at the window. On her sixth time around, Zoey spotted them strolling toward her.

Ivy was holding her ice cream in one hand and Gabi's arm with the other, and Gabi had a cone in each hand. A breeze was blowing the teenager's hair into her face and when she reached to brush it out of her eyes, she accidentally daubed ice cream on her forehead. Stopping short, she turned and showed Ivy what she'd done. Although Zoey couldn't hear what they said, she could see laughter overtaking them both as Ivy wiped it off for her.

When they climbed into the car, Zoey joked, "I hope that wasn't my ice cream you were wearing."

"Nope. It was mine. Peppermint fudge—my mother's favorite flavor," Gabi recollected. "When I was little I used to order it, too, but I could never finish my cone, so Mom would eat the rest of it. My dad tried to convince me to get cherry vanilla, because that's what he liked and he wanted my leftovers, but I refused. So he'd always complain it wasn't fair because he was outnumbered by the two of us. Then Mom would say she wouldn't call that unfair—she'd call it lucky. And Dad would tell her that she was right, he was the luckiest man alive."

Zoey didn't remember that about Jessica and Scott, but she was glad their daughter did.

*

On Thursday, Zoey allowed Gabi to stay home from school again because she said her stomachache had come back and she had another headache, too. It was a stretch to believe her—she'd seemed fine on Wednesday afternoon when she made her first pie with Ivy.

After they'd finished baking, Gabi had put Moby in her room, and treated them to a private performance on her flute. She'd played magnificently and the mini-recital would have been the perfect ending to the day, but the evening got even better when Scott called. He'd been able to add Kathleen to the call, too, and the trio had talked for almost two hours. Which meant Gabi had stayed up late, so Zoey supposed it was possible that sleep deprivation could have upset her stomach or given her a headache. In any case, she had an ulterior motive for not challenging her niece's claim: it gave her peace of mind to know Ivy wouldn't be home alone while she was in Providence at her interview.

It went so well that before she left, the director told her she was their top candidate and they hoped to contact her with an offer by Monday. She was surprised by how anticlimactic their decision felt after so many months of being unemployed, but all Zoey cared about was getting back to Dune Island. She called both Ivy's landline and Gabi's phone to let them know she was on her way. But neither of them picked up, which she told herself was understandable: Gabi hated using her temporary phone and rarely carried it with her and Ivy was probably napping.

Home, sweet home, she thought as she crested the hill on Main Street and flicked on the blinker. Her delight at seeing Nick's truck was parked in the driveway turned to dismay when she noticed Mark's red convertible parked in front of him. *Why is he here?* she wondered. Zoey had barely closed the door to the rental car when Gabi rushed out of the house, her long hair flying behind her.

"What's wrong?"

In one long, breathless sentence, Gabi explained, "Aunt Ivy left the bathtub faucet running upstairs and it flooded the bathroom so I called Nick to ask him what to do and he said he'd come over right away and in the middle of everything Mark showed up and had a meltdown and Aunt Ivy had to take one of her heart pills and then when I was holding the door open so Nick could bring in the equipment to dry the floor Moby got out and I can't find him anywhere!"

"We will, honey." Zoey placed her hands on her niece's shoulders. "First, take a deep breath. Now let it out… Good. Did the pill help Aunt Ivy or did she need to take a second one?"

"No. It worked right away and she said she felt fine again. Nick and I helped her up the stairs so she could take a nap. I stayed with her until she fell asleep and when I came down, Nick told me Mark was taking a walk. So he's still out, Aunt Ivy's in bed and Nick's in the best room checking to see whether the water from upstairs flowed down into the ceiling or along the wall. But I have no idea where Moby could be."

"He's gotten out before but he never goes far. He usually hides beneath the wild rose bushes by the back fence. If he's not there, try using the electric can opener in front of an open window. The sound usually makes him come running. I need to go check on Aunt Ivy and talk to Nick, but if you don't find Moby by then, I'll help you look, okay?"

Zoey hurried inside the house and up the stairs to look in on Ivy, who was sleeping soundly. Since it was a cool, damp day for once, she covered her with a light blanket before going back downstairs and into the best room. She quietly walked over to where Nick was reaching up to skim his fingers across a section of wall near the opposite corner. He swiveled his head, grinning at her. *How could he possibly be smiling still?* she marveled.

"Hi, Zoey. How did your interview go?"

"A lot better than *your* afternoon went," she replied apologetically. "Gabi told me you saved the day. I don't know how to thank you."

"Just wait until you get my bill," he joked.

"Whatever you're charging, it's not enough."

"Actually, you're in luck. I don't think the flood affected this room. But I want to watch this spot for a few days. With sheetrock, sometimes it takes a while for the water to seep through, so I can't promise you there's no damage yet. If a stain shows up, I might have to remove a section of the wall and crown molding so you don't develop a mold problem."

"I never liked that wallpaper anyway." The once pink and red winding roses had faded to brown and maroon, and it was torn and peeling in several places. But in deference to her father's wishes, Ivy refused to change it, just like almost everything else in the best room. "But what I meant was that I can't compensate you enough for helping my family during another crisis. Especially for keeping an eye out for my aunt again."

"She was fine once she took her nitro pill. Well, not fine—she was kind of discombobulated, which is understandable considering all the chaos." From the disgusted look on Nick's face, Zoey knew he wasn't referring to the bathtub overflowing.

"Yeah, my niece said Mark was flipping out. Is that what triggered my aunt's angina?"

"Hard to say. She was already agitated because she'd left the water on, but I'm sure his tantrum didn't help her heart any."

"It couldn't have been pleasant for you, either," Zoey empathized.

"It's okay. I've heard worse."

"Really?" She couldn't imagine anyone spouting off the way Mark did when he was angry. Especially not in front of Nick, an unlikely audience for that kind of vitriol. "You mean you've heard worse from him or from someone else?"

He hooked his thumbs in his pockets and gave her a sheepish look. "From him… the last time you weren't here when he thought you should have been."

"Pft!" Zoey sputtered. "Is that what he was mad about this time, too? That I didn't ask his permission before I left the premises?"

"No, mostly he was going off about the cupboards being painted. Apparently, he's not a fan of white."

"Then I should tell him it's called alabaster," she grumbled, eliciting a smile from Nick. Even when the house was literally falling down around her, she liked it that he appreciated her sense of humor. "I notice he didn't stick around to give you a hand."

"Are you kidding? I was the one who suggested he should take a walk and cool down. Besides, Gabi helped me… until Moby escaped. Do you know if she's located him yet?"

"Shh." Zoey touched Nick's arm to quiet him. She heard a noise and wanted to determine whether Moby was hiding nearby or if Ivy was awake and moving around upstairs.

He leaned toward her. "What's wrong?" he whispered, his mouth enticingly close to her ear. If she turned her head toward him, just a smidgen, her lips would be—

"When you're done making out with the handyman, I want to talk to you in the living room," Mark barked. Then he retreated from the doorway as abruptly he had appeared.

Mortified, Zoey dropped her hand from Nick's arm and stepped away from him. "My cousin is *such* a—"

Nick covered his ears. "Please don't say it. I've heard all the swearing I can handle for one day," he joked, taking the edge off of Zoey's embarrassment.

Then he told her he'd left a fan running upstairs to dry the floor, but he had cut the electricity for the best room, bathroom and a portion of the basement. He'd be back to make sure it was safe before turning it on early the following morning on his way to his other client's house.

Zoey accompanied him outside and moved her car so he could leave. Since street parking was allowed after five o'clock, she didn't pull back into the driveway again so she wouldn't be blocking Mark. *I wouldn't want to delay his departure for even a minute*, she thought.

Once she was back inside she checked on Ivy again before dragging herself into the living room, where Mark was pacing in front of the fireplace. His clothes seemed to hang on him and his face was haggard. Concerned, she asked, "Hey, Mark, is something wrong?"

"Uh, let's see. I arrived here to find the bathroom flooded, Ivy in pain, Gabi in tears and *you* nowhere in sight. Not to mention the paint job in the kitchen looks like—"

"I meant is something wrong with *you*. You seem to have lost a lot of weight in a short amount of time. Have you been sick?"

"I'm sick all right. Sick and tired of what goes on around here."

Why do I even try to show him I care? "Could you please lower your voice? You'll wake Aunt Ivy and it's important that she gets plenty of rest these next couple of weeks." Zoey thought Ivy had called Mark last evening to tell him about the surgery, but in case she was wrong she explained, "She has to have a minor procedure done soon and—"

"No kidding. She told me last night. That's what I came to talk to her about. I understand how a pacemaker will help her heart, but it isn't going to help her memory."

Even though Zoey had concerns about her aunt leaving the water running, too, she knew better than to admit that to Mark when he was in this state of mind. He'd use what she said now to justify taking rash measures—in addition to whatever other scam he'd come here to put into motion—and afterward there'd be no going back.

"We all have things that slip our memory from time to time. I've left the faucet on once or twice when I've been distracted. The only difference between Aunt Ivy and me is that I've got better hearing. So, whenever I've heard the water running, it has jogged my memory and I've turned it off."

"Excuses, excuses. First it was the gas. Then the water. What's it going to take for you to see she can't live on her own—a fire? Don't you care about her at all?"

Zoey was furious. "Don't you *dare* act as if *I* don't care about her when all *you* care about is her house!"

"You're right—I do care about the house. And I'm sorry if you're so jealous that you'd rather see it burn to the ground than to see me inherit it. But I'm not going to stand idly by and let that happen." It seemed like an afterthought when he added, "*Or* watch Ivy get hurt or die in the process."

Before Zoey could respond, Gabi burst through the door with Moby in her arms, bawling. "It's my fault, Aunt Zoey. I did it. I left the faucet on. Aunt Ivy asked me to draw a bath for her and I-I forgot. I was on the phone. I'm really sorry." Her shoulders were shaking so vigorously she nearly caused the cat to tumble to the floor.

"You have *got* to be kidding me. Is everyone in this house utterly oblivious?" Mark jeered.

"I'm so sorry, Aunt Zoey," Gabi repeated. "I-I was afraid to admit it because you're already upset with me about not telling you what I've been doing after school. I thought you'd get even madder when you found out about this and you'd want to send me home. Please don't do that. I have nine hundred and thirty-one dollars in my savings account. I'll pay for the damage, I promise."

"Exactly what *have* you been doing after school?" Mark butted in. When Gabi refused to answer—refused to even look in his direction—he advanced toward her and threatened, "Maybe I should call your father and tell him about the trouble you've been causing here."

Zoey swiftly stepped in-between them. Positioning herself in front of Gabi like a shield, she glared up at her cousin. Then, in the tradition of her great-aunts—first with the policemen, and then with Mr. Witherell—she demanded, "Leave her alone or leave this house."

Mark slammed the door on his way out.

*

Over the weekend, Ivy wept nearly as often as in the days immediately following Sylvia's death. She readily forgave Gabi, who apologized profusely for letting her take the blame for the flood. However, it was no consolation to Ivy to discover that she hadn't been at fault.

"Don't you see?" she cried to Zoey. "I should have been able to recall that I wasn't the one who turned the water on. Whether I forgot to turn it off, or forgot that I didn't turn it on, it doesn't matter. Either way, it shows there's something wrong with my brain."

"I'm not sure that's entirely accurate. I think you're tired and you've had a lot of things on your mind. But after you get more rest and after you've recovered from the pacemaker procedure, if you're still concerned, we'll talk to your regular physician," Zoey suggested, but her reassurance did little to improve Ivy's mood.

Mark's presence in Hope Haven certainly didn't help, either. Fortunately, he didn't stay at the house overnight: this time he used the excuse that the pollen from the trees and grass was bothering him. He'd never mentioned having allergies before, but Ivy fell for it. Zoey suspected her aunt was paying for his room at The Harborview, but she kept her comments to herself. *It's not my money, so it's not my business.* The last thing she wanted to do was create any more tension between herself and her cousin, primarily because it would have upset Ivy.

Mark had already troubled their aunt by telling her that Zoey had made him feel unwelcome on Friday afternoon. He didn't explain in detail, because then he also would have had to admit he'd chosen to leave rather than to dial down his anger, but he said enough for Ivy to know there was conflict between them. She was so anxious about it that Zoey overheard her telling the portrait of Denny, "The kids aren't getting along and I don't know what to do about it, Captain."

So Zoey went out of her way to be congenial to her cousin. It was no small challenge, especially after he ridiculed Ivy's kitchen design, calling it a cross between a checkerboard and an elementary school bathroom. After that, Ivy seemed to lose interest in the remodel and declined Zoey's offer to browse through samples of cupboard and drawer pulls online. Nor did she want to help Gabi bake another strawberry-rhubarb pie. Although she rallied long enough to prepare brunch for Mark on Saturday morning, she was so exhausted afterward that she took a three-hour nap. On Sunday, Mark actually invited *her* out to brunch, a gesture Zoey intuitively mistrusted. But she didn't rock the boat by suggesting it might have been better if their aunt relaxed at home while Mark made her breakfast there.

That evening, as Ivy was half-reclining in bed, twisting her hair around a roller, Zoey reported that Nick had left a message for her saying he planned to remove the tiles from the backsplash on Tuesday. "Isn't that exciting?" she asked, hoping to spark her aunt's enthusiasm about the remodel again.

"Yes, it's fine," Ivy flatly replied. She had been complaining all afternoon that she was too hot. At first Zoey was worried she had a fever but when she took her temperature, it was normal, so she'd opened the windows wide, including those in her aunt's room. The surf was rough and she could hear it slapping the shore across the street.

"Aunt Ivy, is anything wrong?"

She set her brush on the nightstand without putting the rest of her hair up. "I'm just tired. Please stop fussing and turn out the light. I'm getting up bright and early tomorrow."

Zoey was going to ask if that was because she intended to invite Mr. Witherell in for some of the pie Gabi had made on her own—her second attempt was nearly perfect—but Ivy had already closed her eyes and rolled over. So Zoey went to bed early, too. She didn't feel very tired but she was eager for the day to end. Even if it was irrational, she felt as if they were racing against the clock and if they could just make it to the following Monday, when her aunt's surgery was scheduled, everything would be okay.

Meanwhile, she took comfort in knowing Mark was catching the 10:22 a.m. ferry back to the mainland tomorrow. She never did figure out what it was he truly came to Dune Island to discuss with Ivy, but Zoey assumed it had less to do with her health than with *his* needing money. It usually did. But that wasn't her business and as long as he departed on schedule, she no longer cared why he'd arrived.

She must have been more tired than she realized because she didn't wake until her phone rang at 9:30 the next morning. It was the library director calling to offer her the role. Even though the salary was more than she'd been making in her former position, Zoey asked time to consider it. The director sounded disappointed, but she agreed Zoey could have a week to make her decision.

Eager to share news that might cheer her aunt, Zoey whisked down the hall. Ivy's door was slightly ajar and Zoey was pleased to see she was dressed and her hair was combed—the day was already shaping up to be a good one.

"Congratulations, dear. I'm not surprised they'd snatch you up," her aunt said when Zoey told her about the offer. "When did you tell me they want you to start working?"

"It would be sometime in August, but I haven't accepted the position yet. I told them I needed to think it over."

"Why would you hesitate? You remember what I said about not putting off—"

"Yes, I remember, Aunt Ivy," she interrupted. "But it's common professional practice to take time to consider an offer. It's not as if they'll rescind it just because I didn't jump at the chance to work for them."

Ivy's eyes welled and Zoey immediately regretted her sharp tone. She'd only meant to prevent her aunt from worrying she'd lose the offer. As she turned to get Ivy a tissue from the nightstand, she noticed a small, open suitcase on the bed. "Are you packing?"

"Yes. For my trip to Boston."

Zoey was flummoxed. She appreciated that her aunt had been expanding her horizons lately, but an excursion to the city? She must have been pulling Zoey's leg. Either that, or she was planning ahead, giving herself something to look forward to after her surgery. "Boston?"

"South of Boston. Plymouth? Plympton? I forgot. That's why Mark said he'd tell you—because I can't remember all the details. Didn't he discuss it with you?"

"No." The only legitimate reason Zoey could imagine for him taking Ivy on an off-island trip was that he wanted to get a second medical opinion about whether she needed a pacemaker. Still, Zoey wished he had given her a heads-up, too, so she could have gone with them. "Why does he want you to go off-island with him?"

Her aunt zipped her rollers into a cosmetic bag and sat down on the bed. "So I can spend the night at an assisted living facility. Just to see what it's like."

Don't react. Don't react. Stress is bad for Aunt Ivy's heart. Zoey repeated the mantra to herself before asking, "Is now really a good time for that? You've already got an outing this week—your pre-op screening. Couldn't you wait until after you've had your surgery to go to Boston?"

"I suppose." Ivy's palm was pressed against her cheek, signaling her ambivalence. Obviously, Mark had strong-armed her into this trip. "But it might be two months before I feel well enough to travel."

"Two months isn't very long."

"No, but by then the unit that's opening up in September might be rented out."

September? Zoey was losing her battle to keep calm. "You'd move in September?"

"*If* I move, yes, September would be an opportune time for everyone. But I certainly haven't decided anything yet."

"I don't understand. We just started the remodel. And you love this house, Aunt Ivy. Almost all of your memories are here."

"Yes, but you've said it yourself—my memories run deeper than superficial reminders. Besides, this place is getting too hard for me to keep up. I'm too weak. Too forgetful."

It was as if Mark's words were coming from her aunt's mouth. As if she'd been brainwashed. *So* this *must have been what he was harping on during his phone calls to Aunt Ivy and why he'd visited her this weekend.*

"That's why I'm here—to help you. When I leave, I'll arrange for someone else to do the things I've been doing, like shopping and taking you to your appointments. Carla's eager to return to do the housekeeping and we'll get someone to help you with whatever else you need." Zoey paused, letting her words sink in. "You may feel weak now, but Dr. Laurent told us a lot of his patients noticed an increase in energy once they got their pacemakers implanted because their hearts don't have to work so hard any more."

"But what if I don't get stronger or feel better? What if I feel worse?"

Oh. Now Zoey got it: her aunt was frightened. "I don't think that's going to happen. But if it does, we can consider other options then." Zoey sat down beside Ivy, relieved she seemed to be getting through to her. She repeated, "You've got a lot going on right now. Don't you think it would be a better idea to rest up before your surgery?"

"I would prefer that, yes, but I've already told Mark I'll go and he's made all the arrangements. He's on his way over from the hotel to pick me up any minute now."

"I'm sure it's not a problem for him to reschedule."

Mark came into the room just then. Either he had been eavesdropping from the hallway or his timing was uncanny. "Actually, it *is* a problem. I had to call in a lot of favors for this. If Ivy she doesn't stay overnight now, she might lose her position on the waiting list of prospective residents."

"*If* she decides she eventually wants to move, there must be dozens of other places she could consider." *Like one that's closer to Providence, so I can visit her as often as she wants me to.*

"This one is the best quality and the most affordable." Mark addressed Ivy, "Like I said, I went to a lot of trouble to arrange this for you, but if you're not comfortable going, I'll cancel."

"No, that's okay. I don't want you to have to do that." She placed her cosmetic bag inside the suitcase.

"I'll go with you, then," Zoey proposed. "It will be like a girls' night out."

"You can't," Mark objected. "There's only room for two in my convertible."

"We can take the Caddy. *That* will make a good impression." Zoey smiled widely, reveling in his discomfort.

He smiled just as broadly. "They don't let friends or family members spend the night. Only the interested party. Besides, you can't leave Gabi here alone. She might get into trouble. *Again.*"

"Quiet!" Ivy yipped and simultaneously snapped her fingers hard, a warning Zoey remembered from childhood. She rarely ever issued it, but when she did it indicated she was fed up and woe to the niece or nephew who talked back or disobeyed her. "My mind is made up, I'm spending the night—*one* night—in Boston. I'll be ready to leave just as soon as I use the restroom. In the meantime, act like a gentleman, Mark, and carry my suitcase downstairs."

"You sneak!" Zoey hissed after their aunt had left the room. "How could you do this?"

"Didn't I mention I was taking Ivy off-island?" Mark knitted his brows together in phony bewilderment. "It must have slipped my mind. It happens to all of us on occasion. Sorry 'bout that."

No you aren't. You aren't sorry about a thing, Zoey seethed. *But so help me, if anything happens to Aunt Ivy, you* will *be!*

CHAPTER ELEVEN

"It's my fault. If I hadn't left the water running, Mark wouldn't have taken Aunt Ivy to check out the assisted living place," Gabi berated herself for the fifth time on Monday evening. "I think he made all the arrangements when Nick sent him for a walk. I should have confessed right away, the moment he got here."

Zoey usually tried to avoid badmouthing Mark to her niece but she didn't know how to convince her she wasn't to blame except to say, "Mark's been gunning to move Aunt Ivy into a facility for a long time. He probably had it all arranged before he showed up here on Friday. It has nothing to do with you and it doesn't have very much to do with Aunt Ivy. It's all part of his plan to lease out her house so he can receive an income without actually having to work for it."

Gabi swept her bangs to one side. "Do you think he's going to be able to convince her to move?"

"I hope not, because I don't think she really wants to. And because she shouldn't rush into making a decision of that magnitude when she's so emotional."

Zoey was pretty emotional herself. She hadn't been able to eat anything all day because her stomach was tangled up with worry about her aunt. She wasn't concerned about the quality of hospitality and care Ivy would receive at the assisted living facility; on the contrary, the staff would likely give her the royal treatment. But she was worried about her aunt being away from home and with Mark for such a long stretch of time.

He's going to keep preying on her vulnerabilities—her grief and fear and self-doubt—except now I can't be there to offer her a different perspective, Zoey ruminated. Her aunt didn't even have the portrait of Captain Denny nearby to remind her of when she was young and happy and strong. Since Ivy had no support, it would be easier for Mark to wear her down. Zoey wouldn't even be surprised if he coerced her into signing a lease while she was there…

Her catastrophizing was interrupted by Gabi saying, "It would be terrible if Mark took over Aunt Ivy's house, because she loves it here so much. And because I wouldn't be able to stay here any more."

Oh—your mom would be so glad that you want to come back to Dune Island! "I'm sure Mark would let you stay in the house. He might charge you, but he'd still let you visit." Zoey chuckled but Gabi was doleful.

"I mean I wouldn't be able to come back because it wouldn't feel right if I was here and Aunt Ivy was living some place else. Kind of like now. It sort of feels like we're trespassing, doesn't it?" Gabi said and Zoey nodded. "There's still a way we could make sure Mark couldn't take over. We could talk to Mr. Witherell and get him to confirm that he's not really a Winslow—"

"No. I've already told you I don't want Aunt Ivy getting hurt. Not at any time, and especially not now."

"She doesn't ever have to know about it, not even if we discover that Mr. Witherell really *is* Mark's grandfather. But *we'll* know."

"What good will that do us?"

"Because we could tell Mark. And then he'd back off about Aunt Ivy moving because he'd know he's not going to inherit her house."

"But what if that makes him so angry that he tells Aunt Ivy to spite us?"

"He wouldn't do that because he'd be too worried if she found out he wasn't her blood relative, she'd cut off the financial help he's getting from her now."

"How did you know about that?"

"I have my sources. So what do you think of my rationale? Genius, isn't it?"

"In theory, yes. In reality, no. Aunt Ivy's thrilled that she's on speaking terms with Mr. Witherell again. We don't want to risk alienating him by bringing up a subject like that," Zoey added emphatically, "So the answer is still *no*, you are not permitted to talk to him about this. Understand?"

Gabi huffed a sigh and rose from the sofa. "Aye, aye, Captain," she agreed, saluting before she went upstairs for the night.

Within the hour, Zoey was in bed, too. As she watched the curtains billow and flatten in the breeze, she wondered if Ivy was having trouble sleeping tonight, as well. It had seemed so strange not to walk her up the stairs before bedtime, as was their routine. Down the hall, a door squeaked; Moby was inspecting Sylvia's room, as was *his* routine. *Does he miss her still?* she wondered. *I do.*

A few tears moistened her cheeks as she thought of how gentle her great-aunt had been. Zoey remembered that when Sylvia braided her hair for her when she was a little girl, she was so afraid of pulling it that she never wove it tight enough. The braid would come undone as soon as Zoey walked across the room. Or when she'd fill the tub for Zoey's bath, the water was always tepid because she didn't want to burn her skin. *Aunt Sylvia was probably so careful not to hurt anyone else because of the abuse* she *suffered when she was young*, she hypothesized.

For being such a demure, tenderhearted woman, she sure had a bully for a grandson. As Zoey reflected on her cousin's aggressive, selfish behavior, the knot in her stomach tightened. She had the sinking feeling that today represented a major turning point in his quest to push Ivy out of her house. Just like when she was a girl, Zoey found herself wishing her aunt would finally put her foot down and say enough was enough.

Out of the blue, Zoey remembered the one time she'd heard her other great-aunt utter those words: it was on the last day of her life. Sylvia had been so dozy that she couldn't keep her eyes open. So she'd mistakenly thought she was talking to Ivy, not to Zoey, when she'd mumbled, *That boy can only take so much… Enough is enough.*

At the time, Zoey assumed Sylvia had been expressing her concern that Mark would crumble under the stress of his divorce. But now she was gripped with a possibility she'd never considered: had her aunt meant 'take' literally? Had she been trying to convince Ivy not to keep spoiling Mark? Was she saying he'd already gotten enough from them—that he shouldn't take more?

As overheated as Zoey felt, the noisy waves were disturbing her thoughts and she got up to close the windows. She wracked her brain to recollect what else Sylvia had said about her grandson that day. The phrases, "It's not fair," and "Mark doesn't deserve this," popped into her mind.

Wait a second! Zoey's pulse pounded in her ears like the ocean. Was *Ivy's house* what Sylvia was referring to when she said, "Mark doesn't deserve this"?

Her mind frenetically jumped from one supposition to the next: *if* Sylvia didn't believe Mark deserved to inherit Ivy's house, it had to be because she knew that he wasn't a Winslow. And the only irrefutable way she would have known that was *if* she was sure that her husband Marcus Sr. wasn't Marcus Jr.'s father. And *if* that were the case, then the gossip Gabi heard about Mr. Witherell being Mark's grandfather seemed a lot more plausible.

Furthermore, *if* Sylvia really was confessing the secret that she had kept to herself for sixty-some years—a secret that reflected poorly on her and would have wounded her beloved sister-in-law—then it must have been extremely important to her that Mark not inherit the house.

And finally, *if* that were true, Zoey had a responsibility—an obligation to her great-aunt's dying intention—to set the record straight about Mark not being a Winslow. Or at least, to investigate the possibility further.

Dizzy, she sat down on the bed and tried to figure out what to do with this new information. *It's not even new information*, she thought. *It's just a different way of considering my last conversation with Aunt Sylvia.* If she was going to try to use Marcus Jr.'s paternity to prevent Mark from disturbing Ivy's final years and trying to take over her house, she needed evidence, concrete evidence, that he wasn't a Winslow. The only place she could imagine finding that kind of evidence was among Sylvia's belongings. She had already straightened her trunks, but it was worth taking a closer look.

Zoey tiptoed up the attic stairs so she wouldn't wake her niece. For the next hour and a half, she sorted through every single item in her aunt's two trunks, scrutinizing them for any link, however tenuous, between Sylvia and Mr. Witherell. She even read the articles printed on the sheets of newspaper the figurines were wrapped in, hoping for a clue, but she still couldn't find anything to connect them.

Next, she went downstairs to her aunt's room. Several weeks ago, after Mark had finished rummaging through Sylvia's closet and dresser drawers, leaving them in a mess, Zoey had come in to refold and rehang everything. Sylvia had always been fastidious about her clothing and Zoey hadn't wanted Ivy see it in such disarray. So she'd already given the room a once-over, but she conducted a more thorough examination now, turning the pockets of Sylvia's clothes inside-out, flipping through the Bible on her nightstand and even checking beneath the bed and mattress. Again, she came up empty-handed.

Deflated, she crept back to her room and fell into bed. She recognized that her only other option was to discuss the matter with Mr. Witherell. The very thing she'd forbidden Gabi to do because she didn't want to run the risk of Ivy finding out about their discussion. Nor did she want to offend Mr. Witherell or make him feel uncomfortable, especially if she was wrong. How would she even begin a conversation like that? *Desperate times call for desperate measures*, she told herself. But was she *that* desperate?

She was too dazed to decide. Maybe tomorrow after Ivy and Mark returned, she'd have a better sense of whether it was imperative to discuss the subject with Mr. Witherell. After all, it was a remote possibility her aunt would have such an unpleasant experience at the facility that it would permanently sour her to the idea of assisted living. Or maybe tomorrow Zoey would come up with a new, easier way to prove Marcus Jr.'s paternity. But for now, she was just going to have to sleep on it.

*

After Gabi left for school in the morning, Zoey decided she'd take a run and then go shopping so she could make a special meal for Ivy's homecoming, since Mark had texted her that they'd arrive around supper time. Thinking back to the day she'd crossed paths with Phineas in the rain, she timed her route so she'd see him in the same neighborhood again. She figured she should start engaging him in small talk so that if they ended up having a longer conversation, it wouldn't be quite as awkward. But when she didn't spot him, she ran the same course, in reverse. Still no sign. Feeling a mix of disappointment and relief, she gave up and went home.

Motivated by her aunt's return, as well as by the anticipation of seeing Nick that afternoon, Zoey sped through all the shopping, cleaning and baking. After showering, she even had enough time to blow-dry her hair rather than pulling it up into a damp ponytail. And by the time Nick arrived to remove the tiles from the backsplash, she'd also applied a coat of mascara and put on a sundress instead of her usual T-shirt and shorts.

He checked the bathroom floor and the wall and ceiling in the best room before coming into the kitchen. "So far, so good," he reported.

Zoey extended a plate to him. She knew he was on a tight schedule but she'd been looking forward to chatting with him all morning. "Would you like a muffin before you start working? They're chocolate ricotta."

Nick took one. "Smells delicious."

"I hope it is. I'm not half as good of a baker as my aunt but I thought I'd try a new recipe, since it's a special occasion."

He raised an eyebrow at her. "You got the job?"

"I received an offer, yes, but—"

"Congratulations."

"Thanks, but the muffins are in celebration of my aunt coming home today after spending her first night off-island in, well, I guess it was six years ago, for my sister's funeral."

"Oh." Nick brushed a crumb from his lip. "I hope she was off-island for a happy occasion today?"

Not really. "Mark took her for a tour of an assisted living facility."

"Wow. Is she just dipping her toe in the water or is she seriously considering moving?"

"She's serious about it." *Unfortunately.*

"Hmm." Nick reached for a second muffin. "Which facility is she touring?"

Zoey bristled. *What does* that *matter?* "It's called Waterside. In Plymouth."

"I've heard that's one of the better ones."

"That might well be, but it's still not her home. *This* is her home." Zoey made a sweeping gesture with her arms. She felt as if she'd had this conversation before, but with Mark, not with Nick. "You've heard her stories. You're remodeling her kitchen. It seems like it would be obvious to you how much she loves it here and wants to stay."

He held up his hands defensively. "Whether your aunt goes or stays is her business—it's your family's business—not mine. All I'm interested in is whether I should move forward with remodeling this kitchen. Because if there's no need for me to remove these tiles, I've got a major renovation I need to start for another client. So what's it going to be—should I stop yakking and get to work here or what?"

For a second, Zoey was too stunned by his tone to reply. Her cheeks blazing, she plucked her phone from the countertop, turned toward the hallway and replied in a squeaky voice, "Yes, please continue working on the kitchen unless Aunt Ivy tells you not to. I'm going for a walk, so I'll be out of your way."

She hurried outside and down the street. Perching on a bench in the park by the harbor, she wondered why there'd been such a dramatic shift in Nick's attitude. *It's as if I hardly know him—or as if he hardly knows us.* She'd thought he cared about Ivy; that was one of the very things that won Zoey over and made her like him so much. And she'd thought he cared about *her*, too, at least as a friend. But he was acting as if his only connection to them was professional, not personal.

So then were all of those kind, thoughtful, over-the-top nice things he did just an act? Was all of that just so he could retain Aunt Ivy's business? Zoey was doubtful; Nick said he had a major renovation he needed to start for another client, which certainly must have been more lucrative than anything Ivy had contracted him to do.

No, his behavior had to have been genuine. Something must have changed between the time he saw her on Friday and today. *Maybe dealing with Aunt Ivy's heart problem and Mark's temper was too much for him and he decided from now on, he only wanted a business relationship with us? Or maybe he's just stressed out? He has been really busy.*

Zoey understood why he might have been irritated by her yammering on about her family situation when he had work to do, so she didn't blame him for shutting the conversation down. But the way he did it made it seem as if he was shutting their *friendship* down. *Or am I overreacting because I'm stressed out?*

As she was pondering Nick's remarks, Gabi ambled around from behind the bench. "Hi, Aunt Zoey. You look nice." She sat down beside her. "Nick said I just missed you. I didn't see you on my way home so I figured you walked in this direction instead."

"Hi, Gabi. How was your day?"

"It was okay. But I have to tell you something."

Uh-oh. Zoey braced herself. "Is it bad news?"

"It's *sad* news." Her niece glanced toward the lighthouse. "I found out that Mr. Witherell died this the weekend."

"What? No way. Did the kids at school tell you that?"

"Yeah, but I looked it up online, too. Give me your phone, I'll show you."

She handed it to her and Gabi pulled up the obituary online. When Zoey saw the name *Phineas*, she gasped, knowing the rumor had to be true. There was only one Phineas on Dune Island. Or there *had been* only one.

Zoey sniffed as she read the death notice. It didn't take long; in addition to his birth and death dates, it listed his time of service as a lighthouse keeper and named his niece, Melissa Carter, of North Carolina, as his only surviving relative. It said there would be no public memorial or funeral services.

Whether or not he once dated her aunt Sylvia and whether or not he was Mark's grandfather, Mr. Witherell had been a part of her aunt Ivy's history. He'd been part of Dune Island's history, too, and it disturbed Zoey that his entire life had been condensed into a few sentences. "Didn't anyone care about him or know him well enough to write a few words about what he was like as a *person*?"

"I don't think he would have wanted anyone to do that. He didn't like public attention." Gabi patted Zoey's shoulder. "But Aunt Ivy cared about him enough to invite him over for pie. And she knew him well enough to say what he was like. She said it in private, in the stories she told us about him. But that's still kind of memorializing him, isn't it?"

If Zoey hadn't been wearing mascara, she would have given in to the impulse to cry. Partly because niece was right; their aunt *had* known and cared about Mr. Witherell. And partly because Ivy might not have known him as well as she thought she did. Also because Zoey realized her chances of finding out whether Marcus Jr. was Mr. Witherell's son may have died along with the old man.

She warned Gabi, "Please don't tell Aunt Ivy about this tonight. If she finds out, we'll help her cope with it, but since there isn't going to be a memorial service anyway, we should wait to make sure she's rested and in good health before we break it to her."

"Okay, but should we tell Mark? Just in case Mr. Witherell really is his grandfather?"

Zoey hesitated. "Unfortunately, I don't think it would matter that much to him either way and he might blab it to Aunt Ivy. So let's not."

Gabi rose and pulled Zoey to her feet, too. "Let's take a walk to the lighthouse, in honor of Mr. Witherell."

As they strolled, Gabi told Zoey that her history teacher, Mr. Hallowell, lived next door to Mr. Witherell. He said that Mr. Witherell collapsed near his yard, probably as he was returning from his morning outing. A neighbor spotted him lying on the grass, but he had already passed away. "At least he died doing something he enjoyed. But I kind of wish that someone would have been there to say goodbye to him."

Zoey gave her a side hug. "How about if, when we get to the lighthouse, we arrange shells to say, GOODBYE, MR. WITHERELL?"

"That's too flashy for his personality. Let's write it in the sand with our feet instead and then the tide will wash it away."

Without a trace, Zoey thought mournfully. *Just like his past.*

When they returned to the house, Zoey was flustered to see Nick's car still parked in the driveway. She figured if she used the back staircase, she could avoid another awkward interaction with him. But before she and Gabi reached the door, Mark and Ivy pulled up, so they went over to greet them.

Ivy emerged from the car with her hair in disarray and dark circles beneath her eyes. "I was hot so Mark put the roof down on the convertible," she explained.

Take care of Aunt Ivy first, you can deal with Mark later, Zoey told herself as she helped her inside and Gabi followed, carrying her bag. Mark stayed in the driveway, talking on his cell phone. The women stopped in the kitchen so Ivy could get a glass of water.

"Hi, Ivy," Nick greeted her. "Please excuse the appearance of your kitchen."

"Only if you excuse the appearance of my hair," Ivy jested.

Zoey used to enjoy the banter between the two of them but now she wondered if Nick was just humoring her aunt. He *seemed* sincere, but...

Ivy drank her water and announced, "I'll tell you about my trip later, girls, but I'm so tired now, I need to go to bed."

"Aren't you hungry? I plan to make sea bass for supper and I baked chocolate ricotta muffins for dessert."

"And they're delicious," Nick interjected.

Is complimenting my baking his way of apologizing? Zoey half-hoped it was. Maybe now that the sting of their earlier interaction had subsided a little, she could have a candid discussion with him about what he'd said.

"I'll have a muffin for breakfast tomorrow," Ivy said. "Zoey, take my arm, please. And Gabi, take my other one. I'm lightheaded from all that wind."

"Would you like me to carry you up the stairs?" Nick asked, flexing his muscle.

Obviously, he was joking, but to Zoey's dismay, her aunt replied, "You wouldn't mind, would you?"

"It would be my pleasure." Nick wiped his hands on his jeans and scooped her up. Gabi and Zoey followed him as he carried her upstairs.

"Right here is fine," she said when he reached her bedroom door. He carefully set her on her feet. "You're not just the finest craftsman on the island. You're also a true gentleman. Thank you, Nicholas."

With a slight bow, Nick replied, "It's always a pleasure, Mrs. Cartwright."

After he went downstairs and her aunt stretched out on the bed, Zoey pleaded, "Aunt Ivy, I think we should call an ambulance. Or at least we should go to the ER."

"Why? Who's sick?"

"I meant because if you're too weak to walk up the stairs—"

"Who said anything about being too weak? At my age, if a strong, handsome man offers to carry me up the stairs, I'd be a fool to say no."

It was hard to tell to what degree her joke was covering up how crummy she felt. So as Zoey helped her with her bedtime routine, she tried to persuade Ivy to allow her to call her physician and report her symptoms. When her aunt refused, Zoey pleaded to at least let her take her blood pressure and pulse, but Ivy snapped, "That cuff gets too tight. Now shush before your nagging gives me a headache. All I need is a good night's rest."

Gabi eventually left to do her homework but Zoey stayed by her aunt's side until she was snoring. Seeing the state Ivy was in, she felt even more comfortable with her decision not to tell her about Mr. Witherell passing until she was better rested.

Zoey figured that thanking Nick for carrying Ivy upstairs would be a good ice-breaker and went downstairs. But when she got halfway down the hall, she heard Mark's voice coming from the kitchen and she froze, unsure whether she could summon the poise to be civil toward him after he'd brought their aunt home in such rough shape.

"Next week when Ivy's in the hospital overnight, I've got someone coming over to tear up the attic floor. It's all original wood up there, did you know that? Over two hundred years old." He boasted, "I took some photos and showed them to a woodworker I know and he told me he'd pay this much for it."

Mark must been showing Nick a figure because there was silence before Nick replied, "I know a guy who'd pay two-and-a-half times as much as that. He's vacationing in the Bahamas this week but I can set you up with him when he gets back. I can remove the wood myself, no charge."

"Why would you do that?"

"Let's call it a peace offering. I know we've had, uh, a few words since we've reconnected, but I think it would be mutually beneficial if we put that stuff behind us." Nick lowered his voice and Zoey had to strain her ears to hear what he was staying. "This house is going to need a lot of work in the future and I'd like to be the one to do it."

"So you're bribing me?"

Nick chuckled in a way that made Zoey's flesh crawl. "Let's call it a favor. No strings attached. Trust me, you don't want just anyone pulling up those boards. 'Cause if the wood gets cracked or chipped, it depreciates in value, big time."

"Okay, I'll consider selling the wood to your guy and letting you pull the boards up. But he has to make me an offer by Monday."

"It's a deal."

Zoey felt sick to her stomach. She held her hand over her mouth, tripped up the stairs and raced down the hall to her room, where she flopped onto her bed.

Is Nick really so desperate to repay his debts that he'd behave in such an unconscionable manner?! she silently raged. *How could he go behind Aunt Ivy's back and propose a deal like that to Mark, especially after he claimed this wasn't how he did business? And especially after I told him how much it would upset her if he started ripping the attic apart?*

Nick *knew* how precarious Ivy's health already was, but clearly he didn't care about that. All he cared about was how he could profit from her house. He was exactly like Mark: deceptive, self-serving and opportunistic. Only he was worse, because unlike Zoey's cousin, Nick could sustain a really convincing Mr. Good Guy act. And against all of her better instincts, she had fallen for it.

He must think I am such a sucker, Zoey stewed. *And maybe I have been. Maybe Aunt Ivy has been one, too. But as Aunt Sylvia once said, "Enough is enough."*

She didn't know how—especially now that Mr. Witherell had died—but Zoey resolved that before Nick laid a finger on the attic or Mark laid claim to the house, she was going to do whatever it took to find out whether her cousin was truly a Winslow or not.

*

Although Ivy appeared somewhat more refreshed when she came into the kitchen late Wednesday morning, she complained of chest pain twice. Zoey again suggested they call the doctor or go to the ER, but her aunt refused. "I'm going to be at the hospital for hours tomorrow. If anything is wrong with me, they'll find it then."

If *nothing happens to you before then,* Zoey fretted. "But—"

"Zoey, you aren't going to change my mind, so you need to change the subject," her aunt stated firmly. "Let's go into the living room and chat about something else."

Once they were both settled and sipping their tea—iced, not hot—Zoey asked, "What did you think of the *facility*?" She deliberately emphasized the clinical-sounding word.

"The residents were lovely and so was the staff. And the building overlooks the water. A pond, not the ocean, but it was pretty and they have a free shuttle to the public beach on the weekend. The food was decent, too. The chef caters meals to everyone's tastes and medical requirements. But I'll also have access to a kitchen if I want to make something myself."

"What do you mean, 'I'll have access to a kitchen?' It almost sounds as if you've made up your mind you want to move there."

"Yes, dear, I'm leaning in that direction."

Even though Zoey knew this was coming, hearing her aunt confirm it made her heart drop a beat. *There's still time for her to change her mind and there's still time for me to get Mark to back off,* she reminded herself. But how much time? "You wouldn't move before September, would you?"

"No. There's not an opening until then."

Zoey relaxed her shoulders a little. "That's good. By then you should have a better sense of how much the pacemaker is helping your energy levels and—"

"Zoey, even if I feel as energetic as I did when I was fifty, I'm still going to move into Waterside."

So she's not just "leaning in that direction"—she was just trying to break it to me gently, Zoey realized. "If it's because there's too much upkeep involved in taking care of a house this size, like I said, I'll help you hire contractors—"

"That's not it, either. And it's not because of my memory. Or because of my forgetfulness, I should say." Ivy chuckled at herself and set her glass on a coaster on the coffee table before growing somber. "It's not even because I'm lonely for Sylvia, although not a day goes by when I don't wish…"

Zoey leaned forward. "I know, Auntie. I wish the same thing about my sister, too."

Ivy nodded, still not looking up until Moby paraded into the room and trilled at her and she allowed him to leap onto her lap.

"If it's not for any of those reasons, then why do you want to move?" Zoey asked.

"It's not that it's *not* for any of those reasons. But none of those reasons alone is the deciding factor. It's the combination and because the timing is right—for all of us. You could stay here until your job begins. And it'll work out well for Mark, too, since he just found out he has until Labor Day to vacate his home."

"He's going to move to Dune Island in September? Then why would you need to move out?"

"No, he can't move here—there aren't enough job opportunities in his field. But he'll start leasing the house out then, so he won't have to worry about money if he doesn't get a job offer as soon as he hopes to get one. He's been so stressed out about securing employment, he's lost almost twenty pounds in a month's time. He's not sleeping, either. I'm more concerned about his health than I am about mine."

Zoey could have smacked her forehead. Her aunt had mentioned she was concerned about his employment situation and health once before, but she still felt blindsided to learn *that* was ultimately the 'deciding factor' in Ivy's decision to move.

She had severely underestimated Mark's cunning. He was well aware that for every reason he'd suggested Ivy needed to move—her health, her memory, her loneliness, the upkeep of her house—Zoey had already thought of a way to address the problem. So he had shifted his focus. Instead of merely playing up his aunt's declining health and other challenges, he'd apparently been playing up his own.

That explains why she was always so quiet during those marathon phone calls with him—he must have been giving her a sob story about how tragic his situation was. Especially how his health was suffering. He knew *she'd be upset about him losing his appetite!* She could only imagine what else he'd whined to her about whenever he was alone with her.

The brilliance of his scheme was he knew Zoey couldn't do a single thing to change his situation, the way she could for Ivy. Zoey couldn't *make* an employer hire Mark. Nor could she improve his health or cause him to gain weight. For all she knew, he hadn't applied for a single job and he'd purposely been working out for ten hours a day in order to lose weight. But all that mattered was he'd convinced Ivy he was suffering. And a lifetime of experience had taught him that she'd do whatever she could to rescue him. Including moving into an assisted living facility.

Ivy continued, "He's got it figured it all out, down to the penny. I don't have quite enough funding to cover the assisted living costs, but he's willing to share the profits from leasing out the house."

That's big of him. "You've told me why you're not unwilling to move and you've explained how the timing and the move is good for me and good for Mark, but I still haven't heard you say this is what *you* really want to do, Aunt Ivy."

"Oh, I know it will be an adjustment, but I'll get used to it." She laughed. "I'd better—because if I change my mind, I won't get my down payment on the facility back and I can hardly afford that as it is."

"When is that due?"

"Well, today I have to place a call to the trust fund executor and work out a few details, but the assisted living director is willing to wait until the fifteenth."

"Of September?"

"Of June. This coming Monday."

Zoey hopped to her feet. "Uh-oh, I think I hear my phone ringing. That might be the library director."

Her phone wasn't ringing; her ears were. She ran up the stairs, so frustrated that if it wouldn't have upset her aunt, she would have run up the attic stairs, too. And then she would have climbed the ladder and stood on the widow's walk and screamed so vociferously, the islanders would have told stories about it for generations to come.

CHAPTER TWELVE

Since Ivy's pre-op assessment process was slated to take two hours, Zoey sat in the hospital lobby, using her phone to research all the Melissa Carters in North Carolina. After staying up half the night contemplating how she could prove Mr. Witherell was Marcus Jr.'s father, the only plan Zoey had come up with was to contact his one living relative and ask her outright. It was a long shot—a *very* long shot—and she was dreading the conversation, but she was now decidedly desperate enough to give it a try.

She narrowed her list down to three Melissa Carters she thought might be related to Mr. Witherell and gave them a call. The first number was no longer in use. The second number was answered by a child who said Melissa Carter was her nana who had gone to heaven when he was eight. No one answered the third number she called, so Zoey left a voicemail.

Afterward, she walked along Port Newcomb's waterfront, purchased clam chowder from Captain Clark's and ate it on their deck overlooking the water. It was an overcast day and while she usually enjoyed watching the large ferries docking and departing, today the low thrum of their engines set her teeth on edge. She kept checking the time on her phone; she'd asked the receptionist to call when Ivy was done. Since she still hadn't heard anything, she returned to the pre-op department.

"How much longer will it be until Ivy Cartwright's assessment is done?" she asked the receptionist.

"She… th-they had to take her upstairs to cardiology. The nurse was supposed to call you. I'll go get her. She can explain it better."

Zoey's legs felt hollow as she waited for the nurse to come out. She explained her aunt had been exhibiting symptoms—sweating, chest pain, lightheadedness—consistent with a pulmonary embolism. After additional tests, she'd been admitted to the hospital.

"This is the best place for this to happen. If she hadn't come in for the assessment, we might not have caught it in time. I'll take you to her."

"Thank you," she said even though she didn't feel grateful. She felt terrified. And guilty. She should have tried harder to convince her aunt to go to the ER after she'd spent the night at the assisted living facility. And she definitely should have tried harder to stop Mark from taking her off-island in the first place.

At the cardiology wing, she was informed the doctor would be out to see her shortly. She took out her phone and numbly tapped Gabi's number, but her cell was turned off, as usual. She left a message and then a text. Mark had gone back to Boston on Tuesday, but she figured he'd want to know. When he didn't pick up, she left a voicemail and a text for him, too. She felt so desperate to talk to someone that she called Kathleen but when she couldn't reach her, she didn't leave a message.

Three phone calls and that's it. That's my entire family, she thought. *And if Aunt Ivy dies…* She sniffled, on the cusp of weeping. Too bad she didn't keep a tissue tucked in her sleeve, the way her aunt did. The reminder made her sadder, so she called Lauren, but her friend must have been at work and couldn't answer her phone.

Shortly afterward, the doctor came out and said Ivy was resting comfortably. He explained they'd given her medication to try to break up the clot. If it didn't work, they'd resort to surgery. And he said she'd be in the hospital for five to seven days.

"Did this happen because of her arrhythmia?"

"It's possible they're related, but it's just as possible they're not—we'll never know. But we *do* know how to treat her condition and we'll do everything we can to help your aunt feel better soon."

"Thank you," Zoey said, and this time she really meant it.

It was after seven when Zoey left the hospital. If Ivy had had her way, she would have left by five. She thought her niece was making "too much of a fuss over nothing" and said she couldn't relax knowing that Zoey hadn't eaten any supper yet.

"When you come tomorrow, please bring the cribbage board and my coin jar. And don't forget my hairbrush and rollers," she requested.

After saying goodbye, Zoey hesitated outside her room, wondering if she should stay a little longer. But she was concerned because Gabi hadn't returned her calls and Zoey's phone battery had died an hour earlier, so now her niece had no way of reaching her, either.

She caught one of the shuttle buses that departed the hospital every fifteen minutes. When she arrived home she was unnerved to spy Nick's truck in the driveway; there was no one she could have been less happy to see at that moment, including Mark. As she neared the back yard, she noticed Aidan was cutting the grass. It appeared he was almost finished. *Good—they won't be here much longer*, Zoey thought.

"Hiya." Nick rose when she reached the steps, moving aside so she could open the door. "I wanted to check the wall and ceiling in the best room, but no one was home. Is Ivy okay?

Crossing the threshold, Zoey said icily, "Yes, she is. Not that you really care."

Nick followed her down the hall. "Are you upset because of our conversation yesterday? I know I acted like a jerk and—"

She stopped and turned, staring him down. "You weren't *acting* like a jerk. You *are* one. I heard every word of the dirty deal you made with Mark to tear out the attic floor."

Nick jerked his head backward. "I was—I was going to talk to you about that, but I haven't had the chance," he stammered.

"Save it." She jogged upstairs to Gabi's room but there was no sign she'd been back since leaving that morning. Zoey had already called Amy's number from the hospital and left several messages. Where else could Gabi have gone? It was past seven-thirty. She went into her own bedroom, connected her phone to the adapter and powered it on, but it didn't indicate any missed calls. No texts, either.

Nick was waiting for her at the bottom of the staircase, but she breezed past him, down the hall and out the door.

"Aidan!" she shouted twice because the teenager didn't hear her over the mower's engine. She marched across the lawn and clapped her hand on his shoulder. He cut the power and grinned at her.

"Hi, Zo—"

She interrupted him. "Do you know where Gabi is? I can't find her and she isn't answering her phone. I've called Amy but I haven't heard back from her, either."

He gave her a strange look. "I haven't seen her today. But I wouldn't worry too much. Hope Haven is one of the safest counties in the country."

"Aidan, it's important that I find her."

By this time, Nick had joined them. "If he says he doesn't know where she is, he doesn't know."

"He *didn't* say he doesn't know where she is. He said he hadn't seen her today," she argued. "Maybe he's as devious about twisting the truth as his father is."

"Listen, Zoey, if you want to be angry at me, that's fine. But don't call my son a liar."

Zoey ignored him, turning her attention back to Aidan, who was shifting from foot to foot. "I know she used to hang out with a group of kids on Tuesdays and Thursdays. Do you know anything about that?"

"I... uh-I made a promise—"

"You don't have to tell her a thing, son."

The more Nick interfered, the more Zoey suspected Aidan was keeping something from her. She pleaded, "Aidan, this is important. No one will get in trouble. No one will find out you were the one who told me. Please?"

"Dad, she needs to know." Aidan gave his father an apologetic look before telling Zoey, "It's supposed to be anonymous, but for a while she's been attending a group for teenagers of alcoholics. But today's meeting only lasted until—"

"Where does it meet?"

"The community center near the beach. But—"

"Move your truck," Zoey barked at Nick as she dashed inside for the keys. On her way out, Moby slipped passed her legs, bounded down the steps and took off across the lawn. For such a portly animal, he sure could move fast. Zoey didn't have time for his nonsense and she moved just as swiftly in the opposite direction, toward the garage.

Aidan jogged after her. "Gabi won't be there, Zoey. The meeting ended at five-thirty."

Zoey got into the Caddy and shifted into reverse. As she stepped on the gas to back out, the car bucked in fits and starts. When she pressed the pedal harder, the way she'd seen Ivy do it, she sailed backward so quickly she didn't have time to slam on the brakes until after she'd heard a crunch beneath her tires: she had knocked into the picket fence. Knocked *over* the picket fence.

She pulled forward, turning the steering wheel to reposition the vehicle, but in her rearview mirror she saw Nick at the end of the driveway, waving his arms for her to stop. She got out of the car and yelled, "Get out of my way!"

"Gabi's here!" he shouted back. Then he signaled to his son who stood frozen by the picket fence, his mouth hanging open, his hands on his head. "Aidan, leave the mower where it is. We're going."

As they left, Zoey charged down the driveway and embraced her niece, burying her face in her hair. "Where have you been, Gabi?"

Without answering, her niece pushed her arms away and dodged into the house. That's when Zoey noticed a short, round, middle-aged man with a walrus moustache standing in front of a gray sedan parked in the street nearby. A woman, presumably his wife, was sitting in the passenger seat.

"Is everything all right here?" he asked, surveying the splintered fence and the Cadillac parked askew in the driveway, its door open and a warning bell chiming faintly.

"Who are you?" Zoey asked bluntly, wondering why he'd given her niece a ride home.

He explained he was Gabi's history teacher, Gary Hallowell. Apparently she had climbed a tree to get over the fence in Mr. Witherell's yard. The fence was locked from both sides and she'd been stuck for hours until Gary heard her calling for help. He would have reported her for trespassing, but usually she was so respectful and responsible he decided to let it slide. As his eyes darted around the yard, Zoey wondered if he was going to report *her* to the authorities.

She thanked him for bringing Gabi home. "I promise nothing like this will happen again and we'll pay for any damage she did to Mr. Witherell's property."

"She didn't do any damage," the teacher said as he returned to his car. "Nothing like this, anyway."

After parking the Caddy in the garage again, Zoey went inside the house to her niece's room. The teenager was sitting on her bed, her back turned as she faced the window.

"Why would you go to Mr. Witherell's house? You knew he died, so it's not as if you could have talked to him about Mark or Marcus Jr. So why would you try to break in to an empty house?"

Her niece was silent.

"Did somebody dare you?"

No response.

"I expect an answer and until you give me one, you won't be going *anywhere* after school. Not even to band, so you'll need to inform the director you're not going to be performing in the concert."

This didn't elicit so much as a shrug.

Her obstinate passivity was exasperating and Zoey was too spent to try to break through it. As evenly as she could, she said, "I imagine you may have been frightened when you were stuck behind Mr. Witherell's fence. And even though you brought that on yourself, it hurts to know you needed my help and I wasn't there. I promised your mom if…"

Zoey had to stop talking, for fear she'd start bawling. When she spoke again, she went down a different path, saying, "It really upset me when I couldn't find you, because I didn't know if anything had happened to you. But it also upset me because *I* needed to tell *you* something had happened and I couldn't. This afternoon Aunt Ivy had to be hospitalized—"

"She's not in her room?" Gabi whipped her head around. Her cheeks were red but her eyes were clear. "Is she okay?"

"She is now, yes. Or she will be. She has a blood clot in her lungs but they're taking care of it with medication. She'll be staying in the hospital for several days."

Gabi blinked, her mouth opening slightly. Zoey waited for her to speak, but she turned and faced the window again.

"I'll take you to visit her when you get home from school tomorrow," Zoey said and left the room.

After taking a long, hot shower, she considered going downstairs since she'd promised Ivy she'd have "a decent meal" when she got home, but she retreated to her room and stretched out on her bed. She wasn't hungry; she was depleted. Physically, mentally and emotionally; the trifecta of exhaustion.

If she craved anything, it was eight hours straight of sleep. It was a solid plan to keep Mark from putting Ivy into an assisted living facility. Or, most of all, it was a hug and a word of reassurance her aunt was going to be fine; *everything* was going to be fine. It might not have been true, but it was what she needed to hear.

She thought she heard Gabi stirring in the next room, but then she realized it was raining. Zoey disconnected her phone from the adapter and brought it downstairs. As she was walking from room to room, lowering the windows so the sills wouldn't get wet, her phone rang—it was Mark. *Now is not the time for confrontation or conflict*, she reminded herself before answering it. *Whatever he says, I can't react.*

But his compassionate greeting surprised her. "Hey, Zo. I'm really sorry I missed your calls and texts. I left my phone in a friend's car and he just dropped it off now. But I'm really glad Ivy's okay."

"Me, too. I'm thankful they caught it in time." She reclined on the sofa and repeated what the doctor had said about their aunt's condition and treatment.

When she finished, he remarked, "Today must have been pretty tough for you. How are you holding up?"

That Mark's simple inquiry nearly caused Zoey to dissolve into tears was a reflection of how volatile her emotions were. "I'm not great," she sniffed. "Obviously."

He paused before saying, "So, listen, I have a question for you. Do you know what kind of medication they're giving Ivy?"

"Some kind of anticoagulants, I think."

"But that doesn't affect her cognitively, right?"

Zoey rubbed her eyes. "I don't understand what you're getting at."

"I need her to sign a few legal documents, but if she's under the influence of certain substances, her signature might not be considered legitimate."

"*You* might not be considered legitimate," Zoey growled, before hanging up and bouncing the phone against the cushion beside her.

Realizing Mark's initial compassion toward her had just been a front to get her to open up about Ivy's mental state, she hopped to her feet and paced in front of the fireplace. Their aunt could have died—their aunt *still* might die—and all Mark cared about was making sure he could follow through with his plan to push her out of her house in the event she survived.

Now she was boiling mad again. And because she'd taken a hot shower and lowered the windows, Zoey felt physically hot, as well. She tramped into the dark kitchen for a glass of water. As she drank it, a branch tapped the window panes over the sink: Sylvia's rhododendrons. *The minute Aunt Ivy moves, Mark is going have those torn out to let more light into the kitchen*, she thought bitterly. *Nick might even do it for him for free.*

It infuriated her that her cousin had no regard for the things that mattered to Sylvia and Ivy. That he was going to mine her house and yard for whatever would profit him financially and cast everything else aside. And it infuriated her even more that she couldn't come up with any way to stop him. She set her glass down and began to pace.

Rapping her head with her knuckles, she demanded, *Think, Zoey, think!* On her second lap across the room, she stubbed her toe hard against Moby's bowl and sent it skidding beneath the table. Moby! She'd forgotten he'd fled outdoors earlier that evening. Her ire at Mark was instantly replaced with concern for the cat. *The poor thing, out on a wretched night like this.*

She turned on the overhead light and pushed the window further open so he'd hear the whirring of the electric can opener and come running. But when she checked the back steps, he wasn't there. *He must be taking shelter beneath the wild rose bushes.* That was his usual spot to hide whenever he was outside and it started raining. But Zoey knew he wouldn't voluntarily emerge from his haven into the rain, so she switched the floodlight on and stepped outside. Trotting across the lawn toward the hedge of roses along the back fence, she made a kissing sound and cooed, "Moby. Moby. Come out of there, Mobes."

When he didn't, she dropped to her knees beside the sweet, fragrant shrubs. As she parted the abundant lower branches, their prickles scratched her hands. Her pajama top was already clinging wetly to her back from the rain and now her knees were muddy. "Don't do this to me, Moby," she pleaded. "Not tonight."

She continued to crawl down the row, pushing branches aside and peering beneath them until she finally spotted the corpulent creature. She reached in and he allowed her to draw him toward her. Standing, she snuggled him to her chest. "Thought you could fool me, did you?" she asked as she walked toward the house. "I was stashing my cousin's skateboard beneath the roses before you were even born. It's the best hiding place in this yard."

Zoey spontaneously recalled her aunt Sylvia's final words. *For now, it's best to let the past stay buried in the past*, she had mumbled. But then she'd added, *Beneath the roses*. Zoey had attributed the comment to sleepiness. Or to a kind of end-of-life delirium. But now it struck her that Sylvia may have been indicating where she'd hidden the proof of Marcus Jr.'s paternity.

That has *to be it!* She broke into a run, with Moby bouncing in her arms and epiphanies flashing through her mind. She and Mark had just recently reminisced about the time Jessica had snuck off with his skateboard when they were kids and hidden it beneath the rose bushes, to get back at him for his stories about the dentil molding. *Aunt Sylvia was the one who found Mark's skateboard that summer… She couldn't have incidentally discovered it when she was clipping a spray of roses—Jessica and I made sure it was completely hidden from view.*

Zoey concluded her aunt must have looked beneath the roses deliberately, to spare her darling grandson the frustration of searching for the skateboard himself. What if she had known it was the perfect hiding place because that's where *she* had concealed evidence about her relationship with Mr. Witherell? She wouldn't have hidden the evidence inside the house, for fear Marcus or Ivy would discover it. Zoey didn't know whether that evidence was Mr. Witherell's letters or something else, but she was determined to find out.

"Moby needs a towel," Zoey said, handing the cat to a shocked Gabi, who was standing in the doorway. After quickly darting in to put on her running shoes to protect her feet, she dashed to the garage, grabbed a shovel, a hoe and garden gloves and ran back to the wild rose shrubs. Pulling the branches back with one hand, she used the hoe to chop at the ground with the other.

Gabi came out from the kitchen, swaddling Moby in a towel like a newborn. "You're soaking wet. What are you doing out there?"

"Go back to bed." She clumsily pushed the blade into the ground, scooped up a small amount of soil and then chucked it to the side. Again and again.

"Aunt Zoey, come inside!" Gabi pleaded from the doorway.

Zoey kept digging.

Her niece came up behind her. "Aunt Zoey, please stop it."

Zoey ignored her and eventually Gabi left. The rain was coming down in sheets, obscuring her vision, but she kept shoveling and scooping and tossing the soil aside until she'd cleared a hole around the first bush. She pushed on the trunk to wiggle it but its roots were long and intertwined with the roots of the shrub next to it. The thorns bit into her arms and wrists where the gloves didn't cover her skin.

Zoey gripped the trunk of the shrub and yanked it as hard as she could. Instead of uprooting the plant, Zoey lost her grip and fell flat on her butt. She shifted onto her knees again and thrust her hand into the sodden earth. She couldn't feel anything so she took off the gloves and tried again. Nothing but a few stones and roots and sodden dirt. She felt like crying. Like quitting. *I can't give up. This is my last hope for stopping Mark.*

She pushed herself into a standing position and picked up the shovel to start on the next shrub. The movement of a shadow nearby caught her eye. It was Nick; Gabi must have called him. She began digging but he put his hand on her shoulder.

"You've got to stop. You're scaring your niece."

"Don't touch me," she swatted at his arm, splattering him with muck.

"Please come inside, Zoey."

"Who are *you* to invite me into *my* aunt's house, you-you-you— you *traitor!*" She scooped up another shovelful of soil and tossed it sideways, making him jump back.

"I'm not a traitor, Zoey, I swear—" He hopped out of range as she slung more dirt in his direction. "I don't want Mark to remove your aunt's flooring any more than you do. That's why I lied—hey, would you stop throwing dirt at me and just listen for a sec?"

She stopped digging since her arms were tired anyway, but she wouldn't face him.

"I have no intention of ripping up Ivy's floor and I don't have 'a guy' who will pay Mark for the boards. I was lying so he wouldn't let some other contractor come in and reclaim the wood. I knew there was no talking him out of his plan, so I needed to buy time until Ivy was feeling better and I could advise her against having it done—at least while she's living in the house."

The rain pelted Zoey's cheek and ear as she angled her face in his direction. "Why should I believe that?"

"Because it's the truth. And all of my actions have shown I care about Ivy too much to betray her like that."

"But the other day you said—"

"Something really stupid. Something I didn't mean. I was stressed out." Nick stepped closer, his voice going low. "I-I was disappointed."

"Disappointed in what?"

"If you come inside—if *you* invite *me* inside, I'll tell you."

Zoey dropped the shovel and clapped dirt from her hands. "All right. Fine."

Gabi was waiting, looking scared, with a stack of towels. Once Zoey had dried off, she went upstairs to change her clothes. When she came down, Gabi and Nick were in the living room. "I made hot tea but there's also iced tea in the fridge if you want that instead," Gabi said.

"Hot tea is fine. Thanks." Zoey sat down at one end of the sofa. "It's late. You should go to bed now."

"You sure?" Gabi looked apprehensive.

"Yes. We'll talk about all of this in the morning, honey."

So she said goodnight and a very fluffy Moby followed her out of the room. Nick sat down in the armchair opposite Zoey and they quietly sipped their tea until she prompted, "You were going to tell me why you were disappointed?"

He cleared his throat. "Ivy was one of my first clients when I came back to Dune Island. It was after my father died and Aidan had just been through a really rough patch, too. Ivy and Sylvia were really kind to us. The way they treated us… I don't know, I guess I'd say it helped us heal. And it was a privilege to get to know them, to hear their stories, too. So even though I want what's best for Ivy, and even though I heard Mark talking about an assisted living facility at Sylvia's funeral, I was disappointed when you said she was seriously considering moving."

"That's not how you acted," Zoey replied, but her attitude toward him was softening. "You acted as if it was no big deal. You basically said all that you cared about was how her decision affected your work on the kitchen."

"Yeah, that was a defense mechanism." Nick shifted in his chair. "A way of putting some distance between me and Ivy so I wouldn't feel sad about her going."

"Oh, I see." She was touched by Nick's candid admission.

"It was also a knee-jerk reaction to you springing it on me that you'd been offered the job—which is great news, obviously. But I kind of felt like, well, like I'd held down the fort for you at your aunt's house both times you were away on your interviews, and then when it paid off—when you got the job—you didn't even mention it. I had to ask you about it and even then, you glossed right over it, like it was none of my business."

"Oh, no! I'm *so* grateful that you've covered for me during my family's crises. If I glossed over the job offer, it's only because so many other more important things have been going on and I'm not even sure if I want the position. I'm sorry I didn't communicate that better. But your friendship means a lot to me—that's why I was hurt by what you said the other day."

"Yeah, the second I saw the look on your face, I wished I could take my words back."

"They're already forgotten," Zoey said, giving him a small smile. His apology went a long way toward making an awful day a tiny bit better. But other matters still weighed heavily on her mind and she realized they wouldn't be so easily resolved. They might not be resolved at all.

"So, can I ask why you were transplanting roses in dark—and in the rain?"

"I was transplanting them. I-I was looking for something."

"You mean like a buried treasure?"

"I guess you could say that." Zoey rubbed her temples, admitting aloud what she already knew in her heart, "But it turns out that what I thought was a treasure hunt was really a wild goose chase."

"Are you sure? Because tomorrow I could help you dig."

"Thanks, but no." She could know see that it was ridiculous to believe her dignified, ladylike aunt would have buried evidence related to her son's paternity beneath a rose bush. She felt herself blush with shame as she remembered how determined she had been to believe, just a few minutes ago, that all her problems could be solved by digging a hole in the ground. "I'm sorry you had to see me acting so foolishly."

"It's no problem. I've known for a while you don't have enough sense to come in out of the rain," he playfully needled her.

It took a second for Zoey to recall the time she'd refused a ride from him in a rainstorm. "That wasn't because I didn't have enough sense. It was because I thought you were friends with Mark, so, guilt by association, that kind of thing. Sadly, I have a few trust issues."

"My ex-wife was unfaithful to me with more than one man over the years," Nick confided. "So I've developed a few trust issues, too."

Oh! The lightbulb went off in Zoey's mind. *Now I understand why he's been "shuffling" for so long.* She empathized, "That must have been painful."

"It was. But I'm in a better place now. Literally, because I'm living on Dune Island. But my head and heart are in a better place, too." He redirected the focus back to Zoey. "Anyway, I'm glad Gabi called me tonight."

"I am, too. But it really does seem like you always catch me at my most embarrassing moments—probably because I have so many of them." Zoey's chuckle turned into a sob and she covered her face with her arm as she leaned back against the cushion. "I am *such* a mess."

Nick must have known she wasn't referring to taking her pantyhose off in the park or falling between the joists or digging up the roses, because he came over, sat down and put his arm around her shoulder. And in the comfort of his embrace—the hug she'd been craving all day—she told him about Ivy being in the hospital. And Mark's conniving schemes. About Mr. Witherell dying and Gabi jumping his fence. She even told him about Erik bankrupting her.

"Usually being on Dune Island helps me get my life together. It gives me a new perspective. But I've been here for over four months and I'm still a mess—and I've *made* a mess of everything for my family, too." She enumerated her failings, crying, "I've failed to take good care of my aunt. I've failed to keep my niece out of trouble. And I've failed to stop Mark from taking over the house."

Nick took her by the shoulders, gently angling her to face him so he could look into her eyes. "Are you kidding me, Zoey? You haven't made a mess of everything for your family—you've held everything together. I'm convinced, I'm one hundred percent positive, that Ivy and Gabi and even Mark would have been completely lost if you hadn't been here to look after them. Or in Mark's case, to set him straight. You may have made some mistakes, but as you once told me, no one gets it right all the time. The important thing is you've acted out of love. Out of a fierce desire to do what's in your family's best interest." He leaned back again, pulling her with him so that her cheek rested on his chest. Over her head, he said softly, "Ivy and Gabi and Mark are very fortunate to have you."

And I'm very fortunate to have you, Zoey wanted to tell him, but before she could say it, she'd fallen asleep.

CHAPTER THIRTEEN

Zoey woke to Gabi jostling her feet. "Auntie?" She hadn't called Zoey that since she was six or seven.

"Morning, Gabi." She bent her legs to make room for her niece at the end of the couch.

"I have to go to school pretty soon, but I wanted to tell you I'm sorry I scared you yesterday. When you couldn't find me, I mean." Her fair skin was pink around her nose and eyes; she'd been crying. Or she was about to cry.

Zoey propped herself up on her elbows. "I'm sorry I scared you last night, too."

"I also wanted to tell you nobody ever dared me to take my dad's car. I lied. I took it because Kathleen wasn't home and he was drinking and I heard him say on the phone that he'd meet his friend at the bar. I didn't want him to get a DUI or to hurt somebody."

"Oh, sweetheart." Zoey swung her legs off the sofa and sat up so she could put her arm around her niece. "Why didn't you just take his keys?"

"He has, like, four or five sets. I never could have found them all in time."

"I guess that makes sense then." She smoothed her niece's hair back so she could see her face. "Since you're coming clean, do you want to tell me why you went to Mr. Witherell's house?"

"To see if he had a photo of Aunt Sylvia beside his bed, like everyone said."

"Did he?"

"I don't know. The door was locked and I couldn't see in the windows. It was kind of a wasted effort."

"So was digging up the roses. I was looking for a clue for Marcus Jr.'s paternity—I had a crazy idea that Aunt Sylvia might have hidden some sort of evidence there, but no luck," Zoey admitted. She somberly apologized, "I've been a horrible example to you and I am so, so sorry. I let this entire situation get out of hand."

"It's not your fault. I was getting into trouble doing things like stealing cars long before I came here."

"I'm being serious, Gabi. It's time for both of us to give up trying to prove who Marcus Jr.'s father was. And it's time to accept that whether or not Mark is a Winslow, he's going to take possession of Aunt Ivy's house very soon. As much as we want what's best for her and as much as we treasure her home, it's not worth it for us to behave as irresponsibly and recklessly as we've been behaving. And it's not worth feeling so desperate or worried or obsessed. If Aunt Ivy wants to give the house to Mark and move into an assisted living facility—even if he's manipulating her into it—that's *her* decision. Can I trust you to give up trying to prove Mark isn't a Winslow, for once and for all?"

"Yes, you can trust me." Gabi nodded solemnly and Zoey knew she meant it.

"There's something else I'd like you to think about... I love how thoughtful and perceptive you are. Your mom would have loved that about you, too. But it's important that you understand you are *not* responsible for your dad's behavior or for making Kathleen happy or for helping me solve my financial or housing problems, et cetera. You are only responsible for *your* behavior and choices. Right?"

"Right." Gabi was masking her face with her hair again.

"That didn't sound too convincing. What's on your mind?"

"I sort of took responsibility for Aunt Ivy... I lied about lying. I mean, about the bathtub overflowing. *I* didn't leave the faucet running. Aunt Ivy did. She had started to run her bath and then I asked if she wanted to play cribbage while the tub was filling. So we were playing for a while but then Connor called. So I left to talk to him and she must have been concentrating on waiting for me to come back, not thinking about the tub—which seems totally understandable. But when I heard you and Mark talking, he was acting like she was losing her memory and couldn't live alone. So I said I did it. "

"Mm, well, I suspected you might have been covering for her but I wasn't sure so I let it go."

"Why did you suspect it?"

"You were being melodramatic." Zoey imitated how her niece had been shaking her shoulders when she was crying. "That's not your style. You were exaggerating it so much that you almost dropped Moby on the floor."

"I know—I felt so bad about that!" Gabi exclaimed. Then she hastily added, "And about lying, of course."

Zoey fought a smile as she pointed at her niece. "None of that kind of stuff can happen any more. Promise?"

"Yes."

"Good, so do I. And… I hope you'll keep going to your group meetings if you find them helpful." When Gabi's mouth dropped open, Zoey confessed, "Aidan told me—but only because he was trying to help. Or because he was a little afraid of me."

"Just so you know, I don't *like* him, like him. Well, I did at the very beginning but then I found out he's going out with a senior," Gabi said, which made Zoey wonder if that's why she'd been so moody a few weeks earlier. "I'm glad we're friends though. He's the one who brought me to the group and made sure I felt comfortable when I was kind of nervous the first time. He's sort of a big brother. And anyway, I kind of like Connor now."

"Good choice." Zoey grinned. "You'd better get going or you'll be late for school."

"I can hardly wait to hear the gossip about me jumping Mr. Witherell's fence," she said drolly. "And about you digging up the rose bushes."

Zoey laughed. "We're Winslow women. It's part of our heritage to be the subjects of gossip. But we can take it. We're tough—that's part of our heritage, too."

After Gabi left, Zoey noticed that her knees were grimy and she had scratches and thick smudges of dirt on her arms and legs, so she went upstairs for a shower. Within half an hour, she was almost ready to leave to visit Ivy in the hospital, when she heard a muffled tone sounding from the couch—her phone had slipped between the cushions the previous evening.

Zoey slid it out and glanced at the screen. The call was from an area code she didn't recognize until the caller identified herself as Melissa Carter. The woman gruffly asked Zoey why she had called and since she'd just promised Gabi she'd drop the subject of Mark's paternity, Zoey fudged her reply.

After confirming Melissa was, indeed, Mr. Witherell's niece, she said, "I wanted to express my condolences. My aunt spoke very highly of your uncle. She appreciated his vigilance in keeping Benjamin's Harbor safe."

"That's one way of putting it, but I appreciate the thought," Melissa replied. "Sorry if I seemed curt when I answered, but you wouldn't believe the phone calls I've been getting. As soon as Uncle Phin died, the vultures started sweeping in. Most of them want to place bids on his property and I have to refer them to Hope Haven's Search and Rescue, since he donated the land to the association for them to sell. But a few tricksters are after an inheritance, claiming to be his kids or his grandkids. I tell them that would be a miracle."

Zoey's skin tingled. Her curiosity got the best of her and she asked. "Why is that?"

"My uncle was infertile since he was eighteen. Cancer treatments," the woman divulged candidly. "Hey, your aunt didn't happen to be the Winslow girl, did she?"

Zoey swallowed. "Y-yes."

"How about that?! My father told me there was only one girl his brother was ever interested in—the Winslow girl. It never went anywhere, though. It was just as well, since Uncle Phin was better suited for bachelorhood than marriage. He would have made her miserable and he would have been miserable, too. People don't know that about him, but once he got used to being alone in the lighthouse, he wouldn't have had it any other way," Melissa said. "You know what? The attorney sent me a box of stuff from his attic. I saw a photo of your aunt—her name was on the back. I don't have any use for it, so I'll send it to you in case your aunt wants it."

Instead of explaining Sylvia was now deceased, Zoey gave her Ivy's address. After disconnecting, she lingered in front of the window, gazing down the hill toward the water. The day was gray and wet and a thick fog shrouded the harbor. But every five seconds, Sea Gull Lighthouse alternately flashed red, then white. Red, then white. Transfixed, she contemplated what Mr. Witherell's niece had told her. Even though Zoey meant it when she told Gabi she was done pursuing Marcus Jr.'s paternity, she was relieved that she'd inadvertently discovered the truth at last, so there'd be no niggling doubt in her mind.

If she hadn't already accepted that Mark was going to take over the house in September, she might have been more disappointed to find out that Mr. Witherell couldn't have possibly been his father's father. But if she felt any disappointment now, it was on Mr. Witherell's behalf because the only woman he was ever interested in didn't reciprocate his feelings. Not that she thought Sylvia was under any obligation to return his affections. On the contrary, Zoey admired her for standing firm and turning him down—despite his notes or visit to the house—so she could follow her heart and marry Marcus. Yet a part of her wished Mr. Witherell could have found someone else.

Maybe his niece is right—that he really did prefer to be alone. Maybe it was *better that Aunt Sylvia rejected him, for both their sakes.* She smiled to herself, remembering her aunt's truism, "Sometimes, these things have a way of working out for best for everyone."

The long, loud blare of a foghorn snapped her out of her thoughts and she grabbed the bag of items Ivy had requested and hurried to the garage. Since the fence was no longer an obstacle, she drove the Caddy to the hospital. Just after pulling into the street, she spotted Nick coming up the hill in his truck. They rolled down their windows and greeted each other. It was raining but Nick's eyes were all the blue sky Zoey needed for the day.

"You going to visit Ivy?" he asked.

"I was on my way, yes—but if you came here to chat with me, I'll back up."

"No!" He protested vehemently. "Don't back up—I've seen what happens when you drive in reverse."

"Ha, ha. Very funny." He *was* funny though. Funny and thoughtful and handsome. And he'd seen Zoey at some of her worst moments but he'd still come back this morning.

"You should go ahead to the hospital. I just came by to take a look at the ceiling in the best room, since last evening I was, uh, too distracted to do it. I'll pop in and out, if that's okay. Ivy hides a spare key for me near the birdfeeder."

"You came all the way here to do that? What about your other clients?"

"They can wait. This is my priority." He added, "Ivy's materials were delivered so I plan to surprise her and finish the remodel before she gets back from the hospital. Aidan's going to help me in the afternoons. I've ordered new fencing, too, and when it stops raining, he'll take care of the rose bed."

"Thank you." Zoey grinned. "You Armstrong boys are the best in the business."

*

After Ivy put her hair in rollers, she and Zoey spent the morning chatting, playing cribbage and drinking tea, a lot like they did at home. The nurse noticed Ivy was more relaxed with her niece there, so she permitted Zoey to stay as long as she wanted.

While Ivy slept, Zoey sat beside her, texting Lauren and Kathleen. They both felt terrible that they'd missed her calls. After she updated Lauren on Ivy's condition, her friend texted back, asking if Zoey wanted her to come to Dune Island for the weekend for moral support. Although Zoey didn't take her up on it, she was touched by the offer.

Kathleen tried to be supportive, too, asking if it would be helpful for Zoey to send Gabi home now. *NO WAY!* Zoey texted back, appalled at the thought of saying goodbye to her niece earlier than they had planned. She also expressed it was important for Gabi to finish her school year, especially since she was performing in the upcoming concert. Kathleen agreed, adding that Scott was completing his residential program that Monday and they were both looking forward to reuniting as a family once Gabi returned.

Just as her aunt was rousing, she received a text from Nick, inquiring about whether Ivy felt well enough for company. Zoey replied that the doctor recommended limiting visits to family only for the next few days. While she was conveying everyone's well-wishes to Ivy, Mark walked in bearing a big bouquet of roses.

Zoey offered to go get something to put them in and after filling the pitcher a nurse gave her, she dawdled by the sink. Partly because she wanted to give Ivy and Mark a few minutes alone and partly because she felt uncomfortable, knowing she owed him an apology for what she'd said before hanging up on him the night before. Regardless of what she thought about his attitude and behavior, she had been wrong to imply he wasn't legitimately a Winslow.

When she returned to the room, an aide was preparing to take her aunt for another scan. "You kids should go to the cafeteria while I'm gone," Ivy said as she was being wheeled out the door.

Zoey hadn't eaten since lunchtime the day before, so she was all for the idea. She expected Mark to make up an excuse not to go with her, but he didn't.

"Ivy looks really pale, doesn't she?" he asked as they headed toward the cafeteria.

Zoey agreed, although she'd noticed the same thing about *him*, which was odd, considering he usually spent a lot of time in the sun golfing. *No wonder Aunt Ivy's worried about him—he looks awful.*

"She was pale when I took her to Waterside, too," Mark said. "And she kept complaining she was hot. I wanted to bring her home the same day. But she said, 'Stop fussing or you'll give me a headache.'"

"She said the same thing to me when I told her I was concerned about her health."

"I wish I hadn't taken her off the island."

He feels guilty, Zoey realized. As much as she wanted to blame Mark—as much as she *had* blamed him—she knew this wasn't his fault, just like it wasn't her fault. "Aunt Ivy didn't get a blood clot because she left Hope Haven, Mark. She already had it by the time we noticed her symptoms. And you're right—she's stubborn. I tried to convince her to go to the ER or to call her doctor and she refused. So don't blame yourself and I won't blame myself, either, okay?"

He hunched his shoulders toward his ears in a half-hearted shrug. They had reached the cafeteria and Zoey took a tray but Mark said he'd go find a table. After filling a plate at the salad bar, Zoey stood in line to pay for her meal. While she was waiting, she glanced across the lunchroom at her cousin. His arms were crossed against his chest, almost as if he were hugging himself and he was staring out the window, frantically jiggling his leg beneath the table. In that instant, he looked so lost. So alone. *Like a little boy whose parents sent him away every summer because they didn't want him around,* Zoey thought, overwhelmed with compassion.

"Aren't you hungry?" she asked when she joined him. "Their home-made mac 'n' cheese looks decent. That's one of your favorites, right?"

"I only like it when Ivy makes it. It reminds me of being a kid."

Oh—so that's why he always asks Ivy to make him his favorite meals and desserts. Zoey had thought he was just lazy and spoiled. "Yeah, I feel that way about her potato salad. One taste and it's as if I'm on the top of the widow's walk again, watching the Fourth of July fireworks over Beach Plum Cove with you, Jess and my parents, while Aunt Ivy and your grandmother were downstairs drinking tea in the living room."

"Yeah, because Sylvia hated the noise and Ivy was afraid of heights… I remember one time your dad put me on his shoulders while we were up there and your mom was so afraid he'd drop me over the edge that she started crying. I've never forgotten how that felt, sitting on your dad's shoulders, having your mom worried to tears about me, and you and Jessica begging for a turn. It felt like…" He blinked and scratched along his jawline, not looking at her.

It felt like he was part of our family, Zoey realized and her apology tumbled from her lips. "I shouldn't have said what I said last night, Mark. I'm really sorry."

He hunched his shoulders again. "No big deal."

"No, I—" Zoey stopped talking because Mark abruptly stood up.

"I'm expecting an important call in a minute and it's too noisy in here. Tell Ivy I'll be up in a while." He strode toward the exit.

As usual, their moment of closeness hadn't lasted long, but in a way, that made it feel more authentic.

*

Gabi wanted to see Ivy as soon as possible, so Zoey went straight from the hospital to pick her up from school, then brought her directly back.

"Auntie!" the teenager exclaimed, diving into her arms after they entered her room. She nuzzled against her chest for so long Ivy finally patted her back and said if she didn't stop squeezing her, the nurse was going to have to come in and increase her oxygen. Gabi giggled and let her aunt go and then gave Mark a cheerful greeting.

"We won't stay too much longer," Zoey said. "You look tired, Aunt Ivy."

"How can I be tired? I haven't done anything but lie around all day. Didn't you bring my cards?"

"They're in your bag. I brought your coin jar, too."

"Good. Roll that tray table over here and pull up your chairs, everyone," Ivy instructed them. "It's time for a game."

"Mark and I will play against Aunt Ivy and Aunt Zoey," Gabi suggested. "The cousins against the aunts."

"Nah. I want to be Doughy's partner," Mark said. "Is that okay with you?"

"Yeah," Zoey agreed. "We haven't been partners since we were kids. It's about time we were on the same team again."

After playing cards for over an hour—Zoey and Mark won every game—Gabi asked a nurse if it was all right if she played her flute for Ivy. The nurse permitted her to play just one song, with the door closed. Ivy requested "Flight of the Bumblebee," because she said it reminded her of Sylvia and her flowers.

Even more than the last time she performed it, Gabi seemed to play the dizzying piece effortlessly, masterfully. When she was done, Ivy and Zoey burst into applause.

Mark didn't clap but he commented, "I didn't know you were so talented, Jessica."

"I didn't know I was Jessica," Gabi ribbed him. "But thanks, Mark."

His eyes went round. "I called you Jessica?"

"It's easy to do. She looks so much like her," Ivy acknowledged. "But she's one of a kind and so was her mom. Each one with her own special talents and beauty."

"Thank you, Aunt Ivy." Gabi twisted the joints of her instrument apart and put them into her flute case. "I'm hungry. Does anyone want to go to the cafeteria?"

Zoey wasn't hungry but Mark went with Gabi. When they left, Ivy said, "This was such a pleasant day, wasn't it?"

"Pleasant? You're in the *hospital*, Aunt Ivy."

"Yes, but it didn't feel like a hospital because you three kids were here."

Zoey teased, "We could make it feel even homier. I could bring in your portrait of Captain Denny and hang it on the wall over there."

"Oh, I love that portrait but I've found I don't absolutely need it to see Denny. Sometimes, the best way to see someone you love is like this." She lowered her eyelids and the corners of her lips slowly lifted into a smile. As Zoey studied her great-aunt's dreamy expression, she smiled, too. Then Ivy looked at her and asked, "Did I ever tell you the story about my whirlwind courtship with Dennis Cartwright?"

"Once or twice. But I'd love to hear it again."

She patted the bed and Zoey settled beside her and listened to the story of the man who won her great-aunt's heart with a fish instead of flowers.

"Is she sleeping?" Gabi whispered half an hour later when she and Mark returned to the dim room.

"Almost," Ivy answered for herself, without opening her eyes. "Come, say goodbye."

"Goodnight, Aunt Ivy." Gabi kissed her cheek. "I love you."

"And I love you, my great and grand niece," Ivy replied as the teenager picked up her flute case. She signaled Zoey that she'd wait outside and tiptoed into the hall.

"I'll stop by in the morning so we can talk in private," Mark told his aunt.

He's probably going to ask her to sign the paperwork for Waterside, Zoey thought, without a trace of rancor. "Gabi and I won't come until you're done with your discussion. Will you text me to let me know?" she asked.

"Sure." He moved toward the door.

"Give me a kiss before you go," Ivy prompted him.

He swung around and gave her a quick peck on the cheek, mumbling something that Zoey didn't catch. Ivy said something back and then he shuffled out of the room.

Zoey rose from the chair and leaned forward for her turn to kiss her aunt goodnight. "I love you, Aunt Ivy."

"I love you, too." The sheet across her chest rose and fell with her breathing and while Zoey knew her aunt was drifting to sleep, she lingered, reluctant to leave.

"Do you want me to bring a sweater from home tomorrow? Or your bathrobe?" When Ivy shook her head, Zoey asked, "Can I do anything for you before I leave?"

"You've done too much for me already, dear girl." Her aunt peeked at her and then lowered her eyelids again. "It's time for you to go live your life."

"Auntie," she scolded in a hushed tone. She was going to say, "Don't talk like that!" But her aunt was already snoring softly, so she kissed her again and slipped from the room.

*

Since Zoey and Gabi had agreed not to go to the hospital until Mark finished his private discussion with Ivy, on Saturday morning Gabi decided she'd attend her group meeting and Zoey walked to the farm stand for fresh eggs. The air was oppressively steamy, the scratches on her arms and legs from the rose bushes were stinging, and she was bleary-eyed because she hadn't slept for more than three hours the night before, even though she'd been completely drained.

So when she slogged up the driveway and saw Mark patrolling the stretch of bricks in front of his convertible, she bellyached to herself, *What's he doing here anyway? He'd said he'd text. He probably came over because he expects me to make him breakfast.*

When he turned in her direction and she noticed his face was red and contorted into a menacing grimace, almost all of the compassion she'd felt toward him the previous day evaporated. She understood it must have been a shock for him to see a large section of the fence flattened and splintered and a small crater dug around the roses, but couldn't he exercise a little mercy, considering their aunt's condition?

"Hey, Mark," she said but didn't pause on her way to the back door.

"Zoey!" He blared, storming toward her.

She refused to engage with him when he was this angry and when she was this emotionally fraught. "Nick and Aidan are going to fix everything. I'm going to pay for it. It'll be taken care of before Aunt Ivy gets back. That's all you need to know and that's all I have to say."

She let herself into the house and Mark followed her to the kitchen, where she set the eggs on the table. When she turned toward the sink to wash her hands, he was right in front of her, looming, physically stopping her from advancing.

"What is your problem? Move!"

"Zoey!" He took hold of her shoulders. "Listen to me. I—"

"Let go!"

She tried to shove his arms away but he pressed one hand against her back and cradled her head to his chest with the other. And that's how she knew Ivy was gone—because her cousin, who had never been good at demonstrating affection, embraced her.

When Gabi returned from her meeting an hour later and came into the living room where they were sitting on the sofa, Zoey looked up and shook her head, unable to break the news to her. So Mark recounted a second time how he had arrived at the hospital just as Ivy was being rushed into emergency surgery, but that she died before the doctors could operate. Then Gabi dropped onto the cushion on the other side of him and he wrapped an arm around her, too. And the three of them held onto each other and wept, their aunt's chair empty beside them.

CHAPTER FOURTEEN

Because Ivy had specified in her funeral arrangements that she wanted the reception hosted in her home, Mark agreed Nick should focus on finishing the kitchen remodel rather than tackling the attic floor project. Nick told Zoey that was a big relief, since it gave him more time to figure out how to explain that he didn't actually know anyone who was interested in purchasing the reclaimed wood.

They were both surprised Mark didn't want to alter Ivy's kitchen design, but he said since the remodel was nearly done and he was in a rush to lease the place out, Nick should keep going. Without their aunt in the house, Zoey and Gabi felt strangely comforted to have so much remodeling activity going on, as a distraction from their grief. And the final result was striking, from the black granite countertops and white subway tile backsplash to the pendant lighting and new fridge that matched the oven.

Gabi loved it because it still looked retro, and while Zoey agreed, she thought it had a decidedly contemporary feel to it. "Aunt Ivy would have been thrilled. This is exactly the effect she envisioned," she complimented Nick when he finished the project on the Tuesday after Ivy died.

"I'm sorry she didn't get to see it…" He puffed out his cheeks and let the air leak through his lips. "And I'm sorry I didn't get to say goodbye to her."

Zoey touched his arm. "I think she was saying goodbye that day you carried her upstairs. Remember what she told you?"

"She said that I'm a true gentleman and the finest craftsman on Dune Island." Nick rubbed his brow. Or was he hiding his eyes behind his hand? "But I wish *I* told her how I felt about her."

"You didn't have to tell her. She knew because you showed her every time you were with her," Zoey assured him.

Their conversation was interrupted by the doorbell: another fruit and cheese gift basket had arrived. Because of the year-round islanders' bent for gossiping, word about Ivy's death had spread quickly and the residents responded with such a generous outpouring of sympathy that Zoey could hardly keep track of all the flowers, baskets and cards they sent. She offered to share the goodies with Nick for lunch but he had to go make an emergency repair to a client's staircase. So after saying goodbye to him, Zoey sorted the mail.

She was halfway through the pile when she opened an envelope containing a black and white photo, without an accompanying note. Glancing at the snapshot, she recognized that the young, leggy woman wearing Bermuda shorts and a crisp, white blouse was her aunt Ivy. But she wouldn't have guessed the young man standing beside her was Mr. Witherell, were it not for his keeper's uniform and Sea Gull Lighthouse in the background. She'd never imagined his hair as being anything other than white, wispy strands, so she was caught off guard by the dark, thick, curly locks sprouting from beneath his bell-top cap. She was also surprised to see that standing full height, he'd been taller than Ivy by about three inches.

Who sent me this? Zoey flipped the photo over. "Ivy Winslow," was inscribed in faded black ink beside a date that was too indistinct to read. Zoey suddenly remembered her conversation with Mr. Witherell's niece, Melissa. How she'd said there was only one girl her uncle had ever been interested in, the "Winslow girl." Because Zoey thought of Ivy as *Ivy Cartwright* and Sylvia as *Sylvia Winslow,* she had assumed Mr. Witherell was interested in Sylvia. But now she realized Melissa had been referring to Ivy by her maiden name.

Her aunt had never mentioned any romance between her and Phineas. Because Zoey knew the story of their friendship, it was now easier to believe his niece's claim that Phineas's feelings hadn't amounted to more than a passing crush. But if he hadn't been interested in Sylvia, why had he written her such upsetting letters and come to the house to speak to her, as Ivy had told them?

Maybe Ivy had been right; Mr. Witherell believed Sylvia was only marrying Marcus for his money. Perhaps in a misguided attempt to protect Ivy and her brother, he had decided to intervene? Zoey could feel her shoulders tighten as her mind began churning with other possibilities. *I can't go down that road again.*

She set the photo aside so she could share it with Gabi as another reminder not to take gossip at face value. And to prove to her that Mr. Witherell hadn't been in love with Sylvia and he hadn't kept a photo of her by his bedside. But he *had* kept an old photo of Ivy in a box in his attic, probably as a treasured memento of their youthful connection at a time when they both needed it.

Knowing how much Ivy's friendship must have meant to him, just as it had to her aunt, Zoey included the photo on the memory board she created in Ivy's honor for the funeral. The display also consisted of photos of Ivy as a young girl, posing with her brothers and parents. Ivy with her high-school friends. Ivy on her first day of college. Several pictured her with her sister-in-law, and several more with her extended family, including Zoey, Mark, Jessica, Gabi and their parents.

But Zoey's favorite was the black and white photo of her aunt breaking a bottle of champagne over the bow of the *Boston Ivy*, with Dennis eyeing her. "Oh, what a smile he had," she had once said and in this photo, Zoey could tell it was Ivy who'd put the radiant grin on his face.

*

At the funeral, Gabi played Mozart's "Lacrimosa" on her flute and there wasn't a dry eye in the church. Not Zoey's or Nick's. Nor Scott's or Kathleen's. Not Aidan's or Lauren's or Carla's nor any of the other funeral attendees' eyes, including Mark's.

Later that afternoon, when almost everyone had departed from the reception, Zoey was shuttling the platters of leftover food from the dining room into the kitchen when Gabi asked if she wanted to go for a swim.

Zoey wiped her brow. "Not yet, honey. I've got to take care of this, first."

"No, you don't," Kathleen insisted. "We're here to help. You're sweating. Go take a minute for yourself."

Lauren, Scott and Nick echoed her sentiment, so Zoey put on her swimsuit and as they walked to Rose Beach, Gabi linked arms with her. Her niece didn't say anything but when Zoey glanced over, she noticed a tear on her cheek. *She needed a few quiet moments away, too*, she realized.

They continued in silence, dropping their T-shirts and towels in the sand when they got to the beach. The tide was in, so they didn't have far to wade before the nippy water was up to their waists.

They stood together in shared, wordless sorrow, gazing toward the horizon for a long while. Zoey was just about to ask her niece if she'd changed her mind about taking her first swim of the season, when Gabi sucked in a deep breath of air and plunged into the water.

A few seconds later she burst up through the surface about twenty feet away. "That felt *awesome*!" she squealed, so reminiscent of her mother that Zoey wanted to laugh and she wanted to cry. But instead of doing either, she dived forward, too.

*

"Mark really expects you to leave by the end of July?" Nick asked. It was two weeks after the funeral and since he noticed a very faint stain on the wall in the best room, he had stopped by to open it up and check for water damage, which turned out to be negligible. They were chatting in the driveway, since Zoey had just returned from the grocery store and Nick was on his way to another client's house. "That doesn't give you much time."

"For him, I consider it generous," Zoey said with a chuckle.

"Couldn't you stay here and manage the leasing process?"

Zoey wondered if this was Nick's way of telling her he didn't want her to leave yet. He'd been incredibly thoughtful, helpful and sympathetic in the days and weeks following Ivy's death. But their conversations hadn't reached the depth of intimacy they'd shared the night Zoey tried to dig up the rose shrubs. She had thought he'd make a move or say something to confirm he felt the same way about her that she felt about him. It was understandable if he didn't want to ask her out or express his feelings for her when she was grieving. But she hoped that wasn't the only deterrent because a part of her would always grieve her aunt, just as part of her would always draw strength and joy from her memories. And since one of those memories included Ivy's admonition to live her life fully, Zoey decided if Nick didn't make his feelings clearly known by the end of the week, she'd bring up the subject herself.

"As mellow as Mark has been lately, I can't imagine him letting me continue to occupy a room here during prime summer vacation time." Nor could she imagine herself wanting to occupy a room at her aunt's home once it was filled with strangers. In a strange way, now that Mark's plan to lease it out had become a reality, Zoey felt as if she'd lost another family member; the *house*. Her chest felt tight as she said, "Besides, I've got to get used to city living again before my library position starts at the end of August."

"Yeah, I suppose you'll need time to transition." Nick shifted his toolbox to his other hand. "By the way, I found a book in the wall. I left it on the end table in the best room."

"A book *in* the wall? How did it get *in* the wall?"

"My guess is it fell into the open wall cavity from the attic, some time before the house was insulated in the eighties. It would have dropped all the way to the basement because the walls were hollow, but it got stuck on the window header."

"What kind of book is it?"

"A journal or a ledger, maybe. I didn't read it. Anyway, I've got a busy day tomorrow but I can come back and patch the wall some time after five."

Seizing the opportunity, Zoey invited him to come for supper the next evening and he accepted with a smile. After going inside and putting the groceries away, she retrieved the book from where Nick had left it and perched on the settee in the best room. The small, brown, leather-covered volume was encircled three times and tied with yellowed twine. As Zoey picked at the knot, the old string came apart in her hands. She opened the book and read the inscription:

For Sylvia on her 20th Birthday—Love, Mother.

Sylvia's journal? As excited as she was by the discovery, Zoey had a small compunction about reading her shy aunt's private musings. But when she leafed through the first few pages, she saw the short entries read more like a list of daily activities than a diary of confidential reflections. Her aunt had begun the journal by recording details such as:

I cleaned the Baldwins' home today and finished by 6:30.

And:

For supper I made creamed tuna on toast for us girls. I gave Father the ham steak Mrs. Lawrence sent home with me—he said it was too dry without glaze.

Scanning the entries, Zoey danced her feet against the floor when she read:

I've saved enough money from gardening on the weekends to buy a ferry ticket to Dune Island. I leave May 10th. I'll help prepare summer homes for their owners' arrivals and then hopefully one of the families will hire me as their full-time maid for the summer season.

The subsequent pages captured Sylvia's early days of living in a boarding house. It also chronicled her foray into socializing with other young women and men—something she hadn't been permitted to do at home because she was expected to be at her father's beck and call whenever she wasn't working. Sylvia's delight, as well as her innocence, was evident when she wrote about her first dating experiences. Zoey found it sweet that her aunt was so bashful about discussing the opposite sex—even in her diary—that she only referred to the young men by their first initials.

At the bonfire, my roommate Betty met a guy named R. He had a friend named D., who asked Betty if her pretty friend has a boyfriend. He meant me—imagine that?!

D. asked me out. We went to a pizza parlor and then strolled along the Boardwalk, holding hands.

D. took me to Captain Clark's restaurant. After our date he walked me to the door and kissed me goodnight. My first kiss—it was nice.

At the drive-in, D. asked me to go steady. I said yes and then he wanted to neck. I told him I'd like to watch the movie first but he looked so disappointed that I changed my mind. When

I told Betty, she said going steady is one step away from getting married!

Sylvia's account of her budding romance was interrupted by the news she'd begun working as a full-time maid for the Winslow family. She elaborated:

Mr. Winslow is very ill. In addition to cleaning, I help his daughter, Ivy, prepare meals but she's so sweet to me it doesn't seem like work. Sometimes I help care for her brother, M., and he's very pleasant, too.

Zoey smiled at Sylvia's obvious affection for her great-aunt and great-uncle. There was a lapse in-between dates before she indicated Thomas Winslow had died and she'd been asked to move into the Winslow residence. Ivy and Marcus quickly became the subjects of her scribblings:

I'm concerned about Ivy. She hardly eats, she's very pale and I hear her weeping at night. M. doesn't seem as sad as he did right after Mr. Winslow died. His body may be weak but his character is strong.

M. told me, "As pretty as you are, you're more than just a pretty face." He wants to teach me to play chess.

M. is the gentlest, kindest, smartest man I've ever met and he listens to all my silly ideas. Some wealthy girl will be very lucky to have him for a husband one day.

Ivy has been walking to the harbor every afternoon and it seems to be helping her mood. While she's gone, M. and I visit in the living room. He's supposed to be teaching me to play chess, but we talk so much he forgets.

Recognizing that Sylvia and Marcus's love story was unfolding before her eyes, Zoey turned the page in anticipation of learning how she'd ended her relationship with her "steady" in order to date Marcus.

Instead, Sylvia had scrawled:

D. and I met at our usual place but then he took me to a deserted cottage near Rose Beach. He carried me over the threshold because he said that's what he'd do if we were married. I'm so ashamed to admit I gave in to his charms.

Here the ink was splotched, perhaps with teardrops.

I won't ever do that again until after I'm his wife. Once we're married, Father can't make me return home in the fall. I just hope D. will still let me work as a maid here so I can see M. and Ivy every day.

"Oh, Aunt Sylvia," Zoey whispered, wincing empathetically at her aunt's naivete and regret, as well as her fear of her father. The diary continued, documenting an increasingly upsetting sequence of events, some that Zoey remembered from Ivy's stories, and others she'd never known. She quickly read through those excerpts, eager to reach the joyful sections about Sylvia's relationship with Marcus again.

The lighthouse keeper, P., left a note here for me. He must have seen D. and me together because he wrote that I should stop dating him. Why would he suggest such a thing? Doesn't he think I'm good enough?

P. left another note. It really hurts my feelings.

D. asked me to go to the cottage to talk. I thought it was just an excuse for you-know-what but when we got there he said he was breaking up with me. I begged him to tell me what I did wrong so I could change it. When he wouldn't, I cried so hard I was shaking. He put his arm around me and then we kissed. One thing led to another and even though I swore to myself I wouldn't give in to temptation, I did… Afterward, he seemed more withdrawn than before but at least we're still going steady.

P. came to the house to speak with me but I was upset so Ivy made him leave.

D broke up with me for good. He said he was sorry but he's 'real gone' for someone else. That must have been what P. was trying to warn me about. I should have known—my sisters always said no one would ever want to marry me.

When M. caught me crying, he said whoever made me weep like that didn't deserve me. I'm not as sad about D. breaking up with me as I am about leaving Dune Island after Labor Day.

Ivy brought D. home for supper!!! I'm not surprised he'd choose her instead of me and I'm glad she's so much happier now. I pretended not to know him and he did the same. But I wish I hadn't ever gone to the cottage with him. I'll die of shame if he tells Ivy about him and me—or if Marcus finds out!

"No way," Zoey uttered, aghast to discover that D. stood for Dennis. *Ivy*'s Dennis. Captain Denny.

She studied the preceding passages, hoping she had jumped to the wrong conclusion. Then she perused them a third time. But there was no denying it: Sylvia had been going steady with Dennis. She had *slept* with Dennis. And although Zoey already knew what the consequence of that had been, she needed to read about it with her own eyes. Her hands trembled so much she nearly tore the page when she flipped it over. She smoothed it flat and didn't stop reading until she'd reached the last entry in the diary.

M. used all his strength to climb to the widow's walk to watch the sunset with me. While we were up there, he told me he loved me!!! I asked him if he really meant it. He said he never meant anything more and he'd prove it by marrying me right away, if I agreed. (I did, of course—I love, love, love him!) When we kissed, I felt like I was dancing in the stars.

D. and Ivy are engaged, too! He must not have told her about us. It's better this way.

I'm <u>late</u>.

I never dreamed I'd get to have a baby of my own, but I'm sick about the trouble I'm in. If I break up with M., he'll be devastated, whether or not I tell him the reason. Where would I go anyway? I can't return home—I'm terrified of how my father will react. If I tell D., he might marry me but Ivy will be crushed… and I would be, too. I know it's selfish of me, but I don't want to lose M. or end my friendship with Ivy. What am I going to do?

The rest of the diary was blank and Zoey assumed that must have been because Sylvia had dropped it down the wall or it had slid from its hiding place. But she didn't need the journal to know that Sylvia had decided to marry Marcus and keep her son's paternity a secret.

"Marcus Jr. was *Dennis's* son," Zoey said aloud in wonderment.

She sat motionless as the pieces of the puzzle about her aunt's past clicked into place. Zoey was filled with empathy for Sylvia's plight as a young woman and for how her secret had shaped the rest of her life. She realized that while Sylvia may have considered marrying Dennis, it wasn't because she loved him; it was so she wouldn't have to return home to her father. And so she wouldn't have to leave Marcus, the man she truly loved. The man who truly loved her.

As for Dennis… he'd been a player, that much was clear, but he was also the same young man who had died in his attempt to save Marcus's life. So Zoey couldn't guess how he may have reacted if Sylvia had told him she was pregnant with his baby. However, one thing Zoey had no doubt about was that he loved Ivy. It was evident in the stories her aunt had told about him, and it was evident in what Sylvia had written in her journal. *Dennis was "real gone" over his best girl,* Zoey thought, sniffling a little. And his best girl was Ivy.

And what about her? How might Ivy's life have been different if she had known Sylvia's secret? That was another question Zoey had no way of answering for certain. But she suspected if Ivy had found out Sylvia was pregnant with Denny's child, she might not have ever have married him. Might not have ever experienced a relationship she cherished so much that sixty-some years later, the mere sight of Dennis's portrait could make her feel as swoony as a schoolgirl.

What if Sylvia had disclosed her secret later in life, as she'd tried to do shortly before she died? Originally, when Zoey suspected Mr. Witherell may have been Marcus Jr.'s father, she assumed Ivy would have been crushed to discover she'd been deceived for all these years. But that was before Zoey read Sylvia's diary. Before she understood the circumstances and that Sylvia's intentions were to protect Marcus and Ivy.

In light of that realization, Zoey now firmly believed that if Sylvia had followed through with making her deathbed confession, Ivy may have been hurt at first. But ultimately, she would have been as gracious toward her as she'd been toward everyone else. Maybe even more so, because she'd loved Sylvia like a sister.

Of course, in the end, even though she was clearly anguished by the thought of Mark inheriting the Winslow family home, Sylvia hadn't shared the truth with Ivy. But Zoey was almost positive her aunt had compromised by leaving her a clue for when the time was right. Almost positive Sylvia had been speaking deliberately, not deliriously when she said. "For now, it's best to let the past stay buried in the past… beneath the roses."

Strange, though, that she'd hinted the past was buried beneath the roses, when really it was behind the wall. As she stared at the hole Nick had carved above the window, Zoey was struck by the hideous pattern on the wallpaper. *Those* were the roses Sylvia had been talking about! She must have accidentally dropped the diary down the hollow wall from her attic room, and figured out that it had landed behind the wall in the best room. How disconcerting it must have been for her to walk past that rose-patterned paper every day, knowing that evidence of her darkest secret lay behind it…

Zoey was so affected emotionally by what she'd discovered about her family's history that it took a few minutes for her to fully absorb how Sylvia's past had changed her own present. "I can't believe Aunt Ivy's house belongs to me, after all," she said aloud to herself. The realization was staggering. She was elated that she'd be able to continue using the residence as it was originally intended—as a *home*, not a business. Yet Zoey also empathized with Mark, knowing the sobering implications her discovery would have for him.

So when she called him later, she tried to soften the blow by reminding him that he'd still receive his portion of Ivy's trust fund, since he was named specifically in her will. Then, as tactfully as she could, she disclosed what she'd learned about his father's paternity.

Even though they'd both known for decades that the will was incontrovertible, Zoey half expected Mark to threaten to dispute her claim in court.

He was quiet and then he laughed wryly. "I can see the family resemblance to Dennis, all right. I inherited his good looks."

It's just like him to focus on external appearances—although he has a point. Zoey recalled the day Gabi assumed the photo of Captain Denny was Mark's grandfather, probably because she'd subconsciously perceived a similarity between the two men. Still, Zoey thought Mark would have been more upset. Irate, even. Primarily because of the house.

"You don't sound very surprised."

"I'm relieved to find out." Mark explained that when he visited Sylvia shortly before her death, she'd hinted that his father, Marcus Jr., wasn't Marcus Sr.'s son. "She was incoherent during other parts of the conversation, so I thought she was having some kind of hallucination. But then after her funeral, when Mr. Witherell said what he said…"

Zoey's mind jumped back to what Sylvia had written about Mr. Witherell in her journal. He'd undoubtedly seen Dennis and Sylvia going in and out of the empty beach cottage. So while he couldn't have known for sure that Marcus Jr. was Dennis's son, he may have suspected it. His remarks after the funeral could have been his way of trying to keep Mark from taking over Ivy's house, just like he'd once tried to prevent Dennis from two-timing her with Sylvia.

"It's ridiculous, but I'd heard rumors in school and I started to wonder if Mr. Witherell was my grandfather and that's how he knew I wasn't a Winslow. I became obsessed with finding out whether he was or not. I couldn't sleep, couldn't eat, kept losing weight—I was a wreck. I shouldn't tell you this but I even took a strand of hair from Ivy's brush. I was going to have someone run a DNA test but I lost the sample."

You're unbelievable, Zoey thought, as she recalled the day Ivy was so befuddled about where she'd left her brush. But since Zoey had gone to similar extremes trying to find answers, she said, "Not knowing your heritage must have been eating you up inside."

"Yeah. I didn't want to pour a ton of work and money into the house only to find out I had to hand it back over to you," Mark unabashedly admitted. "When Mr. Witherell died, I called his niece to try to find out if I was his grandson, but she said he couldn't have kids. So I figured I'd let my imagination run wild and it was time to put the matter to rest… Anyway, even though I'll lose out on a lucrative leasing opportunity, I'm kind of glad I don't have to deal with the house any more. It's actually been more trouble than it's worth. Besides, I just landed a new job and it's going to keep me on the road a lot."

Zoey earnestly congratulated him, adding, "It goes without saying that you're welcome to visit any time. Just because we're not blood relatives doesn't mean we're not family, you know."

"Thanks." There was a quiet pause before Mark chuckled and said, "But it does mean I've got a better smile—a Captain Denny smile."

*

Zoey and Nick were standing side-by-side on the widow's walk, alone. Scott and Kathleen, who had extended their stay on Dune

Island, had taken Gabi to Captain Clark's and then they were headed to Bleecker's for a cone. The sun had already set, staining the sky orange and yellow, and now dusk was painting the glassy bay deep lavender and the sand black. A brackish breeze cooled the air and in the distance, the voices of summer vacationers rose and fell as they roasted marshmallows over their fire pits or called their children in for the evening.

"I want to tell you something," Zoey said. "But please don't share it with anyone, not even Aidan."

"I won't," Nick promised, the blueness of his eyes darkening with the sky.

Zoey trusted him, even with a family secret like the one about Mark's grandfather. But out of respect for her aunt's privacy, she didn't go into detail. She simply told him that Mark wasn't a blood relative, so she was inheriting the house. However, she did clarify, "And just in case you've heard any rumors, Mr. Witherell *wasn't* his grandfather."

"Wow. That's incredible… Have you told Mark yet?"

"Yes."

"How did he take it?"

"A lot better than I thought he would."

"So what are you going to do with the house?"

"*Live* in it, of course." Since her housing costs were covered indefinitely, Zoey figured she could take a sizeable cut in salary. She hadn't signed a contract with the library in Providence yet, so she could tell them she'd changed her mind and then she'd apply for the local library position, instead.

"Until the end of August?"

"Permanently."

"Yes!" Nick squeezed her tightly before loosening his embrace.

Usually, Zoey relished the moment before a first kiss almost as much as she relished the moments after a sunset. But Nick didn't pause long enough for her to anticipate what was coming next. There was no hesitation, stalling or shuffling before he cupped her face in his hands and pressed his warm, soft lips to hers. Zoey drew back in surprise and then she tilted her chin upward again and they kissed fervidly and repeatedly until they were both breathless.

"Does this mean you're starting to like me now?" Nick asked.

"I may or may not be," Zoey answered coyly as they intertwined their fingers, palm to palm. "And by that, I mean I *definitely* am."

Sliding his other hand between her shoulder blades, Nick drew her close again. By then, the sky was twinkling with pinpoints of light. As they swayed ever so slightly, the words Sylvia had written in her journal as a young woman and repeated again at the end of her life came to Zoey's mind, and she whispered, "I feel like I'm dancing in the stars."

A Letter from Kristin

I want to say a huge thank-you for choosing to read *Aunt Ivy's Cottage*. If you enjoyed it and want to keep up to date with all my latest releases, just sign up at the following link. Your email address will never be shared and you can unsubscribe at any time.

www.bookouture.com/kristin-harper

While I was writing much of *Aunt Ivy's Cottage*, I stayed in a different town on Cape Cod, Massachusetts, than where I usually stay. There were new things to discover and fall in love with there, as well as some similarities between the two places. As usual, I drew inspiration from the setting and fictionalized bits and pieces of it so you could accompany my characters and me to a similar seascape.

I hope that if reading *Aunt Ivy's Cottage* was a fantastic experience for you, you'll share what you loved about it in a review. Your perspective means a lot to me and your enthusiasm makes a big difference in helping new readers discover one of my books for the first time.

Keeping in touch means a lot to me, too, so please don't hesitate to reach out through Twitter, Goodreads or my website.

Thanks,
Kristin

@KHarperAuthor

www.kristinharperauthor.com

Acknowledgments

As always, I'd like to thank my family and friends who cheered me on as I wrote this book. Special thanks to my mother and sisters for the brainstorms and breakthroughs.

Thank you to RD for discussing old houses and repairs; to GD for the flute music; and to LD for input on Moby.

I'm very grateful to AO for letting me stay at her ("little slice of heaven") condo right next to the ocean. It was an inspiration and a respite.

And a big thank-you to my editor, Ellen Gleeson, for her patience, smarts and grace, and to my publisher, Bookouture, for having an all-around creative approach to publishing.

Printed in Great Britain
by Amazon

60403741R00190